Patricia Favier was born in New Zealand of French and English parents but has lived in many countries, including France, Canada and Britain. She began writing fiction and drama in her teens and after completing a degree in history went on to become a journalist and local politician. She co-founded a book publishing company and was for many years its editor. She is also the author of numerous non-fiction titles, as well as a book for young children. She now lives in a small town north of Toronto, Canada with her husband and young daughter, where she enjoys writing, gardening and music.

A MASQUERADE TOO FAR

Little does Léonie, Vicomtesse de Chambois, realise the perils she will face when she takes her brother's place on a French ship bound for the Pacific under the command of Captain François de la Tour — perils that will endanger her heart as much as her life. Her masquerade as a young naval officer enables her to escape an unpalatable marriage and fulfil a lifelong dream, but it leaves her in danger of destroying her own and her family's reputation forever.

PATRICIA FAVIER

✦

A MASQUERADE TOO FAR

Book One of
The French Legacy Trilogy

Complete and Unabridged

ULVERSCROFT
Leicester

First published in Great Britain in 1997 by
Robert Hale Limited
London

First Large Print Edition
published 2000
by arrangement with
Robert Hale Limited
London

British Library CIP Data

Favier, Patricia
A masquerade too far.—Large print ed.—
Ulverscroft large print series: romance
1. Seafaring life—France—Fiction 2. France—
Colonies—History—18th century—Fiction
3. Love stories 4. Large type books
I. Title
823.9′14 [F]

ISBN 0–7089–4240–7

Published by
F. A. Thorpe (Publishing)
Anstey, Leicestershire
Set by Words & Graphics Ltd.
Anstey, Leicestershire
Printed and bound in Great Britain by
T. J. International Ltd., Padstow, Cornwall

This book is printed on acid-free paper

For my father, John Dunmore, for sharing his expertise and passion for French explorers with me. Thanks also to Kate Freiman and Judy Brown for their assistance with the manuscript, and to my husband, Kevin, and my daughter, Erin, for their endless support and love.

1

As the sun rose above the forest to flood the clearing with morning light, two shots rang out. It was, Léonie thought in that brief instant, almost impossible to hear them apart.

Her eyes flew from her brother's outstretched arm to that of his adversary. The Marquis de Vercours stood proudly staring at them, his lips curved in a malicious smile. His gold breeches and coat gleamed in the fresh sun, unmarked by the telltale signs Léonie had fully expected to see.

She turned to her twin brother and a gasp broke from her lips.

Jean-Michel was crumpling slowly into the long dewy grass, a wide, red stain soaking into his shirt.

'*Nom de Dieu!*' Léonie sobbed as she ran to him. 'What has he done to you?' She fell to her knees and cradled her brother's head in her lap. 'Jean-Mich, Jean-Mich,' she sobbed, 'speak to me! Tell me you are not

1

killed by that . . . that . . . *espèce de cochon.* Look at me, speak to me!'

Her brother's eyes were closed and he was breathing in short rasping gasps. With every tortured breath, more blood soaked into his shirt. It tore at her heart to see the pain etched in his dear face. If only she had been born a man, too, she would take his sword and run it through the arrogant marquis's fine, gilded chest. Oh, how good that would feel!

She looked up as she felt a tug on the sleeve of her cloak. Her brother's second, Christian Lavelle, frowned down at her, his face as drained as hers felt.

'Come, Léonie. We must be away from this place. Someone will have heard the shots.'

'Bah!' said Léonie inelegantly. 'So this is how men think to serve their honour — by shooting one another like dogs and then running away. Perhaps I am glad to be a woman after all.'

'I'm sure you are, Mademoiselle de Chambois,' came the oily voice of her brother's challenger. 'Such beauty would never do adorning the face of one such as your worthless brother.'

Léonie glared up at Vercours, making an effort to curb her tongue. 'I do not believe,

2

monsieur,' she responded stiffly, 'that you would recognize worth in another human being if it were presented to you on a gilded platter. You had good fortune on your side, *c'est tout*.'

His laugh was like slime on a stagnant pond. A quiver of loathing ran up her spine.

'I am always lucky, *mamselle*, as your brother surely knew when he maligned me at piquet last evening.' She froze as he bent over her, but he merely retrieved the silver pistol that had fallen from Jean-Michel's fingers and handed it to his second. 'Such hot-headedness is not uncommon in one as young as your twin, of course, though one always regrets the taking of such a spirited life.' He raised a kerchief to his nose as if to ward off the whiff of gunpowder that hung in the still air. 'But such young men will be ruled by passion. Such a wasted emotion, don't you think?'

'What I think, *monsieur*, is that one who cheats at the card table is not fit for the honour of a duel. He should be shot like a dog.'

The marquis's thin eyebrows rose a fraction. 'I believe I feel a sudden pity for your betrothed — de Grise, isn't it? I wonder at poor Alphonse choosing a wife who likes to meddle in the affairs of men.'

Léonie bit back a response. The very mention of her impending marriage depressed her. One day — soon — she would extricate herself from the engagement, despite her father's inevitable fury. But for now, she refused to let Vercours see that his barb had found its mark.

When she made no reply, the marquis merely smiled faintly. 'Good day to you, *mamselle, monsieur.*' Extending the slightest of bows to her and Christian, he turned toward his waiting carriage.

Léonie didn't bother to watch him depart. She was afraid her quick tongue would lend itself to some waspish retort that would merely add to his self-satisfied amusement. Christian disappeared to retrieve the phaeton, and she was left alone in the forest with her brother.

'I see you still spit like a cat,' Jean-Michel murmured as she stroked his forehead. She curved her lips in a smile, relieved that he was at least conscious and well enough to tease. 'But it will do no good against Vercours. He's not known for caring what society thinks of his morals.'

'Let us speak no more of him, Jean-Mich,' she answered, matching his lightness of tone. 'He is a monster, and if you have let him

4

kill you, I promise I will never speak to you again!'

Despite his obvious discomfort and the deep-red stain that grew ever wider from the wound in his chest, Jean-Michel grinned.

'Perish the thought,' he whispered.

Léonie dug in the pocket of her cloak for a handkerchief. It seemed ridiculously small and lacy pressed against the sticky blood that oozed from her brother's chest. In frustration, she tore a strip of cloth from her petticoat and wadded it into a pad.

'Does it hurt terribly, my love?' She applied the makeshift dressing gently to his wound.

He shook his head, though from the lines of pain that edged his eyes and mouth, she knew it was a lie. At that moment the phaeton appeared, rocking dangerously as Christian hurried the horse around the curving path and across the clearing. Together, she and Christian eased Jean-Michel into the seat and Léonie slid in beside him, cradling his head and shoulders in the lap of her cloak. Despite the heavy cloth, blood had soaked through to the cornflower-blue damask of her dress beneath. How would this be explained at home? How could any of it be explained to the satisfaction of their father? Jean-Alexandre, Duc de Chambois was not a man who approved of gambling, let alone duelling, and his ire was not something to be provoked. Léonie knew her mother would forgive them, for she had once admitted that her high-spirited twins were her greatest joy — unlike Robert, the eldest in the family, who took himself so seriously. Léonie couldn't remember a time when he had not spoken and sounded like an echo of their father.

She braced herself as the carriage rocketed out of the park and on to the cobbled streets of Paris. There was no hope for their younger brother Georges, either. At fifteen he was obediently suffering his first year as a cadet at the Royal Naval Academy in Brest, when all he really wanted to do was stay home and read.

She gazed down at her twin. He and she were so alike. The same fiery hair, unpowdered and as red as any in a Titian portrait, the same wide grey eyes and cool skin, the straight aristocratic nose they had inherited from their mother. The main difference between them was that Jean-Michel had grown a man's shoulders, wide and strong, and was two inches taller than Léonie, though she was tall for a woman.

She pressed her lips together and cast an anxious glance at Christian.

'He's so pale. Can you not get home faster?'

6

'And get us all killed in the bargain?' He patted her arm. 'Hold him tight, my sweet. It's not far now.'

Léonie stroked her fingers across Jean-Michel's brow. It was but two weeks since they had turned twenty-one, and he was in his prime, soon to embark with Christian on his first voyage to the vast Pacific Ocean. How could God in his wisdom let such a thing happen? He couldn't let him die: it was unthinkable. What would she do without her soul-mate, the brother she had scarcely been apart from all her life?

The phaeton swung through the gates of the Hôtel de Chambois. A groom scuttled out of the stables and Christian threw him the reins.

'Make haste, Léonie. Fetch Héloïse and let's get Jean-Michel inside. But take care,' he added. 'We don't wish to awaken the household. The scandal would surely reach your parents' ears at Court.'

Versailles, March 1784

François de la Tour rested his finger on the map and looked at the king.

'Your Majesty, I do not underst — '

'It's too costly, Captain. Our purse strings are drawn too tight already. Can you not

7

find a shorter route?'

François opened his mouth to object, but the pallor of Louis XVI's face stilled his tongue. He's gaining weight and looking weary, he thought. Dark lines shadowed the monarch's eyes, making him seem older than his twenty-nine years. François felt some sympathy, for despite the king's political difficulties and the unpopularity of his queen, the man displayed a genuine interest in matters of science and discovery.

'Well, Your Majesty, the Pacific is as far from France as any ship can sail. The journey would take a year or more, ordinarily.'

'But you are no ordinary captain, François de la Tour. Why do you think I chose you for this mission? I want Auguste de Barron found.' The king leaned back in his chair, gripping the gilded arms with puffy fingers. A fleeting look of pain passed over his features. 'I must know what became of him. He was — '

'I will find him, Your Majesty. Or at least news of him.' The king nodded, his eyes closed. François understood something of Louis' concern, for he knew the king counted the famous explorer among his small coterie of real friends. When Barron had vanished on a search for the elusive Southern Continent two years before, it was a painful blow.

8

If France could plant her flag upon the mysterious great land she would become the paramount trading power in the world, and Louis' bankrupt government needed that badly.

François returned his attention to the map spread before them on the gilded table.

'Perhaps it may suffice to shorten our visits, particularly in Africa and French India, but that will limit our potential for trade.'

'We do not require you to trade,' mumbled the king.

The captain pursed his lips. His officers would be disappointed. Trading between ports brought lucrative profits to augment their poor naval salaries. But from the expression on the king's face, he knew better than to demur on their behalf. He tugged at his scarlet waistcoat, impatient for this interview to be over.

'What of the South China Seas?' Louis asked suddenly, sitting up to lean over the map again. 'I fail to see why your expedition must travel north of the equator when your goal is eastward to the Pacific.' He poked a bejewelled finger at the map. 'Would your vessels not sail more directly via this route?'

The captain stared with foreboding at the Sunda Strait that led from the Indian Ocean into the heart of the East Indies.

'It is dangerous, Your Majesty. That coast is a haven for brigands and the winds and tides are uncertain. It looks commonplace upon a map, but — '

'*D'accord*. Then it's settled. Be back within the twelvemonth, de la Tour. You may find me especially generous if you bring Barron with you.' The corners of the royal lips twitched in the first hint of a smile François had seen. 'Perchance I'll make you Bishop of Bordeaux — you'd be the only honest cleric in France!'

François looked away, not wishing the king to see that the very idea of political patronage was repugnant to him. He was no more religious than most men, but he felt God and good government made uneasy bedfellows.

'I am of course most grateful, Your Majesty,' François replied, 'but I fear the sea is my only calling.'

'So I've heard.' He felt Louis stare at him keenly. 'That affair with your family when you were away in America — I was sorry to hear of it, but you must not blame yourself, Captain. Fate is a fickle mistress when she chooses to deal a hand.'

François frowned, rising to remove the weights from the map and gather his papers.

He did not trust himself to respond. The pain was still too raw.

The king seemed to understand that it was a subject he did not wish to discuss. He shrugged. 'One last thing, before it slips my mind. I er — *c'est à dire*, my wife — '

'Your Majesty?'

'Well, confound it all, Marie Antoinette came stomping in here dressed in that ridiculous dairymaid's outfit she's besotted with these days — '

'Shepherdess,' François corrected, maintaining a neutral expression. If the king chose to criticize his wife's foibles so openly, that was his affair. He was, after all, the king. But it would be folly for François to agree.

'Shepherdess, milkmaid — all trumpery if you ask me. I know she finds life at court something of a trial, but I sometimes wish — ' The king seemed to recall himself suddenly, and coughed. 'No matter. It would appear one of her ladies-in-waiting has a boy called up for your expedition. Chambois. He's a viscount, good family. His father has a pretty sound mind and with luck, the boy does too. Anyway, she craves your indulgence, asks that you watch out for the whelp, help him wipe his nose. That sort of thing.'

11

François raised his eyebrows. 'How old is he?'

'Damned if I know. I merely promised to convey the lady's wishes. The queen will doubtless ask if I remembered.'

François bowed. 'I will do my utmost to fulfil the queen's wishes,' he said. Though he disliked being asked to show favour to anyone, he could scarcely naysay the monarch.

But Louis was no longer attending. Clearly, for the king the interview was closed, and he had turned to stare out the window at the early evening sun sparkling on the fountains behind Versailles.

François furled the map, bowed deeply to the king's back and left the royal apartments. As he descended the marble staircase he felt his spirits lift in anticipation of the voyage. At last the final formality was completed, his ships were ready and he was eager to depart.

His carriage waited in the cobblestoned courtyard, the horses frisky and eager.

'Take me to the naval shipyards at Brest,' he ordered the driver. 'We stop only to change the horses and eat.'

'But, that's four days — '

'Get me there in two and I'll pay you double.'

The driver jumped into his seat without further objection. François smiled as he slammed the door behind him and slumped into the seat, loosening his fine lace cravat with one hand and tossing his dark blue tricorne on the floor with the other.

He hoped the winds in the Atlantic could be as easily tamed.

★ ★ ★

Léonie had fetched her old nursemaid Héloïse — or Nounou, as she and Jean-Mich had always called her — and with Christian's help, they had settled their patient on to the cot in Héloïse's bedchamber.

'Quick, child, find Marie. Tell her to bring bandages and hot water.'

Léonie obeyed instantly, out of habit, for although Héloïse was a servant, she was also a second mother to the twins. She had come to the Hôtel de Chambois as their wet nurse, the penniless widow of an army officer left with a young infant daughter to support. Marie had been first playmate, and then abigail to Léonie, and they had never been separated for even a day.

With her daughter's help, Héloïse peeled off Jean-Michel's silk shirt to expose the still-bleeding wound, muttering under her breath.

Léonie felt herself blanch at the sight of the long metal tweezers Marie held out to her mother. She looked down at her toes to compose herself.

'*Eh bien, petit,*' the old nurse scolded Jean-Michel. 'Now you find out there is one thing worse than being shot in a duel! Grit your teeth and pray to Our Lady that this will be over soon.'

Léonie clutched her brother's hand tightly as Héloïse pressed the wicked-looking tweezers deep into the wound. Jean-Michel opened his mouth to scream but Christian clamped a hand over his face before he could awaken the household.

Léonie kept her eyes firmly on her brother's face, as pale as the sheets on which he lay. She was relieved to see him faint before Héloïse's cruel instrument could discover the ball and pull it from his torn flesh.

'Pass me that bottle, Marie.' Deftly, Héloïse poured alcohol on to the wound. Jean-Michel flinched, but his eyes remained closed.

Léonie's glance met Christian's in a mutual message: what if he dies? A cold dread passed up her spine. How could a silly game of cards have ended thus? Was a man's honour worth the taking of a strong young life?

She would never believe it was.

14

Léonie was bathing her brother's face with a cool towel when his eyes opened twenty minutes later. His chest had been bandaged and he wore a clean white shirt. He stared up at her for a second, and then a faint smile touched his lips.

'You thought I was dead, *ma soeur*,' he whispered. 'But 'twill take more than a bullet from Vercours' silver pistol to send *me* to Hades.'

Léonie threw the cloth down in a pretence of anger. 'Dead? You were sleeping like a babe after Nounou's gentle nursing, just like when you were a child. You always did take more than your share of attention.'

Her twin groaned and rolled his eyes. 'I remember none of this. 'Twas always little Léonie who scraped her knee and had to have it kissed better. Is that not so, Nounou?'

Héloise clucked in mock disapproval.

'I see you are better. Marie is fetching some broth. You must regain your strength quickly lest you stay in my bed and these poor old bones have to sleep on the floor like a dog. Not that I mind, of course,' she added, raising her hands to stem any objections that might be forthcoming. 'I never gave a thought to my comfort when you were small, and I am well practised now, *mon enfant*.'

Léonie winked at her brother as the nursemaid poked at the meagre fire in the hearth.

'I will eat the broth, Nounou,' Jean-Michel said gravely, 'I am sure I will be instantly restored, and then Christian and I can be on our way.'

'On your way?' Léonie's eyes widened with alarm. She looked from her brother to his best friend.

Christian tugged at the lace at his throat. 'We . . . we are due in Brest, Léonie. Our ship sails in five days.'

'Five days? But it must surely be five days' journey by coach! And the roads — mud and mire and vagabonds. Why you would have to leave this very morning!'

The men exchanged glances. It was a fleeting look, but Léonie read its meaning as easily as she had when they had all been children together.

'Nounou,' Léonie implored, pulling the nurse away from her prodding at the coals. 'Tell him he mustn't go.'

'Go? Child, what are you saying? Your brother is very sick. He must stay in bed for at least a week, and then, God willing . . . '

Jean-Michel attempted to laugh off the women's concern, but his hand as he waved it at them was as weak as a newborn's. 'You fuss too much. Women always do. I have to be on board before the *Aurélie* sails, and that is that. Father will disown me if I break my contract.'

'You should have thought of that before you accepted the Marquis de Vercours' challenge,' Léonie retorted smartly. 'When news of the duel reaches Father's ears he will be furious anyway.'

'Vercours will tell no one,' Christian said. 'He earns his reputation by legend.'

'I don't understand.'

'By his very silence, *ma soeur*,' Jean-Michel assured her. 'He will never admit to a single duel, yet he is reputed to have killed more than a dozen men.'

'So,' Léonie said, impatient with such talk. 'All of Paris and Versailles will know of this by nightfall, and yet no one will have told them. Do you think that will make Papa a happy man?' She shook her head at them. 'Christian, you will have to go to the ship alone.'

'Impossible!' Jean-Michel cried. 'I have waited two years for this chance to see the other side of the world. If you think a little hole in my shoulder will stop me, you are sadly mistaken.'

Héloise harrumphed. 'Jean-Michel de Chambois, you will go nowhere. There is plenty to be seen on dry land in France — and Europe, no doubt, though I'm not sure it is safe to eat the food anywhere else. I never did trust those Italians, and as for the Germans, they are all for eating that foul pickled cabbage and singing loud songs. No, you must stay right here in Paris until you are well.' She wiped her hands on her apron. 'As the saints are my witness, if you move out of this bed, it'll be into a box on its way to the cemetery.'

Then, as though horrified by such a black thought, she blessed herself quickly, three times.

'*Voila!*' Léonie said triumphantly.

'I have to go. My career depends on it.'

Léonie spread her hands in frustration. Why was he being so mule-headed?

'Christian, can't you persuade him that to attempt such a journey would be insanity? Jean-Michel would surely die, and then how would the family's honour be served?'

At that moment, Marie returned bearing a tray. She set it down beside the bed and shyly passed Jean-Michel the spoon.

'Does *monsieur* desire me to to assist him with his broth?'

'Of course he does, child,' her mother grumbled. 'You can see for yourself he's as weak as a baby.'

Between them, the two women helped their patient to sit up a little and Marie began feeding the soup to Jean-Michel, who appeared to be enjoying all the fuss. How like a man, Léonie thought in frustration, to be as helpless as a kitten one moment and then off to conquer the world five minutes later.

She pulled Christian's sleeve and led him to the hearth.

'Christian, have not you yourself told me many times that when ships leave on such expeditions as this, they are often delayed in port for days or even weeks? The *Aurélie* may not leave when you expect at all. Why, she may lie at anchor awaiting the weather or the tides for many days, and by then Jean-Michel will be well enough to travel.'

'I wish it were so, but Capitaine de la Tour has a reputation for impatience. If the tides are right, he'll not wait an hour.'

Léonie felt tears of helplessness rise in the back of her eyes.

'Oh, Christian, what are we to do? You heard Nounou: if Jean-Michel makes this journey, he will surely die.'

Christian made no reply and Léonie could sense they were all at an impasse. She stared across the room at her brother, ghost-pale against the pillows, and tapped her foot.

'I have it!' she cried suddenly, causing

19

Marie to jump and spill the contents of the spoon she had been directing toward Jean-Michel's mouth.

'*Bien*, child!' Héloïse scolded her daughter. 'You have ruined another sheet with your clumsiness.'

'Listen,' Léonie said, clapping her hands with delight as the plan crystallized in her brain. 'I have the perfect solution! *I* shall take Jean-Michel's place on the *Aurélie*. I shall be the one to voyage to the other side of the world. And Christian, you shall help me!'

2

The silence in the tiny room was absolute for a few seconds. Léonie stood, hands on hips, her eyes brimming with excitement, and waited. Christian broke the silence first.

'You are mad, Léonie!'

Héloïse jumped up from the bed with such a rush Marie spilled more soup on the sheets. 'What are you saying, *ma petite?*'

Jean-Michel merely raised his eyes to Heaven.

'Well, I don't see why you must be so

slow-witted, all of you,' Léonie replied tartly. 'Have not Jean-Michel and I played this trick a thousand times in our youth? Even starchy Robert has been fooled as often as not . . .'

'Don't speak of your brother that way,' Héloïse interjected automatically.

' . . . And no one on the *Aurélie* will know what Jean-Michel looks like — except Christian, of course, and he would never betray me.' She clapped her hands in delight at the very thought of the adventure. 'In fact, with Christian at my side, I will be the consummate young officer and will bring great honour to my brother's name.'

'You'll be found out in an instant,' Jean-Michel grumbled. 'Tell her, Christian.'

'He's right, Léonie. The moment you take up your — Jean-Michel's — duties you will expose the lie, and then we'll all be ruined. My God, they'll set you down at the first landfall and leave you to your own defences. Me? I'll probably lose my commission and be fed to the sharks!'

'Fiddle!' she replied, cross that they were not entering into the spirit of her enterprise. 'You think I am just a silly girl, fit only to simper behind my fan at Court. But Jean-Michel has shared his lessons with me for so long, I feel I know everything already about life at sea. Did you not let me study your books on astronomy and mathematics, Jean-Mich? And the letters you wrote of your voyages to the American War — did I not read them so many times I have their contents by heart?'

'You can't work a sextant worth a damn, *ma soeur*,' her brother answered drily.

'Since you are not assigned as a navigator, that does not signify. I can sketch well enough, and I have read your books on plants and can tell a coconut from a breadfruit.'

'In theory,' Christian said.

'But of course! This will be 'Jean-Michel's' first voyage to the other side of the world. When I have seen these wonders with my own eyes, then I will know them by their smell and taste, just like the other naturalists aboard. Oh, Christian,' she implored him, 'please try to understand. It's like a wonderful dream. To travel across the world and see places as faraway as the stars — places that women can only dream of! I shall be the most travelled woman on God's earth!'

'No, you won't,' Jean-Michel said from his bed. 'There was a woman — what was her name, Christian? Baret? That's it — Jeanne Baret. Dressed herself up like a valet and travelled all the way to Tahiti before she was found out.'

22

'*Voilà!*' Léonie said triumphantly. 'So it can be done. And was this woman thrown off the ship?'

'No,' her twin replied. 'But then her captain was Monsieur de Bougainville, and she was under the protection of one of his botanists.'

'Then I shall be safe,' Léonie said, satisfied. 'Christian will be my protector.'

'Protector be damned,' he countered. 'Who will protect me? I shall be the laughing stock of the navy.'

'Is that all you care about? Here I am, willing to sacrifice myself to save the reputation of my family and my wounded brother, and you are worried the sailors will laugh at you. No, my mind is made up. I shall sail with the *Aurélie* and that is that. Marie, you will come to my chamber and help me dress. Christian, you will think what to do with my brother while we are away at sea. For my part, I shall write a note to my father telling him I would rather be an old maid than marry someone I do not love.' She laughed. 'I shall say I have decided to become a nun. That will provide entertainment for the gossips!'

Before anyone could protest further, Léonie spun out of the room with Marie trailing in her wake.

'*Mamselle*, should I fetch you some breakfast?' Marie whispered as she scurried up the wide marble staircase behind her mistress.

'I have not the least need of it, Marie. We have so much to do, I could not possibly think of food.'

'But *mamselle* — a little nourishment,' the maid persisted as the two women entered Léonie's bedchamber. 'It will settle your nerves. Clear your head.'

Léonie laughed as she threw off the bloodstained cloak she still wore. Her usually nimble fingers tore at the black velvet bows that held her echelle bodice together, fumbling in her haste so that one came off in her hand. What did it matter? The blue gown was ruined anyway, stained deep with her brother's blood.

'My sweet Marie. All our lives you have been trying to be my conscience, but you need bother no longer. I am going on this voyage for the honour of my brother — and my family. No amount of cook's delightful pastries and coffee will soften my determination. My mind is completely made up.'

'But, *mamselle*,' Marie objected dismally as she helped her mistress out of the gown, 'to go aboard a great vessel filled with men — so many men of all classes — and . . . ' Her voice faltered and her wide brown eyes filled with tears. 'Please say you will not go. Tell me this is all a jest.'

'No jest, just a wonderful happenstance — one that will never come my way again. Don't mistake my delight for any unfeelingness toward my beloved twin, Marie, for I am truly saddened by his state. But what's done is done. If you were in my place, you would go too.'

'Never!' Marie responded in horror.' 'Twould be my ruin — as it will be yours.'

'Nonsense!' Léonie was annoyed by such timidity. She didn't want to analyse her plan like some stuffy old actuary, for she knew this wasn't something any sensible woman would do. The trouble was, the things ladies were expected to do didn't interest her in the least. If she was going to have any adventure before her youthful days were done, this was surely her one, heaven-sent opportunity. She kicked off her bloodstained blue satin shoes.

'Go quickly to Jean-Michel's chamber and bring me his clothes. Ask his valet to pack for *monsieur's* departure. Tell him only that Jean-Michel has been detained *en route* and that Monsieur Lavelle has come to fetch his belongings for the voyage.' She saw Marie hesitate and waved an impatient hand. 'Quickly, now!'

As her abigail left the room, shaking her head, Léonie could no longer suppress a giggle of mischievous delight. She ripped off her torn petticoat and brocade corset and wondered how many months would pass before she once again donned such feminine garb. Then she turned to examine herself critically in the mirror. She was slightly built, but the padded shoulders of Jean-Michel's frock coats would counter that. She was tall and long-legged. That was good. And her breasts were small. For the first time in her life she was pleased by that observation, though she knew she would still need to bind them down. It would never do to take chances.

Is it possible? she wondered. Can I really carry off so bold a scheme? The *Aurélie* was a new ship to Jean-Michel and Christian. If luck was on her side, there would be no one aboard who knew Jean-Mich; no one who could expose her as an impostor. But would she expose herself?

She turned from the mirror and rummaged feverishly in a drawer until she found an old muslin fichu, then tore the fine cloth into wide strips and began to wrap her chest.

Her brother had taught her much about his

26

navy life, and she had been an eager pupil, but would it be enough to carry the ruse? She had never set foot on a ship before; never clapped eyes on a great ocean. How would she tell a capstan from a sheave hole?

She tucked in the ends of the breast bandage, feeling her spirits fall a notch, but then recalled that Christian would be at her side. He had been the twins' closest friend most of their lives and looked after her like a brother.

She folded the remaining strips of muslin to add to her belongings. With Christian's aid, the plan would work. It had to, for all their sakes.

Within minutes, Marie returned with Jean-Michel's travelling clothes. The velvet coat widened Léonie's shoulders admirably and made her feel quite the man, but her brother's new dove-grey breeches were too loose at the knee, and Marie had to resew the buttons. Then Léonie encountered a problem she could not overcome.

'Marie! What am I to do? His boots and shoes — none of them fit.'

'Perhaps some cotton in the toes?'

'It will not suffice, Marie. I cannot possibly spend months in footwear meant for a giant. You must find me some others.'

'But *mamselle* . . . '

'Georges has smallish feet, and he's away at the Académie. Bring me all the shoes suitable for a gentleman of the navy. Quickly!'

Marie obediently set out on another mission and Léonie was left to straighten the lace at her throat and practise striding up and down her boudoir in a manner becoming to a young officer of the realm. She was just attempting an elegant bow, putting her best foot forward in her stockinged feet, when the door burst open and Christian appeared.

Léonie grinned. 'Well, *mon ami*? How say you? Will I make a dandy for the ladies yet?'

Christian closed the door and threw himself into the nearest *chaise*.

'Dammit, Léonie. This is the most madcap scheme you've brewed up yet. You can't imagine you'll get away with it.'

Léonie bristled. 'If I fail, it will be because you, dear friend, had not the stomach for it.'

Christian jumped out of the chair, striding across the room to her with a movement that Léonie envied. Perhaps if she were to practise . . .

'Léonie, listen to me! This is the real world. Going to sea is no frivolous adventure. There will be men of all kinds on board, from the roughest sailors to the tough captains who force them on, though they be dying from want of food and clean water. And even the sleek new ships of the French Navy are no place for women.' He lifted one of the long red curls that lay on the shoulders of her man's frock coat, and grinned wryly. 'Not forgetting that wearing Jean-Michel's clothes will not make a man of you!'

'I am not a child, Christian. I know there will be dangers and discomforts. But I am my brother's twin. I can fight with swords and pistols as well as either of you, and I don't faint when men swear or fall ill.' She picked up a brush and attacked her hair with savage strokes. 'I have nursed the peasants in my father's domains through the devastation of typhus, and I have held children while they died.' She shook her brush at him. 'And all without getting the vapours and needing a man to rescue me.'

'It's not the same.'

'I think it is not I who am afraid, Christian Lavelle.'

He sighed, running a hand through unpowdered, blond hair, which had grown increasingly dishevelled since the events at dawn.

'I confess, I am afraid I shall forget myself and call you Léonie.' He turned to stare bleakly out the window. 'Damn it all, after so many years, how shall I ever remember to call you Jean-Michel?'

She grinned impishly. 'Simple! Don't look at me. If you concentrate on my clothes, you will see your friend, the naval *enseigne*, and not his sister, *n'est-ce pas?*'

'That depends,' he replied, finally grinning, 'on whether 'he' is wearing shoes.'

Léonie looked down at her toes, encased only in white silk stockings, and laughed.

'Marie has gone to fetch some from Georges' room. Jean-Mich has grown feet like a seven-league duck.'

At that moment, both Marie and Héloïse entered, the maid bearing an armful of footwear, the old nurse carrying a sack.

Christian shrugged and left the women to their plotting as Léonie pounced on a pair of low-heeled black pumps and found they fitted well enough.

'*Voilà!* Now I am transformed,' she crowed, drawing herself up tall for the inspection of the other women. 'Don't you think I look very fine, Nounou?'

The old nurse shook her head in silent remonstrance.

Marie led her young mistress to the *poudreuse*. Léonie sat obligingly before the mirror and giggled at the image of a young gentleman having his hair dressed by an abigail at the feminine toilet table.

'I think we will abstain from perfume of roses today, don't you, Marie?' Léonie teased as the girl began brushing her hair with long smooth strokes.

'You are determined, then, to embark on this foolishness?' Héloïse asked, setting her mysterious sack on the floor and crossing to Léonie.

'Perfectly.' Léonie watched the old woman in the glass.

'*Eh bien.*' Héloïse reached into the voluminous pockets of her black skirt and withdrew a large pair of scissors. 'If your mind is truly set on this *sottise*, we must cut your hair.'

Léonie's eyes widened.

'Perhaps you did not notice, *petite*, that young men who shun their wigs, do not wear it long like this.' She held up a lock of long red hair.

Léonie swallowed. 'Do it, Nounou, if there is no help for it.'

Héloïse closed the shears on the hair with a resounding snip. Six inches of bright auburn curl fell to the floor, but Léonie gritted her teeth and refused to mourn. Hair would grow again. Her brother's career could not be so easily resurrected.

It took only minutes to cut, then trim the

sides into suitable pigeon's wings. Marie tied it back with a simple black riband.

'I am ready,' Léonie said quietly, standing up and turning to face them. The women stared at the transformation of the Duc de Chambois's only daughter.

'Now I am no longer Léonie de Chambois, fiancée of the awful Marquis de Grise who smokes cheroots and smells of garlic. Now I am Jean-Michel, Vicomte de Chambois, sub-lieutenant in His Majesty's Navy.' She made a leg.

Marie blessed herself, hugged her mistress fiercely and ran from the room in tears.

'Don't fret,' Héloïse said. 'I will send Marie with your brother to my sister's house on the Rue d'Antoine. He will be safe there, and Marie can nurse him. When he is well enough, we will find a safer place outside Paris until this madness is over and you return, God willing.'

'Bless you, Nounou.' Léonie hugged her. Héloïse had been as close to her and Jean-Michel as their own mother. Leaving her would be almost as hard as bidding farewell to her twin. She turned to the small chiffonier that stood by the bed, and from the top drawer withdrew a small ebony box decorated with a Sèvres motif.

She took a velvet pouch from the box and pressed it into the old woman's hands.

'Give this to Marie with my blessing. She must not worry about money whilst I am gone. With this, she can live quietly until my return, and then we shall all be reunited.'

'But *mamselle*,' Héloïse murmured, tears glistening in her eyes, 'this is too much. Marie has simple needs, and she can occupy herself on my cousin's farm . . . '

'Take it, Nounou. It is little enough for the worry she will have on my behalf.'

Héloïse wiped her eyes with her hand and slipped the pouch into the folds of her skirt. She reached for the sack on the floor.

'If I must accept your gift for my daughter, *petite*, then you will honour me by taking this on your voyage.' She held out the bag. Léonie took it cautiously. Its aroma reminded her of a summer field at haymaking.

'What is it?'

'Use it as you will, child. It will ward off the foul sea air.' The old nurse touched her nose with one arthritic finger. 'I have a *cousine*. It was a terrible scandal to the family when she married an English sailor, and still I am the only one of all my family to remain her friend. She writes to me once, twice a year. Marie composes letters in return — my hands, you know, they do not handle the quill so well these days.'

Léonie knew that was a falsehood — Héloïse had never had reason enough to learn to write her own name, let alone a whole letter.

'My *cousine*, her husband made many great voyages. Twice his ship was wrecked beneath his feet, but he survived. And he learned, on those long journeys without sight or smell of land, that the most terrible scourges of the sea can be eased with this.' She pointed to the sack. 'I prepared these for your brother, but they are yours now.'

Léonie smiled at the passion with which Héloïse believed in the magic of a few herbs. But if it would make the good woman happy and ease her worry, it was nothing for Léonie to add it to the meagre belongings she would take on the voyage.

'*Merci*, Nounou. I will think of you each time I use it, and its sweet smell will remind me of my beloved France.'

And with that, she turned, straightened her shoulders under her brother's coat, and strode manfully from the room.

3

'I can smell it, Christian!' Léonie cried in delight as she peered from the window of the coach. Impatiently she scrubbed at the dirty glass to get a clearer look at the distant horizon. There it was at last. A long band of hazy blue — the Atlantic Ocean.

Despite the crisp spring day, she pushed down the window and leaned out, filling her nostrils with the tangy breeze. Never in her life had she seen the sea, and its smell was so tantalizing, so exotic, it filled her with unbearable excitement.

Christian leaned around her and pulled the window down sharply. 'You'll smell the sea until you're sick to your bones of it, Léonie,' he said. 'And you'd best practise your voice. There's a guard post ahead.'

She looked down at her man's attire, which felt almost natural after the dreary journey from Paris. Her breeches were thick with dust and her white stockings were a grimy grey. She studied her fingernails, wondering if four days without rose water had been enough to disguise their girlish delicacy.

The coach, emblazoned with the crest of Christian's uncle and guardian, the Prince de Charigny, stopped only briefly at the post and then rolled on over the ever-busier road.

'Thank goodness for your uncle's carriage,' Léonie sighed as they were waved through without inspection.

'My uncle loses few chances to remind people of his power in France,' Christian remarked somewhat grimly. 'And my cousin Dominic was only too keen that he should provide our transport to Brest.'

'I thought your cousin hated you.'

'With all his soul, if he has one. He wants to be sure I go to sea in the hope I won't return. He took great delight in describing all the evil sicknesses abroad in the world that I might succumb to if I had the chance.'

Léonie shuddered. 'He sounds perfectly horrible, even if he is your cousin.'

'Not just my cousin, Léonie. As he loves to remind me, while I am but a commoner living under sufferance in his father's house, he is a duke, one day to become the Prince de Charigny himself.'

'May the good Lord help France,' Léonie mumbled.

They were approaching the main gate of Brest now and Léonie brushed away thoughts

36

of Christian's unfortunate upbringing. This was what their weary days on the roads had been for and she felt her excitement rise as the journey neared its end.

The town was small compared to her beloved Paris, and yet it bustled with a life and vigour all its own. Shopkeepers and artisans, wealthy merchants and sailors — all seemed to jostle for space in the crowded streets. They passed markets and foundries, and clattered down streets boasting elegant houses sequestered within walled gardens.

Finally the carriage stopped in the enclosed courtyard of an inn. The sign swinging in the breeze proclaimed it *Au Bon Sauvage* and bore the picture of a black man, naked, save for a few feathers and shells.

Christian stepped out first to make sure the courtyard was deserted, then signalled to Léonie to follow. She snatched a glance at the strange depiction of mankind half a world away. Whatever would Héloise say if she realized that Léonie might soon be employed in rendering such illustrations herself?

The innkeeper's eyes bulged when he saw the crest of the Prince de Charigny on the coach in his yard. He blustered about, calling to the servants to prepare the best rooms and promising the travellers that baths and a fine meal would be brought directly.

They were shown to the parlour and left alone. A cheery fire crackled in the grate and Léonie sank gratefully into a chair, allowing herself the masculine liberty of stretching her legs straight out before her. It felt good to be finally free of the confines of the coach.

'Well,' Christian said as he stood with his back to the blaze. 'Now is the hour of truth, my sweet. You've been Jean-Michel for four days and no doubt you'd be glad if I sent for some clothes more appropriate to your, er . . . gender. You may return with my uncle's coach to Paris.'

Léonie straightened in her chair. 'Never! Christian, why must you keep asking me this? I have not travelled halfway across France just to turn around and run home like a coward.' She frowned at him. 'And you must stop calling me your 'sweet' before someone hears you and thinks we are . . . what is the word . . . ?'

'Never mind,' he assured her hastily.

'*Bien*. Then let us not speak of it again.'

He sighed, his blue eyes suddenly so weary that Léonie felt a pang of guilt.

'Forgive me, *mon copain*,' she said, reaching out to touch his hand lightly. 'I never meant for this to be such a trial to you. It is not to plague you that I wish to do this, but to save my brother's career.'

She stared down into the bright flames that danced over the logs in the grate. 'I cannot succeed without your help, but perhaps I demand too much of our friendship — and of your love for my brother.' Christian squeezed her shoulder gently.

'My swee — , *mon ami*,' he corrected, 'I am as anxious as you to help Jean-Michel. You and he are the only real friends in my life, the only family I've cared about since the sickness took my parents. Believe me, I am thinking only of your own safety. A ship is no place for a woman, even if the American War is over.'

Léonie gave him an impish grin. 'But I am not a woman, Christian. I am an *enseigne* in His Majesty's Navy. What better place for me than aboard one of his fastest ships?'

If Christian harboured any further misgivings, he was forced to keep his own counsel, for a servant entered bearing a creditable meal of soup and crusty bread, meats, fish, and several freshbaked tarts. They ate sparingly; baths, and reporting to the ship were uppermost in their minds.

Within the hour, they were bathed and dressed in their blue and red naval uniforms, smallswords at their hips. The journey to the port itself was short and as the bustling town gave way to warehouses and shipyards, a forest of masts appeared in the sky. Léonie had expected a few ships, but the sight that met her eyes left her speechless with wonder.

Row upon row of corvettes and frigates, storeships and traders stood shoulder to shoulder. Everywhere there were men shouting, hammering or rolling barrels as they prepared the giant vessels for voyages to all parts of the known — and unknown — world. Longboats bore sailors and officers, both merchant and King's Navy, to ships riding at anchor, and the sounds of shipbuilding echoed off the façades of the tall buildings that fronted the harbour.

She felt Christian's hand on her knee and jumped.

'Try to look as though you've been here before, Leon — *Jean-Michel*,' he said with a twinkle in his eye. 'Your brother was a naval cadet at the academy here, after all.'

'But it is so . . . ' There were so many questions Léonie wanted to ask, but Christian was right. This would all be second nature to her brother and she must act her part well. This next hour was vital.

She followed Christian from the carriage. A boy was employed to bring their belongings and the coach quickly disappeared into the narrow streets on its journey back to Paris.

'Which is the *Aurélie*?' Léonie asked as she danced aside to avoid a man pushing a barrow laden with provisions.

Christian raised his hand to point and then cursed under his breath. He shoved Léonie roughly down behind a stack of wooden barrels that smelled strongly of dried fish.

'What — ?'

'Shh!' he growled, his arm pinning her beside him. 'There is someone I know,' he muttered grimly. 'Worse, it is someone who knows Jean-Michel.'

Léonie regarded him with dismay. 'Who?' She peered cautiously from their hiding place, following his line of sight. Walking steadily along the wharf was a tall, thin man in the uniform of a naval officer. His beaklike nose protruded from beneath his hat and he walked with a crabwise gait that betrayed a lifetime of bad posture.

'Roussillon,' Christian said tersely. 'He instructed us in the art of scientific illustration at the *Académie*. If he boards the *Aurélie* we are sunk.'

'You mean he might be on the same voyage? And he's an artist? *Quelle catastrophe!*' Léonie groaned and slid down behind the barrels once more. 'I shall have to work with him. He will know instantly that I am not Jean-Michel.'

41

'He's gone aboard.' Christian swore again, and then realized his indiscretion. '*Pardon, ma petite!*' For a moment, he stared thoughtfully at Léonie.

'What?' she asked impatiently. 'What is it?'

He shook his head. 'I must be getting as addlebrained as you, my sweet, but there is just a chance . . . '

'What chance? Christian, you said yourself that the man knows Jean-Michel from school . . . ' She nodded, suddenly wondering if her thoughts were following the same lines. 'But that *was* several years ago. Perhaps . . . '

'Exactly. He taught us when we were in our very first year at the Hôtel St-Pierre.'

'When Jean-Mich was but sixteen,' she continued slowly. 'Five years. Much can change a person in five years, Christian.'

He grimaced. ''Tis a terrible risk, Léonie. And what if there are others aboard like Roussillon?'

Léonie almost let herself contemplate the truth of that argument, but stopped just in time. What good would she do Jean-Michel if she ran away at the first scent of danger?

'If this Roussillon has not seen my twin in five years, Christian, he surely can't know how tall Jean-Mich has grown, nor whether he shaves. Won't he simply consider him a young cadet who has taken longer than most to reach his manhood?' She got to her feet and brushed the dust off her dark-blue frock coat. 'Come, we are going aboard.'

Christian looked at her for a moment, then took the hand she proffered and let her help him up. 'We have both taken leave of our senses,' he said as he led the way toward the vessel.

Léonie stared up at the frigate as they climbed the gangway. The *Aurélie* was an impossibly beautiful ship, smaller than most, but sleek and fine. Her hull was copper-sheathed, which, as Christian had described to her during their journey from Paris, would give the ship greater speed and save time otherwise required for careening during the voyage. Her tall masts were festooned with ropes and ratlines like some giant tangled loom, the spars heavy with furled sails. Only the pennant bearing the royal fleur-de-lis fluttered in the breeze. Around the many small-paned windows in the high stern, gilded woodwork glowed in the soft spring sunlight.

But it was the quarter deck that brought Léonie to a standstill.

Christian obtained quick directions from a passing *matelot*, and then tugged on her arm.

43

'Don't stare! You're supposed to be used to all this, remember?'

'But Christian,' Léonie hissed, keeping her voice low. 'It looks like a barnyard! What are all those cows doing tied to the mainmast? And the longboats — they are full of sheep!'

'What did you expect?' he murmured as he led the way to the captain's quarters across the crowded deck. 'That we would eat nothing but dry biscuit on the voyage?'

'Oh.' The realization that these creatures were destined to be her dinner silenced Léonie. She followed him without further ado, though her eyes darted this way and that, taking in the pigs rooting happily about in the gangways, and the countless barrels and sacks of provisions that seemed to fill every corner of the deck. There were even nets of fish hanging to dry from the lower reaches of the shrouds, giving the ship the air more of a marketplace than of a vessel about to embark on a great voyage.

No one paid any attention to the two young officers as they crossed the quarter deck. Léonie found it surprisingly easy to walk, for the ship barely stirred on the gentle swell. Christian had filled her head with dire warnings of storms and rolling decks, doing his best to weaken her resolve, no doubt, she thought as she stepped around some men lashing barrels together.

She followed him down a steep flight of stairs, snatching off her hat and ducking her head just in time, and then along a narrow companionway lit by a single lantern hanging from a peg. They stopped beside a closed door.

'Well, *mon ami*,' said Christian softly, 'there is no turning back now. Remember your salute for Capitaine de la Tour.'

Léonie looked up at him, squared her shoulders and tried to smile bravely, though her insides shook like fresh blancmange.

'I will, for Jean-Michel's sake.'

'For *your* sake,' he reminded her with a quick glance over his shoulder. 'From this moment on, you *are* your brother.'

Léonie's heart pounded as Christian raised his hand to knock. This was it. The moment of total commitment. Whether she would be discovered or not, whether she would contract some terrible illness during the voyage and die, there could be no turning back. She gripped her hat beneath her left arm and took a deep breath.

From within the cabin a rich voice commanded, '*Entrez!*'

Léonie followed Christian into the room. It was a small study with cupboards and drawers filling every available space. Beneath the four-paned window that looked out over the stern of the frigate was a long walnut desk, polished to a mirror. The captain sat with his back to them at that desk, head bent over an assortment of maps and charts. She could see only the breadth of his shoulders and his coal-black hair tied in a riband at his nape, yet he seemed to fill the entire room.

He turned to them, his eyes looking at Christian before coming to rest on Léonie's face. She felt immediately impaled by the glance, by midnight-blue eyes that cut through her fragile façade like a sword through butter. Oh no, she thought dismally, he has seen through my disguise. Forgive me, Jean-Mich.

But the captain said nothing. His eyes roved over her hair, her eyes, her mouth, her uniform. She fought valiantly against a blush as his scrutiny turned to her legs. If only he would think of her as a promising youth and not as a woman whose body should by all the laws of nature be decently clad in layers of silk petticoats. Finally he looked back at her face, but she could read nothing in his expression.

Christian saluted and Léonie remembered herself just in time.

'Christian Lavelle and Jean-Michel de

Chambois, at your service, *Capitaine*,' Christian said.

'Which are you?' he asked Léonie. His voice was deep and rich.

'I — I am the Vicomte de Chambois,' she replied, cringing as her voice came out in a girlish squeak.

The captain harrumphed. She was surprised that he wore plain brown breeches and a white shirt with a simple ruffle of lace at throat and wrists. She had expected the captain of such an expedition to outshine everyone in his dress, and yet the simple clothes suited him, emphasizing the pugnacious angle of his jaw and the determined flash in his eye.

He stood, his head almost reaching the beamed ceiling until he lowered himself to perch on the edge of the desk. 'I understand you may need some help to wipe your nose, Chambois. Looking at you, I begin to understand why. I wonder if you bothered to pack a razor?'

'*Capitaine*?' She heard his soft laugh and felt herself colour. Just as she was about to defend herself, he turned to Christian. 'And you, Lavelle. Are you a duke's whelp also?'

'No, *Capitaine*. I am a commoner under the protection of my uncle, the Prince de Charigny.'

47

The captain's black eyebrows rose a fraction.

'Well, my young peacocks. You look very pretty in your uniforms. Wear what you will this evening, but tomorrow we sail and you will dress in plain working breeches and warm jackets. The Atlantic is cold at this time of year.'

He turned to the small window and stared out at the harbour beyond. 'I run a fast ship, and speed demands efficiency. It is my experience that officers and men alike work best when they leave their social class behind in port, so I allow no use of titles aboard the *Aurélie*. You are officers, nothing more. You will work with men who are your naval or scientific superiors, who will teach you much, and if you earn the respect of your fellows it will be on the strength of your talents and your application to duty.'

He turned to them again as though suddenly remembering to whom he was delivering this speech. Clearly it was one he had repeated many times this day.

'I demand much of my officers, but I think you will find me a fair man. Nonetheless, I am no one's nursemaid. Since you two appear to be well acquainted, you may share a cabin.'

Léonie was about to object when she

recalled the alternative. It would be infinitely better to share a room with Christian than to be left to swing a hammock with the other juniors. She stole a glance at him. He was a gentleman and she trusted him. Somehow they would manage.

The captain was rummaging in a drawer. 'And since you have more experience, Lavelle, I shall pass the queen's request on to you.' He straightened, having retrieved some documents. 'Her Majesty wishes this young whippersnapper to return unscathed — '

'My mother,' Léonie sighed. The captain looked quizzically at her. 'My mother is one of Her Majesty's ladies-in-waiting, sir. I apologize if her concerns have inconvenienced you.' She had no desire to commence the voyage at odds with the captain. He didn't look like a man to tangle with.

'There's no need. I prefer my men to return alive and healthy. It's one of the reasons I make my voyages swift.'

'All the same, sir — '

'I said we need speak of it no more, Chambois!'

Léonie took a step back, surprised by his flash of anger. Christian had been right — she would have to get used to taking orders.

She stood in subdued silence, waiting while

49

the captain perused the documents in his hands. Then he raised his head and looked directly at her. Her heart began to beat uncomfortably fast, but she maintained her demeanour, avoiding his eyes by observing his muscular legs encased in close-fitting calfskin breeches and knee-length boots with silver buckles. He was everything Alphonse de Grise could never be; a man of innate strength, at ease with himself. She doubted anything could shake Captain de la Tour. Why could her father not have found a match such as this for her? At least she might have learned to love him, for she found much to admire, despite his intimidating air.

She found the idea curiously disturbing and reined in her thoughts sharply. What painful irony it would be to fall in love with a man aboard the ship, while she herself was disguised as one of their sex. That would be true punishment for her deceit, and it was too cruel to contemplate.

She realized with a start that she hadn't taken in a word he'd said.

'I beg your pardon, *Capitaine*?'

'I said you have seen some interesting service for a boy. You sailed with La Pérouse to Charleston, according to your dossier?'

Léonie thought fast, trying to recall her brother's vivid correspondence on the subject of the American War.

'Yes, sir. We captured a British frigate and nearly lost our mast to a cannonball.'

The shadow of a smile passed across the captain's face. 'I seem to recall the British vessel lost all her masts.'

'You were there, *Capitaine*?'

'For some years. But that is in the past.' He studied the personnel files again for a moment, then tossed them down on his desk.

'Very well. You, young Lavelle, are assigned to the chief navigator, Pierre Grévin. Consider yourself fortunate. He is the best in the navy. Our mission is built on haste and I would have none but the most experienced to guide our course. Learn from him.'

'With pleasure, Captain.' Léonie could hear the delight in Christian's voice.

'Now you, Chambois. Your dossier says you are talented as a botanist. You have the opportunity to enhance that skill with Monsieur Duplessis. He is a *savant*, not a naval man, and is less than enthusiastic about my rules. He calls himself the Comte du Plessis, though there appears no record of such an honour. As a civilian scientist of some repute, perhaps it is not undeserved. You may address him that way if it will help smooth your association.'

51

Léonie had little interest in the physical sciences, unlike her brother. But she was resigned to keeping up appearances. She only hoped she could.

'Your second master tells me he knows your work,' the captain continued, 'though I fear he finds little to praise. Roussillon tells me he attempted to teach you the finer points of illustration while you were at the *Académie*, with only modest success.'

Roussillon! The man they had seen from the dock. Léonie stole a glance at Christian, but his expression betrayed nothing.

At least drawing was a skill she both loved and excelled in. As long as her disguise was convincing, she would enjoy this part of the voyage. 'I believe Monsieur Roussillon may note some improvement in my work,' she replied with a wry smile. Her brother would not thank her for this!

'I am pleased to hear it. You may divide your time between your superiors as suits the needs of the voyage. Should confusion arise, you may defer to me.'

'Thank you, *Capitaine*.'

He turned and reached for a small bell on his desk. A boy of about fourteen appeared.

'Vincent, escort Messieurs Lavelle and Chambois to their cabin.'

Léonie flushed as his eyes lingered on

her. She saluted stiffly and escaped behind Christian and the young servant.

Exhilaration bubbled up inside her as they entered a tiny room with two small cots built one atop the other into the wall. Despite his obvious suspicions, she had convinced Captain de la Tour that she was indeed Jean-Michel!

Surely it must be a good omen.

* * *

François de la Tour stood at his desk and stared out at Brest harbour. The familiar scene barely registered in his mind, for he was thinking of the young urchin dressed to the nines in his naval uniform. Was it his flame-red hair that had lit up his study so? Or his flawless skin?

He shook his head. The eyes. There was something about those calm grey eyes that had hit him in the chest with the force of a cannonball. The boy had regarded him with such coolness, with such . . . audacity, as though he were challenging him in some way.

Could he have lied about his identity? The *dossier personnel* listed him as barely twenty-one, yet he seemed more like a lad in his teens.

53

Lavelle seemed straightforward. A clean, professional-looking young man of twenty-three. If he were half as good as his naval record claimed, the chief navigator would be glad to have him along.

But Christian Lavelle was not the problem. Chambois was. Damn, but the boy was memorable.

François ran a hand through his hair, pulling some of the strands free of the riband at his nape. Roussillon would know, he thought. He'd been acquainted with Chambois. He would know if the boy were an impostor.

The captain slumped back into his chair and forced his mind on to the subject of the next morning's tides.

'Say your prayers well tonight, Chambois,' he muttered to himself, 'for you'll need God to protect you if I discover you're a fraud.'

4

Dinner in the *grande chambre* was an elaborate affair. To Léonie's surprise there were almost as many dishes as she would have expected at the Hôtel de Chambois:

pigeon bisque, or partridge and chestnut soup with crisp white rolls, dishes of tender lamb, chicken and fresh-caught Breton fish, and a variety of elegant pies and tarts, as well as vegetables and snow-white rice. The wine was excellent and flowed freely, loosening tongues and causing several of the gentlemen *savants* to brag about their expectations for the journey. There was talk of wondrous plants and animals and the untouched innocence of peoples in far-off lands. Some even questioned whether it was right to bring European culture to such noble savages, perhaps tainting them with concepts they could not hope to comprehend.

Léonie, who had entered the wardroom in a state of some anxiety, had managed to face the curious glances of her fellow officers with equanimity. Gradually, as the meal progressed, she had relaxed, delighted to find herself a part of the hubbub, and marvellously free of the need for feminine conversation and wiles. To find gentlemen of all ages actually listening while she expressed her ideas was a novel and exhilarating experience. She did, however, have to repress an urge to giggle at the luscious freedom of leaning back on the bench seat and stretching her legs out in front of her, but she had to concentrate each time she opened her mouth to speak, lest it was the voice of Léonie and not that of Jean-Michel that came out.

As the evening wore on, it became easier, except in one regard: Captain de la Tour seemed troubled. Several times Léonie glanced up and caught him staring at her. Twice he looked deeply into her eyes as though searching for something, and then turned away, leaving her trembling from the unexpected contact. The third time, she met his gaze squarely, for her apparent acceptance by the other officers emboldened her. If they found nothing odd, neither should he.

She heard her name suddenly and glanced across the table. Charles Duplessis, chief botanist and self-styled count, was wagging a plump finger in Roussillon's face.

'I will not tolerate it. Science takes absolute precedence over your childish doodles. He cannot be spared, and there's an end to it.'

'Childish doodles!' Roussillon nearly exploded with anger. His face turned as purple as the wine as he glared at the *savant*.

'While one must make allowances for those who are not officers of the navy, Monsieur le *Comte*,' he added with cutting emphasis, 'may I remind you that without the services of talented artists such as myself your work is worthless! Would you present King Louis with a bundle of shrivelled leaves instead of a beautifully executed drawing of the living specimen?'

He waved a hand at Léonie and smiled in triumph, displaying a row of bad teeth. 'No, my dear count, this young man is my responsibility.' Léonie smiled to herself. Clearly the man harboured no doubts as to her identity despite her earlier misgivings. 'To me has fallen the duty of converting his amateur dabblings into works of art, and I am never lax in my duty. I shall require him for at least seven hours a day.'

Seven hours! Léonie tried to imagine how she would survive being sequestered with the odious Roussillon for most of her daylight hours. She cast imploring eyes toward the captain, only to discover him staring at her over his glass again. His brows rose a fraction.

'Gentlemen,' he said, in a voice that told her he was accustomed to this argument between them. 'Monsieur Chambois will allot his time equally between science and art. Pray do not let us have arguments about such things before we even leave port.'

'*C'est impossible*!' huffed Duplessis. 'The work of science requires total dedication. Total!' He spread his fat fingers in supplication to François, but the captain merely stared across the table at Léonie, ignoring the man.

Léonie couldn't help staring back. His eyes were blue-black in the light from the lanterns suspended from the rafters. She noticed a faint scar above one eyebrow that gave him a slightly piratical air, but it was a brooding quality in his face, his intensity, that made her spine tingle. She sighed with relief when he got up from his place at the head of the table.

Captain de la Tour raised his glass so the ruby-red wine caught the light in a flash of fire, and waited while the others scrambled to their feet. Léonie noticed that both Roussillon and the botanist, Duplessis, seemed rather unsteady. It could not be the ship, for the harbour waters were so still she had barely felt the ship rock since they came aboard.

'To the King!' said the captain.

There were acclamations of 'King Louis!' from all sides, and 'Amen!' from the ship's ageing priest, Father Cassel.

When they were again seated, Léonie noticed the captain's place was empty. She jumped when his hand descended on her shoulder.

'Chambois, I would speak with you.'

She rose and followed the captain to the

end of the room. He placed one foot on the side of the cannon that was roped there in case of battle, and rested his arm on his knee, for he was too tall to stand easily in the low-vaulted room.

'Sir?'

'I have been observing you this evening, young man, as I believe you're aware.' She nodded, her heart pattering beneath her blue frock coat. 'I consider that your looks present me with a problem.'

Léonie swallowed, for speech was impossible.

'Under normal circumstances, all officers are rostered for the weekly inspections below decks. I am relieving you of that task.'

Léonie bristled. 'That will not be necessary, sir. I wish no special favours, nor I believe, would my mother, who made her entreaty to you via . . . ' Her voice trailed off as his face grew black with rage.

'I am not in the habit of having my orders questioned, Chambois, especially not by baby-faced sub-lieutenants! You will not conduct inspections. That is all.'

Léonie knew she'd been dismissed, but she returned his gaze with asperity, for she had no wish to be treated like a child.

'May I ask the reason, Captain?'

He leaned toward her across the cannon, poking a finger into her chest. It hurt, despite the bandages that protected her disguise, but she pressed her lips together and stared him straight in the eye without flinching.

'Because I cannot ensure your safety, boy. This is a ship full of men without women. If you need further explanation, ask your cabinmate.' He turned away, ducking to avoid the beamed ceiling, and strode to the door.

'Gentlemen,' he said as he gripped the door handle. 'We sail on the morning tide. I suggest you get some sleep, for there's rough seas coming when we've cleared the coast of Finistère and you may not get your chance again for some time.'

Then he ducked through the door and was gone. Léonie stayed by the cannon, feeling shaken by her encounter with the captain, until the first of the gentlemen had taken his advice and retired to their quarters. Then she, too, left, escaping to the small cabin she shared with Christian and shutting the door with relief. She tossed off her coat and gave herself a brisk toilette in the porcelain bowl that sat with its matching water jug on a small washstand.

The tiny cabin glowed softly in the lantern light with only the faintest moonbeams penetrating the small window. The ship creaked softly in the light wind as Léonie brushed out her hair. Despite the tension of the evening meal, now that she was safe in her little haven she felt exhilaration that she had fooled them all, even the captain who seemed to have spent the entire meal studying her in minutest detail.

Tomorrow, she thought with growing excitement. Tomorrow the expedition would be gone from France, out into the mighty ocean bound for the far-off Pacific. What would they find? Would they accomplish their mission or be forced to return with no news for the king? And what if their own expedition proved as doomed to mystery as that of their quarry, Captain Barron? Jean-Michel would not be able to continue the deception forever, and her parents might never know what became of their only daughter.

She set down the brush and stared up at the heavily beamed ceiling. From above came the sound of cows moving restlessly as the ship rose and fell on the water. She pitied the poor beasts. To be taken from the quiet pleasures of the field and confined on the rocking deck of a ship only to end in a stewpot, seemed an unworthy fate.

The wind eased for a moment and then buffeted the *Aurélie* with a light gust. Léonie steadied herself against the uneven rise and fall of the wooden floor and quickly stripped off her clothes. In a few minutes she was climbing into her *couchette* in Jean-Michel's nightshirt and pulling the blankets up under her chin. She picked up the white nightcap that lay on the desk beside her bunk and grinned wickedly.

What would sweaty Alphonse, the Marquis de Grise, make of his runaway betrothed if he could see her now? She pulled the cap over her head and flicked its peak over her shoulder. Alphonse's pale watery eyes, and his nose that was constantly red and puffy from taking snuff, were not memories she would hold dear to her heart on the voyage.

Her thoughts turned to the captain. Such a contrast made her want to laugh aloud. Instead of a pale, vacuous expression were eyes of midnight blue, as hard as flint. In place of the sagging paunch and gouty legs was a fine-muscled body that bespoke strength and vitality.

Léonie sighed and snuggled down beneath the covers. What sweet torture this voyage would bring — to be so near such a man and yet have him so utterly beyond her reach.

★ ★ ★

François de la Tour stood outside the door with his hands clasped firmly behind his back and stared at the toes of his shoes. What was he doing here? Was he mad?

Beyond the door he could hear sounds of the boy moving about, preparing for bed. His movements sounded light and quick, stirring something in François that he couldn't understand.

Chambois was so young, so vulnerable. And yet he had spirit. It was ridiculous. Never in all his seventeen years in the navy had he concerned himself with one member of his crew in such a fashion.

Perhaps the clue lay in the boy's very youthfulness. It was the only explanation. He stepped up to the dark wood-panelled door and raised his fist to knock.

And yet . . . ?

His hand fell to his sides and he turned away. It would not suit. It was not his habit to make personal visits to the cabins of his officers in the middle of the night, especially not those of his juniors. How would it look?

'Damn me for a fool,' he muttered. It was only right that he see Chambois and reassure him about that unpleasant squabble between Roussillon and Duplessis. He had promised the lad he would not let him become a trophy, and he meant it.

It was a thin excuse, but for the moment, it was the best he could think of.

★ ★ ★

The tap on the door was quiet but unmistakable. Léonie, who had been about to doze off, opened her eyes in alarm. Then she remembered. Christian had said he would give her half an hour to undress before he came down.

'*Entrez!*' she called.

But it was not Christian's head that ducked through the door. It was the captain's.

Léonie stifled a squeak of dismay and clutched at the bedclothes, tugging them to her chin.

'Capitaine de la Tour!' she muttered, keeping her voice low.

He closed the door and stood in the middle of the tiny cabin, seeming to totally fill the space. All the lessons of her gentle upbringing surged through her. A lady could never receive a gentleman alone in her bedroom when she was *déshabillé*! Such an occurrence was unthinkable! She must ask him to leave instantly.

But she was not a lady. Not any more. She was a man, as was he, and she must

64

act like one, no matter how compromising the circumstances.

'Please,' she stammered. 'Be seated, sir.'

He grabbed at the only chair as though desperate for support, and perched himself as far away from her as he was able. He seemed so ill at ease, Léonie was momentarily alarmed. Had something happened? Had someone betrayed her after she'd left the wardroom?

He was staring at her again, his eyes almost black in the soft light from the lantern. Léonie felt a blush stealing up her neck and pulled the covers higher.

'Did you wish to speak to me, *Capitaine*?'

He cleared his throat and looked down at his hands.

' . . . I just came to . . . '

What has he come to say? Léonie wondered. And why wouldn't he just say it and leave before the pounding of her heart became so loud it drowned out the rising wind outside?

He looked up, meeting her eyes again. The encounter was so sudden and so powerful it felt like a bolt of lightning had passed between them.

And then, just as quickly, it was gone.

The captain moved his chair closer to her bed.

'I wanted to see that you were not distressed,' he said with a frown. 'You seemed such an *ingénu* tonight in the company of the others, so very . . .'

'I can look after myself, thank you, Captain,' Léonie interrupted, wishing she could put some space between herself and the man. If he got any closer he would surely see her lip tremble. She tried not to notice the intoxicating mixture of sea air and male strength that surrounded him, but it was impossible. The potion was as entrancing as a harvest moon.

His voice grew quieter and slightly apologetic. It growled over her skin, filling her mind with the wildest imaginings.

'I was concerned about your work assignment. It was not my intention to throw you to those old wolves on your first evening. Duplessis and Roussillon have an ancient rivalry, but it's more bluster than storm. You must understand . . .'

'I do,' she replied quickly, relieved that was all that had prompted his visit. 'And thank you.'

But if she had expected him to leave, she was grievously mistaken. He frowned, tightening his jaw so that its hard lines turned to stone. Where was Christian? Why wouldn't he come and rescue her?

66

She jumped as the captain's fingers closed suddenly over her hands. His touch was rough and warm, not at all like the puffy digits of those whose lives were spent at Court. He drew her hands toward him and turned them to the light. Beneath his grip, her fingers trembled. Fire seemed to flow from his touch, yet it did not burn but incited flames that licked along her arms and into her very soul. She blinked and tried to focus on something else.

'They are too soft,' he growled, and then released her, pushing back the chair and leaping to his feet.

'Damn it, Jean-Michel de Chambois. You are a liar, and I will not have liars aboard my ship.'

Léonie's mouth opened in shock. '*Monsieur?*'

He turned, towering over her where she lay. She was grateful for the shadows cast by the upper bunk though they weren't enough to shield the fury of emotions in the captain's face. He shook a finger at her.

'Your records are false, any fool can see that! Perhaps they were enough to pass muster with your previous commanders, but not with me, young man!'

'I — I don't understand . . .'

'Pray don't lie, you young rogue. I should

67

have you tossed off this ship this very minute, but I know your family has the royal ear and I'd not be thanked for it . . . When did it all begin, this masquerade, eh?'

He stopped his ranting and glared down at her, his face only inches from her own. Léonie could see the frustration in his eyes and yet her only thought was how soft and enticing his lips were, set in that face of steel.

'I do not understand, *Capitaine*,' she said softly.

There was a moment of silence broken only by the creaking of the ship on the swell. Léonie held her breath, letting her imagination share a tiny flight of fancy as she fought the urge to tilt her face upward and invite his kiss.

But then sanity returned. She was Jean-Michel, and Jean-Michel did not want to be kissed by another man! The very idea was repulsive and unthinkable.

Only Léonie knew its irony, and it was one she must endure, for all their sakes.

The captain straightened suddenly, clamping his hands behind his back. He turned to the window and peered out at the dark harbour.

'Give me your true age,' he ordered coldly.

'And if you tell me an hour over sixteen, by God I'll . . . I'll . . . '

Léonie interrupted him quickly before he thought what he might do. 'There is no falsehood, Captain. I was born on March 10th, 1763, at our estates in the Loire valley. Please, you may ask Monsieur Lavelle. He is just two years older and we spent most of our childhood together.'

'1763! Impossible,' he growled. 'How can you be twenty-one and not have felt a razor near your face? Even the young cadets upstairs have played at being men by now. But you . . . you . . . '

'I am sorry, Captain,' Léonie said as bravely as she could, feeling as though her world — and that of her family — was about to fall apart. Forgive me, Jean-Michel, she pleaded her absent brother, for what I must do to save us both from this! 'It is true that in my family the men hold hard to their youth. My father is fifty-five, yet you would think him barely forty.'

'And does he shave?'

She felt a grin dimple her cheeks. 'I have not asked him, *monsieur.*'

The captain stared down at her for a moment, probing her face until her knees trembled beneath the covers. Then he laughed, a deep rich sound that filled the small room.

'Very well, *mon petit*, since you insist on being a babe of twenty-one and I have no evidence except your pretty face, I shall take your part — for now.'

He crossed to the door.

'I am concerned for you, Jean-Michel,' the captain said, turning finally. 'On a ship there are few distractions to wile away the weeks at sea, and some men grow more restless than others. You can share this cabin with young Lavelle, and I have excused you inspection duties. Beyond that, I can do little to protect you but offer you my own quarters as a sanctuary.'

His blunt words shocked Léonie. 'Th-thank you,' she blustered, reddening unmercifully.

There was an uncomfortable silence while the unspoken dangers hung between them. Then there was a tap at the door and Christian entered. He stopped in astonishment when he saw who was in the room.

'*Bonsoir*, Lavelle,' the captain said gruffly. 'I had expected you would remain above to play at piquet with the other young bucks.'

Christian looked quickly from Léonie to the captain and back, momentarily lost for words. 'A . . . no, *Capitaine*. I have no desire to pass the voyage in gambling.'

'You best be abed, then,' he said. 'We sail at dawn.'

He nodded to Léonie and ducked out of the cabin, leaving stunned silence in his wake.

'*Nom de Dieu!*' Christian growled as the door closed on the captain. 'What is going on, Léonie? Already the officers are murmuring that the captain has an unhealthy attraction for you, and now — '

Léonie felt herself pale at his words. '*Quels imbeciles!* It is nothing. He is concerned, that is all.'

'For what, my sweet? Your pretty boy's face and charm?'

'Don't be beastly, Christian. He came to reassure me that I need not fear the rivalry between Duplessis and the odious Roussillon. And . . . ' She bit her lip.

'And?' Christain asked, staring down at her, arms akimbo.

'And . . . he came to accuse me of lying about my age to the navy.'

Christian spread his arms expressively. 'So! I knew something troubled him. He stared at you throughout dinner as though no one else existed. And his eyes . . . '

'Are they not extraordinary?' Léonie asked, sitting up suddenly. 'So rich and deep a blue, like the night sky at harvest-time. Ah,

71

Christian, he is such a man. Although I am Jean-Michel on the outside, inside I am a woman whose eyes have seen perfection.'

'Léonie, no!' Christian sat upon her bunk and grasped her hands. 'This is madness! You must not think like this, not even for a second. To allow such feelings will make your disguise impossible. You will give yourself away before the week is out. Do you not see the terrible danger?'

'Danger?' Léonie laughed. 'What danger can there be in love from afar, Christian? My dreams are my own. They shall not be despoiled by reality.'

Christian groaned. 'I knew some such would happen, though I had not thought of this. Léonie, listen to me. If you let yourself harbour such romantic notions, they will surely show in your face, and those magic eyes you speak of that stare at you so? — they will see. And then we will all be disgraced — you, me and Jean-Michel. Now do you understand?'

Léonie sighed and slid beneath the covers. 'You are right, Christian. I must be strong for all our sakes. But oh, how I wish Papa had ordered me to marry a man such as Monsieur de la Tour . . .'

'He could not, my sweet,' Christian said more kindly, as he got up and unbuttoned

72

his frock coat. 'Your father would never allow you to wed a man without social standing.' He laughed. 'He once told me, in all seriousness, that much as he admired my character, unless both my uncle and Dominic were to die, and I could become the Prince de Charigny, he would not allow me to bid for your hand. I think he thought to quash any such thoughts before they could be born.'

'You never told me this!'

' 'Twas ten years ago,' he mused. 'Your father was anxious to strike early.'

'Bah!' Léonie said in disgust. 'My father is too much concerned for what the king will think. How could a man wish a disagreeable reptile like the Marquis de Grise on his only daughter?'

'Because,' Christian replied with an edge to his voice, 'he has land and power. And Capitaine de la Tour and I are but loyal naval officers, destined to grow old before our time in the service of the king. Now turn over and shut your eyes so I may disrobe without offending your pretty, aristocratic eyes.'

Léonie grinned impishly at him. 'Perhaps I will peek?'

Christian gave her a threatening glare and snuffed out the lantern.

5

The creaking of timbers awoke Léonie slowly. She lay staring up at the oak struts of the cot above her head, then threw back the blankets and sat up.

The ship is moving! she thought.

Gone was the gentle rise and fall she had experienced in Brest harbour. In its place was a wild sea that tossed the *Aurélie* in a motion more akin to riding a wild pony. Léonie clung to the sides of her narrow bed unsure whether to laugh or cry.

'Christian!' she called, suppressing a wild giggle as the ship lurched and her head nearly smacked the wall. 'Are you awake?'

No answer. She spared one hand to knock on the bed above her, but still there was no reply.

'*Tiens*,' she muttered, struggling to lower her feet to the floor. 'He is gone without waking me. No doubt he thinks 'Jean-Michel' needs his beauty sleep!'

She clutched the tiny writing-desk bolted to the wall and pulled herself up. It was barely light. Through the window a pale sky lurched alarmingly in and out of sight with every plunge of the vessel.

She washed quickly, bound her breasts in a fresh muslin bandage, and dressed in shirt and breeches, tumbling to the floor twice before she discovered that sitting on the bed was the best way to dress on a rolling deck. Mindful of the captain's command, she snatched her wool coat from the trunk at the foot of her bed, and staggered from the cabin.

As she stepped on to the deck, the salt wind stung her face yet it filled her with wild exhilaration.

I did it, Jean-Michel, she thought. They have put to sea with me in your place! She clung to the wide spray-slick rail and stared around her.

Already the port of Brest was far behind, swallowed by the swirling morning mists. Far to the north, the Pointe de St-Mathieu slid in and out of view, its medieval abbey cresting the headland like an ominous watcher.

Léonie turned from the rail. She would have no such gloomy omens dampen the start of this adventure.

A sailor brushed roughly past her carrying a wooden bucket filled with mash. He stared rudely at her as he hurried toward the poop deck and the squawking chickens. Léonie envied the man's seasoned gait.

Still clinging to the rail, she searched for Christian, wondering if he were at the duty bench. But as her eyes sought him out through the gloom, she felt her skin prickle. Standing at the helm without even a coat to protect him from the chill April wind, stood François de la Tour. The plain white sleeves of his shirt flapped in the breeze as he held the wheel on course. His powerful legs were braced against the deck and his black hair blew back in the wind that fought to free his locks from the imprisoning riband at his nape.

She felt his eyes on her and knew she must do something. But what? Was she supposed to be somewhere, employed at her scientific duties at this hour? Perhaps she should go below, seek out one of her two masters — Duplessis for preference — and see if they required her services.

It seemed the safest thing to do. And yet unaccountably she released the rail and crossed the quarter deck, steadying herself by clutching at ropes and barrels as she went.

Her heart was pounding by the time she reached the captain, and though his gaze was occupied by the choppy ocean, she sensed that he had watched every step she had taken in her brother's shoes.

'You have lost your legs, Chambois,' he said, his voice carrying easily over the wind. 'If you think this is rough, wait until we've cleared the peninsula!'

Jacques Le Brun appeared at his elbow. Léonie had been so occupied in crossing the deck she had not noticed the first officer.

'*Capitaine*,' he said in his level voice, 'I beseech you to turn back. To risk the expedition on such a day is foolhardy.'

The captain frowned. 'You worry like a woman, Le Brun. I will hold my ships in port only for a real storm. But this . . . ' He chuckled at the wild grey waves whose white caps grew clearer as the sky lightened. 'This is but a fortuitous breeze to speed us on our way.'

He looked up and barked some orders to a group of sailors in the rigging. Immediately they scrambled to loosen ropes, and the huge mainsail billowed out above Léonie's head, snapping as it caught a gust of wind.

'But, sir,' Le Brun persisted, 'the fishermen have returned to port already. Surely it would be wise to wait until tomorrow — '

'Tomorrow! Tomorrow I aim to be gone from the sight of France. In twelve days we shall be in Tenerife and then you may exercise your caution on some delightful Spanish maidens!'

He threw the lieutenant a broad grin that transformed his stormy face and made Léonie's heart quiver. Standing there clutching the helm, he looked like some wild pirate, not at all the image of a naval commander. It made her own adventure feel all the more dangerous — and exciting. Le Brun gave the captain a stiff little bow and disappeared.

François turned toward her and Léonie knew she'd been caught staring.

'Come here, boy,' he said, moving to one side of the wheel.

Léonie let go of the banister she was holding and stepped beside him. His eyes were dark as midnight as he looked her up and down.

'Very fine,' he said with a touch of mockery. 'I see you have on your best gold buckles. That should appease the gods of the sea.'

She looked down at her feet, clad in her brother Georges' best shoes that she had worn the night before. Her glance sped to his own footwear.

'I . . . I do not have boots such as yours, *Capitaine*.'

'Then you'd best acquire some at first landfall. This is not Versailles, you know.'

'*Non, monsieur,*' she replied meekly.

'Have you stood at the helm before?'

78

She shook her head, hoping it was a believable answer. Where was Christian when she so desperately needed him?

'Place your hands here . . . and here,' the captain said, grasping her fingers and placing them on the heavy polished wheel. A tingle of awareness spun through her from the warmth of his hands, but she pressed her lips together and stared out front, wondering what she was supposed to be looking at. Beyond her, the deck of the frigate was obscured by busy sailors, alarmed farm beasts, and a forest of masts and ropes.

She felt a hand press down on the top of her head.

'Down here, *petit*,' said the captain, amusement clear in his voice. 'This is not the road to Paris. If you want to find your way, you'd best follow the compass.'

Léonie was grateful for the gloomy dawn as she felt herself blush at her foolish error. She struggled to hold the heavy wheel on its heading, bracing her feet apart as she had seen him do. But slowly the needle swung away, creeping a few degrees to the north. The helm was so heavy, the ropes that controlled its movement like deadweights. She could feel the captain watching her, leaning his back nonchalantly against the banisters that led up to the poop deck, and she felt the metallic taste of panic on her tongue.

He's testing me, she thought, angry with her own inadequate strength. She battled with the wheel, pulling it back with all her might, but still the compass swung barely one degree to the southwest.

Just as she thought her shoulders were about to burst from their sockets, the ship lurched violently. With an undignified shriek, Léonie lost both her grip on the wheel and her footing, and crashed into the captain.

Powerful arms gripped her like iron bands. Léonie gasped as her hands splayed against the thin cotton of his shirt and she felt the solid muscle and sinew beneath. His body was warm and vibrant, despite the cold, and she could clearly feel his heart beating beneath her fingers. She struggled to regain her feet, but was somehow suspended above the deck. For a second she froze as she realized he was holding her up, pressing every inch of her body against his own. Then she heard him growl, low and throaty as he set her down on the pitching deck.

Scarcely daring to breathe, she risked a glance at her commander. He was staring at her with eyes black with fury and something else Léonie could not comprehend.

She turned away, burned by his anger. The

ship! She made a grab for the wheel, but the helmsman stood calmly in her place, his wiry arms controlling the frigate with all the ease of a lifetime of experience.

'We've cleared the peninsula now,' the captain said, as she stood staring at the man. 'The helmsman will keep us on course for the coast of Africa.'

'Oh,' she replied, feeling stupid that he had to explain something so basic. What must he think of her?

She looked up, but he was staring out at the grey ocean, his hands clasped behind his back as though he, too, had been burned by the contact of their bodies. Clutching her shaking hands together, Léonie waited for him to speak. Surely he had felt her feminine curves as he held her against him for those precious seconds? How could such a thing be hidden from a man so worldly wise?

She blinked back the tears, staring down at the scrubbed boards beneath her feet, and wished the deck would swallow her up.

No doubt now he would accept Jacques Le Brun's entreaty to wait out the storm. In a few hours they would return to port and she would be publicly disgraced and thrown off the ship, all her efforts to help Jean-Mich in vain.

A hand touched her arm. Léonie jumped.

'Don't blame yourself,' the captain said gruffly. 'Le Brun will no doubt castigate me for letting a pup like you swing on the helm in such seas.'

She looked up, relief washing over her. 'Then you are not angry that I endangered your ship?'

'Don't sound so surprised. Damn it, I'm not an ogre. I drive my fleet hard and fast in the king's name, but I don't throw lives away. I have a hundred and sixty souls aboard this ship and another hundred and twenty on the *Mousquetaire*. Do you think I would risk them just to show you what a babe you are?' He shook his head, but his voice grew softer. 'Chambois, you have much to learn and I plan on seeing that you do. This voyage we are embarking on will either kill you or make you a man.' He paused, his dark-blue eyes intense. 'Which is it to be?'

Death or discovery? It was a bleak choice, but she was not ready to give in. She had promised Jean-Michel that she would and could do this. Never in her life had she let her brother down.

She tilted her chin defiantly and stared at the captain, but he had turned away, summoned to speak with the chief navigator.

Léonie watched him walk away at Grévin's side, annoyed that she had lost her chance to answer. And yet in truth she had no notion what her answer might have been. How would Jean-Michel respond to such a challenge? The question made her smile. He would stand tall as an arrow and look at the captain man-to-man. There would be no trembling at the knees on her twin's part.

But Jean-Michel was already a man. If François de la Tour had met the real Sub-lieutenant Chambois, such a challenge would never have been issued.

'Young man,' called a voice from the poop deck. Léonie looked up to see the chaplain, Father Cassel, beckoning.

She clambered up the stairs, keeping a very firm grip on the railing. This time there were no warm arms to catch her if she fell!

The old priest stood beside the chicken coop at the back of the sloping deck.

'It is time.'

'Time, *mon père*?' Léonie asked with a puzzled frown.

'To bid farewell to France, my son.' The wizened chaplain gazed back at the vanishing strip of headland with a wistfulness that surprised Léonie. For her, this was the beginning of an adventure. A chance to flee a loveless marriage and a life of utter emptiness. But she looked, to humour him.

'You miss France already, Father?'

He sighed gustily. 'One cannot miss what one has seldom known, so it is said. And yet . . . '

'And yet?' she asked gently, sensible of the sadness in his voice.

Then he seemed to gather his wits, turning to her with a bright smile.

'We must not wish ourselves where we are not. That is not the way to do God's will, is it, my son?'

She bent her head and smiled at the priest. His back, buckled from his advancing years, made him inches shorter than Léonie, and she found it strange after the captain's exceptional height, to have to look down at a man.

'Is it God's will that sends you to sea, *mon père?*'

'But of course. The sea has always been my life. So many voyages, so many sights I have seen, that I dare say many of them are lost to my poor memory now. But there is always the ocean . . . always.'

The ship's bell sounded suddenly and the priest blinked.

'Seven o'clock,' he said. 'I must prepare for the *angélus.*' He looked at Léonie. 'You do pray with us, do you not, Jean-Michel? A young man should never neglect his Maker, especially not at the start of a great voyage.'

84

'Of course,' Léonie assured him hastily, as her mind revised Christian's explanations of the daily routine. Prayers, breakfast, then the morning shift.

'You must not concern yourself with the captain's ways. He is a great commander, but a little help from Our Lord never goes amiss, eh?'

'I am not concerned, *mon pére*. He assured me this was not really a storm.' She helped the priest to the steps, but between the old man and her own land-legs, they would make a funny sight should anyone be watching.

'Ah, this is but little. Capitaine de la Tour likes a strong breeze to fill the sails. I'm sure we shall make a record journey to the Pacific this time.'

'You have sailed with him before, then?'

He frowned as they made a slow descent of the stairs. 'Many times. I cannot recall . . . So many wondrous sights and yet always God takes His price.'

'I don't understand,' Léonie said, as she took his arm to guide him towards the *grande chambre*. 'What price?'

The priest turned toward her. 'You will know, Jean-Michel, sooner than I would wish. It is why we pray, *n'est-ce pas?*'

* * *

The midnight bell had just sounded when François de la Tour snuffed out the wick in his lantern. He stood for a moment at the window in his cabin, watching silver moonlight catching the soft peaks and valleys of the Atlantic Ocean. The ship's even motion usually soothed him. But not tonight.

For four days he had observed the young man. At work, at meals in the *grande chambre*, and at prayers. There was something about Jean-Michel, Vicomte de Chambois, that simply did not fit the description of the robust young man described in his dossier.

It was more than his physical innocence. There was something eager and untested in those wide grey eyes. Something . . . almost childlike.

François leaned his forehead against the heavy pane of glass and stared out at the ghostly seascape passing by.

He was growing fond of the boy. Much too fond.

Perhaps the dossier was not his. Mix-ups were not unheard of.

Chambois was said to have earned a commendation during service across the Atlantic with Lafayette's troop ships, yet François knew from bitter experience how demanding that had been, for he, too, had earned distinction, during the siege of Charleston in '79. He shook his head. Try as he might, he simply could not see the lad distinguishing himself with sword and pistol. *Nom de Dieu*, when the boy had fallen that first day at the helm, he had weighed less than a feather!

But then, his first days at sea on the *Aurélie* had shown the *enseigne* no weakling, for he was one of the few who had suffered no seasickness. Perhaps his strength was of a different kind.

The captain wiped a tired hand across his brow. It was but four hours till the early watch and he had been on his feet most of the day.

He began unbuttoning his chemise, wishing he could forget all about Jean-Michel de Chambois. But the young sub-lieutenant intrigued him, and the more fascinated François became, the more painful it would be should he ever discover some other 'truth'.

★ ★ ★

The captain was right about the weather off the coast of France. The *Aurélie* and her little supply ship, the *Mousquetaire*, ran before the wind like a pair of galloping stallions, yet no

87

real storm developed.

But he was wrong in his calculation of time. It did not take twelve days to reach the Canary Islands off the coast of Africa. It took ten.

'My God,' said Christian as he and Léonie stood on the poop deck and watched the men working the capstan to lower the anchor into the bay at Tenerife. 'He drives this ship like the Devil's at his back. At this rate we'll be home again before Jean-Michel's wound is healed!'

'Shh, Christian!' Léonie hissed in alarm, looking over her shoulder lest someone had overheard. 'It is not my wish to be cast off here and left to live my life among Spaniards.'

'What's the matter, *Jean-Michel*,' he teased. 'You don't like Spanish wine?'

'It is inferior to that of our own estates,' she replied with a tilt of her chin.

He grinned, staring across the bay at the gigantic mountain that dominated the island. 'Get used to it, *mon ami*. You'll not get too much vintage Loire in these parts.'

Léonie jumped as she felt a hand on her shoulder. From the frisson that went through her, she knew instantly who it was.

The captain nodded to them both and braced one boot against a cannon. Léonie's pulse fluttered as it always did when he was close.

'You will enjoy our stop here,' François said, pointing at the mountain. 'Duplessis is twitchy to gather his young naturalists the moment we reach land, and drag you up El Pilón.'

Léonie swallowed. The chief botanist had talked of nothing else for most of the voyage so far, but she had not imagined the mountain would be so big. 'It is . . . higher than I had expected,' she murmured.

François grinned, a flash of white teeth in the morning sun. 'We shall travel part of the distance by wagon, never fear.'

'We? You will join the expedition, then?'

He nodded, scanning the mountain hungrily. 'I've not climbed Teide Peak since before I sailed to the American War. My legs could do with a stretch as much as yours, Chambois.'

Léonie said nothing. She had a sudden yearning to find a quiet courtyard and spend a day sipping cool exotic fruit juices, reading poetry and fanning herself. It took some resolve to cast such feminine desires aside and make herself eager for a hot, dusty trek up the side of a mountain to gather botanical specimens.

★ ★ ★

By the time the expedition returned, Léonie could barely put one foot in front of the other. They had walked and climbed and scrambled to the roof of the earth, or so it seemed. Her back was weary from bending to gather rare plants under Duplessis' sharp gaze, and despite the wide-brimmed straw hat she had worn, her neck was burnt from the unrelenting sun.

If there was one thing she had learned that day, it was that Léonie, Vicomtesse de Chambois, was not born to the botanical sciences. She had watched the captain striding up the volcanic slopes as though such exertion energized rather than sapped the strength in his limbs. And though she had neither the breath nor the opportunity to talk to him, during their short respites to sip water and eat oranges from the trees that hugged the mountainside, she had felt his eyes searching her out among their little group.

The *Aurélie* had never looked as beautiful as when they returned to the ship in the longboat. Dusk was falling, crimson and gold across the western slopes of El Pilón, and the rhythmic strokes of the oars nearly sent her to sleep on the spot. But Christian, who had also joined the expedition, nudged her awake.

90

When they reached their cabin, Léonie let her thoughts dwell on one little luxury she had always so taken for granted at home — a hot rose-scented bath. It was a heavenly impossibility, so she made do, as always, with a quick wash from the enamel basin in her cabin.

Much as she longed to simply tumble into her bunk and fall into a dreamless sleep, Christian would not permit it.

'We have but two days here and then many weeks until our next port of call. You'll curse yourself for missing a night ashore, my sweet.'

Léonie's protestations fell on deaf ears and finally she struggled into her scarlet breeches and dark-blue frock coat. She balked at the weight of the smallsword, but Christian strapped it on her anyway and jammed her tricorne on to her head before pushing her out the door.

And now they sat, in falling darkness, on the terrace of an open-air café, sipping a sharp but pleasant red wine that did, after all, remind Léonie of her father's estates in the Loire. At one end of the wide stone terrace a swarthy Spaniard played swirling music on his guitar while a girl in a tight scarlet dress that unashamedly bared her knees danced with wildly sensuous movements.

Léonie could barely keep her eyes off the dancer. Nothing could have been farther from the courtly dances of the French court, performed sedately to the latest Mozart minuets. And yet there was a wild earthiness to the performance that excited Léonie.

She watched the dancer lift some black wooden castanets from the low wall that bordered the café, then leap back into her dance, spinning and turning as the instruments clattered in frenzied accompaniment. From the corner of her eye, Léonie noticed a tall man dressed in the uniform of a French naval officer step on to the terrace. The swirling dancer spotted him at the same moment and wove herself around him in a blur of red silk and brown legs.

Léonie caught her breath, staring at Captain de la Tour as the woman's openly seductive dance entrapped him. For the first time in her entire life she experienced jealousy as she saw his eyes travel the length of that sinuous — and oh so womanly — body.

She turned away, but not before she felt his eyes light upon her. Christian murmured a quick warning, but in seconds the captain stood at their table.

'*Bonsoir, mes petits,*' he intoned gravely.

'I trust you are rested after our little stroll up El Pilón.'

'Of course, *Capitaine*,' Christian replied, standing to offer him a chair. He signalled the waiter for more wine. Léonie caught an unmistakable frown darken her friend's brow.

The captain spun the chair around and sat astride, facing Léonie across the small table.

'I'm glad I found you, Lavelle. I believe Pierre Grévin wishes to speak with you. You'll find him at the Marinero Féliz, near the dockyards.'

'Now, Captain?'

François raised one black eyebrow. 'I assume he did not mean next week, Lavelle.'

Christian coughed, gave his commander a stiff bow and turned to go. For a second he hesitated then looked quickly between Léonie and the captain. 'Will you be all right, Jean-Michel?' he asked quietly.

Léonie grimaced at the thunderous expression that suddenly blackened the captain's face. 'Be all right?' he bellowed. 'Dammit, man, the boy is safe enough from these Spanish hooligans with his commander. He'll never get to be a man if you hover around him like some guardian angel. Be gone, I tell you!'

Christian, wisely, vanished into the night. Léonie hid a smile behind her glass of blood-red claret. She sipped the strong vintage, intoxicated by the heady mixture of wine, music and the scent of orange blossoms. She looked up, purposely avoiding François' gaze, and stared at the bowl of stars piercing the night sky.

'This is a very beautiful place,' she murmured.

The *mozo* set a new carafe of wine on the rough wooden table, and placed a clean glass beside it. François tossed a few coins on the waiter's tray and poured himself a glass. He held it out to Léonie.

'To fair winds and God's speed.'

Léonie touched her glass to his. '*Santé.*'

The café was filling up with a mixture of local merchants and seafarers from some of the numerous ships anchored near the *Aurélie* in the bay. There were even a few red frock coats of the British Navy among the revellers. Although France and England were no longer at war, the emotions fired by the American Revolution had yet to cool, and there was no cordiality between blue coats and red.

'So, my young *vicomte*,' said the captain. 'You and your faithful watchdog are not enjoying a night of debauchery in the whorehouses, eh? What's the matter, you don't like women?'

Léonie almost choked on her wine. She set the glass on the table.

'I have no taste for painted women,' she replied, avoiding his eyes.

His lips twitched with amusement. 'Any woman will look good to you by the time this voyage is over.'

Léonie knew that would not be so, but she could scarcely explain why, so she turned her attention to the couples who had begun to dance in the centre on the terrace — local girls teaching their sensuous movements to a handful of delighted sailors.

'Perhaps it is not their painted faces you dislike,' François continued, an edge to his voice that she'd not heard before. 'Perhaps you prefer to mix only with the flighty socialites of Paris and Versailles.'

She stared at him, hurt by his tone. 'I have no great admiration for the women of my class, Captain. But there are some I value.'

He laughed, but it was a mirthless sound. 'Like your *maman*, perhaps? I am told she is a great favourite with Marie-Antoinette. Does she prefer to play shepherdess or milkmaid at the palace toy farm?'

'Neither!' Léonie snapped, uncomfortable to hear him criticize her mother, even though his feelings on the subject so closely matched her own.

'Ah! I fear I have touched a nerve.' He tapped a finger thoughtfully against his glass. 'But then, you have sisters, no doubt, whose ambitions are perhaps as great as your mother's?'

She blushed and averted her face. 'I have one sister,' she mumbled, 'and she finds life at court suffocating.'

Léonie risked a peek at him then, anxious to judge how he would absorb this information. His eyebrows rose a fraction.

'Indeed. Then how does she find air to breathe?'

'She . . . she has gone away,' Léonie replied lamely. 'To a convent.'

'A drastic step. The air at Versailles must indeed be too rich for the girl.'

Léonie wished she could explain her predicament to him — and then realized she could. She would, after all, be recounting the unhappy situation not of herself, but of her 'sister'. She sipped her wine and looked the captain in the eye.

'My father had arranged for my sister — Léonie — to be married to a man almost as old as himself. A marquis. He is very wealthy and has great influence at court, but she does not — cannot — love him.'

'Your sister, I take it, is a romantic,' François observed drily.

'She is young and frets at the chains of propriety that bind her. So she ran away to a nunnery.'

'No doubt that pleased your father.'

She shrugged. 'I do not know. He is seldom home.'

There was silence for a while. Léonie watched the captain refill his glass and fiddle with the stem. He seemed almost angry, as though the story disturbed him.

'You . . . you do not admire the aristocracy, *Capitaine*?' she asked at length.

He looked up. 'Admire? No, I do not admire. I have been at sea and at war too many times, seen too much suffering, to hold admiration for a troop of peacocks with nothing better to do than strut about the ballrooms of Versailles. They waste their lives plotting amorous conquests of each other's wives and squandering France's greatness.'

Léonie was astonished by his outburst. 'I see you have become a follower of the new thinking. The war in America has changed many attitudes in France.'

'You were there, Chambois,' he replied, looking up at her suddenly. 'Did it not occur to you that if the colony were French

97

instead of British, we might have fought on the losing side?'

Léonie opened her mouth, but could think of no answer. She took refuge in her drink, helping herself to more from the nearly empty carafe. She was confused, heady with wine and the unexpected pleasure of having a man talk to her of something so real, so vital, as politics. Yet she was also stung by his rebuff for all that she and her family represented.

She wondered why he had chosen this café to pass the evening. Why was he not with the first officer or his old friend the surgeon? What had made the captain seek out her lowly company?

Fate was playing cruel games at her expense, punishing her for her deceit by throwing into her path the very kind of man she had always dreamed about — only to make him utterly beyond her reach. For surely, even if she were not damned in his eyes for her disguise, the very social fabric from which her family was woven would repel and disgust him.

It was as well, she thought, suppressing a sigh.

The captain signalled to a Spanish girl leaning against the stone wall of the café.

She crossed toward them, swinging her hips seductively.

'*¿Señor?*'

The woman was not much older than Léonie, with ruby lips and flowing black hair. She wore a simple red and black skirt with a wide belt that emphasized her narrow waist and ample bosom, and her feet and legs were bare.

Léonie wondered if the captain had decided the maid would be better company than she. She watched him tuck an arm around the girl, speaking to her in fluent Spanish, of which Léonie understood not a word. But she understood the girl's seductive laugh and felt bitterness rise in her throat.

He threw a gold coin on the rough wooden tabletop and the girl snatched it up.

'*Voilà*, Jean-Michel,' he said, his good humour apparently restored by the wench. 'I have bought you the price of your manhood.' He pushed the girl around the table to where Léonie sat, open-mouthed. 'Did I not say this voyage would either kill you or make you a man?'

'*Capitaine?*' She earnestly hoped it was the strong Spanish wine that made her tremble so suddenly.

He laughed. 'You said you had no great love of society ladies, so Carmelita here will teach you what you've never learned at Versailles — and a great deal more, besides. Pray, don't thank me,' he said, holding up a hand in protest. 'Consider her services a gift from your captain. I detest the thought that one of my officers should risk his life on my ship without at least once experiencing the pleasures of the flesh.'

Léonie was transfixed with horror. The wretched girl was leaning over her now, her bosom mere inches from Léonie's bulging eyes. Christian had never thought to warn her about this!

'It-it is quite unnecessary,' she stammered.

But the captain was having none of it. He winked at the girl and said something rapid in Spanish, which caused her to giggle and grab Léonie by the sleeve. Léonie resisted, feeling a hot flush of embarrassment as she heard cheers from other tables nearby.

As the prostitute bent over her, stroking her face with her fingers and murmuring encouragement in broken French, Léonie shut her eyes and prayed for divine intervention.

How would she talk her way out of this disaster? What on earth could she do? If she refused the girl, it would only confirm the gossips' suspicions. Léonie swallowed. How could she refuse . . . ?

And then an idea presented itself, giving

her a sudden desire to giggle. She drew a deep breath of sweet night air to give herself courage and reached for the girl. She patted her curvaceous bottom affectionately, took her arm and got up from the table.

Hoots of bawdy laughter rose into the night from all around as she led the prostitute away toward the street.

But as she passed François, the dangerous glitter in his eyes made her heart beat wildly and caused her to wonder if she had indeed made a wise decision.

6

Palace of Versailles, May 1784

Alain de Vercours stepped back into the shadows and observed the Marquis de Grise bear down on the little group entering the Galerie des Glaces. But it was not King Louis that drew his attention. It was Eléanore, the Duchess de Chambois, as beautiful and tantalizing as ever he remembered. Oh, how he had wanted to bed that raven-haired beauty.

He still did. But the passion of his youth

was gone. Now he wanted to steal her from the ducal bed and show her what she had missed these more than twenty years. He leaned his back against the window alcove and watched her from beneath hooded lids, letting his lurid imagination conjure up some of the things he would like to do to the duchess. Things that had earned him a fearful reputation among the whores of Paris.

Perhaps she would be amused. A smile twisted Vercours' thin lips. No, *she* would not be. But it would amuse him greatly, for a while.

His attention was drawn back to Alphonse de Grise. The odious creature was clearly angered with the duke and duchess, for he shook his fat ruby-ringed finger in their faces. Vercours felt a stirring of interest. There was so little to occupy one's attention these days at Versailles, and he was bored with piquet.

He pushed himself away from the window and moved easily through the crowd until he was close enough to hear snippets of the conversation by the door.

'I'll be damned, so I will Your Grace, if I'll see myself made the laughing stock like this without . . . without . . . '

'Without what, *monsieur*?' asked the Duc de Chambois in an icy voice. Vercours could clearly see the duke struggling to hold his temper in check.

Alphonse spluttered with rage, but his anger made him even less coherent than usual. Eléanore tapped her ebony fan on the sweating nobleman's sleeve and smiled her prettiest.

'Calm yourself, my dear Alphonse. I am sure Léonie will be found and all this can be cleared up.' Her words piqued Vercours' interest and he edged closer. 'I really do not know what the child can be thinking,' continued the duchess. 'Your betrothal should have pleased her. Such a suitable arrangement.'

De Grise appeared somewhat mollified. Vercours watched him wipe a large white kerchief across his sweaty brow. 'Well, to be sure, Your Grace, the girl is young. As was my first wife, God rest her soul. But I was promised your daughter and I mean to have her!'

So, the lovely Léonie needed to be found, did she? Maybe there was something to interest him at court after all. Vercours well remembered his conversation with the firebrand the day he'd killed her brother. He smiled to himself. If he could not have his sweet revenge on the duchess, he could always bed the daughter. He had a liking for sweet young flesh — especially when it covered so enticing a little tigress.

Suddenly he felt Eléanore's eyes upon him. He inclined his head, expecting her to glance away as she had always done in the past. But she did not. She pointed her fan and tugged on her husband's arm.

'*Voilà*, Jean-Alexandre,' she cried. 'There he is. Speak to him at once. I demand it!'

Chambois stared into the crowd. His dark-red brows — the only clue that beneath his powdered wig he wore a mane of hair as red as his daughter's — creased into a frown.

'I believe you are right, my dear. Vercours, I would speak with you.'

Vercours raised one eyebrow in amusement, waiting while the duke pushed his way past a group of young nobles to confront him.

'You require my advice, Your Grace? I regret I must disappoint you, but I am not the perpetrator of your ravishing daughter's disappearance.' He let a note of mockery touch his voice. 'More's the pity.'

Chambois' voice was ice cold. 'If I for one moment suspected you were, sir, I would not waste my breath on you. One bullet would do admirably, I'm sure.'

Vercours coughed and tugged at his lace cravat, for the room was hot. The duke appeared not to notice. 'However,' he went on, 'a gentleman would not skulk about in corners eavesdropping upon the conversations of others.'

'You flatter me, Your Grace. I have been called many things, but seldom a gentleman.'

'I find no dispute with that,' Chambois continued. 'However, perhaps you would humour me by discouraging the tittle-tattles who insist you've killed my son in a duel. Jean-Michel, as I have just this evening assured the king, is engaged upon one of His Majesty's ships bound for the Pacific.'

Vercours grew very still as anger spread up his spine. He kept his voice low and even as he spoke.

'And pray, Your Grace, when did this expedition leave France?'

'On the first day of April, I believe, and if the *vicomte* had not been aboard, I assure you the Ministère de la Marine would have informed me immediately.'

'Indeed,' Vercours replied softly. For a moment he stared at the duke, turning this information over in his mind. Then he bowed and forced a smile to his lips. 'Clearly, the gossips have created an impossible tale, have they not, Your Grace?'

The duchess appeared at her husband's side, her expression full of loathing as she stared at Vercours. 'How could you permit people to say such dreadful things, *monsieur*? Have you no idea how it pains a mother's heart to hear such lies?'

He stared at her, letting his hooded gaze travel from her wide grey eyes and full mouth down to her décolleté neckline and the still-youthful curve of her bosom.

Eléanore blushed, opening her fan and fluttering it as a shield in front of her.

'I take it I have your word that you will correct this outrage?' Chambois continued doggedly.

Vercours inclined his head, then watched the pair turn away and disappear into the crowd. A servant offered him a glass of champagne, and he took the drink automatically, sipping it as he mulled over this new intelligence in his mind.

He was certain he had inflicted a mortal wound upon the boy. He had never been wrong before. And yet, within five days the *vicomte* had sailed away as though the duel had never happened? It was not possible. It could not be.

Angry with sudden doubt, he set the champagne down hard on a table and made for the door. He needed fresh air and time to think.

As he crossed the wide terrace at the rear of the palace and made for the Orangerie, he could hear titterings from some of the nobles who strolled in the cool evening air. Damn Chambois. If Jean-Michel were indeed alive and well, he, the Marquis de Vercours, would be the laughing stock of the court.

He had almost reached the Orangerie steps when an idea came to him. He stood for a moment looking down at the orange trees in their wheeled pots below, a slow smile spreading to his lips. How simple! How sweet the revenge!

Quickly, he returned to the Hall of Mirrors where he finally found Alphonse de Grise breathing all over the newly presented daughter of an Italian prince. He felt almost sorry for the girl, who was vainly trying to edge away.

Vercours held a scented kerchief to his nose and tapped Alphonse on the shoulder.

'I would speak with you, de Grise,' he said, winking at the grateful Italian, who quickly excused herself and fled.

'*Hein?* Me? Now listen, Vercours. I'll not play you at cards, nor fight with you for the eyes of a woman, so you'd best look elsewhere for your devilish amusements.'

Vercours smiled. 'I merely wish to offer my condolences, *monsieur*. I hear the beautiful Vicomtesse de Chambois has, er . . . shall we say taken her leave somewhat . . . unexpectedly?'

The marquis's eyes bulged and his port-wine nose grew scarlet. 'How the devil . . . ?'

'I regret that the palace is abuzz with the news.' He sighed ostentatiously. 'Secrets are not the stuff Versailles is made of.'

'Secrets? The place thrives on them — spreading them around like honey for the wasps! A man can't get the clap these days without the ladies giggling behind their accursed fans every time he passes. Damn idle chatter.'

Vercours found his sympathetic expression becoming harder to maintain. The man was a reptile. Even *he* couldn't wish such a blustering fool on the spirited young Léonie.

'So,' he prompted, 'it is but a rumour. You are still engaged to be married to the Vicomtesse de Chambois?'

'Engaged? I'm engaged, all right. All signed and sealed. But damn me if the girl hasn't taken it in her head to become a nun!'

'A — nun?' Vercours asked softly, suppressing a desire to laugh outright. He grappled with the idea of the young firebrand meekly accepting a life of prayerful obedience, but it was too much.

'So her note said,' de Grise went on. 'Left without so much as a by-your-leave to her father, she did. Took her maid and ran off like a fox before the hunt.' He laughed, spraying spittle over the front of Vercours' scarlet coat. 'Vixen'd be more like it, eh?'

Vercours gently wiped his kerchief across the droplets staining his coat and suppressed a snarl. 'And did her note indicate the whereabouts of this . . . convent?'

'Eh?' Alphonse asked, his watery eyes narrowing suddenly. 'You're damned interested in the girl all of a sudden, aren't you, Vercours?'

'My interest is purely on your own behalf, *monsieur*. I have some influence with the Church. Perhaps I can be of service in returning your betrothed to your loving arms.'

'Eh? Well, I must say. That's most generous of you. Most generous.' He thought for a moment, stroking a pudgy hand across his abdomen. 'I think it was Switzerland. Now what town did Chambois say? Bern? No. Ah — I have it — somewhere in the Vaud district. A Carmelite house. Didn't say which.'

'If I were to return the errant lady to you — say prior to your nuptials . . . When did you plan to marry, exactly?'

'Eh? Well — All Saints, it was. Plenty of time for her to come to her senses, I expect.' Alphonse stared at him, shoving a large pinch of snuff into one nostril and sniffing loudly. His eyes watered and he spoke on the rise of a sneeze. 'What's it to you, anyway? Meddling in other people's — ' He sneezed. Vercours ducked just in time.

'Fear not, my dear Alphonse,' he said, as he wiped something unmentionable from his cuff. 'I've had my eye on that remarkable pair of greys you purchased from Foucault. How say you to a small wager?'

'You want my horses?'

Vercours shrugged to feign disinterest. 'A fair exchange for my trouble, I would have thought.'

'You'll bring her back unscathed,' de Grise sputtered. 'I'll not have second-hand goods.' Vercours nodded. 'Very well, man. You have till the day before the wedding on November 1st, not a day more. I wish I could say I was in danger of losing my greys, but if you knew the chit as I do, you'd know better.' He snorted and turned away, leaving Alain de Vercours staring after him with undisguised loathing.

Tenerife, April 1784

The victorious smile on Léonie's lips did not last long. By the time Carmelita had led the way up the narrow stairs of a bordello in the stench-ridden dock quarter of Santa Cruz, she was wishing herself back in the safety of her cabin.

Resolutely, she climbed the last of the stairs, flattening herself against the wall as a pair of urchins in ragged clothes pushed rudely past.

'*Entrar*,' Carmelita murmured, opening the door of a dank little room where a single candle burned in a dish on the nightstand. Léonie followed reluctantly.

The Spanish girl closed the door and immediately crossed to the bed, unbuttoning her crimson blouse as she went.

'Wait!' Léonie cried in alarm. Carmelita's hands paused.

'*¿Señor?*'

'No,' Léonie answered, pulling off her tricorne and twisting it in her hands. 'That is . . . you wouldn't understand.'

The girl stared, her eyes wide and suspicious. 'Your *capitán*, he says you need to make love to a woman, to make you a man for the first time. He pay me well.'

Léonie coughed, looked away from the comely bosom that was now half exposed, and strode to the window. She flicked aside the filthy curtain and peered down at the street.

This was madness, yet she felt committed

now. The prostitute was waiting, ready to perform the abomination without so much as an ounce of concern. How could men do this? Come to a place like this — buy a woman as though she were of no consequence? Where was romance, and courtship? Did men not need those wonderful secret moments Léonie had yearned for? The hints, the stolen glances across a crowded room that spoke of love?

She knew Paris was awash with prostitutes, of course. But she had never thought about them, never imagined what going with one might be like. And now here she was in this diseased hovel with a young girl ready to offer her the most precious gift a woman could bestow on a man . . .

She dug into the pocket of her breeches and withdrew a shining gold Louis. Turning to Carmelita, Léonie held it up so it caught the candlelight.

'Would you like to earn a little more than my captain paid?'

The girl licked her lips at the sight of the coin. '*Sí, Señor.*' Then she frowned, clutching her half-open blouse with fingers. 'But I am not like some girls. I do not — '

'Don't worry!' Léonie assured her hastily, not wanting a list of the sordid tricks that were too terrible even for one versed in the art of paid sex. 'I require nothing of you that I would not ask of any God-fearing woman.'

Carmelita cocked her head on one side and stared at her strange visitor.

'Do up your blouse,' Léonie ordered and then waited while the puzzled girl did as she was bid.

'For you to earn this gold Louis, I require two things. Firstly, your absolute silence.' The girl nodded warily. 'Secondly, a large bath filled with hot water.'

Carmelita stared. '¿*Queréis un baño, Usted?*'

'Yes, I require a bath.' At the café it had seemed like the perfect use of the opportunity the captain had presented her. Now, in this awful place, Léonie wondered if there even were such a thing.

Suddenly, Carmelita burst out laughing. 'First the French *capitán* pays me, then the *señor* pays me — for a bath!' She giggled.

'If you can't help me . . . ' Léonie said stiffly, pocketing the coin.

The girl's eyes widened. 'Oh, *perdone!* I am sorry, I do not mean to laugh. It is just . . . the *capitán*, he said you were — '

'Never mind!' Léonie interrupted her hastily. 'Can you provide a bath or not? And I require clean towels and soap.'

113

Carmelita nodded, grinning, and opened the door.

'¿*Señorita!* Remember, silence if you want your gold!'

Within minutes, she was back, carrying an armful of miraculously white towels and a bar of golden soap. Behind her, eyes averted, came two older women carrying a large metal tub which they placed in the centre of the floor. They returned with buckets of hot water to fill the bath and then discreetly withdrew, all without a single glance at Carmelita's strange customer.

Carmelita stood holding the towels and soap. 'You wish that I undress you, *señor?*'

'No!' Léonie gestured to the bed that was draped with a grubby red blanket. 'Put the towels down. I have no further need of your services.' She tossed the coin across the room and Carmelita caught it in a flash.

'You wish me to go?'

'*Gracias.*'

'But — '

'I shall require the room for one hour. Make sure that I am not disturbed, understand?'

The girl nodded and with one last look at her strange benefactor, slipped out of the room. Léonie turned the rusty key in the lock and heaved a sigh of heartfelt relief.

She undressed quickly and slid into the

deliciously warm bath, soaping herself all over and revelling in the feel of water on her skin. Since boarding the *Aurélie*, the only washing she had been able to do was a sponge bath once a day. It would be two months before they would again make landfall, and Léonie was determined to enjoy this unexpected good fortune.

She closed her eyes and imagined herself in a huge marble bath sprinkled with rose petals. As she drifted off into her imaginary world, she envisioned her lover carrying a fragrant red rose. He sat on the edge of the bath and stroked her shoulder, softly, sensuously, with the petals of the rose, leaving a trail of dewy moisture on her skin. She looked up, her heart drowsy with love.

It was François.

The image was so tempting she couldn't resist. She lay in the water with her eyes closed and gave her imagination free rein over her senses. Just for once. It was so delicious to think of herself as a woman for a while, to dream of what might have been, even if in her heart she knew it was impossible.

Her skin quivered beneath the soft strokes of the rose as in her mind she watched François' face descend slowly toward her. A tiny sigh escaped her lips as she raised her face for his kiss . . .

★ ★ ★

Three weeks later, as the ship languished in the Doldrums near the Equator, Léonie stood barefoot on the quarterdeck, her thumbs tied by a rope that bound her to Christian on one side and a naval cadet on the other. Beyond them, three other officers were similarly secured. On the portside, beyond the open space occupied by one of the longboats, which was now filled with seawater, stood a row of *matelots*, also tied in a row by their thumbs.

She held her breath. One hundred and sixty faces turned up in the fierce noonday sun that hung directly overhead, and waited.

A blood-curdling scream rose on the humid air and then eight shouting, squealing, tar-blacked bodies, as naked as heathens, hurled themselves down from their perches in the rigging. Behind them came the boatswain, the clockmaker, the engineer, the master carpenter and the chief armourer, all dressed in the most outlandish fashion Léonie could imagine. The boatswain, who clearly headed the strange procession, wore a horned tiara to distinguish him from the other celebrants in their sheepskins and ram's horns. Barking and mewing, and generally sounding like escapees from Bedlam, the bizarre group

116

followed the blackened boys down to the deck where they began leaping and dancing around their prisoners in a feverish frenzy.

Léonie stood her ground as one of the naked boys — whom she recognized only with difficulty as the captain's young valet, Vincent — slithered between her and Christian and began cavorting around them, making wild gestures and screaming like a banshee. Léonie averted her eyes, though there were so many of the urchins she could barely focus on anything that wasn't indecent. The boys were tarred with lamp-black and decorated with feathers that floated off in the sticky heat as they danced and sweated around the deck.

'Shut your eyes, Jean-Mich,' Christian ordered as he, too, endeavoured to avoid his clothes becoming smeared by the offensive substances on a small black body.

'Christian, you never told me crossing the line would be like this! I thought we would have a special meal prepared by the cook, and maybe a bottle or two of something from the captain's reserve!'

He grinned. 'Relax, *mom ami*. All neophytes must endure this the first time they cross the Equator. And I'm told' — he ducked to avoid a tar-sticky feather that was floating with intent near his face — 'that it gets worse!'

Léonie groaned. Her thumbs were sore from their confinement in the rope, and the chaos around her was aggravating a headache that sailing in these sultry waters seemed to bring.

Suddenly the noise subsided. 'Father Line' sat upon his 'throne' specially made by the carpenters for the occasion, and proceeded to read a proclamation. The prisoners had to say 'I swear' after each of these ridiculous bans, promising that they would repeat this farce with all first-timers on future crossings, that they would never make love to the wife of an absent sailor, and so on. Léonie began to giggle as the horned masqueraders began asking who would buy their freedom. But with Christian's warning fresh in her mind, she was glad to drop some coins into the basket held under her nose.

Within seconds she was free. She quickly sought shelter from the sun beneath the shade of the poop deck, where the wardroom servants, seeming to be the only sanity in so much madness, passed her a cool drink. Wine was already flowing amongst the crew on this special occasion, and some of their number grew bawdy on the mixture of alcohol and relentless sun.

Léonie found herself searching the assembled crew for the captain. She spotted him leaning against the starboard rails talking to the surgeon. He seemed so relaxed, as though this chaos was nothing to concern him.

He turned his head suddenly and stared straight at Léonie. She raised her glass a fraction in salute and looked away. Since that evening in the café in Santa Cruz, he had been standoffish, and Léonie was puzzled that her acceptance of the gift of the prostitute should seem to have angered him. She missed the few chances she'd had to talk with him about the voyage or her work during the first leg to Tenerife. She sighed and turned her attention back to the quarter deck.

Christian was in the thick of the battle that raged around the longboat. He had been hustled on to the flat blade of an oar and now sat suspended over the water-filled longboat.

'Do you buy your freedom, Lieutenant Lavelle?' yelled one of the drunken *matelots*. Christian reached into the pocket of his dovegrey breeches and withdrew a coin which he threw at the man.

'There, you vagabond,' he replied with a laugh. 'Now let me down!'

'Let him down,' yelled the sailor, winking at the man who held the oar. He promptly released it, sending Christian tumbling into the longboat with a mighty splash. Léonie ran to the boat, ready to berate the ruffians, but Christian was chuckling as he struggled from his baptismal waters.

'Are you all right?' she called.

'Hey,' slurred a huge bear of a man behind her. 'Lookee — the little officer is worried his friend can't swim!'

'He don't need to swim, Dupont. He can walk on water like all the snuff-noses!'

Léonie ignored them and reached out a hand to Christian, but he had jumped from the boat and was eagerly accepting a water-filled bucket from Vincent. He disappeared into the crowd, searching out the perpetrator of his drenching. Clearly he was entering into the spirit of the day. Léonie turned away, then jumped when a beefy arm was wrapped suddenly around her shoulders.

'Say, my friends, do you think it right the nobs keep this little morsel all to themselves, eh?'

'Not a bit of it, Grandet. Here, give the lad some wine. He needs to mellow up.'

Léonie felt real alarm. The blood began to pound in her ears as three men started to herd her away down the for'ard steps to the lower deck. They were each a foot taller and a hundred pounds heavier than she, and she looked around wildly for an escape.

They were at the steps now, pushing her down, but so close that she lost her footing and stumbled. The one called Grandet caught her by the arms and threw her across his shoulders. In seconds, she found herself alone with the men in the 'tween deck, where the stench of human sweat was almost choking in the airless heat.

'Let me go, you brutes!' she cried, genuinely alarmed. 'How dare you touch an officer! Let me down this instant!'

'Squeals like a girl,' said the third man, with an evil laugh that made Léonie's skin crawl. Grandet set her on the deck, pushing her down on to a pile of hammocks. She crawled backwards, eyeing the three monsters, until she felt the unyielding shape of the bulkhead block her retreat.

'You'll not escape us down here, pretty boy. This is the 'tween deck. No fancy officers down here to protect you.'

'Twenty-two days at sea, Mascarin,' said the third sailor, 'and you're an animal. Leave the boy be. If the captain hears of this, he'll have you flogged.'

'Bah!' spat Mascarin as he approached Léonie. She could smell his putrid breath from two feet away and felt her stomach heave in protest as his filthy unshaven face drew close. He was on all fours now, crawling toward her where she cringed among the stinking hammocks. She felt among them for something, anything, she could use as a weapon, but there was nothing. Only sweat-stiffened sailcloth and short ropes for attaching the beds to the ceiling at night.

Just as the lurching sailor's fetid mouth was almost on her, there was a roar and Mascarin toppled sideways.

François stood behind the men, Christian and two soldiers at his side. In his hand was a wooden bucket, which he had obviously used to fell the sailor.

'Place these men under arrest!' he barked, glaring at the trio with such ferocity that Léonie trembled, although she was so glad to see him.

He knelt before her, grasping her hands which shook violently now it was all over. 'Are you all right, *petit?*'

She nodded. The concern in his dark-blue eyes touched her and she had to struggle not to burst into womanly tears.

'I'm not hurt, *Capitaine*, thanks to you.'

As the captain helped her to her feet, she saw Christian's pale face behind him. He looked stricken that such a thing could have happened. She gave him a wobbly smile.

'I'm fine, Christian. I promise. The brutes had drunk too much of Father Neptune's wine, 'tis all.'

The soldiers removed the now subdued matelots and François helped Léonie to the steps. She blinked as they reached the bright sunlight once more, and allowed herself to be led toward the safety of the wardroom. She didn't care if she never took part in another crossing of the line as long as she lived.

On deck the fracas continued. As she walked between François and Christian, a sudden movement caught her eye and she turned just in time to see a bucket of seawater being thrown in her direction. She tried to duck, but it was too late.

The reveller ran off, hooting with delight, and Léonie stood there, dripping from her hair to her knees. She looked down at the puddle forming around her feet and froze in horror. The impact of the cold water had made her nipples harden and had glued her shirt to her skin.

Her small round breasts, which in deference to the intense Equatorial heat she had left unbound, stood clearly outlined beneath the thin cotton for all on deck to see.

7

Le Château Aristide, June 1784

'Catch me quick and kiss me quicker!' Jean-Michel called over his shoulder as he took the steps two at a time and made for the apple orchard with long strides.

Marie wailed as she endeavoured to keep up and nearly tumbled headlong into the sweet spring clover that grew thickly beneath the blossom-covered trees. She was too out of breath to speak as she stumbled on after the viscount. The intoxicating scent of apple blossom filled her senses as she followed, more sedately now that he had disappeared beneath the snowy boughs.

'Marie!' he called, his voice light and teasing. She stopped for an instant and then turned in the direction of the rope swing that they had discovered during their first days on the Franche-Comté estate.

'There you are at last,' he said, the letter still clutched firmly in his hand.

'Please give it to me, *monsieur*. I beg of you,' she implored.

He shook his head, his grey eyes sparkling. 'Kiss me first, little one. 'Tis the price of news today. And don't call me *monsieur*. Do you want someone to hear?'

She shook her head, eyeing the letter in his hand and judging how far she would have to reach if she were to snatch it from his fingers.

'Uh-Uh!' he cried, raising it high above his head. 'You'll not get it that way, my girl.' He laughed. 'Come now, one simple kiss. Is it so much to ask?'

'Jean-Michel,' she said reprovingly, wishing he would stop tormenting her. All these past weeks since they had fled Paris, she had been yearning for some news from home, and now it was finally here, he would not give it to her. She let her eyes dwell a moment on his lips. A simple kiss? Simple for him, perhaps. How many times in her dreams had she imagined such a kiss? And yet that was all she could have, Dreams. The likes of a lady's maid could never harbour such yearnings for the Vicomte de Chambois.

She gazed at him in silence, standing just beyond his reach where he sat on the swing beneath the tree.

'A gentleman would not tease a lady so,' she said, trying not to smile at the impish expression he wore.

'But I am not a gentleman, sweet Marie. I am but a humble stable hand in the service of your uncle Jacques, who is himself no more than chief groom for the ancient Comte de Vaux.'

'He is not so old.'

'Marie, Marie! He is so decrepit he thinks the Sun King is yet on the throne of France! And thank heaven for it. If he were anything less than a recluse in his dotage, he might be tempted to visit Versailles and catch some idle gossip that would destroy our cosy hideaway.' He shook his head. 'No, we couldn't have had a happier position than at the Château Aristide. We are safe here.'

Marie sank to the grass and leaned her back against a trunk, facing him. 'But it is not right, Jean-Michel, for you to be a servant. You should be out upon the seas seeking adventure, and my mistress should be rehearsing her wedding vows to milord Alphonse.' She sighed. 'Such a fearful mess.'

The viscount's eyes darkened and he leaned toward her, wrapping his fingers around her chin and turning up her face. Tears of despair blurred her eyes but did not fall.

'My poor, sweet Marie. You were ever our conscience when we were children. But you must not take this madness on your shoulders. 'Twas none of your doing.'

She trembled beneath his touch, wishing she had somehow been able to help them. After her mother, Léonie and Jean-Michel were the two people most dear to her in all the world, and her heart was heavy with dread whenever she thought of the terrible life her mistress must be living.

'Come to me,' he said softly, drawing her to her feet. He wrapped an arm around her waist and pulled her into his lap. 'Here, take your letter.'

She blinked away the unshed tears and kissed him shyly on the cheek.

Jean-Michel stared at her for a second, and she felt the fire in his gaze. She looked away, embarrassment burning her face. With fumbling fingers she broke the seal on the paper and unfolded it. Another letter tumbled out.

'What's this?' Jean-Michel asked. It was addressed to Héloïse in Christian's handwriting and the seal was broken. He opened it. Inside was a letter from Léonie, penned in Tenerife. At the top she had written:

Dearest Nounou
Please give this to Jean-Michel so he may copy it in his own hand and send it to Papa. I dare not send it myself, for no

one can imitate his hand! I am well and having such an adventure! I pray nightly for my brother's health, and for Marie's forgiveness for entangling her in this sorry affair. God protect us all.

'It's from my sister.' His lips curved in a fond smile. 'As sharp as a fox still, I see.'
'What does she write?' Marie asked, her own letter forgotten for the moment.
' 'Tis her — my — report to Papa. It is the custom to write home at every port, so the mail can be carried by ships returning to France. I must copy it or Papa will recognize her pretty script in an instant.'
He dropped the letter to the grass. 'But read yours first. I am anxious to know the gossip from Paris.'
Marie tried very hard to ignore the firmness of his hands around her waist and bowed her head over her mother's letter. It had been penned by her cousin in Paris, but the voice behind the words was clearly that of Héloïse.

Ma chère fille, Marie read. *There is great uproar at the Hôtel de Chambois. Monsieur le Duc roars like a bull and Madame cries quietly in her chamber. All the servants have been interviewed and I*

128

have had to go to confession three times for the terrible lies I have had to tell, may God forgive me! Three times Milord has made me repeat these blasphemies, yet I have not betrayed you.

Jean-Michel shook his head. 'Poor Nounou. Her knees will be quite worn out from all that praying!'

Marie turned to him, wishing he could see how serious all this was. 'It is no game, *monsieur*. Maman must pray forgiveness for such falsehoods, even though she has uttered them for the most honourable of reasons.'

'You are right, of course, *petite*,' he replied solemnly, though Marie was almost certain he was secretly laughing. 'It is a very serious business. Go on, read the rest.'

She looked at him for a moment and then turned with great misgiving back to the letter.

Monsieur le Duc was so enraged by Léonie's note that he set out at once for the convent to bring his daughter home. But, hélas she was not there, though he tells no one this. He makes Madame la Duchesse tell people that Léonie felt a sudden and irresistible vocation. But there are many raised eyebrows. I fear our young

*vicomtesse is too well known for her zestful
ways. I pray that some other scandal will
make them forget our little mystery until
the time comes for God to deliver Léonie
safely home from the terrors of the sea.*

Marie paused and the letter fluttered in
the light summer breeze.

'What is it?' Jean-Michel asked. 'Marie,
you are trembling.'

'I am sorry, *monsieur*. It is just that I, too,
have nightmares for Léonie. What can have
happened to her, trapped on a great ship
. . . with all those . . . those . . . men!'

Jean-Michel smiled, stroking her hair with
his fingers. 'You worry too much, little one.
She has Christian at her side, don't forget.
He will take care no harm comes to your
mistress.'

Marie looked at him, trying to assess his
belief in his own words, but his eyes told
her little. She so hoped he was right, though
the misgivings remained. She lifted the letter
again, smoothing the creases.

*There is news of that evil rake, the Marquis
de Vercours. Beware this man,* ma fille *for
he can destroy us all! I have heard from
Géricault, his butler, who is courting my
second cousin, Mathilde — you remember,*

she works in that little millinery shop on the Rue Beaupré — anyway, Géricault says that Vercours has set his heart on finding the vicomtesse and returning her to the Marquis de Grise. His spies are at this very moment searching France for news of her!

'Damn!' Jean-Michel muttered.

Marie blessed herself but continued reading.

Géricault was quite certain from the instructions he overheard that the marquis does not know exactly which convent she went to. But you must warn Jean-Michel, ma petite, for there could be spies in Franche-Comté even as you read this. Ah me, I do not know which way to turn or what to do. This is all such madness.

It is too dangerous for you to write to me. You must send a letter to my sister on the Rue d'Antoine.

God be with you both.

They sat in silence when Marie had finished her mother's letter. From beyond the orchard they could hear the tinkling of the horses' harness as the farmhands ploughed the cornfield below the château, and from all around them came a chorus

131

of bees gorging themselves on apple blossom and sweet clover.

'So,' Jean-Michel said at last, letting the swing move slowly back and forth but still holding tight to Marie's waist. 'Vercours thinks to expose us himself, does he? No doubt he is disappointed he did not kill me the first time.'

'What can you mean?' Marie asked, aghast.

He slid her from his knee and stood up. 'He means to discover our plot, *ma petite*. Why else would he interest himself in Chambois affairs?'

Marie pressed her mother's letter against her bosom and stared at him in horror. 'But what possible reason could he have, Jean-Michel?'

His laugh was soft but made her shiver.

'For revenge, Marie.'

'Revenge? He almost kills you with a pistol, and yet you say it is he who seeks revenge? I do not understand.'

Jean-Michel turned and stared at her for a moment. 'No, Marie. You are so sweet and so innocent, it is not in you to comprehend what can drive a villain like Vercours to do the things he does. But you see, many many years ago, when Papa was courting my mother, Vercours too, had his hopes.'

'The marquis wished to marry Madame?'

He laughed shortly. 'Perhaps. At least he wished to have sport with her, so I have heard. But she would not have him and she married my father instead and refused to take Vercours as her lover. My mother, you see, for all her faults, is a woman of character. And she truly loves my father.'

'So now *Monsieur* de Vercours will try to destroy Madame?'

The vicomte's jaw flexed with sudden anger that made Marie tremble. 'He will destroy us all if we grant him the smallest chance.'

The Equator, June 1784

The tap on the door came a mere heartbeat after Léonie had wrapped her breasts in fresh muslin and shrugged into a clean shirt.

Christian ducked under the lintel and closed the door softly behind him.

Léonie's fingers grew suddenly stiff and clumsy as she fumbled with the ties at her neck. She took a quick breath and summoned the courage to ask the question she so dreaded.

'Did he see? Did everyone on deck observe me?'

'I saw.'

133

The blush crept into her cheeks no matter how hard she tried to will it away. 'And — ' She couldn't bring herself to say the captain's name.

'I don't know. Maybe. Maybe not.' Christian ran a hand through his fair hair, which had lost its riband during the mêlée on deck. She noticed that his clothes were still damp. 'Dammit. Léonie, I'm sorry. I should have been there with you, not joining in with the rabble. Your brother will have my blood for this, quite rightly.'

'I'm supposed to *be* Jean-Mich, Christian. You wouldn't cosset him so. He would never stand for it.'

'But you are not Jean-Mich. Those cutthroats would never have touched your brother. The captain is right to say I should watch you more carefully.'

'He said that?'

'Just now. Can you not see my ears are scalded?' He grimaced, dropping on to her bunk and wiping his eyes with one hand. 'Damn but it's hot. If only the wind would blow us from this accursed nothing of a place.'

'It will pass, *mon ami*,' Léonie said gently. 'Perhaps we shall see a breeze before night is out.'

'Perhaps. But for now, I am sent to

summon you to the hearing.'

'Hearing?'

'The captain considers that as the injured party, you have a right to hear him pass sentence on those men. He's waiting in the *grande chambre*.'

Léonie tried to swallow the sudden lump in her throat, but it wouldn't move. 'You mean I have to face them again? After what they did — tried to do — to me?'

He jumped up quickly and wrapped a brotherly arm around her shoulders. 'I'm sorry, my sweet. It will be quick, and you need not face the brutes. Stand behind the men and it will all be over in a blink. It is the captain's way. He wants you there.'

She nodded, stricken by the thought of those three vile seamen leering at her, their eyes undressing her for who-knew-what unspeakable acts.

She left the cabin without a word.

At the door to the wardroom, she paused, listening to François' angry tones as he berated the men. She considered turning back and seeking the sanctuary of her room, but knew that would not be the act of a gentleman. It would not be Jean-Michel's choice.

Resolutely, she let herself into the wardroom. Heads swivelled in her direction, but she barely noticed the *matelots* who waited chained at wrists and ankles between two armed soldiers. To their side stood the sergeant, stiff and sweating in the intense heat, but it was François who claimed her immediate attention and made her heart speed like a runaway horse. He stood tall and in command with his back to the ornate windows at the stern of the ship, a clean white shirt open halfway down his chest in deference to the heat, revealing a scattering of black hair that made Léonie's palms itch.

For a second there was silence as her eyes held the captain's gaze. He seemed to see right inside her and Léonie felt unaccountably naked. Had he seen her breasts in that brief moment on the deck after all? And if so, what would he do? With all her quaking heart, she prayed he would at least wait until after this ordeal with her attackers was over. Her shame, if her secret were uncovered before them, would be unbearable.

'Ah, Chambois,' the captain said at last. 'You are just in time. Come and stand before these foul wretches while I pass sentence.'

Though she would rather have waited by the door until it was all over, Léonie had no choice but to cross the room and stand in front of the men. If he were to expose her now, the shame would kill her.

'You have offered the gravest of insults to the person of one of my officers,' he said to the men. 'It is my intention that all aboard the *Aurélie* shall know how seriously I view this crime, and how severely such behaviour will be dealt with.'

He was going to make an example of them? Léonie felt the sweat forming beneath her breast bandage as she wondered what terrible fate awaited her attackers. She clasped her fingers behind her back.

'Accordingly,' the captain continued, 'each of you will be dealt thirty lashes in front of the assembled crew, followed by hard labour until we reach port, at which time you will transferred to a home-bound ship in irons.'

Dear God in Heaven, Léonie prayed as she stared at the floor. A wave of bile rose from her stomach, her temples began to pound and the room grew suddenly airless and black. If I don't get out of here, I shall be violently sick, she thought in panic. She felt the boards beneath her feet sway and forced herself to breathe. Sweat ran in rivulets down her back.

But the captain was not finished. 'Monsieur le Vicomte de Chambois will be afforded the opportunity of administering any or all of this punishment himself — at his own discretion.'

Her? He expected her to take a whip to the bare skin of a man and scourge him? Once, as a child, she had witnessed a man flog his dog half to death while the miserable cur grovelled at his master's feet. After the nightmares had subsided, she had vowed she would never again stand by and watch such cruelty. Not from man to beast, nor from man to man. Never. This far she would not — could not — go. Not even for the love of her brother.

Léonie stared at the captain, aware vaguely that he — that they *all* — waited for her response. She had to move, lest she faint dead away. She strode across the wardroom to one of the cannons that stood lashed to the floor and laid her hands on the cool metal. She pretended to stare out the window at the tired grey sea, surreptitiously drawing deep, even breaths. Slowly the dark mist cleared from her eyes and she could focus.

'Well, *Monsieur l'Enseigne?*' the captain asked. 'What is your decision? We are waiting.'

She pushed herself away from the comforting chill beneath her fingers and struggled for a calm, disinterested tone.

'With the greatest of respect, *Capitaine*, I would prefer to choose some other punishment.'

There was a moment of stunned silence.

'I see. Perhaps you do not find my sentence sufficient for the insult upon your person?'

An idea was forming in Léonie's mind, and she paced back across the long room as it crystallized, stopping behind the men, whose eyes darted out at her nervously. She had seen them blanch when the captain had decreed their fate. Thirty lashes could kill a man. They knew that and so did she. From their terrified faces it was clear they feared she would increase their flogging. After what they had subjected her to, she felt some small satisfaction at their discomfort.

But for the moment Léonie remained silent. She reached out to the sergeant and with a flick of her wrist, drew his sword from its scabbard. The man's mouth dropped open in surprise, but she swivelled away before he could move.

Slowly and deliberately, she strolled behind the prisoners with the sword held loosely in her hand. A slight smile curved her lips.

'No, Captain, your punishment seems not quite fitting to me.'

'Not fitting?' François all but roared. 'What else would you have me do — feed them to the sharks one piece at a time?'

'Perhaps. But that, too, would be a kindness.'

'A . . . kindness?'

She smiled to herself as she saw she had gained the total attention of everyone in the room. Léonie was beginning to enjoy this game.

'Would you permit me, Captain, to pick a . . . more appropriate punishment? One that fell a little closer to the admonition of the Old Testament — 'an eye for an eye', isn't it?'

François' gaze narrowed. He stuck his hands in his pockets and stared at her across the heads of the men, who shifted nervously in their chains.

'What do you suggest?'

Léonie lifted the sword and trailed its razor-sharp point up the back of the man she shudderingly remembered as the one who had so nearly torn off her clothes on the 'tween deck. Mascarin. He smelled of filth and stale wine, and though she longed to abandon this whole sorry affair and seek what fresh air she could find on deck, she made herself raise the sword slowly up his stinking back. He cringed. She pursued, letting the point of the sword snag the rotten cloth and rend it slowly in two.

'Please, *Capitaine* — ' the wretch began to blubber. 'We meant the boy no harm — '

'Silence!' Léonie barked, then stole a glance

at François to see if her presumptuousness had incurred his ire.

But he seemed amused. There was a faint gleam in his eye and one corner of his mouth was unmistakably turned up.

Encouraged, Léonie continued. She lifted the sword to Mascarin's filthy neck and toyed with the riband that bound his hair. She heard him suck in his breath, felt the eyes of all three prisoners darting in supplication at the others in the room, but no one moved. Then she flicked the tip of the sword expertly, slicing through the ribbon and freeing the wretch's hair.

'Ah. That's better,' she said softly. 'Such a pretty maid you will make.'

She heard the captain's laugh, rich and full across the room.

'I see your game, *mon jeune*,' he said. 'Pray continue. The wretches' lives are in your hands.'

Léonie bowed her head in acknowledgment. 'Then I wish the men to be made to wear women's petticoats, with ribbons in their hair, and to work thus attired until we reach the tip of Africa. Perhaps this will show the crew what will become of those who think it fair sport to treat an officer of the King like a common harlot.'

Despite the heat and their sun-swarthy

complexions, the men paled visibly. Léonie handed the sword back to the sergeant, who issued sharp commands to the soldiers and the procession filed out.

She watched them go, but could not suppress a sigh of relief when the door closed.

'So, *mon petit*,' came François' voice from behind her. 'You exhibit the wisdom of a young Solomon, I see. The men will not thank you for their skins. They would rather be flogged like men than made to look fools in front of their fellows.'

'Then my purpose will be well served, *Capitaine*.'

'Yes,' he replied, staring at her. 'I believe it will.'

★ ★ ★

Night had fallen like molasses over the ship. Black and sticky with Equatorial heat, the air seemed to press down upon Léonie as she stood at the stern of the *Aurélie* and stared out at the inky ocean.

'At least we are moving,' Christian murmured at her elbow.

She nodded.

'The wake glistens so. I never imagined it would be quite like that, all froth and phosphorescence.' She sighed. 'After today, the last thing I expected to feel was any appreciation for the beauty of the sea.'

Christian's eyes caught the faint light reflected from the water as he looked down at her.

'It was not a day I wish to remember. I would give anything to have spared you such an abomination, my sweet. No woman should ever have to suffer such debasement — especially not one of your station.'

Léonie bit her lip, thinking not so much now of the terror of her abduction, but of how close she had nearly come to being forced to witness the mutilation of her attackers.

'It is over, Christian. 'Twas not your fault, and once we make landfall in Cape Town and those brutes are taken from the ship, I will breathe easier.' She clasped her arms across her chest, feeling suddenly chilled despite the sultry heat. A blackness that had nothing to do with the late hour seemed to invade her being. She could not put a name to it. Could not quite reach out and identify what troubled her. Yet it lay, dark and threatening in her mind.

'What is it, Léonie?' Christian asked, touching her arm. 'You are shivering.'

She forced a laugh, though it sounded

unsteady to her ears.

'Take care, Christian. Though all the ship's abed, they say even albatrosses have ears.'

'There's no one on deck except the helmsman below, and he's probably half-asleep. Tell me what troubles you.'

'I don't know. Nothing. Everything.' She stretched out a hand to the starless sky. 'This. What am I doing here, Christian? You were right, all of you — this is total madness. I thought it was such a fine adventure to take my brother's place once more, like when we were children. But the moon does not work its magic on the fantasy any longer. We are so far from France, from those we love and cherish. Now we have only the endless oceans for company, and men who would slit our throats for sport. And still I must play my part. I must be brave and stand day after day in my brother's shoes. I must show all the honour and strength of a gentleman, even watch men — ' Her voice broke on a sob as she tried to say 'flogged'.

'Hush, Léonie! Don't think on it. Soon we'll reach the Île de France. There will be balls and fine dinners and all the good things of life for a while.'

She pushed him away, fearful lest someone

prowling the midnight deck might spot their embrace.

'It will be well for you, *mon ami*,' she said sadly, 'to enjoy such pleasures. But for me it promises only further torture. How will I be able to bear the sight of the captain flirting and dancing with the ladies, while I . . . while I am dressed like a boy puppet?' She shuddered. 'I think I would rather stay aboard and work on my sketches.'

They were silent for a moment, staring out across the oily waters toward the faint glimmer of light from the *Mousquetaire*. The supply ship sailed two knots off their stern, keeping just in sight but not close enough to endanger either vessel in case of a sudden storm.

'Perhaps . . . ' Christian murmured.

Léonie looked at him. 'Perhaps?'

'You know I have a cousin on the Île de France?'

'Madame Dumont? Was it not some of the petticoats you were bringing her that we gave the sergeant for the prisoners to wear?'

He nodded. 'They were for her maid, but there are plenty more in the hold. I was planning to take advantage of her hospitality while we are on the Île de France, and of course I would take you with me. Angelique is very sweet and full of fun.'

'I thought she was in mourning?'

'She is. Her husband was killed in a pirate raid not quite twelve months ago. He traded with French India for silks and spices — an irresistible target for some of the brigands on the seas.'

Léonie shook her head. 'Poor woman. To be so alone and cut off from her family.'

'On the contrary, she loves the life. There is much to keep her amused, and soon she will put off her widow's weeds and marry once more, I have no doubt. In fact,' he whispered conspiratorially, 'I have several trunks of the latest gowns for that very occasion packed in the cargo.'

'No doubt your cousin will be delighted with your thoughtfulness, Christian, but none of this makes me feel better.'

'Don't sulk, Léonie. I am getting to it.'

'Christian, though we are only making a few knots on this breathless ocean, I fear we shall arrive at the Île de France before you reach your point!'

'My point, my sweet, is that you shall wear some of those gowns.'

'What are you talking about, Christian! The heat of the Equator has softened your head.'

The excitement in his voice only deepened Léonie's depression. The prospect of balls and dances might enthral Christian and the widow Dumont, but for her, it meant more misery. More time spent watching the man her heart ached for grow further and further out of reach.

'Think, Léonie! We will both of us stay with my cousin, where sadly Jean-Michel will take to his bed with a fever. Meanwhile, you will appear as the beautiful — ' he gesticulated at the ocean as he sought a name ' — Hélène de Lisle, visiting with your distant cousin, the widow Dumont. She will be your chaperon, and you her companion as her days of sorrow draw to a close.'

Léonie regarded him dubiously. Could such a plan hold any chance of success? Could she parade in front of her fellow officers — right beneath François de la Tour's very eyes — and yet be taken as anyone other than the impostor she was?

What if she wore a fashionably grey wig to cover her flaming curls, and a touch of powder and rouge? Maybe a judicious patch or two would help to disguise her face and avert suspicion.

'No. It would be folly, Christian.'

'But why? No one would suspect.'

'But your *cousine* — surely she would have something to say?'

He grinned. 'A lot, I imagine. And she will adore the plan. From her letters, it seems mourning is not the most exciting time of one's life — especially not for an attractive fun-loving woman only four-and-twenty years of age. She will welcome such a diversion.'

Despite her misgivings, Léonie felt a quiver of excitement. It would be a double masquerade — a woman disguised as a man disguised as a woman. She giggled suddenly as she foresaw the delightful potential of the idea. If she could not have François de la Tour because both her station and her assumed identity forbade it, she could at least make it possible for a few days on an island in the middle of the Indian Ocean. It was too delicious to contemplate.

And too dangerous.

8

François stared at the note that lay on his desk. It was full of angry flourishes and sweeping allegations of slothfulness and plain stupidity. Whichever way he considered it, the memorandum boded ill for Jean-Michel de Chambois. How could the boy have been so careless? He'd warned him that Duplessis was a man to beware. Did he deliberately court disaster?

The captain gazed gloomily at the rain beating against his small study window. Darkness fell quickly on the Indian Ocean, especially when rain closed in, wrapping everything in a cold wet mantle. He scrubbed a tired hand across his brow. He would be glad to make Port-Louis. He'd driven both ships hard on his mission so far, stopping only briefly in Cape Town at the southernmost tip of Africa, for he was anxious to reach the Pacific and solve the riddle of the missing Barron expedition. But they must rest at the Île de France. He needed his crew fresh and healthy to tackle the dangers ahead.

François dropped the offending memorandum on his desk and leaned closer to the glass, listening to the mournful wind whistling against the timbered frame. It was late June. At home in Beligny the blackbirds would be summer-fat and the vines heavy with fine Bordeaux grapes ripening slowly in the southern sun.

He stared at his reflection and frowned. He was never homesick. Especially not now, when there was no longer any reason for him to return to the Gironde. He had made his choice between the land and the sea, and the sea had won.

He shook his head to dispel the feelings. Perhaps, after all these years, life on the high seas was losing its attraction.

A knock on his door made him jump.

'*Entrez!*' France faded and the rain sweeping in across the Indian Ocean sounded suddenly loud against the glass.

He watched Jean-Michel walk stiffly into the study and close the door. The boy seemed paler than usual. Had his summons scared the lad? François looked closely at him, but received only a calm grey-eyed gaze in return. His imagination was clearly playing tricks on him tonight.

'Sit down, Chambois.' He indicated the only chair in the room. He himself leaned against his desk from where he could better examine the young sub-lieutenant he'd come to feel so protective toward. He didn't relish this interview.

François picked up the memorandum and frowned. Jean-Michel's innocent expression tempted him just to tear the damn missive into shreds and be done with Duplessis and his whining. But the man did have a point . . .

'I have a letter that concerns you, Chambois.' The boy simply gazed at him,

150

waiting. Why did the room seem so warm suddenly? François wondered, pulling at the lace at his neck. 'I — ' God, but the boy was pretty enough to be a maid.

'*Capitaine?*'

François dragged his attention back to the paper in his hand. 'Where was I? This complaint. It seems your work leaves Monsieur Duplessis less than satisfied.'

He felt a twinge of remorse as he saw Jean-Michel's face pale still further. Dammit, he was getting soft where this lad was concerned. Ever since those roughnecks attacked the boy at the Equator, François had kept a close eye on him. He told himself Chambois was different, that he brought a gentleness to the ship, and that after all he *had* been asked to look out for the young *vicomte* by the king himself. But that wasn't it. He knew he'd have been concerned regardless.

'M-monsieur Duplessis is not satisfied?' he heard Chambois ask. His voice trembled, François was sure of it.

'See for yourself.'

He thrust the sheet into the boy's hand and turned away, calling himself all kinds of a fool for having let this lad become such a favourite. François de la Tour did not have favourites. He had always been fair to all his men, treated them equally, even the conceited *savants* like Charles Duplessis, though the vanity of the man irritated him.

'Well,' he asked without turning from the window, 'what have you to say?'

'I am sorry, *Capitaine*. I do my best.'

'Your best?' François turned, clamping his jaw momentarily against a choice epithet. 'He says you have absolutely no talent and appear to have forgotten everything you ever learned.'

Jean-Michel tilted his head and his red curls caught the lantern light like sparks from a fire.

'Monsieur Duplessis is not easily pleased.'

François was tempted to laugh. The boy had no lack of courage, to be sure.

'That is not for you to judge, young man. You work under his instruction, but your duty is to France. Do you think you serve your country well with such an attitude?'

A glint of moisture seemed to come into the *enseigne*'s eyes, but he made no answer, nor did he make further excuses. François admired that.

'Did you bring me your sketches?'

Jean-Michel nodded and handed him a folio. For an instant, François felt the brush of the young man's fingers on his hand as he took the sheaf of drawings. The result was electrifying. He stared at his hand, unable to comprehend the sensation. How could he feel such fire from this . . . this . . . boy? Such feelings were the stuff of *grand amour* — something François had never encountered, not even with — He clamped his mind shut on the memories, focusing on the present, which perplexed him greatly. That he could burn at the touch of a man — even one as pretty as Chambois — made him dread his own sanity. There was nothing for it, he would have to seek out Father Cassel, beg his advice, before this moon-madness took hold.

'*Capitaine?*'

Jean-Michel's voice snapped him back to the present. He sifted through the sketches, glancing only quickly the first time, then studying them more closely.

'I don't understand,' he said slowly, mystified. 'You executed these yourself? All of them?'

'*Ah non.* These are just a few I have done since we left Africa. You see — ' François froze as Jean-Michel's slender finger pointed to one particularly fine drawing, touching the heavy parchment dangerously close to his wrist. 'This one here shows the view from Table Mountain with the *Aurélie* and the *Mousquetaire* far below at anchor.'

'So I perceive.'

153

'Are they . . . are they to your satisfaction, sir?'

'To my satisfaction?' Was the boy mad? 'Jean-Michel, they are superb. Now at least I understand why the chief artist has been so tight-mouthed about your work for him. The old scoundrel's jealous!'

He saw a pink blush steal into the *enseigne*'s cheeks, as pretty as any court lady could concoct. With an effort, he forced his mind to the purpose of this meeting.

'So your art is impeccable. But your science . . . Duplessis threatens to send his memorandum to the navy once we reach Île de France. It will be a mark against your record. And yet here you are producing scientific drawings of a standard I have never seen on any voyage.'

'Thank you, *Capitaine*.'

'Don't thank me, dammit! Don't you understand? Your dossier states that you are a *poor* artist and a talented *botanist*!' François drew a breath to steady his frustration. 'Explain it to me, Chambois,' he said wearily, leaning his back against the wall. 'I do not understand why you are deliberately wasting your talent for botany. Do you hate Duplessis so?'

'Not at all. I like him better than Monsieur Roussillon. It is just that . . . well, I have

154

never seen such sights. There is so much to record, so many wonders to capture before we sail on and all is lost! The cataloguing of specimens . . . it is very worthy, of course, but . . . '

'But you are bored, is that it?' François laughed briefly. 'I think I understand your point, jaded as I am by the magic of faraway places.' He scratched the back of his neck, looking down at the troubled face before him. 'What are we to do with you, *petit*? I've had not a moment's peace since you stepped on my ship and I doubt I will have till we dock in Brest once more.'

The grey eyes were suddenly downcast. 'I am sorry, *Capitaine*. It is not my intention to cause you pain.'

'You do not cause me pain. It is the likes of Roussillon and Duplessis who do that. What you cause me is confusion.'

The copper-coloured head lifted again, the wide eyes stabbing his heart with their childlike innocence. He was suddenly struck with how wan the boy looked.

'Jean-Michel, are you ill?'

The *enseigne* looked down at his hands and merely shook his head. Damn me, thought François, how could I be so blind? The boy is sickening under my very nose

155

and all I care about is that fool botanist's complaints.

He went to the door and opened it, bellowing for his valet.

'Vincent!' he said, as the boy appeared in the passageway, 'fetch the surgeon at once.'

His command to the cabin boy snapped Léonie out of her misery. She had been racking her brains for a solution to the problem of Duplessis' report but none was forthcoming. And now he was going to have the doctor examine her — in his presence! Her plan — and her disguise — would be undone in an instant. She had warned Christian to be sparing of the powder and not whiten her cheeks too much.

'Please,' she implored him. 'I am not sick, just a little tired.'

The captain shut the door and stared down at her, his midnight-blue eyes so intense that her hands trembled. She clutched them tightly in her lap.

'You are too pale, Jean-Michel. I have never seen you this way, and though we make landfall in the morning, I'll take no risks with the health of my officers. The surgeon will see you now.'

'It's no more than a touch of fatigue,' she pleaded. 'I shall be well once I have had a night or two ashore. I plan to stay

156

with Monsieur Lavelle at his cousin's house, where I shall soon regain my strength.'

'Lavelle has a cousin in Port-Louis?'

'A Madame Dumont. Her husband was a merchant trader with French India, but he died a year past. Christian is bringing her many supplies from France.'

'It will be well that you rest with her, then. But you will still let Montauban see to you tonight. It could be some contagion and he may need to bleed you.'

'Bleed . . . ?' Léonie swallowed. Her 'illness' wasn't meant to alarm him this much, only to explain Jean-Michel's retirement to bed once they made landfall!

'Don't worry, *petit*,' the captain said, mistaking her concern completely. 'Montauban is a good cutter. We're lucky to have him aboard.'

Léonie jumped up from the chair and forced a bright smile to her face.

'I am sure he is a great surgeon, *Capitaine*, but his skills should be kept for those in need. As you can see, I am perfectly well — '

'Sit!' François ordered. He pressed her back on to the chair. Léonie froze under his hands, afraid to breathe as spirals of sensation flowed from his touch to the very pit of her stomach, making her want to cry out, but not with pain. She didn't dare raise her eyes to his. They would give her away in an instant.

Vincent opened the door and announced André de Montauban. The surgeon had clearly been readying himself for bed, as he lacked his usual moth-eaten wig and his half-bald pate gleamed in the poor light.

'So who have we here, François? What, not young Chambois?'

He snorted. 'Young lad like you should be at home in your mother's arms, not dashing about the globe picking up uncivilized ailments. We don't have the strength of the savages you know, lad. 'Tis fine for them to be catching these things; they're used to it.'

François released his grip on her shoulders and Léonie's heart beat a little less wildly, though she remained so acutely aware of him, standing close behind, that every breath was an ordeal. Her desire to flee to her cabin was overwhelming. With great effort, she smiled at the old man.

'Monsieur de Montauban, I'm sorry you were disturbed, but the captain is quite mistaken. There is nothing at all the matter with me except for the lack of a good night's sleep in a bed that does not rock with every wave. Half the crew are anxious to make

158

landfall at the Île de France. The land air will do us all good, don't you think?'

She could feel François glowering, even from behind her. The surgeon was uncertain now, and frowned first at her and then at the captain.

'Truly,' Léonie persisted, taking advantage of his confusion. 'I will visit you tomorrow before landfall so you may see for yourself.'

'Well . . . you do seem sprightly enough. A little pale perhaps, but . . . ' He looked to the captain for guidance. 'I could always bleed you a little — '

'No!' Léonie stood up quickly, but checked her outburst as the captain frowned. It would not do to protest too much, and she could see he remained unconvinced.

'Jean-Michel, let the man at least see if you have a fever.'

'Captain, I am perfectly well, I assure — '

She gasped as François' hand enclosed her arm. 'Let *me* see.'

He pulled her toward him and laid his other hand across her brow. It was impossible to look away although she knew she must. Their eyes locked together in some strange battle dance as she sought to evade his probing. How she wished they would reach Port-Louis within the minute! She couldn't bear another moment of this travesty without giving herself away, for the more he touched her the more in danger her disguise became. She knew if she couldn't free herself and become a woman, the intolerable tension would force her to expose her secret. Like a person mortally afraid of heights, she could feel herself being drawn inexorably over the precipice she dreaded.

His strong fingers stroked her brow and she shut her eyes, feeling darkness swirl around her. You can't faint, she thought. You must keep your senses. But surely her fever was raging beneath his touch?

When he said nothing, she pulled away. 'You s-see, Captain, I am not hot at all,' she lied, stepping back quickly.

'You try, André. Damned if I can tell.'

She allowed the doctor to feel her forehead and then backed away toward the door.

'*Voilá*. No fever. No sickness. Now may I retire, Captain? I am needed to help catalogue the last of the African specimens at dawn, and I do not think Monsieur Duplessis will appreciate tardiness, do you?'

Without awaiting his permission, she let herself out and fled to her room.

In the safety of her cabin she flopped on her bunk and sucked in huge gulps of air. She still trembled when she imagined François' rage had she been forced to remove her shirt for the surgeon!

She lay staring up at Christian's empty bunk, concentrating on the rise and fall of the ship until her heartbeat had quietened. Thank heaven they were about to make landfall and she could escape the close confines of the ship.

She got up, used the commode and then, as was her custom, emptied the chamberpot carefully out the window into the rainy night. She wondered if her monthly curse would return once she was on land, for to her relief it had disappeared after they left Tenerife.

She was feeling calmer now as she scrubbed the white lead off her face, for she disliked *maquillage* of any sort. As she towelled her skin dry she began to look forward to the coming days of freedom. And then a terrible consideration began to occupy her mind: what if François de la Tour had no interest in her as a woman when they reached the Île de France? What if he ignored her or treated her with polite disinterest?

How ever would she bear it?

Paris, June 1784

Alain de Vercours tapped a jewelled finger on the papers spread before him on the desk. They were full of bumbling and

161

bluster but contained not one morsel of information. Though he had offered lucrative remuneration to the ferrets he'd sent to spy her out, the beautiful young Vicomtesse de Chambois had indeed disappeared.

He read the note aloud, a mocking tone in his voice that disguised the contempt with which he regarded his so-called informants. 'We regret, Milord, that none of the Carmelite houses in the cantons of Switzerland can offer any information, blah, blah. *Imbéciles*!' He tossed the offending paper back on the desk, strolled to the window and gazed down upon the chestnut trees in bloom along the boulevard. This quest to locate the young lady had grown from an amusing bagatelle into an obsession.

The stakes, as far as that reptile Alphonse de Grise was concerned, might be no more than a pair of fine matched greys, but to Vercours they held far greater promise.

He rang for his manservant, remaining at the window with a small smile upon his features, until the lackey entered.

'Géricault,' he said without turning. 'Since it appears France contains only poseurs and simpletons, I have a task for you, one ideally suited to your somewhat reprehensible past.'

He chuckled softly and began to explain.

Port-Louis Harbour, June 1784

'You still aboard, Yves?'

'Indeed,' Father Cassel sighed, raising a thin hand to guard his eyes from the warm morning sun. 'I make no haste to see more of the world, François. It becomes so familiar after all these years, does it not?'

The captain grimaced. 'Too familiar.' He leaned his elbows on the rail and stared out at the harbour, dotted now with small vessels scurrying to and fro between ship and shore. Much of the activity was centred on the supply ship, giving the *Mousquetaire* the air of a tall dragonfly beneath a swarm of gnats. From the *Aurélie*, a steady flow of boats carried the eager crew towards Port-Louis, the excited voices of the sailors carrying across the water. It was a perfect day to arrive at the Île de France, but somehow, François had not the stomach for it. He would rather a dreary, rain-swept welcome to match his present mood.

Jacques Le Brun and the other officers appeared on deck wearing their dress uniforms of scarlet breeches and dark-blue jackets trimmed with gold, swords at their hips, as gaudy as the island paradise they were about to visit.

'Are you ready, sir?' the first officer asked.

François stared at his staff, trying not to search the group for the one person who so filled his thoughts. It was no use. The fiery head shone in the sun like burnished copper, drawing his attention. Child-wide grey eyes stared solemnly back at him.

'*Capitaine*?' Le Brun asked again. 'The longboat is waiting.'

François dragged his gaze from Jean-Michel and tried to concentrate on what his lieutenant was saying.

'*Non, merci*. Take these young dogs with you. The padre and I will follow shortly.' He looked at the young *enseigne* again and beckoned to him as the officers moved off. 'Chambois. How fare you today? Are you well?'

The boy still looked pale. Too pale.

'I have no fever this morning, *Capitaine*,' he replied, looking over his shoulder at the departing officers. 'And I am sure that I shall recover quickly once we are ashore.'

François reached out a hand to tilt the boy's face up into the sun. The feel of soft skin beneath his fingers sent a jolt through him and he dropped his arm instantly. Although he did not turn his head to see, he knew Yves Cassel had observed his action, and he felt a wave of frustration at his own stupidity.

'Well, make sure you do rest. You are excused from this afternoon's official parade on the Champ de Mars. It will be a tedium easily dispensed with and you'd best save your strength. Duplessis is expecting you to join an expedition to the mountains in search of the dodo.'

Was he dreaming, or did his words spark a flash of alarm?

'The . . . dodo? But there have been no such creatures seen for a hundred years, Captain. They are said to be extinct.'

So, the boy's knowledge was not so poor, after all.

'You are correct, Chambois. But he has hopes of recovering some bones. I am told the king is especially curious about the creatures.'

Chambois nodded, but François could sense his reluctance. For a moment he weakened — almost excused the boy — but then reprimanded himself. It was too bad if the lad preferred other attractions in Port-Louis. His duty to the chief botanist was clear, whether it was to his taste or not.

'I will visit you ashore,' François said, then turned back to the rail before he relented and offered to make the boy's excuses to Duplessis. 'Make sure you rest well, young man.'

165

'Yes, sir,' came the meek reply. When François looked back he was gone, scrambling down to the longboat with as much eagerness as a young cadet. Maybe he wasn't so sick after all.

'He's a good boy,' the old priest murmured as the boat pulled away from the side of the ship. 'All this is new to him. He'll adjust.'

New? The notion startled François. Maybe that was it. The old man had put his finger on it so simply, while he — he had been blind to the obvious. And yet 'new' made no sense. None at all.

'Our voyage is scarcely novel to the *vicomte, mon pére*. He's made several voyages of length. Fought against the English in the American War, even earned a commendation. And yet . . . ' He glanced at the priest's impassive profile. 'What do you mean, Yves? Perhaps I mistook your words.'

The priest turned to him, his expression benign. 'It is a matter of innocence, my dear François. The boy is — how can I explain — an *ingénu*. He retains that which so many in the king's service lose so lamentably soon — the priceless gift of wonder.'

'An innocent.' François grimaced. 'I gathered that when I first set eyes on the lad in Brest. And then in Tenerife . . . ' He shuddered

166

as he remembered how he'd purchased that common harlot and all but shoved her on the boy. 'Make you a man,' he'd said. Hah! If François was truly honest with himself, he'd admit he'd felt no little envy for Chambois' singular clarity of mind, as though he were able to observe the world with the delight of a child and yet somehow remain unsullied by it.

'Perhaps I am guilty of the sin of envy, *mon pére*. I wish I had even half an ounce of Jean-Michel's innocence.'

'But you do not, François. And neither do I, though I struggle to retain my delight in God's work. But when we have witnessed so much of the dark side of this earth, it is sometimes hard to praise the Lord for His masterpiece. You must not blame the boy.'

Blame him? François nearly laughed aloud. It was not for his own lost innocence that François blamed Jean-Michel de Chambois: it was for the unsettling feelings that drew him to the boy. Feelings that any red-blooded man would never — *should* never — have for one of his own sex.

He glanced over his shoulder at the deck, deserted now except for a small group of soldiers who stood guard at the other end, well out of hearing. He took a deep breath and stared up at the endless blue sky that hung above the Indian Ocean. What better time to pour out his heart to the ship's priest? After all, just because he was captain didn't mean he was immune to occasional weaknesses of the spirit suffered by normal men.

Ah, but this was different. This was something so alien to François' nature, how would the old priest react? They had known each other so long. So many voyages together, so much sickness and death. And yes, in those early years, so much delight in the miraculous world around them.

But he had nothing to confess, had he? He'd managed to control his thoughts — so far. François gripped the rail so hard his knuckles turned white. He was a man. A man with normal desires, normal appetites. Why did this particular young officer torment him so, day and night, waking or sleeping?

Was he losing his mind?

The touch of Father Cassel's fingers on his hand startled him.

'You could try telling me, my friend. I am a confessor, remember?'

François stared at the wizened hand trapping his own. Was his troubled heart so easy to perceive?

'I . . . don't know how to begin, *mon père*,' he responded finally on a sigh. 'There are feelings. Feelings . . . I've not had to face before. I'm not sure you would understand.'

Father Cassel released his hand and nodded sagely, staring out toward Port-Louis. 'So, you are finally discovering that you are not invincible. I had despaired of it, over the years.'

'Invincible? I was never that, Yves. It is my very inadequacy that drives me.'

The priest nodded. 'Ah.'

Ah? François thought. That's all his old friend could say — ah? 'I thought you guessed.'

'I try never to guess. God sees everything with perfect clarity. Why should a poor sinner of a priest like me waste what short time he has upon this earth by trying to imagine how people think?'

The captain chuckled briefly. 'Because people would prefer to have you meet them halfway, Father.'

Yves Cassel nodded, looking up at him gravely. 'And right now, you would wish me to 'guess' that you are troubled by your feelings for Jean-Michel de Chambois, *n'est-ce pas*? That you are afraid for your masculinity?' He shook his head. 'It is not the way of God, François, that a priest should pre-empt the confession. I can hear your sins — offer guidance perhaps — and

169

give absolution, but only you can bare your soul. This challenge comes to you direct from your Maker.'

For a second, François stared at the old priest, then he sighed.

'You know, Yves, you may be old, but you still have a way to see things that puts me in mighty fear of the hereafter.'

9

After the unprepossessing aspect afforded by the simple buildings of the town of Port-Louis, La Maison Dumont startled Léonie with its elegance. The carriage, which for the tedious journey from the harbour had jolted mercilessly over the crude roads, now settled into a gentle swaying motion as the black coachman turned the horses on to a pebble-white driveway. The road wound beneath a canopy of trees whose scarlet flowers seemed to attract a veritable aviary of exotic birds. Léonie knew Monsieur Duplessis would expect her to recognize them — as undoubtedly Jean-Michel could — but she was far too absorbed in the rich sights and smells of the plantation to care.

170

Within minutes the house itself came into view. White and wooden and encircled by an impressive terrace, it stood facing the drive, its wide stone steps seeming to welcome her with open arms.

'It's exquisite, Christian,' Léonie murmured as the coach swept up to the door and stopped. 'You did not tell me your cousin was rich. I had expected a comfortable trader's dwelling, but this . . . '

He laughed, jumping down from the carriage. Léonie followed.

'In truth, I did not know what to expect myself. But when you meet Angélique, you may understand that she attracted a man of no little wealth to her marriage bed.'

At that moment, a petite figure in a haze of blue silk threw herself headlong down the steps toward them.

'Christian! Christian, is it really you at last? I thought your ship would never arrive and I have been waiting so many days.'

The vibrant figure enveloped Christian in a hug and Léonie stepped back as the woman stood on tiptoe to kiss him on both cheeks.

'Ah, Angé, you are as pretty as a picture. The colonies have been kind to you, it seems.' He swung her off her feet in a hug and then deposited her back on the step, turning her to face Léonie, who was once again feeling a trifle nervous about sharing her scandalous secret with a total stranger.

'*Bien*, who is this, *mon cousin*? You have brought another officer to brighten La Maison Dumont.' The china-blue eyes stared at Léonie for a moment and then creased with a sunny smile. 'La, but what a pretty boy! The young ladies of Port-Louis will positively swoon with delight. How do you do, *mon jeune*? You may kiss my hand.'

Léonie blushed, but did as she was bid, showing a respectable amount of leg as she bowed over the delicate fingers.

Christian introduced them and within moments they were being shown to their rooms. A black manservant carried Léonie's trunk to a comfortable suite on the second floor and withdrew wordlessly. Another came in with a jug of cool water and filled the elegant Sèvres bowl on the table, leaving a fluffy white towel before also slipping away.

Léonie crossed to the French windows that opened on to a private balcony. The air was deliciously cool, redolent with fresh-tilled soil and tropical vegetation. Beyond the elegant formal gardens with their pebble walkways lay acres and acres of mango and coffee trees as well as many crops she could not yet identify, and to the north lay the sea, sparkling like a jewel in the late morning sun.

She turned as the door to her room opened once again.

'Christian,' she said, crossing to him quickly. 'I am afraid your cousin will not take kindly to our plan. What if she is scandalized by the whole idea of my posing as Jean-Michel and will not help us? Can you be sure she'll not go straight to the governor and tell him our secret? Or even to the captain?'

He ran a hand through his hair and shrugged. 'I can make no promises, my sweet. Only let me speak to her. 'Twould be best if you remained here meanwhile.' His eyes softened as he glanced down at her fingers which still gripped the brim of her tricorne. 'Don't worry, Léonie.'

She stood in the middle of the room until the sound of his footsteps had faded, then turned and gazed about her. She looked at her waiting trunk, but felt no desire to open it. There was nothing in it she wished to wear.

She tossed the hat on the bed and sank on to a *chaise-longue* by the fireplace, staring into the empty hearth with unseeing eyes.

'How is it with you, Jean-Michel?' she murmured aloud. 'I trust you are enjoying this foolish adventure more than your headstrong sister.' And then she stood up, annoyed to have allowed herself such self-pity. She had entered into this journey — this masquerade — to save her brother's life, and no sacrifice came easy. She had wanted to see the world. Well, this was the world. A place full of wondrous and wondrously alarming things, to be sure — and poor cosseted Léonie, Vicomtesse de Chambois, having witnessed them, knew she would never be the same again.

Five minutes later, the servant who had carried her trunk tapped quietly on the door and bade her follow him downstairs. With heart in hand, Léonie entered the salon, expecting the worst.

'Ah!' her hostess sighed as the door closed once more. 'But of course, I see it now!'

Léonie met the woman's eyes, expecting disdain, even revulsion. What she got was the merriest twinkle she could ever remember.

Angélique skipped across the room, grasped Léonie's hands in her own and kissed her soundly on both cheeks. Then she stood back, holding her at arms' length while she inspected her disguise from head to foot.

'It is very good, my dear. Very good indeed. You had me quite convinced that your pretty looks were simply those of a handsome boy strutting in his officer's garb, but now that I look again, I can see the woman in you.' She reached out a hand and touched Léonie's hair. 'Such colour! Like flames from the heart of love! Christian,' she said, turning to where he stood watching from beside the window, 'we must disguise this hair or Léonie will be undone in a moment. Oh, *pardonnez-moi*, I may call you Léonie, may I not? It is such a lovely name and I have so few young friends in this place. But of course, if you prefer I shall try to call you *Vicomtesse*, though it makes you sound very stuffy.'

Despite her nervousness, Léonie felt the laughter bubbling up inside. The woman was charming. Open and honest and without a trace of rancour at being asked to protect the honour of a stranger.

'Of course, *madame*. I am not much for titles, myself.'

'Angélique, please. We must be friends. The best of friends. You will call me Angé, and I will call you Jean-Michel when you are dressed thus' — she brushed her fingers over the blue sleeve of Léonie's uniform, — 'and Léonie when we are alone, and . . . what did you say she shall be called on the island, Christian?'

'Hélène de Lisle.'

'*Ah, oui, la belle Hélène* when we are in skirts!' She grinned impishly, her oval face creasing with mischievous dimples like a child. Léonie felt herself relax. She would be safe. If anyone could help her during the next days, she felt certain it would be Angélique Dumont.

You are most kind, *mada* — Angélique,' she corrected. 'I am sorry to bring such deception into your house, but I trust Christian has explained the necessity that drove me to take such a risk?'

'Deception, fiddlesticks. Diversion is more like. I have been in mourning for my poor Armand this past twelvemonth and I cannot wait for the governor's ball and my return to society.'

'A ball?'

'This very night, my dear. It is the perfect chance to try out the ruse, *n'est-ce pas?*'

Léonie felt herself pale at the suddenness of it all. To go from Jean-Michel, naval officer, to Hélène de Lisle, society lady, in so few hours.

'I'm not sure. It's so soon. What if someone recognizes me?'

'She's right, Angé,' Christian agreed with a frown. 'No doubt most of the officers will be there. It's too risky. Should Léonie's disguise be uncovered by the captain or one of the senior officers, that would be bad enough. But to be exposed in front of the whole of polite society here on the Île de France would be intolerable. I do not think we should go.'

Léonie knew he was right, but felt curiously let down nonetheless. After so many dreary weeks at sea, the thought of a lively ball — with her dressed once more as a woman — was irresistible.

'*Non, non*, my loves!' Angélique replied, her blue-black curls bobbing vigorously as she shook her head. 'I shall lend Hélène a wig' — she stared sadly at Léonie's hair — 'though it breaks my heart to cover such glorious locks. You will be the talk of the town, my dear, and I shall be truly launched back into our little island society with everyone wanting to know about my beautiful relation from — where shall she be from, Christian?'

He shrugged. 'It matters not. There are so many vessels in the port. Choose one that has left in the last day or two.'

'Of course.' Angélique tapped a delicate finger against her chin and strolled across the room deep in thought. 'There was a ship that left last evening. The *Troubadour*. Now where was it from? India? Yes, I believe it was on a voyage from Pondicherry to

Cape Town. It will do nicely. There were several ladies aboard, but none, I think, who remained here when she sailed. It shall suffice.' She winked at Léonie, her blue eyes sparkling. 'Very well, you sailed here from French India on the *Troubadour* to spend a few days with me, whom you have not seen since my wedding five years ago to your uncle Armand.'

She reached out an arm and drew Léonie to the door. 'Come, we have so little time and I am all agog to explore the contents of the trunks Christian has brought me from Paris. Why, I have not seen a Parisian gown in two years. No doubt you will think us woefully behind the times with our *couture*, my dear, but I shall expect you to describe what the ladies at court are wearing now, to the very last detail!'

Léonie raised her eyebrows at Christian as she allowed Angélique to lead her from the salon and up the wide staircase to yet another suite of rooms.

The bedroom in this one was larger and more feminine, with a lace-covered chiffonier and gilded chairs that bespoke the opulence of the reign of Louis XIV.

Her hostess closed the door firmly and whispered, 'Christian has explained that Jean-Michel is unwell and must take to his bed, so

178

we cannot have the lovely Hélène disturbing his rest, now can we?'

Léonie giggled, relishing the sudden freedom to do so. She tore off her frock coat and threw it on the bed, kicking off her brother's silver-buckled shoes with equal delight.

'So,' Angélique asked as she helped her remove her smallsword and uniform with all the comfortable intimacy of a sister, 'tell me about this *capitaine*. He must be quite a man to have you taking such risks.'

The image of François' strong face filled Léonie's mind in an instant. With it came bittersweet memories of the sparks that passed between them whenever he looked at her. Or when their hands touched.

How could she explain what she felt? It was a secret so deeply disguised she doubted she could ever share it with another soul. She pondered for a moment, wondering how to dress her response in words this bubbly young widow would understand, when Angélique blithely continued.

'Of course, Léonie, you are taking a great risk of another kind. You must remember there is more than one kind of man. Most are sensible to the attractions of women, of course, lest where would we be in this world?' She gave a silvery laugh. 'But there are some — and I don't say your beloved captain is one of them, *naturellement* — but there are those who prefer the company of handsome young boys!'

★ ★ ★

Prefer boys? Angélique's words burned through Léonie's mind for the thousandth time since Madame Dumont had cast them so casually into the conversation earlier in the day. And for the thousandth time, Léonie shivered.

It could not be. François de la Tour was a man whose very presence sent fire dancing through her veins. The night before their landing in Port-Louis, when she had passed him her folio of drawings and their fingers had touched, had not lightning arced between them? She had felt it as surely as she had felt the motion of the ship beneath her feet. And his eyes, those fathomless pools of midnight blue, had they not flashed with recognition?

She reached out and picked up the sapphire and diamond brooch Angélique had given her for tonight's ball. The stone cast a magical glow, as deep and mysterious as her captain's eyes.

She stared into its translucent depths. When had she begun to think of him as

180

'her' captain? The stone gazed back, mute in the captured candlelight.

'I will not believe it of you, Captain,' she whispered to the jewel. And yet her fingers trembled as she pinned the brooch to the neckline of her lace fichu and settled it amongst the soft folds. In a few short hours she would meet François for the very first time as a woman. It was a moment she both dreaded and desired with all her heart.

She picked up the first of the matching ear-rings, marvelling at the beauty of the diamonds as she pinned them to her ears. The transformation was miraculous, even to her own eyes. Although it was but three months since she had last worn a gown, it felt like a lifetime. The young woman whose likeness appeared in the mirror before her bore no resemblance to the young officer she had become. Gone were the amber curls. In their place, a wig of powder grey, high upon the head and laced with silver and gold filigree. Gone, the sun-browned face of a young man. With the help of a modest application of ceruse and cheek rouge and the judicious application of a single heart-shaped patch at the corner of her eye, the elegant creature's resemblance to 'Jean-Michel' de Chambois lay only in her eyes themselves.

She jumped as the door burst open.

'Ah, but you are *ravissante*! Let me look, my dear. Stand up! Turn around!' Angélique clapped her hands, her face dimpling with delight. 'Exquisite! You will be the talk of the town. Your *capitaine* will not be able to contain himself.'

There it was again. *Her* captain. Léonie's heart pattered wildly for a moment.

'This is a madness, Angélique. He will recognize me, I know. I have this terrible feeling here . . . ' She pressed her hands against her breast.

'Nonsense, my love. Why even I barely recognize you. With your hair covered and your sailor's colouring so artfully disguised, why I wager even Christian will barely know you, and *he* is anticipating your transformation.' She reached out and expertly twitched the heavy folds of Léonie's skirt into place. 'Captain de la Tour expects no one except Jean-Michel in his dress uniform, and I shall soon put that notion from his head when I tell him how my dear Doctor Mirabeau has insisted the boy remain in bed two more days at least! La, I cannot thank you enough. Such a wickedly delightful way to re-enter society after my bereavement, do you not think? All the most eligible gentlemen will be pestering me for your introduction.'

Léonie blushed. 'You exaggerate, Angélique.

182

With you in that beautiful cerise gown the last person who will be noticed is me.'

Her hostess executed a dainty pirouette before the cheval mirror and giggled.

'It *is* rather delicious, I agree, but still 'tis sweet of you to say so.' She dropped on to a gilded chair and leaned back, looking suddenly older than her four-and-twenty years. 'Ah, Léonie, in truth I am in no less of a fluster about tonight than you.'

'But Angélique, I thought you had been looking forward to coming out again?'

'So I am. But it is six years since I was last unspoken for. One becomes accustomed to a husband's protection. It leaves one free to talk and flirt with the gentlemen, to be sure, but for me there was never anything more than that.' Her light-blue eyes were filled with a sudden sadness that made Léonie's heart ache for the young widow. 'I loved my Armand, you see, though he was twice my years. It was to my great sorrow that he died so soon and without an heir.'

'You wished for children?'

'Doesn't every woman?'

Léonie made no reply. It was not something she'd thought much about. Her dreams had been of love and romance and adventure — of finding a man she could lose her heart to, rather than meekly submitting to a loveless marriage.

'Did you — ?' She wasn't sure quite how to phrase her question. 'Was Armand . . . your own choice in a husband?'

Angélique looked up, her eyes wide with astonishment.

'No, indeed! It was all arranged. We did not meet until the night before our marriage, though we were betrothed for many months.'

Léonie was appalled. 'But why so late? What if you had detested the man?'

'We could not meet. I was in France and my betrothed was here in Port-Louis with his ships.' She smiled at Léonie. 'But I loved him at first sight. He was like a father to me, as well as a lover. And he had the most beautiful dark eyes. I do think the eyes of a man reflect his soul, don't you?'

Léonie pictured a set of eyes as fathomless as the deepest ocean. Many times she had thought to see things in them. But she was never sure. Perhaps it was mere wishful thinking, an imagination overwrought by circumstance.

Unable to reply, she merely nodded and turned away to find her fan.

'My dear *Vicomtesse!*' Angé was on her

feet in an instant. 'I have upset you!'

'Not at all, you have been most kind.' Léonie kept her eyes on her fan, her grip awkward after so many months without practice. '*Imbécile!*' she rebuked herself as it fell to the floor.

Angé reached it first. She retrieved it and looked up at Léonie.

'My dear child, you are crying!' She took her arm and pulled her to the *chaise-longue*. 'Come sit here. This will never do.' A moment later she pressed a glass of cognac into Léonie's hand.

Léonie held the glass, feeling silly as the moment of despair passed. 'I'm sorry, Angé, please accept my apologies. You have been so kind, already — '

'Nonsense!' Angé sat beside her. 'I love a good cry myself from time to time. 'Tis nothing to be contrite about. Now if I am not mistaken, there is more to you and this Captain de la Tour than you have pretended, *n'est-ce pas?*'

Léonie looked up at the woman. Her cornflower-blue eyes were full of real concern, and Léonie was so very confused. She felt that if she didn't talk to someone she would explode.

'Very well.' She set down the glass untouched and gripped her ebony fan. 'You

185

are right, *madame*. I was drawn to him like a helpless moth from our first meeting. I tried, oh so very hard, not to let myself think of him, knowing how hopeless it was. And Christian warned me. Yet he was always there, watching me, looking out for me. It was as if he knew, and yet I am sure he doesn't.'

'So, you have fallen in love with him.'

'No!' Léonie was horrified. 'I can't. At least, I haven't. I don't think. Oh, Angé, I don't know.' She covered her face with her hands for a moment and then looked up. 'I always thought that when I eventually found someone to love, I would feel about them the same way I feel about Jean-Michel or Christian, only stronger. But this is different.' She got up and strode across the room, swinging around to face Madame Dumont. 'I can't eat without the food sticking in my throat. I can't sleep without dreaming of him. I feel agitated, so very agitated. When he is near me I can scarcely breathe, yet I want to be with him all the time!' She wound her fingers around her fan. 'Sometimes I even make up silly excuses to speak to him, but nothing helps. I still feel this way. It's like an illness.'

Angé laughed. 'I cannot wait to meet this paragon. If he can make you so head over

186

heels in love with him, he must be a splendid specimen indeed!'

Léonie stared at her in dismay. 'It cannot be, *madame*. If ever he discovered who I really was his anger would know no bounds. And if he does not, then I am nothing but a boy to him. He does not love me, he doesn't even know me. He is simply doing his duty as an officer.'

Angélique tilted her head, a little smile touching her lips. 'He has this effect upon others?'

Léonie frowned, putting one foot on the windowsill and resting her hand on her knee. 'I don't — ' She stopped as Angé giggled. 'What is it?'

Angé let forth another peal of laughter. ' 'Tis you, dear heart! You will truly make an intriguing addition to the Port-Louis social circle if you don't concentrate your mind.'

Léonie was quite perplexed. 'What do you mean?'

'You are striding about the room and otherwise behaving like the perfect gentleman,' she replied, still giggling, 'but the gown quite spoils the effect!'

Léonie looked down at her stance in amazement, gave Angé a horrified look, and then dissolved into laughter with her.

10

Léonie was not enjoying the Governor's Ball. She scanned the room as often as she dared, hiding her nervous glances behind her fan, the glittering scene all but lost upon her. Crowds of Port-Louis' finest bobbed and jostled and filled the scented night air with the tinkle of laughter and courtly conversation. The long room blazed with candles and in all the corners, tall palms dipped their fronds as though in time to the latest Mozart tunes favoured by the musical ensemble.

He is not here, she thought miserably, her gaze once again flitting to the grand entrance where yet another group of guests was being announced. Despite her fear of being immediately recognized by the captain, Léonie felt hopelessly depressed. She remembered how she had struggled to contain her excitement all day long as she prepared for the ball, hoping against hope that the ruse would work — that the captain would not only notice 'Hélène de Lisle' but would fall instantly in love!

And now he was not here. Hélène was attracting admiring glances from strangers, but she didn't want their attentions. She wanted the eyes of only one man looking at her tonight. Midnight-blue eyes. François de la Tour's eyes.

She leaned toward Angélique and whispered behind her fan.

'He is not coming! What am I to do?'

Her companion merely giggled. 'My, you are impatient, little friend! The night is barely begun. Your captain is fashionably late, *c'est tout.*'

Léonie stifled a sigh and resumed her observation of the door. Fashionable it may be. But to her pounding heart, late was just late.

Christian brought her a glass of champagne. 'Here. Perhaps this will calm your nerves, my sweet.'

'I am not nervous,' she retorted, sipping the bubbly wine, cool from the cellars.

'Well, I am. Who's to say the captain won't take one look at your big grey eyes and accuse you of being a ship's harlot on the spot. Worse,' he added glumly, 'he'll accuse me of having brought you on board for my own — '

'Christian!' Angélique rapped him smartly across the knuckles with her fan. 'Such language! Go away, Cousin, if you must be in so black a mood.' She winked at Léonie. 'We ladies are out for some excitement tonight. Surely one night of frivolity is not too much to ask.'

Christian made no reply, but Léonie could feel his concern as he stood stiffly at her elbow. She poked him in the ribs, trying to bring a lightness to her tone that she was far from feeling.

'Don't worry, Christian. Your uncle the prince will protect you. And if he won't, I will.'

'I do not know which I dread the most, my sweet.'

★ ★ ★

It was nearly eleven and still the captain had not joined the company. She had danced two cotillions and a minuet with faceless strangers, then begged off further entreaties. Angé had disappeared in search of amusement, and Christian was dancing with some attractive young débutante in a white gown. Léonie's heart grew more and more heavy as the night wore on. No matter how hard she tried, she could not fool herself much longer. And as she faced the reality that François would not appear, a blackness

190

of spirit settled ever deeper over her heart.

And then she saw him. Half a head taller than any other man in the ballroom, Captain de la Tour was advancing straight toward her with Angélique Dumont clinging to his arm.

He looked magnificent in his dress uniform, tall and straight, with broad shoulders and a tilt to his head that made other men cast envious glances his way. She seldom saw him in uniform and he took her breath away. She knew she should pretend not to notice him since he was officially a stranger, but her eyes refused to obey. Wide-eyed, she could only stare, her heart racing with a mixture of fear and elation.

* * *

François had left it as late as propriety allowed. But finally, he'd had to come. His valet, young Vincent, had dressed him meticulously in his formal garb, attached his gleaming smallsword at his waist, dusted off his tricorne and polished his glossy black shoes with their gold buckles. Made him feel like a damned fop, but there it was.

He realized his escort had stopped beside some potted palms. She was a pretty thing, very persuasive, and his efforts to sidle out of her invitation to be introduced to her undoubtedly comely niece were totally ineffectual. Oh well, if he had to be bored silly, it might as well be with her as any other of the frumpish and ill-educated fan-flutterers at the ball.

'*Voilà, Capitaine*,' Madame Dumont was saying, fingers nudging his elbow. 'May I present my dearest friend and niece, Mademoiselle de Lisle.'

François looked up with resignation. The young lady's face was hidden behind a fan of astronomical proportions that fluttered like a damned butterfly in front of her face.

'Mademoiselle de Lisle's father is an administrative official in Pondicherry,' Madame Dumont was saying. A clerk's daughter, thought François, quashing a sigh. 'But she is staying awhile here with me on her way home to France.' His escort giggled with an almost conspiratorial tone, which struck him as strange from someone he scarcely knew. 'I am certain you will have much in common. Hélène, *chérie*, may I introduce Capitaine de la Tour, commander of the *Aurélie* and the *Mousquetaire*.'

François bowed, wondering if the fan would ever stop fluttering like some suicidal moth. Lower it, woman, he thought to himself, and let me see the worst.

She did. And François gazed into the most bewitching pair of grey eyes he had encountered since . . .

He frowned. Somewhere deep in the recesses of his mind strange feelings were stirring, yet he couldn't quite grasp them. He let his eyes rove over the woman's unexpectedly lovely face. Oval, with a slightly pointed chin. Her coiffure was the height of fashion, which struck him as odd, powdered white as snow and threaded with gold and silver. An administrator's daughter? These damned colonial officials were getting mighty fancy all of a sudden, he thought. Mademoiselle de Lisle curtsied low and he caught a glimpse of firm white breasts cupped into the silken fabric of her décolleté bodice. The sight took his breath away and made old yearnings stir abruptly into life. He coughed as she straightened and took the hand she proffered.

François pressed his lips to her fingers ever so gently, though why he bothered to make contact at all, he knew not. It was not his style. For a moment he stared at her small hand, so sunbrowned for a young woman of her obvious station that he was quite taken aback.

'*Mademoiselle,*' he said, relinquishing her hand. Why did she seem so nervous?

193

'*Capitaine*.' At that moment, Christian appeared and Léonie was dismayed to see the captain turn away with a quick nod to her and Angé. He took Christian's elbow and pulled him aside. It was not hard to hear their conversation.

'Lavelle, where's the boy? I do not see him with you tonight.'

A dull red flush crept up Christian's neck. 'Er, he is unwell, Captain. He wished to be allowed to rest tonight.'

'Damn. I tried to have the surgeon bleed him, but the lad would have none of it. I must go to him.'

Léonie looked aghast at Angélique. She, too, had overheard them speak and stepped up quickly.

'Indeed, Captain, there is no need to trouble yourself. Jean-Michel is in good hands. Why I myself summoned my own dear Dr Mirabeau to tend the gentleman.'

'Madame, you are most kind, but — '

'And he assured me that there is nothing wrong with the boy that a few nights' rest will not cure.' She laid a pretty hand on his sleeve and smiled up into his face. 'There is absolutely no cause for you to distress yourself, my dear Captain. Come, will you not take some refreshment with us?'

And with a wink over her shoulder at

Léonie, who stood rooted to the floor, Angélique bore the captain away.

As they watched the pair move into the crowd, Léonie let out her breath slowly and took Christian's arm to follow.

'He didn't know me, Christian.' She wondered if the words sounded as hollow to him as they did to her own ears.

'Then why so glum? Surely 'tis what you wished.'

'Of course.' She made an effort to sound breezy. 'But I did rather hope . . . '

Christian laughed softly. 'Aha. Methinks you are just a trifle jealous, perhaps. You think Angé will sweep him off his feet.'

'I do not!'

He merely raised his eyebrows as they passed through the doors into the supper room.

'Well, perhaps,' she grumbled.

Christian tried to tempt her with the fantastic array of dishes laid out on long tables in the anteroom, but her stomach felt tied in knots.

'I can't, Christian. Eating is the farthest thing from my mind.'

'You must, my sweet, you've lost too much weight since Africa. If you want to go on wearing your brother's uniform, you'd best stock up a little before you waste away.'

But she couldn't pay attention to food. She followed him up and down the table as he ate, but her attention was elsewhere, trying to catch a glimpse of Angélique and the captain, to no avail. Finally, he persuaded her to try the exotic fruits piled high on a silver platter. She lifted a morsel of pineapple to her lips and found it surprisingly delicious, but it didn't incite her appetite. Christian excused himself and went in search of one of his fellow navigators, leaving her deep in thought by the table. She sipped a glass of burgundy and glanced idly about her, straight into the eyes of Father Cassel.

He was studying her so intently from across the room that her traitorous cheeks flamed instantly. In a panic she turned, bumping into a man at her side and spilling her dark wine like a blood stain all over his blue velvet coat. One strong hand reached out to steady her before her swirling skirts could send her sprawling, while the other lifted the now-empty glass from her fingers and set it upon a nearby table.

'Oh, *pardon monsieur*, I am so clumsy. I have ruined your frock coat!' Léonie stared in dismay at the ruined jacket. 'I shall of course pay to have it cleaned, if you would allow — ' She looked up.

'Oh!' So unprepared was she to be staring

straight into François' eyes that her legs buckled under her. I am going to make a complete fool of myself, she thought as she sagged against him, but there wasn't a thing she could do to prevent it. In a trice he scooped her into his arms and strode through the French windows on to the terrace.

The night air was cool but no match for the heat that flowed from the intimate contact between their bodies. Léonie closed her eyes and slid her hands about his neck.

'Never fear, *mademoiselle*,' he said. 'You are in safe hands.'

Safe? She was in mortal danger. Yet at that moment there was nowhere else on earth she would rather be.

He set her upon a stone bench overlooking the formal gardens. Reluctantly, Léonie opened her eyes, drank in the fresh scented air, and endeavoured to smile at her rescuer.

He was kneeling before her, still holding one of her hands as though afraid she might faint away again.

'You are . . . most kind, Captain. My apologies once again. I fear I have totally ruined your evening — and your jacket.' She took a lacy kerchief and began to mop at his coat, dabbing at the stain.

'Stop! That's really not necessary,' he said,

giving her a smile that lit up his eyes and softened his features, rendering her powerless to speak. She looked down to find her hands enclosed in his.

Why was he being so nice? she wondered. And yet he was restrained, with the courtesy one would reserve for a stranger. It made her feel wretched to deceive him so. He didn't deserve it. She pulled her hands free and stood.

'Forgive my clumsiness, Captain. I shall of course pay for the injury I have caused you.'

'Injury?'

'To your coat. It is quite ruined.'

He looked down and shrugged. 'Please do not concern yourself. We are all subject to momentary lapses from time to time.'

He would hardly consider her behaviour these past months to be a momentary 'lapse', she thought. 'Nevertheless, I'm sure you have more important things to occupy you than rescuing silly young girls.'

Deep inside, Léonie knew that she must flee. She despised her own selfishness for ever engaging in this masquerade. Christian was right — no possible good could come of it. She had been thinking only of herself.

Music began drifting out from the open windows. Léonie couldn't bear to remain with him in such a romantic spot feeling as she did, but she allowed herself one last lingering look at him, a tall dark shadow in the moonlight. She knew she must leave, for both their sakes, yet she wanted to throw herself into his arms and seek his forgiveness.

'I believe I should like to dance, *mamselle*,' François said with a smile. 'But as you so rightly pointed out, I am no longer fit to be seen indoors.' He took her hand. 'Perhaps we could dance here?'

Léonie's heart beat wildly as she looked into his face and contemplated dancing with him alone under the tropical moon.

'No! That is — I am not much for dancing . . .'

He frowned, his dark eyes searching hers. 'I see.'

'No, Captain, you don't.'

He stood away from her, hands clasped behind him. 'Then explain it to me.'

She looked down, fiddling with her fan. 'I fear I cannot, sir.'

Then he laughed, a soft rich sound. 'Why I do believe you are shy, little Hélène.' He took her hand once more and pulled her out into the centre of the terrace. She followed meekly, feeling unequal to the task of inventing a reason to desist further.

Perhaps one dance, she thought. What harm could it do?

The sweet melody wafted over her as they danced a stately minuet. Léonie gazed up into his face, watching the moonlight illumine the rugged planes of his face, the black waves of hair at his temples, the flash of fire in his eyes. Slowly, she began to relax, forgetting her guilt and enjoying the moment.

'Pardon me, *mamselle*, but I have the strangest feeling — ' He fell silent as they turned, and then when they faced each other again said, 'Could it be that we have met previously?'

Léonie's hands trembled suddenly and she pirouetted away from him, grateful for a chance to collect herself.

'I — I very much doubt that, Captain. I am quite certain I would remember if we had.'

Suddenly the moon did not seem so romantic anymore. Its light exposed her relentlessly when she yearned for dark clouds to hide behind, to obscure her from his searching gaze. This sweetest of moments was soured by layer upon layer of duplicity. Whatever he thought he saw in her, it was a falsehood, and she knew him well enough by now to know that he would revile her for it.

'My apologies, *mamselle*.' François said as the music ended. 'Perhaps instead of dancing you would prefer to talk?' He offered her his arm and she laid her fingers on it with the lightest of touches, for fear he would sense her nervousness. They turned and strolled along the terrace. 'Tell me about your home. French India is the next port of call for my ships and I would be interested to know how things are. I myself have not visited the colony for some years.'

★ ★ ★

'Christian, we must rescue our pretty friend,' Angé whispered fiercely as she gazed through the open doors on to the terrace. 'I mislike the way your captain is eyeing our Hélène, as though she were a canary and he the cat.'

'I thought you two had concocted this ruse just so he could do that,' Christian responded drily.

Angé gave him a quelling glare. 'My dear boy, he is in extreme danger of realizing our masquerade, and if he does, you will be as much to blame as Léonie, to be sure!'

Christian grimaced. 'And I thought a few days ashore would give me a respite from all this intrigue. No wonder sailors consider women aboard bring bad luck.'

'Pah!' his cousin responded as he led her toward Léonie and the captain. 'You sailors have more superstitions than women have diamonds.'

Christian rolled his eyes, but she saw him grin.

They found the captain and Léonie standing awkwardly on the terrace. It was plain to Angélique that Léonie was wound as tight as a bowstring. They were deep in conversation of some serious nature, the captain's fine lace cuffs catching the moonlight as he emphasized a point.

'We have found you at last!' Angé exclaimed. 'Fie, you are in serious mood tonight, *Capitaine*. I expected you to be reading my niece poetry from the stars themselves on such a fine evening, not bemoaning the woes of the world.'

'We were discussing some of the grand sights of southern India, *madame*,' replied the captain stiffly. 'But it seems your niece was not much interested in her surroundings there.'

Oh, Lord, thought Angélique. Poor Léonie. I should have told her something of the place so that she could at least make her story convincing. 'My dear Captain, young girls such as Hélène are not interested in the colonies. Their heads are full of fashion and romance! You have surely been too long at sea.' She tapped him with her fan, tucking her free arm into his and steering him back toward the safety of the ballroom. 'If you do not understand these things, how will you ever care properly for a loving wife?'

Léonie saw anger flash in François' eyes.

'Madame, I assure you I do not seek to encumber my life with a wife. My ships and my men are responsibility enough.' With a sharp bow to Léonie and Christian he turned on his heel and disappeared down the terrace steps into the darkened garden.

'Oh dear,' Angé sighed as they watched him vanish into the night in the direction of the stables and carriages. 'I fear your captain is a thorny bush. We shall have our work cut out if we are to trim his prickles.' She linked her arm through Léonie's. 'I'm sorry, my sweet. I never thought that he would question you on Pondicherry. 'Twas thoughtless of me. Shall I invite him to tea tomorrow and see if we can make amends?'

'He's coming anyway,' Léonie said with a sigh as she lowered herself on to a bench. 'He wants to visit 'young Chambois' as he calls him, first thing in the morning and see for himself how the boy fares.'

'Oh no!' Christian raised his hands in defeat. 'This gets too complicated for my blood, Léonie. You are going to have to end the charade — and the sooner the better. We must just take the consequences, whatever they might be.'

Léonie frowned. She had entertained similar thoughts herself just an hour ago, but it was too late for that. The captain had plied her with questions concerning her supposed life in India, and she had prevaricated as best she could, though her answers, by their very vacuity, displeased him. Clearly he thought her a self-absorbed young woman without an idea in her head. To show him up for a dupe now and face his scorn, would be more than she could endure.

She shook her head. 'I will not have you and Jean-Michel disgraced because of me. Your uncle will disown you on the spot, not to speak of what my father might say.'

'Well what are we to do?'

'I must pretend to be Jean-Mich once more.'

Christian snorted. 'And who will play the part of the mysteriously ignorant lady from India? Me?'

Ange giggled. 'Let's not test the charade too far, my dears. Léonie is right. We shall cope very nicely in the morn. Why you will take young Hélène to see the sights of the island in my carriage, and I shall chaperon the visit between my poor sick young visitor and his devoted captain!' She waved an airy hand as she beckoned them to follow her back into the ballroom. 'Come! Let's not waste this perfectly delicious evening by moping over such a trifle.'

11

Trifle it may have seemed, but it was enough to keep Léonie tossing and turning in her bed that night. By dawn she was weary and heartsore, filled with a strange homesickness.

She rang for Yvette, her black maid, the only servant in the house trusted to keep the secret of her disguise, and dressed simply in a gown of blue-and-white dimity, for the day would be warm. It would be hours before she need assume her role as Jean-Michel for the captain's visit and she enjoyed the feel of loose petticoats billowing around her legs.

No one except the servants was yet about downstairs, and Léonie wandered freely through the house. In the library she discovered a clavichord, and with a cry of delight sat at the keyboard, resting her fingertips on the keys. In her present mood, this was a discovery indeed, a poignant reminder of home and of the life she had tossed aside so lightly.

Her fingers began, almost of their own accord, to pick out a tune, aimlessly at first and then following a melody as though it were just yesterday that she had last sat to play in her father's house. The music soothed her like a breath of cool air.

Léonie closed her eyes, letting it flow over her. On and on she played, feeling the tensions fall away, until the sun rose in the tropical sky and streamed into the room. She imagined she was her old self again, a young woman in love with life and with scarcely a care in the world. She dreamed of summers in the Loire valley, falling blossoms giving way to ruby-red apples and golden pears in the orchard, of a carefree life filled with thoughts of poetry and love . . .

★ ★ ★

François de la Tour stood in the doorway of the library where he had been ushered by a lackey, and stared. Hélène was far more beautiful in the morning light than he remembered from the night before Her simple cotton gown emphasized her slender

206

form, creating a picture of sweet innocence that took him by surprise. Her eyes were closed, long dark lashes brushing her cheeks, and her small mouth bore a light smile of pleasure in her music. He wondered what she was thinking about. Perhaps a lover left behind in the East, or an imagined tryst in France?

François disliked the sensation of spying on another person's reveries — and Hélène de Lisle was clearly captivated by some delight this morning — so he stepped into the room and closed the door firmly.

'Oh!' Léonie's eyes flew open and her hands stumbled across the keys. The very last person she had expected to see at this hour was the captain. 'Good morning, Captain. You are . . . that is, Madame Dumont did not expect you so early.'

He inclined his head. 'My apologies, *mamselle*, but I have much business to attend to this morning and I was anxious to enquire after the health of young Chambois. It seems you like to rise with the birds yourself.'

Léonie got up from the clavichord stool. It would not do to tell him that she had been unable to sleep for fear of her next encounter with him.

'I rose early to be ready for a tour of the island with Monsieur Lavelle,' she replied. 'I must not keep him waiting. I shall inform Madame Dumont that you are here, though I doubt she is awake as yet. Perhaps some breakfast while you wait?'

'If you will keep me company, I could not refuse. I think I owe you some civilized behaviour after my performance last evening, don't you agree?'

'I'm sure I was not much better, sir.'

He smiled, transforming his expression to one of such warmth that Léonie felt all her determination to avoid him dissolve. She knew she should excuse herself, yet being near him like this — like a woman — made her feel so wonderfully alive.

She rang a tiny silver bell, explained their requirements to the servant who appeared, and led the captain out through the French doors, searching for some small talk, to cover the pounding of her heart.

'Meals are served on the terrace until the day becomes too warm. I expect you prefer to spend time out of doors after weeks cooped up on the *Aurélie*.'

He laughed. 'Indeed it is a treat to breathe clean air on dry land,' he replied gravely, following her out into the dewy morning. 'But no doubt you felt much the same after your own voyage from India.'

Léonie averted her face. 'Yes, of course.'

She chose the chair with its back to the sun, so she had more comfort to observe her companion. In an instant a black child appeared bearing a parasol and stood silently to shelter her from even these early rays of sunlight. It made her uneasy. She waved the boy away.

'There are so many servants on this island,' she commented, toying with the lace tablecloth. 'I can't imagine how they can afford so many. Perhaps they have been spared the strictures we've had in France.'

François' eyes narrowed. 'You've heard about the economic troubles from as far away as Pondicherry?'

The gaffe made Léonie blush. She laughed it off as best she could. 'I receive letters, naturally, but one can only sense such things.'

'I believe I was altogether too harsh in my judgement of you last evening, *mamselle*. I never dreamed French politics would excite you when you appeared indifferent to the situation in India. Yet you must understand that these Africans are not servants as they would be in France. They are slaves.'

'Slaves!' The word tasted bitter on her tongue. 'You mean they are not free to come and go as they please? Are they not even paid?'

'They are kept.' He shrugged. 'It is not to my taste, either. But the French India Company's success was built on importing coffee and sugar and spices — gathered by slaves — for re-export to Europe. It's business.'

'But it's not right! People must have their own lives, their own freedoms, even if they are poor.'

The captain sat back, eyeing her like some specimen under one of Duplessis' microscopes. 'I had no idea you would hold such firm notions on matters most women do not care to discuss.'

'Is it so bad to know right from wrong?'

'Not at all.'

'But it surprises you.'

'Perhaps I am too used to pragmatists.'

Léonie frowned. Pragmatism was her father's favourite notion, especially when the subject was arranged marriages.

'For myself,' she replied somewhat haughtily, 'I prefer idealism. It is more honest, even if one is made to suffer for it sometimes.' As I will, she thought with a pang, when you learn the truth about me.

A silver coffee urn was brought to the table, suspending conversation momentarily. The rich aroma made Léonie's mouth water and she accepted a cup gratefully. It felt like hours since she'd awoken and she was surprised by how hungry she felt.

She sighed with pleasure as she set down her cup. 'The Île de France is a truly bountiful paradise, slaves or not,' she said. 'I almost think I could stay here.'

'And do what?' he asked wryly. 'Marry one of those cheroot-smokers who were making your fan flap last night?'

She giggled. 'I had to hide behind a potted plant just to escape some of them! There are too few women in the colonies.'

The warmth of François's laugh made Léonie's heart skip a beat. It was so nice to sit here on the terrace in the warm morning sunlight, enjoying a conversation with him. So wonderful to discover that she could be herself, even if 'Hélène' *was* a fiction wrought from necessity.

Nearly an hour passed while they consumed their leisurely breakfast. The captain, with some prompting from her, described the voyage of the *Aurélie*, and she was amused to hear herself — as Jean-Michel, of course — described as a talented young man with a hot head and a soft heart. If only he knew!

She realized François had stood up.

'Your company is a pleasant distraction, *mamselle*, but I have allowed time to slip by unchecked. If you will excuse me, I must

211

visit young Chambois and be on my way.'

Léonie's hand flew to her mouth. She must delay him, at least until she could assume her twin's identity. He must not find the boy absent from his bed!

'Oh, but Captain, Angélique — Madame Dumont — will be down presently and would never forgive me if she did not escort you on your mission of mercy.' She touched the captain's sleeve, thinking to persuade him to be seated once again, but the contact took her breath away and she found herself staring into his eyes, quite forgetting what she wanted to say.

It seemed to affect him too. He laid his hand atop hers, pressing it into the thin fabric of his sleeve. The warmth of his skin made her fingers tingle.

'It would please me very much if' — he was looking down at her as if uncertain whether to continue — 'if you would consider riding with me this afternoon, when the worst heat of the day is gone. I am told the sands near here are a wonderful place for horses to stretch their legs. You do ride, *n'est-ce pas*?'

Léonie blushed with real pleasure. 'I would be delighted, Captain.' At that moment Christian and Angé stepped on to the terrace, and Léonie was relieved to see from their expressions that they understood the situation instantly. 'Ah, here is Monsieur Lavelle ready for my tour of the island. I must hurry, *Capitaine*, if you will excuse me.' She fled indoors, hoisted up her dimity gown, and took the stairs two at a time.

Within minutes, Léonie lay once more abed, her wig gone, her red curls tied back, her face scrubbed and pale against the feather pillows of Jean-Michel's bed in the darkened sickroom. She did not have long to wait, though counted in pounding heartbeats it felt like a lifetime.

Angé preceded the captain into the room. Léonie pretended to be dozing and remained so until she felt her hostess touch the sleeve of her nightshirt.

'Jean-Michel. You have a visitor. Wake up, *petit.*'

Léonie opened her eyes slowly, then shut them again as though against the light, while in reality she was controlling a terrible and untimely desire to laugh. Slowly she made herself focus on the room, frowning with the effort.

'*Capitaine!*'

He sat on the edge of the bed, his thigh pressing against hers through the light sheet. 'How are you, Chambois? I would have sent André de Montauban to you, but Madame

Dumont says her own surgeon has been seeing to you.'

Léonie nodded. 'I am much improved, thank you,' she replied softly. It would not do to let him think she was fully recovered. Not just yet. She yearned to be Hélène for just a little longer. 'Please don't trouble yourself.'

Angé slipped out of the room with a wink over the captain's shoulder that only Léonie could see. Léonie coughed to cover a sudden giggle, and then felt contrite as she saw the concern in François' face.

The pressure of the captain's muscled leg against her own was sending a flush of heat all the way to her thigh. She lay back against the pillows and tried to ease her body away.

'Do you have a fever, young man?' The captain reached out and placed his large brown hand across her forehead, then against her cheek. 'You feel warm.'

If I am no more than warm, Léonie thought, spare me a real fever! It took considerable effort to lie there and allow him to touch her so intimately, even if it was without his full knowledge. Every touch of his fingers burned her skin and made her tingle in places she hadn't known existed. When his fingers set to exploring the tender skin beneath her ears, she knew

214

he was feeling her neck out of concern for goitre or some such disease, but that didn't make it any easier to breathe.

'Good heavens, Chambois, you're as tense as a sparrowhawk. Don't tell me you're afraid of doctoring?'

It was a gift of a lie and she took it like a drowning man grabs a rope. 'I try not to be.'

He dropped his hand, frowning. 'Well you've nothing to fear. There's nothing obvious. Perhaps after all it is just fatigue. Is your work too much aboard the *Aurélie*?'

'No! I love my work. And I will do better at botany, I promise.'

He nodded, apparently satisfied, and stood. Léonie took a breath as she saw he was about to leave.

'Captain, I am sorry I was unable to attend the Governor's Ball last night. Did you enjoy the diversion?'

'As much as ever. Which is not much to say.'

She frowned. 'I don't think I take your meaning, sir.'

'I dislike such events, Jean-Michel. Small-talk bores me to my buckles. However . . . '

'However — ' she prompted.

He opened his mouth as if to explain, and then apparently changed his mind. He

215

crossed back to the bed, stared down at her for a second and then touched her arm in a fleeting gesture. 'Get well, Chambois. This is a beautiful island and once we sail we'll not see its like again.'

Léonie lay under the sheets after he left, her eyes tight with tears. His touch had felt so magic, so full of compassion. And yet he was a man no one could ever suspect of such sentiments. How very special he seemed. How perfectly, how absolutely unobtainable.

★ ★ ★

It was past four o'clock when Hélène de Lisle mounted her horse sidesaddle, wearing a borrowed riding gown of Angélique's, and rode down the rutted country lanes towards the beach in the company of François de la Tour. The peak of the day's heat had subsided, leaving the air cool and rich with the scents of black earth and damp foliage.

For the first mile they rode in silence except for calling to their horses. Léonie was glad of a chance to concentrate on the awkward saddle. At home she had finally persuaded her father to allow her to ride astride in a special divided skirt of her own invention, for she abhorred the back-breaking side-saddle.

They passed beyond the sugar plantations and travelled for some distance over rocks. The familiar sound of ocean waves grew ever nearer and soon they rode out on to flat white sands that seemed to stretch for miles.

François reined in his horse. 'Would you care to race, *mamselle*?'

'I hardly think that a chivalrous request, Captain,' she replied in a teasing voice, 'considering the difference in our saddlery.'

His eyebrows rose in mock surprise. 'Would chivalry be served by a handicap, perhaps?'

Léonie inclined her head with a laugh, kicked her heels and set her mare to galloping down the hard-packed sand. Soon she heard the heavy beat of his horse bearing down upon her, and in a flash he had outstripped her more dignified passage and was in the lead.

He stopped beside an upturned boat and waited till she came up, laughing and breathless. 'You are most uncavalier, sir, to treat a lady so! Your handicap was but a breath behind me, I declare!'

He grinned. 'What would you have me do, *mamselle*? Walk?'

She harrumphed with spirit. 'I would have you swap mounts with me, sir, if you dare.'

'Swap mounts!'

'If you think you can handle my gentle well-bred mare, of course,' she added sweetly.

He was off the stallion in a flash and reaching out to hand her down from her horse. With as much dignity as she could muster in her voluminous skirts, she stepped on to the hull of the old boat and attempted to mount astride François's big grey stallion. Her skirts rode up her calves, exposing her slim-fitting ankle boots and an indecorous length of leg. Léonie pretended not to notice the captain's staring, or the half smile curving his lips.

Soon it was her turn to smile as she watched him attempt to balance in the clumsy side-saddle.

'Damn things! How on earth . . . ?'

'Are you experiencing difficulty already, *Capitaine*?'

'Of course not. Nothing to it.'

They faced back down the beach. The captain identified a landmark for the finish line and the two horses surged forward together. Léonie felt the power of the grey, and combined with her secure position she and the horse flew together across the white sands. She was carried away with the exhilaration of the ride, noticing only as she passed the appointed spot that she had easily outdistanced the mare. She reined in and turned the stallion, waving a gloved hand at the captain as he lumbered up. He was clearly not pleased, either to look so foolish or to have been so soundly trounced. Léonie tried not to giggle.

'Women may be the gentler sex, Captain, but they often have the harder task to bear.'

He grinned somewhat sheepishly. 'Anyone who can ride like this earns my total respect.'

She took pity on him. He really did look uncomfortable. She slid off the grey and handed him the reins. 'I think you'd better have this manly beast back, Captain. You quite overwhelm the little mare.'

Once remounted, they let the horses amble along in the small waves that lapped the shore. The sun was growing low in the sky and Léonie knew they would soon have to turn back, but she felt so free, so relaxed with François, that she had no wish to hurry.

'The sea is a strange beast, do you not think so, Captain? So tame and peaceful one minute and then filled with fury the next. What drives it, do you suppose, into such rages?'

He laughed. 'The moon.'

'Of course, the moon. How strange that

219

one tiny moon can control these vast seas. To what possible purpose, I wonder.'

'That is for someone higher up to say,' he replied, pointing upward.

'Do you enjoy living your life upon the oceans?' she asked gently, watching as he gazed far out across the sea, deep in thought. 'Do you not sometimes wish for a normal life in France. For a family, perhaps?'

A blackness passed across his features, hardening the angle of his jaw. He turned away, but she could see the tension in his broad shoulders. 'I do not know the meaning of 'normal', *mamselle*. I keep my thoughts confined to my current mission, whatever it is. That's why naval men make poor husbands: they are wedded to the sea.' He looked quickly at her. 'You would do well to remember that.'

Then he turned his horse out of the shallows and spurred it up the beach. Léonie followed in silence, stunned by the bleakness in his face.

They left the beach and picked their way among rocks leading to a shady valley divided by a small stream, then dismounted so the horses could drink before releasing them to browse on the sweet grasses of the valley floor.

Léonie herself was thirsty from their ride

and knelt on the rocks, cupping her hands to capture the cool clear water. It tasted better than the finest wine and she drank again and again, until suddenly aware of the captain watching her. His expression was deep, unreadable, and she felt a flush rise in her cheeks. She stood up and wiped wet hands on her skirts.

'What colour is your hair?' he asked.

She reached up with one hand to touch her wig, and sought an answer, for she dared not tell him the truth, and yet more and more she found it hard to lie to him. He stepped close, bending his head so his eyes could roam across her features.

'You have an exquisite face, yet you cover it with powders and patches. And your hair . . . Will you not let me see it, so I can remember the real Hélène when I am once again at sea?' He reached out and stroked her temple with one finger, sending darts of fire along her skin. She tried to think of a response, but his touch sent her thoughts into a whirlspin. Over his shoulder she saw the sky flame red as the sun began to set.

'My hair is . . . the colour of the sun,' she whispered, for her voice refused to be any stronger.

'Golden, like my mother's was.' He slid his hand behind her neck, stroking upward at the constraining wig. 'I wish you'd let it fall, free and natural, so I could touch its softness, for I'm sure it would feel like the finest silk.'

Léonie feared that he would tug off her disguise and expose her deceit, but instead he lowered his mouth and kissed her. She had not even the time to cry out before the crushing warmth of his lips claimed her senses. He tasted wild and free, like an ocean storm, his lips devouring hers with a passion that exceeded her wildest imaginings. She felt herself respond, opening her lips like a flower opens to the sun, sliding her fingers beneath his riding jacket and pressing them against his muscled chest. She felt his body press against her, felt his hunger, and responded with a primitive urge of her own that took her totally unawares. He wrapped his arms tightly around her and she knew she never wanted him to let go.

Suddenly he released her, holding her at arm's length for a second and then crushing her once more to his chest. He stared up at the canopy of trees, his cheek resting on the top of her head.

'I'm sorry. I know that was wrong of me, yet you seem to create needs in me. Needs I thought I was no longer prey to.' He let her go and turned to crouch beside the stream, dousing his face with a splash of cool water.

Léonie's heart was pounding so fiercely she could scarcely breathe. She touched his shoulder. 'You make me feel strange, too.'

He stood up and wiped his face on his sleeve. 'You have your whole life in front of you, Hélène. You are pure and innocent, and you will find a good man in France, one who will cherish you as you deserve. That person is not me. I am world weary. I have seen too much of life and death and things that will haunt me all my days.' He tucked a finger beneath her chin to raise her drooping face. 'Take my advice: find a man who will put your happiness above all else.' And not spend his life half a world away, he thought bitterly.

Who is this child, he wondered, letting his hand trail along the edge of her fichu, that she welcomes the unbridled passion of a battle-scarred naval officer? Does she not know how precious her innocence is? No matter how drawn to her he felt, he would not take advantage of her trust. Nor could he be there if she needed him.

Suddenly his finger stilled. He pushed her fichu aside, frowning. Against the milky skin of her collarbone lay a small heart, the size of a gold locket but black as soot.

'What is this?'

Léonie pulled abruptly away, covering

herself. 'It's nothing. A scar, no more.'

'That's not nothing,' he replied. 'It's a tattoo, and not a very good one. How did you come by such a mark?'

Léonie sighed. She knew him well enough to be certain he would insist upon an answer. 'It was an accident. When I was a child I loved to ride astride my horse. One day I had a fall and the locket I was wearing was crushed into my skin.'

'That must have been most painful.'

'It was. My father, when he heard what had happened, was so angry with me for riding like a boy that he rubbed ink into the wound, so that it would remain forever as a reminder that I must be a lady.'

'That is an outrage!'

She shrugged. ' 'Twas long ago. I have forgiven him.' As I hope you'll one day forgive me, she added silently. For she could scarcely tell him that she was dressed as Jean-Michel at the time in order to take part in a jousting contest. Her father inflicted the mark so that they could never dupe him by changing places again.

She reached for her horse's bridle, sad that the magic of their passionate embrace had been so quickly broken. 'It will soon be dark. We should return to the house before we lose our way.'

No sooner had they mounted than the forest quiet was broken by a crash that echoed down the valley. It was followed almost instantly by shouting and wailing.

'My God,' François said, spurring his horse up the hill toward the road. 'What was that?'

Léonie gave chase, her horse faltering occasionally as she hurried over the uneven ground. The dreadful sounds of wounded animals drove her on and she reached the road just a second behind François. On the far side, a heavy wagon pulled by bullocks lay on its side in the ditch. One of the animals was dead, the other bellowing in pain. She looked away as François crossed to the beast and drew a pistol from his saddle-bag. The shot created a moment of dread silence and then the wailing began again. Léonie threw herself off her horse and ran to a black woman who lay screaming in pain on the ground. At her breast she held a tiny babe, barely a few weeks old. Léonie knew it was dead before she touched it, but she drew it away gently and placed it nearby on the ground, speaking soothingly to the woman. Two small children huddled beside their mother, whimpering, black eyes round as saucers.

François appeared at her side. 'The father

is dead. How is the woman?'

Léonie shook her head. She feared the worst, for there was thick blood oozing from a terrible gash on the woman's neck, and her left leg was broken, probably her hips as well. But she had no wish for the children to hear such news.

'What happened?' she asked the woman gently, cradling her head in her lap and attempting to staunch the blood with the hem of her riding dress. The dark eyes gazed up into her face, trying to focus, but from the woman's lips came only the sounds of agony.

One of the children crept up to François and clutched his leg. The captain seemed uncertain what to do, but then knelt in the dust and took the child onto his lap, gathering in her brother at the same time. He held them in the circle of his arms while they trembled and sobbed. After a few minutes the boy seemed to gain some control.

'The carriage was going so fast,' he hiccoughed.

'Carriage? What carriage?'

'I don't know, sir. It was racing along. My father tried to get out of the way but the bullocks were old.'

'Did it hit you? The carriage?'

The boy shook his head. 'But the bullocks went off the road there' — he pointed a bony finger — 'and fell amongst the rocks. The wagon turned over . . .'

He began to sob again and François held the children as tightly in his embrace as he had so recently held Léonie. She watched anger war with compassion in his face and her heart filled with love for him.

'Take the children,' she said softly. 'They look to be unhurt. I will wait here with the mother while you get help.'

He frowned. He didn't want to abandon her in this isolated spot, especially as darkness was falling. The rural areas were full of *marrons*, escaped slaves who roamed the countryside, robbing and causing mayhem. But the children couldn't be left, and they were too young and defenceless to send for help on their own. He lifted the snivelling children on to the saddle of Léonie's mare, then turned back to her.

'Take this,' he said, passing her his pistol. 'It has been reloaded. Let me show you how to use it.'

'There's no need, Captain. I am perfectly capable of pulling a trigger if I have to.' She tucked the bulky weapon beneath the folds of her skirt. 'We shall be fine. Please don't worry.'

He looked down at her, as bloodied as her patient as she sat on the road tending to the injured woman, and yet as unconcerned as any man aboard ship in the height of battle. He felt better leaving the pistol with her and she seemed happy enough to have it. François shook his head. Hélène de Lisle was indeed an enigma, one minute disinterested and the next as worldly-wise as any man. He grabbed the mare's bridle and threw himself up into his own saddle, but as he urged the horses into a trot he caught a disturbing flash of a face that was hers and yet not quite hers; someone familiar and yet unknown to him. The vision flitted through his mind so fast he couldn't grasp it, but it left him with a deep feeling of unease.

★ ★ ★

By the time the men arrived bearing a palanquin litter on long poles, it was dark. The woman was dead. Léonie still cradled her head, though it was no longer necessary to stem the blood. Her hands and arms were sticky, her dress ruined, but she sat holding the woman's lifeless form, rocking slightly and singing an old French lullaby in the moonlight. François felt an ache in the back of his eyes as he led the rescue party to her. She looked up at him, her eyes bright with tears.

228

'Now they have no one, François. They have no mother and no father. What will become of the children?'

The palanquin bearers took the woman's body and that of the tiny infant and bore them away, then the captain lifted Léonie to her feet and held her against his chest.

'Don't trouble yourself. They are safe at the Maison Dumont for the moment. Which is where you are going right now.'

'You went to Angé's house for help?' Léonie struggled out of his arms in dismay. What if he had asked to see Jean-Michel?

'Of course. It was the nearest settlement. Why would I not go there?'

'No reason,' Léonie mumbled, reaching to untie her mare from where the captain had tethered it to the broken wagon.

They rode back in silence, each absorbed in their own thoughts.

12

The remaining days on the Île de France passed quickly. Léonie met with the captain in her alias as Hélène de Lisle only twice more, once at an evening of cards in the home of a retired sea captain, and again when he called to visit Jean-Michel and found her at home instead. But the double act was wearying and it was no longer possible to pretend that the sub-lieutenant remained ill. She had to resume her duties as a naval officer, accompanying Duplessis on several expeditions in the volcanic plateau to gather specimens. They collected a wide variety of exotic plants, some strange lizards and many birds which they would attempt to keep alive until their return to France, though taxidermy was an unpleasant skill she'd become adept at for their all-too-frequent failures.

A few days before they sailed, Léonie donned her borrowed women's garb and made an excuse to Angélique that she wished to visit the shops in Port-Louis for some 'essentials' no woman aboard ship for months at a time could be without. She borrowed a carriage and asked the driver to take her to the town orphanage.

It was a squalid affair, little more than a hut and with a mud floor. Inside it was dark, the air rancid with the smell of cooking and ill-kempt babies and children. She could see no sanitation and preferred not to ask how the children were expected to perform their ablutions. She pressed a lacy white kerchief to her nostrils.

The woman in charge of the establishment seemed to know who she was and there was much commotion from the back room. Suddenly the two black children Léonie remembered from the accident were presented, looking a great deal cleaner than their counterparts, no doubt especially to impress this important visitor.

Léonie was not sure why she had come. She had simply been unable to forget the children's plight. She thought she wanted to see for herself if they were coping with their grief. Now she knew the reason.

'The children are to come with me,' she told the woman coldly. 'This place is not fit for animals.'

The woman, a half-caste of uncertain origins, drew herself up in anger. 'We do the best we can. If it were not for this home, these children would be running wild in the mountains like a bunch of no-good *marrons*.'

'They would be better off!' The angry voice made both the women start. François de la Tour stood menacingly in the doorway, slightly stooped to accommodate its mean proportions. As he stepped into the hut Léonie could see he was angry; angrier than she had ever seen him. Except once.

Except when he had rescued her from those would-be ravishers aboard the *Aurélie*.

'Captain!' She was flabbergasted to see him. 'What brings you here?'

'I might ask you the same,' he replied. The children ran to him, wrapping their skinny black arms about his waist. The woman moved to pull them away lest they spoil his frock coat, but he sent her a chilling glance and she faltered.

' . . . I do not wish them to dirty your fine clothes, sir.' The woman smiled through broken teeth, bobbing a little curtsey.

'They would not dirty me if you had not left them to wallow in this cesspit like pigs at a trough,' he replied coldly. The woman blanched. 'I shall speak to the governor about this today. Before my ships leave Port-Louis, you, *madame*, will be looking for other employment. Good day.'

Taking Léonie's arm, he ushered the children out into the sunshine.

'But Captain, what shall we do with the poor waifs?' Léonie asked as they walked away from the stinking hovel.

François grimaced. 'I have no idea. But I wasn't going to leave them there. Nor any of those other poor infants. No doubt when they are considered old enough for service, someone will wash them, burn their

232

flea-infested clothes and then sell the babes for a good price. Children are in demand as slaves.'

'Oh, how horrible,' Léonie murmured, squeezing the hand of the small girl at her side. 'What is your name, *petite*?'

'Danielle, *madame*,' replied the child shyly.

'It's *mamselle*,' Léonie chided her quietly.

The girl turned her huge black eyes to François whose hand she still clung to. 'But I thought you and *Monsieur le Capitaine* were . . .'

Léonie blushed, glancing quickly at him only to receive a crooked smile in reply. 'We are acquaintances, Danielle. *C'est tout.*' Then she had an idea and turned to François.

'Could we not take them with us? I . . . I mean, could you not take them aboard your ship? You must have need of servants. I'm sure they could be useful.'

He stared quizzically at her, but seemed to accept her blunder as a simple *faux pas*. 'I could take the boy, but I allow no females aboard my ships, *mamselle*.'

'Why . . . why not?' she faltered.

'The men would mutiny. Women bring bad luck on a boat.'

'That's preposterous! Surely you do not

give credence to such superstition?'

The line of his jaw was grim. 'It is out of the question. She would never be safe, and it would be cruel to separate her from the only family she has left.'

Léonie nodded sadly. 'You are right, but we must find them a home. Perhaps Madame Dumont will take them in. I shall take them back with me and beg her mercy.'

François handed her and the children up into the carriage, quelling the scandalized stares from the driver with a single glance. 'I think that is the best option, and I would come with you to add my own entreaties to your aunt, but I have urgent business with the governor as a consequence of all this.' He kissed her fingers quickly and signalled the driver. Léonie had only a moment to wave before he was gone.

★ ★ ★

She did not see François again until the morning of their departure. Her trunk was packed, her uniform pressed and ready, but she was in no hurry to leave and ambled among the flowerbeds in Angélique's garden dressed in a white gown embroidered with tiny golden flowers, enjoying her last freedom as a woman. Danielle walked at her side, carrying a basket in which Léonie was placing roses and forget-me-nots.

The child looked up as they heard a horse approach. '*C'est Monsieur le Capitaine*!' she squealed, dropping the basket and dashing across the lawn to welcome him.

Léonie watched as François swung his leg over the saddle and jumped to the ground, catching the little girl in his arms and swinging her around. She smiled. They looked so natural together, so relaxed. How could he be determined never to marry when he was so wonderful with children?

He should be a father, she thought sadly. For such a man to be alone all his life would be a waste. With a start she realized that *she* wanted to give him children. The sudden image of her holding a baby in her arms — his baby — made her ache with longing, and she turned away, bending to collect the blooms that had fallen from Danielle's basket.

'Mademoiselle de Lisle?'

His voice startled her. She had not heard him cross the lawn.

'Good morning, *Capitaine*.' She looked around. 'Where is the child?'

'I sent her inside so I might speak with you alone.' He bent to help her, picking up the roses and placing them into the already overflowing basket. Léonie stared at his strong brown fingers, realizing this would be their last meeting under such circumstances. There was so much she wanted to say to him, so much she wanted to do, but it was all impossible. Now she would have to go back to her pretence of being a man, hiding her emotions, being nothing to him once more. She blinked as unbidden tears stung her eyes.

Suddenly he reached one hand under her chin and lifted her face. 'My dear Hélène, you are crying.' His eyes dark with concern, he helped her to her feet and led her to a small stone bench. 'Surely you are not trying to flatter me that I shall be missed when my ships have sailed?' His voice was gently teasing as they sat on the bench. Léonie sniffed, wiping her nose with a lacy kerchief and removing her hand from his too-warm grasp.

'You flatter yourself, Captain. I merely pricked my finger on a thorn.' She sucked the imaginary wound, avoiding his eyes.

'A most vexing injury, indeed,' he replied gravely, taking her hand and examining it. 'Perhaps I can help. Does this make it better?' He kissed her finger, his breath teasing her skin. 'Or this?'

Léonie shut her eyes as spirals of fire

trickled along the path of his lips. Then he turned her hand over and kissed her palm. She pulled her hand away abruptly. This would never do. It was not at all how she had envisioned this scene. She had planned to be courteous but distant, making him aware that while she had enjoyed his company, she was not troubled by his departure. She must not let him think Hélène de Lisle felt anything for Captain de la Tour but a passing interest. It would never do for him to pine for a phantom lover once they were at sea together. She knew it was ludicrous to feel jealousy toward her own alter ego, but she couldn't help herself.

She jumped off the bench, gathered up the basket and headed toward the house. He was at her side in an instant, strolling along as though nothing had happened.

'Where will you go when you return to France, *mamselle*?'

'To relatives . . . in the Dordogne,' she replied evasively.

'Won't you at least tell me where, so I may call on you if I find myself nearby?'

She stopped walking and turned to face him. 'To what possible purpose, *monsieur*? If I am not mistaken, you have made your life's vows to Mother Ocean, have you not?'

He frowned, clasping his hands behind

him. 'I made no secret of my feelings, *mamselle*. I simply wished . . . ' He stopped, as though he wasn't sure what he wished, or how to explain.

'You simply wanted what, sir? To keep all your cards? To play with a young girl's dreams, perhaps?' She shook her head, sad yet satisfied at the hurt creeping into his eyes. 'You have chosen the wrong lady for your games, Captain. I thank you for your company, and for your compassion toward those poor children who lost their parents, but I think it quite unlikely we shall ever encounter one another again.'

She turned to head up the steps of the house, but he caught her arm and spun her back to face him.

'Just like that? I thought we had become . . . friends, but now you toss me away like a bent coin when it suits your mood. What kind of woman are you, Hélène de Lisle?'

She was wounded by his accusation, though his reaction was exactly as she needed it to be. Nevertheless, part of her yearned to fall into his arms and confess the lie, to tell him what was really in her heart — that she loved him hopelessly. But she stood her ground, concentrating on the lace at his cuffs, for she knew to look into his eyes would be to expose her soul.

He was waiting. The question, it seemed, was not merely rhetorical. She made herself look up, staring at him for a moment, trying to memorize the way he looked at her, at a woman.

'I am not a person who forgets, Captain, but neither am I as raw as you take me to be. I wish you a safe and successful voyage.'

She left him there at the bottom of the steps, though she could feel his eyes burning into her as she walked up into the house. At the door she turned and looked back. For a second their eyes met and then she closed the door firmly and went to cast off her female persona and transform herself back into his *enseigne*.

Danielle was waiting in Jean-Michel's room, her dark eyes round as saucers. She had known the first night she had been brought to Angé's house that the Vicomte de Chambois and Hélène de Lisle were one and the same, and her girlish nature revelled in the excitement of such a ploy.

'Still he does not realize who you are, *mamselle*,' she said, clapping her hands with delight.

Léonie smiled, tired by the task before her. 'No, Danielle. But 'tis a hollow victory.'

The girl frowned as she helped her out of the white gown.

'If I have made him a little in love with Hélène, how will I ever make him fall for the real me, even if he were to discover my existence?' She sat still while the child fumbled with the wig and lifted it from her head. That was one item of clothing she would definitely not miss. Her head was hot and itchy from the thing, and she relaxed as she felt the tines of her hairbrush sliding over her scalp. 'Aah, that is good, Danielle. You will make a wonderful lady's maid.'

The girl dropped on to her knees at Léonie's side. 'Please, *mamselle*, take me with you. Then I could be near both you and the captain. Please, don't leave me here.'

'Child!' Léonie took her small hands in hers. 'You know that's impossible. You heard the captain say so yourself. And Madame Dumont will treat you well. She has promised that you and your brother will learn to read and write and be taught many skills that will help you make a life for yourselves. She could not have been kinder.'

'I know,' Danielle responded, her shoulders drooping. 'But we want to be with you and *Monsieur le Capitaine*.'

Léonie hugged the child. 'I will make you a promise, Danielle,' she murmured into her hair, 'if you are a good girl and learn your

240

lessons well, I shall send for you when I am back in France.'

'You mean it? You would really bring us to come and live with you? Both of us?'

Léonie nodded. 'I promise. Now, dry your tears and help me get dressed or I shall miss my ship!'

Danielle wiped her tears on the back of her hand and giggled. 'That would make *Monsieur le Capitaine* very cross, I think.'

★ ★ ★

The *Aurélie* sailed out of Port-Louis late in the afternoon, followed at a few leagues' distance by the *Mousquetaire*. François was intent on making best use of the westerly monsoons to blow the expedition across the Indian Ocean, and his timing, as people so often observed, was impeccable. They reached the east coast of India in mid July, sailing into the French colony of Pondicherry without incident.

The expedition stayed only long enough in India to restock before sailing east once more toward the Sunda Strait and the Dutch settlement of Batavia, where they would make a final resupply before passing through the East Indies and out into the vast Pacific Ocean.

Léonie found her botanical work at Duplessis' side growing daily more fascinating, though she still preferred her tasks under her other master, Roussillon, for whom she continued to produce excellent drawings. On the one hand, Duplessis became less of an ogre as her own interest and therefore her application to botany increased. Roussillon, however, clearly felt 'Jean-Michel' to be too cocksure and resented his artistic skills. Léonie merely smiled to herself, amused at the woe she would create in her brother when he learned how respected his artistry had become.

Everyone was keen to make port in Batavia, but before they crossed the Equator the winds sighed away and the once-full sails sagged and hung limp. By nightfall a dense fog had arisen, cloaking everything in languid steam.

The ships waited, dangling like wraiths in sea-level clouds. The ocean was oil smooth with barely a swell, and not even the creaking of timbers broke the unnerving silence.

The fog was so close it rendered the sextants useless, and the water was too deep for the anchors, so they drifted aimlessly, cut off from all sensation in a soundless world. Nobody could work, conversation was sparse, and the tension gave Léonie a headache.

On the second morning the captain ordered the vessels made battle ready and Léonie had to strap on her smallsword and matching silver dagger, something she had never done except on formal occasions when in uniform. They merely added to the burden of coping with the suffocating heat. But no matter how hot she was, she would not go without her breast wrap, for the memories of crossing the Equator in the Atlantic were all too fresh in her mind.

Jacques Le Brun, the first officer, scratched his head over the orders. He himself felt there was no real danger, except from boredom and frustration. Wary of creating panic among the crew, he sent Léonie to ask the captain if he required *all* the cannons readied.

She knocked on the door of his cabin. There were voices from within and she was momentarily disappointed, for she'd had little chance to be alone with François since their departure from the Île de France.

'*Entrez!*'

She opened the door. François was ripping off his stockings while Vincent stood holding his master's boots.

'*Oh, pardon, monsieur,*' she said automatically, turning to leave.

'Don't be an ass, Chambois,' François

replied, barely casting her a glance. 'Do you have some news?'

Léonie chided herself, but stayed near the door, trying not to watch as young Vincent helped the captain undo the buttons at his wrists. 'Monsieur Le Brun wishes to know if he should order all the cannons made ready, *Capitaine*.'

'Damn me if Le Brun hasn't got wax in his ears! When I say 'battle ready' I *mean* battle ready. What does he think we'll defend ourselves with — ship's biscuits?' He waved the valet away as he began to unfasten his shirt. 'Vincent, go tell the first officer that cannons don't prepare themselves. Oh, and for good measure, tell him that his captain's blood runs cold this morning.'

'*Capitaine?*' Vincent's eyes grew round.

'That's right, boy. Cold. He'll understand.' He shooed the valet out of the cabin and wiped a hand across his brow. Though the small window by his bedside was latched open, not a breath of air entered the room and the heat was intense.

Léonie wondered how he could feel cold in such humidity. 'Are you ill, Captain? Do you wish me to send for the surgeon?'

François laughed, ripping off his sweat-soaked shirt. 'My blood runs cold, Chambois, but not for lack of health. I have a sixth sense for danger that has not let me down once in all my years at sea.' He picked up a cloth from a white enamel bowl set on the commode and began to rub himself vigorously, splashing the water on to his skin until it ran in rivulets down his chest and back.

Léonie tried not to look but her eyes were impossibly drawn to him. Jean-Michel would think nothing of it, she reminded herself, but she felt as though she were peeping through a keyhole. It wasn't right.

She jumped as the washcloth sailed across the cabin toward her. 'Wake up, man. Here, scrub my back for me.'

'Ah, well, I really should . . . '

He was looking at her, waiting, seeing only her twin, she knew.

'What's the matter? You haven't seen a scar before? Don't worry, it doesn't hurt. Not any more.'

She'd been too shocked to notice the ragged tear that ran from beneath one armpit across his muscle-hard belly. It was a raised welt, red in places, purple in others as though he had not been spared infection either. A scattering of hair hid the lower part where it disappeared into . . . She blinked and looked away.

'I'm sorry, Captain.' She dipped the cloth

in the cool water and began gingerly wiping his back.

'Harder, man!'

Léonie took a deep breath and made herself do it. At least she was behind him so he couldn't see her scarlet face. His skin was warm and bronze, slick with the heat of the day. She reached up and rubbed the cloth across his shoulders, feeling the muscles ripple beneath her touch, and then he turned to face her, so suddenly that she had to reach out and steady herself. Her free hand slapped on to his chest, her fingers burying themselves in the coarse black hair that was scattered there. For a second neither moved, then Léonie pulled back as though scalded. She handed him the cloth and turned away.

She heard his soft chuckle. 'You're the strangest young officer I've ever had aboard my ship, Chambois. Anyone would think you'd never seen a man's body before. I thought you had brothers.'

Léonie knew her cheeks were on fire and kept her face turned resolutely away, fighting for control. 'I do, *Capitaine*. But they are not built quite to your . . . specifications.'

He laughed. 'You flatter me, young man. Here, pass me those breeches on the bed.'

Léonie picked up the pants and handed

them to him, only to realize that he was now stark naked and holding out his hand without the slightest embarrassment. Léonie opened her mouth, then shut it, passing him the clothes in a paroxysm of embarrassment. She thought suddenly of Marie, wondering how her timid little maid would react if she could see her now? Léonie fought a hysterical giggle that bubbled up, covering it with a cough.

'What did you say, Chambois?'

She looked up, relieved that François was once again clothed, at least below the waist. 'Nothing, sir. I simply wondered why you believe we are in danger.' She knew why *she* was.

'We are too close to Sumatra for my liking. The coast hereabouts is crawling with brigands, mostly Malays or renegade Dutchmen. If we happen upon them they'll not take the time to discover that we have little on board of great value. A few trinkets to offer the natives in exchange for information, some brandy . . . Little enough for their trouble, except the gold we carry to buy supplies.'

'Surely the mist protects as well as blinkers us?'

He had pulled on a clean shirt now and held out his wrists to her. Reluctantly she

247

fiddled with the small buttons, doing her best to avoid touching his hands.

'Preparing for the worst is just a precaution, Chambois,' he said more gently. 'You need not alarm yourself.'

'I am not afraid to fight,' she said with a tilt of her jaw.

For a moment he looked down at her, then he stooped to pull on his boots. 'That won't be necessary. You will remain below with Vincent and the other boys.'

'Captain!' Léonie bristled. If he thought she would hide like a coward while the man she loved was in danger, he knew her not at all. 'I am not a child! I can look after myself.'

'You will stay below.' His jaw was firm, but Léonie's indignation made her ignore the warning glint in his eye.

'You forget, Captain, that I sailed with Lafayette. I will not cower beneath the deck like a snivelling brat.'

'*You* forget, Sub-lieutenant,' he said, his voice hard as steel as he strapped on his sword, 'that I am your commanding officer. You will obey me.'

Léonie's nerve faltered, but only a little. She drew herself up and stared straight at him. 'I promise only one thing, *Capitaine*. That I will do my duty.'

For a moment there was silence. François' eyes were black with rage and she was wondering if she had gone too far, when there was a sudden commotion from the deck above.

They stared up at the ceiling, startled. Léonie looked at François, wide-eyed with fright, but before she could speak, the heavy bell on deck began to toll wildly and there was a pounding on the door.

'*Capitaine!* Capitaine de la Tour! Sir, we are under attack!'

François grabbed his dagger and shook it at her as he ran for the door. 'Stay below, Chambois, and save your pretty neck — for your mother's sake, if not your own!'

He was gone in an instant. Léonie listened to the shouts above and hesitated for barely a second. She flew up the companionway to the deck, close on his heels.

13

As she reached the quarter deck, Léonie stopped, a cry of terror stuck in her throat. A black ship under full sail loomed over the *Aurélie* in the mist, like a vulture with outstretched wings. Though its canvas hung limp as their own, it moved and twitched as hordes of dark-skinned men slithered down swaying ropes and ratlines and dropped on to the deck of the *Aurélie*, shouting and yelling with blood lust.

Léonie flattened herself against the wall of the companionway and looked feverishly about her. The captain was gone. The deck was so crowded with men running, fighting and screaming that it was almost impossible to see friend from foe. And the noise was deafening as orders were shouted, wounded men screamed and the livestock, tied securely around the masts, bellowed and squealed in panic.

'God save us,' Léonie murmured. Perhaps the captain had been right to order her to stay below. But she would rather die here in the open than be found by these savages cowering in her cabin. She drew her weapons.

As she stepped out of her hiding place a grappling hook landed on the deck beside her, ripping into the timbers until it found purchase against the railings. Without a moment's hesitation, Léonie sliced through the rope. Below, a dozen men fell into the sea.

She ignored their screams. There was

no time. As she turned she saw Christian fighting hand-to-hand with a brute of a man. Then from behind, a Malay ran toward him, an evil kris dagger in his hand. Léonie screamed his name and he turned just in time. In a second she was at his side.

'What the hell are you doing!' he bellowed. 'For God's sake go below!'

'And miss a good fight?' she shouted, suddenly enjoying herself. This was like old times, fencing with her brothers.

She lunged at the Malay, catching his sword arm. With a howl he dropped his weapon. His mistake was in trying to retrieve it. Léonie shut her eyes as she felt her rapier pierce his chest.

'Dear God,' she cried under her breath. 'I have killed a man.'

But there was no time to worry. No time to feel. Two more invaders dropped on to the deck, their eyes on her. Léonie backed slowly up the companionway to the poop deck. The first man lunged with his sword. She blocked easily. The second took advantage of her distraction to scramble up the balustrade and get above her. She was trapped.

'Come on, you brutes!' she taunted, angry with herself for letting them corner her. She parried with her dagger in her left hand and her smallsword in her right, cursing the sweat pouring off her skin and stinging her eyes. So much for being a lady, she thought cynically.

One of the men grasped a wicked-looking knife by the blade. She ducked instinctively as it sang past her ear and dug into the wood behind her. Using her sword as a block, she stabbed with her dagger and felt it connect. Without checking to see what damage she'd inflicted she turned to block an attack from the other man. Their swords clashed, jarring her hand, for his heavy cutlass was more than a match for her light rapier. She raised her boot and kicked out as hard as she was able. The man was off balance and the blow caught him in the belly. She watched as he fell to the deck below.

'Chambois!'

She turned as she heard her name bellowed above the chaos. Above her, the captain was fighting a man bearing a formidable steel sword. Léonie felt her heart flip over. She couldn't bear to lose him. Not now. She ran up the stairs, slipping on a slimy patch of blood and yelping with the sudden pain as she banged her hip on the step. Then she was up again.

As she reached the top deck, the *Aurélie* was rocked by an explosion. The sound of cannon fire stunned her for a moment. She looked back, fearing the worst. Below on the quarter deck a fire had broken out on the gangway beside the longboat. There were sheep down there, and pigs, many of them killed outright by the small cannonball that had ploughed into the deck. The noise of panicking animals was almost drowned out by the fighting that still raged all around. And then the *Aurélie* returned fire. Six volleys, all at once. They hit the pirate ship broadside. The huge mainmast shuddered and then toppled slowly into the sea. Dozens of men fell with it, their screams swallowed in the pandemonium.

Léonie's stomach churned, but she knew she couldn't afford to think. At least there were no more men landing on the *Aurélie's* deck now, though the ship still swarmed with brigands.

She felt someone grab her arm and turned, dagger drawn. It was François.

'Damn you, Chambois! I ordered you to stay below!'

'And let you die? I don't think so, Captain.' Her eyes widened as a man with blood running from a head wound lunged at the captain's back. Léonie pushed François out of the way, for there was no time to explain. The attacker's sword passed between them

253

and he lost his footing. Léonie helped him over the rail and looked triumphantly at the captain as the would-be assassin fell to the quarter deck with a grunt.

'I think you need me, Captain.'

He made no comment, though the glint in his eye told her he would not forgive easily.

There was another blast from the cannons. The ships were close enough that men could jump from deck to deck, and the gunners' aim was deadly. As the clouds of acrid gunpowder began to clear, the Frenchmen cheered. The black ship was badly holed and her decks were on fire, flames leaping up the rigging and exploding in the sails that hung from her two remaining masts. In seconds, fire lit the misty sky with an eerie glow.

But it was not over. There was little activity now on the poop deck. The captain was already below helping defend the gunners on the quarter deck. Léonie saw several Malays lying dead, their blood seeping into the sand that had been spread about. Then she spotted Alexandre Roussillon, his head twisted unnaturally as he lay against the mizzenmast. She bent over the artist, but she had no need to feel for a pulse. His neck was broken and he had a deep gash in his chest.

Léonie began to retch. 'I can't do this,' she thought. 'I am not Jean-Michel. This is not how it was supposed to be . . .'

She felt better when she'd emptied her stomach over the side. She wiped her face on her sleeve and started down to the quarter deck. The smell of blood and gunpowder almost overwhelmed her, but she made herself ignore the heaving in her stomach. So far she was unharmed, and that was more than she had a right to be.

There was no sign of François. The black ship was starting to sink, slowly settling into the sea like a dying whale. Some of her men had panicked and were leaping from the deck of the *Aurélie*, some of their own accord, others at the point of a sword. The oily waves surrounding the vessels were tinged red with the blood of dead or severely wounded men tossed overboard.

Léonie felt unbelievably tired. Both arms ached from fighting, she was covered in blood and sand, and her nostrils were full of the stench of death.

She crossed to the portside in search of Christian and the captain. Instead she found Vincent, François' cabin boy, holding a wooden bucket in front of his face as he tried to defend himself. His attacker was laughing, a toothless cackle that sent shivers down Léonie's spine. The futility of Vincent's defence gave her renewed strength. She yelled at the man, lunging with her smallsword, but she was a split second too late; her yell had distracted the boy. He dropped his guard just long enough for the Malay to slash his kris across his throat. Léonie saw Vincent's eyes widen with shock before he crumpled to the deck.

'Vincent!' Léonie felt blind rage fill her. She screamed with rage, leapt on the Malay and stabbed him in the back without a second's thought for the evil weapon the man held.

'He didn't deserve to die! He was just a little boy!' The Malay slumped to the ground and she fell with him, the last of her energy spent. But the man was dead. She pushed the body away and stood up, tears streaming down her face. 'I don't care,' she sobbed, trembling with exhaustion, her hands, still holding her weapons, dangling at her sides. 'I don't care. He had no right to kill an unarmed child!'

She let her dagger fall to the deck and raised her hand to wipe salty tears from her face. Too late to see a burly man in black shirt and breeches raise his pistol. Too late to see him take aim at her heart. But as the bullet tore into her body, knocking her to her knees, she felt the scorching pain and smelled the powder.

I wonder if this is how . . . Jean-Mich felt . . . she thought. And then her world went black.

* * *

François could see it was almost over. The black ship was finished, sinking slowly into the misty sea like a dying serpent, and many of the attackers were fleeing while they had the chance. He thanked his lucky stars they had made the guns ready in time, for their superiority over the pirate ship lay mostly in cannon.

He wiped his face on his sleeve to clear the sweat and looked along the deck. A few skirmishes continued, and some prisoners were being led away.

Christian Lavelle appeared at his side, his expression concerned.

'Have you seen Chambois, sir?' he asked.

François felt a jab of fear. 'Not since we were up on the poop deck. I ordered him below.'

Christian grimaced. 'I doubt he'd follow your advice sir. He's quite a fighter when the mood takes him.'

'So I noticed,' François replied grimly.

257

'You search below. I'll check the decks.'

He took the stairs to the upper level two at a time, but though he found Roussillon's body, there were no other Frenchmen. 'God rest your soul, Alexandre,' he murmured, stopping long enough to close the man's eyes and lie him flat on the deck. Then he returned to the helm. Grévin sat on the bench deep in discussion with the helmsman.

'Pierre, you are wounded.' François was struck by the ashen colour of the navigator's skin.

Grévin tried to shrug it off, but the effort cost him much pain. His greying hair was sticky with blood and his left arm hung useless at his side. He tried to stand, but the captain pressed him back on to the bench.

'You must go below and let the surgeon fix you up.'

Grévin gave a short laugh. 'Cut me up, you mean. No François, I'd rather you did it. Your aim is probably better.'

'Take him below,' François ordered the helmsman. But Grévin bade him wait.

'I have news, Captain. A messenger came from the *Mousquetaire*. They were unseen and untouched in the raid. It seems there was but one ship involved in the attack.'

'That is good news indeed. We'll send

the prisoners to them in exchange for some healthy men to work the *Aurélie*. Once this blasted fog lifts we'll still have some days' sailing to reach port, and who knows if there are more pirates out there searching for trapped vessels like ours.'

Father Cassel appeared, his clothes soaked with blood from tending to the sick and dying. His face was haggard, but his eyes lit up when he saw François, then clouded again at the sight of Grévin's injuries.

'Come, my friend,' he said, taking the navigator's good arm.

With François helping, they got the man down the companionway to the wardroom and laid him on the heavy wooden table, which had been pushed up against a wall to make room for the cannons to be fired. The room smelled of powder and blood, but it was better than the deck. François threw open the windows for what little breeze might care to enter.

He stood looking down at his officer, his heart heavy with dread.

'Just do it, sir,' Grévin grumbled, trembling now with shock.

François heaved a sigh. 'Damn it, Pierre, couldn't you have stayed in one piece? You know how I detest this.'

'It's the captain's job,' Grévin replied

firmly. His eyes were glazed with pain. 'If you don't, I'll die.'

Father Cassel went to get François' medical kit, which he was called upon to use whenever there was a battle or there were too many sick for one surgeon to tend. It was the part of his job he least liked, but he knew he was good at it. He knew his duty.

Mercifully, Grévin fainted and the removal of his smashed arm was over quickly. With Father Cassel's help, François bandaged the wound and dressed the superficial gash on the navigator's head.

Already from the deck came sounds of hammering, as the ship's carpenters removed broken timbers and repaired the damage caused by the enemy's cannons.

'I must begin the burials,' the priest told Francois. 'In this heat we can't wait till tomorrow.'

'No indeed. Tell the men there shall be a wake of two hours only. Give them double rations of wine. They have fought well, to a man.'

Suddenly he remembered Jean-Michel de Chambois. He wondered if he'd been found, and ducked his head into the cabin the lad shared with Christian Lavelle, but it was empty. Perhaps that was a good sign; perhaps it meant he remained unharmed. It would be just like Chambois to be down below helping Montauban tend the wounded.

As he closed the door, he saw Christian coming up the companionway from the forecastle. His face was a mask of concern.

'You haven't found him.' It wasn't a question. One look at Lavelle's face told him it was true. Francois felt a terrible rage fill him. 'Damn that boy! I ordered him to remain below!'

Christian shrugged, wiping a tired hand across his brow. For a moment François fancied the lieutenant was crying.

'You were good friends, Lavelle.'

'We grew up together.'

François saw the pain in his young officer's eyes and felt the guilt flash again. 'Damn!' he growled, smashing his fist into the wall. Then he turned and strode up the stairs.

François found Chambois half-hidden by a fallen sail, face down on the deck with one arm flung across twelve-year-old Vincent. Neither moved. Beneath them a pool of blood had congealed and flies were already gathering.

He dropped to his knees, reaching out unwilling hands; hands that would tell him the worst. But as he lifted Chambois' lifeless body, he groaned.

'Dear God, he's alive!' There was no point

261

in checking young Vincent. The boy's eyes were open but they saw nothing but another time, another place. Gently, François pressed the lids closed, touching the child's cheek for a moment. 'You were a good boy, Vincent. May God enjoy your company as much as I have.'

He picked Chambois up and carried him to his cabin, where he laid the *enseigne* gently on the cot. His shirt was soaked with blood and stained with filth from the battle.

'You fought bravely, Chambois. I hope you'll be as good a patient.'

Awkwardly, for the boy was as limp as a rag doll, he removed Chambois' scabbard and bloodied boots and tossed them to the floor, then unfastened the buttons of his shirt and peeled it gently away from his body. Beneath, François was puzzled to find what had once been white linen strips. Now they were blood-soaked, like old bandages, though François knew of no previous injury that would have necessitated such treatment. There was a ragged wound in the *enseigne*'s left side, close to the wrappings. François took his knife from his pocket and cut them. 'This will hurt less if I do it fast, boy,' he murmured to his unconscious patient. Then he tore the bindings away.

Léonie felt the terrible wrenching in her side and screamed. Then she opened her eyes and stared straight into François' face. 'Holy Mother of God,' he said.

14

François had never felt so stunned in his entire life. Perhaps it was the fatigue of battle or the shock of losing Vincent that was making his eyes play tricks. But the more he stared, the clearer the vision became.

He sat on the edge of the cot and stared uncomprehendingly at Jean-Michel's chest. There was no doubt about it. The Vicomte de Chambois was most definitely a woman.

His eyes finally travelled to her face, so familiar and yet now that he looked anew, he felt he was seeing it for the first time. Her eyes were dark smudges in her face, her skin ghost-pale apart from a vivid streak of blood across one cheek. A woman. He'd had a woman beside him fighting hand-to-hand with a bunch of bloodless pirates . . . She could've been killed. By rights, she should have been! And how would he explain *that* to the Admiralty?

She tried to sit up. 'I . . . I'm sorry . . . '

'You're sorry!' he roared. 'Do you have the slightest idea — '

She lurched toward his lap. ' . . . but I'm going to be sick — '

He grabbed the chamber pot just in time.

'Damn me for a fool,' he berated himself over and over as he held the woman's shoulders and she emptied her stomach. 'How could I have been so absolutely, utterly blind?'

He fetched a cloth and dampened it from the water jug. 'Wipe your face.' He knew he sounded brusque, but sympathy was not high on his list of feelings at this moment.

She did as he bid and then sagged against him. Her eyes closed and her breath came in short gasps.

François felt some of his fury fade as a burst of compassion flowed through him. She was so small. Why had he never noticed that before? While she was tall for a woman, her frame was as slight as a young willow, and she felt almost childlike leaning against him.

'Your wound is bleeding again,' he mumbled, putting his hands awkwardly around her and easing her down on to the bed. Her bare skin felt hot and silken and despite his turmoil, François felt an unmistakable surge in his loins. The reaction made him catch his breath. He let her go, trying to concentrate on her trickery, trying to stop his suddenly whirling mind from wondering what she looked like without her navy breeches.

Then she opened her eyes and looked straight at him. It was a disconcertingly direct gaze, trusting and unafraid, and it refuelled his anger. How dare she be so comfortable in his presence? He wanted to yell at her, shake her, make her understand what a terrible predicament she was in. What a mess they were all in. He wanted to shake some fear into her, make her tremble, he wanted to . . .

Kiss her.

François looked away sharply, his face burning. My God, it was true. He wanted to kiss her. How could he? How *could* he go so rapidly from concern for a junior officer to wanting to make love to her? He curled his hands into fists to stop himself punching the wall. You fool, he thought. You always felt something for Chambois, you just refused to see it, refused to bring your feelings into the open and figure them out like a rational man. You were afraid. Afraid . . . of what? He sighed, wiping beads of sweat off his forehead with his bloodied sleeve. He made himself face the truth though it pained him — he'd been afraid that he had romantic feelings for a boy, that's what.

'Captain . . . ?'

Startled from his thoughts, he looked down at the woman. She was holding one hand to her ribcage, while the other tried to pull the sheet over her breasts. 'Would you . . . ? That is, I don't want the surgeon to . . . '

'Of course. I — I'll get my bag.' He hurried to fetch his medical kit, closing his mind to the thousands of questions that buzzed around in his head like hungry flies. There would be plenty of time for thinking later. Right now he had a ship full of wounded men to consider, the continued danger of being becalmed, and the risk of disease adding to their miseries in the tropical heat.

When he re-entered her quarters, he saw she was close to tears. It should have given him satisfaction, but it didn't. He busied himself preparing his instruments to avoid the temptation to wrap his arms around her.

François peeled her fingers away from the sheet and eased it away from her. She gave in, but her cheeks flamed and a little more of his anger dissipated.

'I need to . . . ' His voice trailed off as he looked at her legs. It wasn't as if he'd

266

never . . . Then he realized it was true — he *had* never removed breeches from a woman before.

She seemed to understand and tried to help him undo the buttons, until their fingers touched. François pulled back as if burned and she looked away, leaving the task to him. The fastenings were sticky with blood around her wound and he cut the cloth away in frustration. Then he covered her with the sheet — for the sake of his sanity as much as for her modesty — and eased the pants down her legs, dropping them on the floor with relief.

Finally he began to cleanse the wound. She flinched, but made no sound. 'You're lucky,' he said as he finished.

'Lucky?' Her voice was faint, but her tone wry. 'If being shot equates to good fortune, Captain, I trust I may . . . avoid ill-luck at all costs.'

He smiled, despite himself. She was plucky, he had to give her that. 'You are fortunate the wound is not worse. It's only a flesh wound. The ball missed your ribs.'

'How very considerate of it.'

'It means I don't have to dig about in your . . . armpit,' he replied, repressing a blush with savage determination. He finished cleansing the wound, rinsed the cloth and began to wipe away a smudge of dried blood on her collarbone.

Suddenly his hand paused, jolted into stillness by a whole new flush of hard, furious anger. Beneath his hand lay a small mark. A heart. A black heart, carved into milk-white skin.

He stepped back as if stung. 'Hélène!'

Léonie was too startled to speak. She had forgotten about the tattoo. It brought back a flood of memories. Memories of him touching her tenderly, his fingertips caressing her throat and neck, his lips warm and seductive against her skin, against her mouth . . . She trembled, suddenly ice-cold. His anger filled the room, and though she longed for the presence of mind to explain everything to him, after all that she'd seen and endured that day, she didn't have the strength.

'May . . . may I have a blanket?' she stammered, fighting tears that burned her throat as she tugged the sheet up to her chin.

His eyes were thunder-black as he threw the washcloth into the bowl and reached for a blanket from the end of the bed. He tossed it to her. Léonie refused to ask for help, but as she fumbled to draw it over herself with her good hand, he picked the thing up and spread it over her legs. He was breathing hard and she could almost taste his fury. She couldn't blame him. He was right to hate her.

But she was so cold. As she tried to pull the blanket up, he stopped her.

'I'm not finished.'

'But you said there was no ball.'

'So I did. But I still have to dress your wound. If infection sets in there will be nothing I can do.' He turned to his bag and removed a small flask of cognac. Léonie's eyes widened. 'You'd be advised to faint,' he said coldly as he uncorked the neck. 'No doubt you're accomplished enough at that, being a woman.'

She bit her lip, refusing to rise to the bait. She'd show him she wasn't just a fainting violet. Faint, indeed! She wouldn't give him the satisfa —

She screamed as the alcohol entered the hole in her skin, burning worse than the bullet that had started all this. For a moment dizzying sickness swamped her and then she fell into a welcome black hole.

When she awoke, he was dressing her wound somewhat awkwardly, trying to avoid her breasts as he wrapped a fresh bandage around her ribcage. The searing pain was gone, replaced by a throbbing ache. She watched as his fingers deftly bound off the end of the bandage. He didn't speak, seemingly absorbed in the task. Then he rummaged in her trunk until he found a clean white nightshirt. In silence he helped her into it. In silence she endured the pain the movement cost her, then sank back on to the pillows.

'You are shivering less.'

'I feel much better, thank you Captain,' she replied in a faint voice. It was a lie, and by the frown on his face, she knew he saw it. He picked up the flask of brandy once more.

'No, thank you.'

'I was not asking your permission.' He held her head, tipping the bottle against her lips. Léonie opened her mouth obediently and let some of the fiery liquid trickle down her throat. She coughed, but the cognac warmed her, giving her limbs a comforting lethargy.

'Now you will rest. I have men to bury and more wounded to treat, and then I will give consideration to your presence aboard my ship. You will of course be set down when we reach Batavia, which, God and a good breeze willing, will be soon.' He returned the flask to the bag and snapped it shut. The sound echoed in her throbbing head. 'You will, of course, consider your liaison with Monsieur Lavelle at an end. I shall have Roussillon's quarters made ready for you and you will remain there — alone — until we reach port.'

'Monsieur Lavelle!' Léonie was appalled at the meaning in his words. 'Captain, I — '

'Spare me the details, *mamselle*. No doubt it amused you both to use my ship for your love tryst.' He thought of how he himself had courted her during their stay in Port-Louis and felt a flood of rage heat his face.

'But Captain, you don't underst — '

'On the contrary, I believe I understand far too much, far too well.'

He slammed the door behind him.

Léonie stared up at the underside of Christian's cot, listening as the captain's footsteps faded away. He'd given her no chance to explain. And now he thought she was Hélène, and that she and Christian had been lovers all this time. She turned her face into the pillow and let the hot salty tears flow.

★ ★ ★

It was stifling on the starboard quarter deck that afternoon as François and Father Cassel led prayers over the bodies of thirty-seven men and officers. Six of those had died of their wounds since the battle and there would certainly be more as shock and infection added to the grim tally.

Finally, only one small sail-enshrouded body remained. As the old priest went forward with his prayer book, François felt a terrible sadness in his chest. Vincent had been with him three years, had served him bravely and well. No child deserved such a death.

The drums, draped in black cloth as a mark of respect, beat out their final tattoo. François waved the men back and took the end of the plank in his hands.

'Farewell, my young friend. May God give you eternal rest.'

Then he raised the board and let the canvas-wrapped body slide into the sea below. The splash as it hit the surface was muffled by the fog-laden air, then the leaden waters closed over the child and sucked him down forever.

For a long while afterward, François stood at the rail staring down at the pale oily surface of the sea. He felt someone come to stand at his elbow.

'Well, *mon père*, let us hope we have no more days like this during our voyage,' he murmured. He heard a slight cough and turned, only to find that it was not the priest, but Christian. He felt a burst of anger fill his veins.

'I have nothing to say to you, Lavelle.' He saw the young man blanch.

'You — you found Monsieur Chambois, then, sir?'

François gave a sharp laugh. 'You could say so.'

'Captain?'

He rounded on the lieutenant. 'Monsieur Lavelle, I have just buried thirty-six of my best men plus a boy who was like a son to me. I do not care to play games. You will find your . . . *paramour* in Monsieur Roussillon's old quarters recovering from a bullet.'

Christian's face was ashen. 'My paramour! Captain, I assure you — '

'Don't waste your words, man. You'll need them to save your own skin soon enough.'

'I assure you, Captain, that I am prepared to take full responsibility.'

'Oh you will, Lavelle,' the captain replied, his voice quiet and dangerous. 'Believe me, you will.'

'Our actions were in a noble cause, Captain. It was not a frivolous action. I trust you will take that into full account.'

'In due course, I shall take everything into account, young man, and those who have taken such liberties with the French Navy — and especially with my command — shall certainly be held to account. Now leave me. I do not wish to think about you or that . . . that woman below deck!'

He turned back to the sea, anger boiling inside him. Then he realized the young officer was still there.

'Dammit, Lavelle, are you deaf? I said I wished to be left alone.'

'I — I heard you, sir. But . . . I simply wondered who had attended . . . her wounds?' He said the word 'her' hesitantly, looking about him to see whether this conversation had been overheard, but there was only a group of sailmakers further up the deck, busy at work and murmuring among themselves.

François sighed. 'I did. For the moment you may be assured that no one else knows of this. It was a simple wound, and for a woman, Hélène showed remarkable bravery.'

'Hélène?'

'I recognized her scar,' François growled. 'I wonder it never came to light before we were all made to look fools.' Especially me, he thought savagely, remembering how he had taken delight in discussing the qualities of Hélène de Lisle with the bed-ridden Jean-Michel. 'How the hell did he — *she* — manage to be two people at the same — '

But when he turned to look, Lavelle had gone.

★ ★ ★

Léonie lay alone in Roussillon's quarters, the nine-gun salutes for the dead echoing in her head long after the last splashes of bodies sliding into the waves outside her open window had ceased. She'd wanted to be there, had wanted to pay her last respects to her art master, despite his harsh tongue and superior ways.

It seemed strange to think she would never have to endure his caustic remarks again. Stranger still to be lying in his bed, staring at his books on his shelves. She turned her head and gazed across at his cluttered desk, pens and charcoals littering its surface, for there had been none of the usual need to tidy everything away in case of heavy seas. The ship creaked once or twice as a slight swell created a tiny movement in the hull, but otherwise there were no sounds except for distant hammering from carpenters repairing the ship.

Then she heard footsteps. There was a sharp knock and before she could call out, the captain entered. Léonie's heart jumped at the sight of him, and she chided herself for being stupid. From the thunderous set of his brow, he wasn't here to cheer her up.

He was dressed in full uniform, but the blue and scarlet scarcely reflected his mood. His face was haggard, his shoulders slumped. He cast his eyes over her and then around the room.

'He was busy,' he muttered, clasping his hands behind his back. 'Roussillon. When the battle broke out, he was in the midst of something.'

Léonie nodded. 'We'd been working on a series of sketches of rare plants. Some of the specimens were dying. We needed to record them before . . . '

Her voice trailed off as her eyes encountered his. Why were they talking about drawings, when so much else was clearly on both their minds? His gaze burned her, drove into her, reaching somewhere deep inside and causing a pain that was quite unlike the dull throb in her wounded side.

'I think you owe me some explanations, *mamselle*. Honour me with some element of truthfulness for once.'

She was stung by his tone. It was no less than she deserved, but she was at a loss to know where to begin.

He clasped his hands behind his back, slapping the ball of one fist into the palm of his other hand, staring out the open window.

'What did you hope to achieve by this masquerade, Hélène? Were you simply seeking an adventurous journey to shock your parents?' He laughed, though it had a bitter sound. 'I'll warrant you've encountered rather more adventure than you bargained for.'

'No, I . . .'

'No, of course, I forgot the irresistible Monsieur Lavelle. With his family connections he would make a handsome catch for a minor official's daughter. Did he promise you his hand, or did you think to make yourself indispensable to him by offering him your body for the voyage?' He turned to stare at her, contempt in every line of his face. Léonie bit her tongue to keep from crying out, for she couldn't bear to hear another poisonous word.

'It wasn't like that!' she protested.

He leaned over the bed, his voice like flint cutting her to the quick. 'I promise you, it was a serious miscalculation. The Prince de Charigny would never countenance marriage between a commoner and his nephew. You clearly do not understand the class you aspire to. It's a closed shop, *mamselle*, and you cannot buy there.'

'Captain, please — '

'Answer me one question, Hélène,' he went on angrily. 'Just tell me what you did with the real Vicomte de Chambois. Did you kill him? Is your desperation to become the wife of a nobleman so great that you would stoop to that? You certainly do not lack skill with weapons.'

Léonie's eyes filled with tears and this time she made no effort to stop them. She turned her head to the wall, unable to bear the sight of François in such a vile mood. How could he even think that she would be capable of such things? Did he have so little respect for her? Did he regard her with such total contempt? Christian had been right; letting herself fall in love with him had been a terrible mistake.

She flinched as his hand descended to her cheek. He turned her face toward him. 'Don't,' he said gruffly. 'I can't stand to see you cry.'

She wiped her eyes on the sheet, suddenly angry with him. 'How can you be moved by my tears, when you believe me capable of murdering a man for the sake of his berth on a ship? Surely such a woman would be worthy only of contempt?'

278

He dropped his hand, turning away. 'I'm sorry. That was cruel, I know. I'm just trying to understand how we came to be in this position.' He ran a hand through his hair, dislodging several strands from its bow. He looked so tired, suddenly, staring down at her, that her heart twisted painfully.

'There is so much to explain, Captain. So very much that you don't know. Will it make any difference?'

'I need to know.'

'And then?'

'I don't know.'

She almost felt a flare of hope, but it died when she observed the shuttered look on his face.

'You had so much compassion for those children in Port-Louis. Can you not find a little for me?'

He looked at her in silence and for a moment there was a flash of understanding. She was sure he was remembering the same things that were passing through her own mind.

'You will need to be kind,' she whispered, 'to forgive me so much.'

He pulled out the chair and sat down, flicking his coat free. He leaned his elbows on his knees and covered his face with his hands. Then he reached out and took her hand, rubbing the flesh on her palm with the ball of his thumb. 'Explain it to me, Hélène. In the past two hours, I have been saying prayers with Father Cassel, watching the bodies of my men slide into the sea forever, and while I did that, over and over again, do you know what I was thinking about?'

She shook her head.

'I was thinking about you. About how you looked riding that stallion along the beach. About how you danced in the moonlight at the governor's ball. About how the sun touched your cheek the morning we took breakfast on the terrace at Madame Dumont's house.'

A sense of profound loss filled Léonie's heart. She knew she had been lucky to have had even a short time of happiness with François, and that when she confessed the whole story to him — as she knew she must — she would lose him forever. She focused on her hand imprisoned in his, blinking back tears. His fingers were warm and brown, his hands strong and capable. Hands that could kill a man with deadly accuracy one moment and tend wounds as gently as a nursemaid the next. She didn't know if she could bear to lose those hands; didn't know if she could face life without him. But she knew she had to find out.

'I remember those things, too,' she murmured, easing her hand from his grasp.

'And yet — '

'No.' She looked at him. His eyes were dark with pain as the question hung between them like a poisonous cloud. 'Christian Lavelle and I were never lovers. Not before we came aboard the *Aurélie* and not since.'

He stared at her. 'Why should I believe you? Either of you,' he added, when she was about to tell him he could question Christian as well.

'Christian and I have been friends since childhood. He . . . agreed to help me. But only because I offered him no choice.'

'How could you have such a hold over him? You told me yourself you are an official's daughter. What did he do to place himself so much in your debt?'

'Nothing. He was — is — quite blameless.'

His eyes narrowed suddenly and he became very still. 'You are not Hélène de Lisle at all, are you?' he said finally, his voice so cold it made her shiver. 'That too, is a lie.'

She nodded, staring down at the bed.

'Who are you?'

'My name is Léonie de Chambois. I am Jean-Michel's twin sister.'

281

15

François stared at her as though disbelieving his own senses. A thousand thoughts flew through his head, none of them pleasant.

'You are Jean-Michel de Chambois's *sister*!' He almost spat the words. 'A viscountess, dressed as a man . . . aboard an expeditionary ship for months on end without so much as a servant for a chaperon . . . are you mad?'

Léonie flushed but gave him a determined stare. 'I had no choice.'

'You had no choice? No *choice*!' He jumped up from the chair, pushing it back with such force that it crashed into Roussillon's desk, scattering papers and pens on to the floor. 'I'll say you had no choice — no choice about such a ridiculous prank.' He drew a frustrated breath, running his hand through his hair as he stormed across to the window and back. 'You have destroyed yourself and your family. Dammit, Hélène — or whatever your name is — your father is a duke! What in the name of heaven do you think the king will say?'

Léonie sat up, throwing off the sheet and turning her legs so she was sitting over the edge of the bed. Pain seared through her, but it was welcome compared to the agony his accusations were creating. 'If you would just let me expl — '

'Oh no! You can't talk your pretty way out of this one, young lady. This is not the Hameau and you are not Marie-Antoinette playing at shepherdess. This is real life, and you've seen a great deal more of it than is fitting for a woman of gentle birth. Dammit, you went with a . . . a prostitute in the Canary Islands!'

Léonie couldn't help grinning at the horror on his face. 'But Captain, you purchased the woman especially for me. A lady could hardly refuse, could she?'

He had the grace to turn beet red, but it did nothing to soften his mood. 'You have a great deal of explaining to do, *Vicomtesse*. I suggest you get to it before I lose my temper entirely.'

She pressed her lips together to still their sudden trembling, for the banked rage behind his eyes made her believe every word he spoke. 'Very well, Captain. But please . . . my name is Léonie.' She knew he disliked the use of titles aboard his ship, and had come to understand his republican attitudes, but his chilled expression served only to widen the yawning social gap between them. He despises me because my father is a duke, she thought helplessly.

'Very well, Léonie. Let us hope that is still your name tomorrow and that this will be an end to your chameleon lives.'

She ignored the barb. 'My brother was unable to take up his orders in time,' she began. Those events so long ago seemed so remote, almost ethereal now.

'I don't understand. Apart from death, nothing should have prevented his joining the expedition.'

Léonie folded her hands in her lap. 'He was grievously wounded, Captain. In a duel.'

'A duel!' François stormed up and down the tiny cabin again like a caged tiger. 'And no doubt the young fool got himself into this predicament over some inconsequential bit of skirt?'

She shook her head. 'He accused a man of cheating at cards.'

François let his hands drop to his sides. 'Ah, of course. Every gentleman's occupation. We wouldn't want a young nobleman to give his mind to serious matters too often, lest he fatigue his intellect.'

Léonie's head snapped up. 'Your sarcasm is unwarranted, Captain. My brother loved his career in the navy. He was determined to come despite his wound, but Nounou said the journey would kill him.'

'And who, pray, is Nounou?'

She bowed her head. 'Our old nurse. She has been with us since we were babies.'

François shook his head. 'That was not long ago.' He retrieved the chair and sat heavily on it. 'You expect me to believe that your brother was hurt and could not travel to Brest, so his twin sister donned his breeches and *voilà*, all is well with the world?'

It sounded lame, even to her ears. 'There was more than that,' she added, getting up awkwardly and going to the window to stare out at the leaden sea. 'I . . . I was betrothed to be married.'

'Betrothed? To whom?' His voice sounded strange, as though the words choked him.

She turned and looked at him, knowing her answer would be but another nail in the coffin of their relationship. 'The Marquis de Grise.'

'*Alphonse*! That fat old . . . You promised to marry him? What on earth for?'

She turned her gaze back to the sea, her heart leaden. Nothing seemed to matter any more, not so long as François despised her. 'My father arranged it, the king approved. I had refused all such other arrangements and he would no longer countenance my opinion. If I did not marry Alphonse, he said I should have to live out my days in a convent.'

François reached up and took her arm, forcing her to turn from the window and face him. 'And were you not in favour of becoming a marquise? Surely it was a better option than destroying yourself with scandal.'

She stared down at the hand imprisoning her arm. Tears blurred her eyes. 'I — I couldn't bear the man. He was so old. And he wheezes, and — ' She looked up at him suddenly. 'But you must know him. You called him Alphonse.'

He released her arm. 'By reputation only.'

'I never gave my promise, and as the time grew near I knew I never could.'

He shook his head. 'Léonie de Chambois, do you realize what you have done? You have destroyed your reputation, as well as that of your brother and your family. You have used me to escape your obligations in France. I'd almost like to believe that you were just some bored little nobody seeking excitement. At least then I could just drop you on some island. But what can I write in my log now? 'Stowaway: Léonie, Vicomtesse de Chambois, daughter of the Duc de Chambois, favourite of King Louis XVI.

Set down at first landfall. Whereabouts unknown.' The king would have no trouble choosing *my* next destination when he read that — the Bastille!'

Léonie's eyes filled with unbidden tears. His words cut into her heart like a rapier, twisting and turning as the implications of her actions were spread before her. 'I did not think . . . That is, I only wanted to give myself time, to see the world and experience a little of life before I consigned myself to the drudgery the rest of my days would bring. Being some aged nobleman's wife or being a nun — it made no difference to me.'

She sank down upon the bed again as weariness filled her. The captain's face bore no trace of the compassion she had so hoped to find. Instead it was shuttered, etched with anger.

'I require your word that this is the very last version of events to which you will subject me, *Vicomtesse*.'

She sighed. 'It is the truth.'

'I wonder you can tell after all the lies you have practised these last months,' he retorted. Before she could protest, he strode to the door and opened it. 'Rest assured, that whatever consequences shall befall you as a result of this grotesque prank, your accomplice will most certainly be discharged from His Majesty's service with dishonour.'

The door shut behind him with a resounding bang.

* * *

Her accomplice! With her good arm, Léonie picked up a brass paperweight from the table beside the bed and hurled it at the closed door. She heard the captain's steps pause for an instant and then resume their tread up the companionway toward his quarters.

'How dare you!' she raged, feeling a storm of tears welling up now that he was gone. 'It was not Christian's fault! I don't care what you do to me, but you shall not destroy him. My father is a confidante of the king and you are — you are a mere — ' She forced herself to speak the very words she had never wanted even to *think* throughout the whole voyage. 'You are a mere *naval captain*!'

She rolled back on to the bed, curled up her legs and rolled herself into a ball. Sobs tore into her chest, wrenching at her bandages. Waves of agony from her wound ripped through her body, but she welcomed the pain. At that moment she knew she would welcome death if it came knocking, though she doubted she would be granted such a blessed release.

288

A knock on the door stilled her tears. '*Qui est-ce?*'

'It's Christian. May I come in?'

With total disregard for the pain, Léonie flung herself off the bed and pulled open the door. 'Oh, Christian, can you ever forgive me? I have ruined everything. Everybody.' She hugged him, feeling new, gentler tears as his encircling arms gave her comfort. 'You were right. I was stupid — more than stupid — to give my heart free rein. Why was I so short-sighted, Christian? Whatever made me think I could get away with it? Why didn't you stop me?'

He held her away from him and looked down at her, amusement softening his weary eyes. 'My dearest Léonie, whatever makes you think I could stop you doing something you'd set your heart on?'

She sighed, wiping the damp from her cheeks on the kerchief he offered. 'I know you're right, Christian, but if I could share some of the guilt perhaps it would not weigh me down so.' She sat back on the bed, wincing as her bandages tugged. 'The captain is out for your blood. I shall have to write to Papa and beg him to intervene on your behalf with the king.'

Christian unbuttoned his blue frock coat and threw it on the desk, then sank into the chair and rubbed his hands across his eyes. Léonie noticed for the first time that he still wore the shirt and breeches he'd done battle in, for they were splattered with blood like his boots.

'You are tired, *mon ami*,' she said, suddenly feeling very selfish to be worrying about herself. 'There is wine in Roussillon's trunk there beside the desk, and glasses, too. He liked to sip before we began work each day.'

He waved the offer away. 'It will take more than burgundy to save us, my sweet. I have just had a most unpleasant interview with the captain. I gather you have given him the real story at last.'

'Of course. Did you think I would not?'

'He thought you were Hélène last time I saw him.'

'Oh,' she said in a small voice. 'That's a long story. But I put his misconception right as soon as he would allow.'

'And now?'

She raised her hands in defeat. 'He says he will court-martial you and set me down at first landfall.'

'He can't afford to do that. The king would never countenance such an action. No matter what your sins, you are still a duke's daughter.'

'And what of you? You are rightfully of higher rank than I, as the Prince de Charigny's ward.'

Christian shook his head. 'I am a commoner as far as the world is concerned. The prince has a natural son. When my mother cut herself off from society by marrying her music teacher, she abandoned all *noblesse* for her children. The world is less forgiving than you think. It is only by the grace of my uncle that I enjoy his protection at all. When he hears of this, he will abandon even that slim obligation.'

Léonie felt a chill run up her spine. 'What are you saying?'

'I am finished, my sweet. The navy will not have me and without the support of my uncle . . . '

She reached out and touched his hand. 'Oh, Christian. I could never abandon you. Never. You are the kindest, most noble soul I have ever known. Jean-Michel will help you, too. You know he will.'

'If he lives,' he replied darkly.

'Surely you do not think — '

'He was very badly wounded, Léonie. I have spent hours at Father Cassel's side today helping him give the last rites to men with lesser wounds.'

'But Jean-Mich is so young,' Léonie

cried. She couldn't bear the thought that he might be dead. She couldn't, wouldn't let herself think it. To imagine something might somehow make it come true.

Christian stood and picked up his jacket. He touched her cheek as he moved to leave. 'I'm sorry, Léonie, but we have had no news since we left France in April, and won't until we have completed our mission and are returning — if you and I are still aboard the *Aurélie* by then.'

Stricken, Léonie searched deep inside her soul for any clue, any special feeling she might have overlooked. Then she shook her head. 'No, Christian. If Jean-Mich were dead I would know it. I have always known when he was in trouble.'

'From a few miles away, perhaps. But we're half a world away, my sweet.'

She shook her head. 'I will not believe it,' she insisted, as he blew her a kiss and left the room.

She lay on the small hard bed, listening to the occasional creaking of the becalmed ship, trying not to dwell on the wet blanket of heat that enveloped the room. How she longed to be up on deck, though she knew all the able-bodied men on the ship would be there, so it would hardly afford her any peace. And she was tired, drained by the battle, by her injury and by her arguments with François. She didn't want to think about anything right now. She blew out her lantern and lay staring through the open casement at the misty night. Finally, she slept.

But sleep, while it rested her body, filled her mind with feverish images. Instead of Malay pirates falling into the sea at the point of her rapier, it was Jean-Michel, his eyes wide in death. Instead of Vincent dying in her arms, it was François . . .

★ ★ ★

Sleep also eluded the captain. After two hours tossing and turning on his narrow bunk he threw off the light sheet, pulled on his breeches and shirt and went above. The air on the poop deck was not much cooler than the steam-bath of his room, but the lack of walls around him eased his mind. The quarter deck below was a clutter of sleeping bodies as the sailors sought fresh air. Some lay propped on their elbows playing cards or talking in low voices. Above, the huge sails hung soggily from the masts.

François leaned on the railing and gazed into the black night. Fog blanketed the sky, allowing no stars to penetrate, yet it seemed to be lifting a little from the surface of the oily black sea. He scanned the dark. There it was! The *Mousquetaire*, dimly showing the glow of lanterns from her wardroom and deck, lay off the portside, no more than half a league away. François felt greatly reassured to see the little storeship. It made him feel less like his own vessel had wandered into a timeless dimension, somehow cut off from the world, like an ancient Greek ship lost in Hades.

'I see you cannot sleep, either, my boy,' said a voice at his elbow.

Lost in his musings, François jumped. Father Cassel smiled, the whites of his eyes catching the light from his lantern as he set it on the broad balustrade.

'I was wondering if we have somehow sailed into a bottle, Father,' the captain mused. 'Somewhere out there, the real world goes on without us. Winds blow, ships pass by. But here we are, corked up in this black airless hole.'

The old priest chuckled. 'Then eventually we will wash up on the shore and someone will let us out.'

'Aha! But where, Father? And will we all have suffocated by then?'

He felt the priest touch his sleeve. 'You are maudlin, tonight, François. It will pass.'

François sighed, his mind suddenly flashing

with memories of Léonie's ashen face as he ripped the bandages from her chest. It had been playing over and over again in his mind. Would it never stop? He shook his head to chase the vision away.

Father Cassel pulled his arm, forcing him to look directly at his old mentor. 'Perhaps you had better tell me what you have discovered, my son.'

'What I have . . . ?' François frowned, then enlightenment hit him like a blast of cold air. 'Dammit, Father. You knew! Why did you say nothing to me?'

The priest merely raised his eyebrows. 'I know many things. I do not necessarily pass them on. It's the nature of my profession, keeping secrets. Anyway, what would you have done?'

'Done!' he thundered. Suddenly he was aware that raising his voice was causing some of the men below to look up. He dropped his tone to a vehement whisper. 'I would have put the woman off the ship and rid myself of a liability.'

'I rather felt she was an asset. She almost saved young Vincent's life, you know.'

'No, I didn't.' He frowned. The memory of the boy still twisted in his heart. 'Nevertheless, she could have got herself killed. We could've buried her at sea,

never knowing who she really was . . . '
The thought pained him so much it took his breath away. Why on earth should he care? he wondered.

'Ah. So you have discovered her identity, then?'

'Indeed I have.'

'And?' the priest asked gently.

François turned from the inky sea to stare at him. 'At first I thought her to be Hélène de Lisle. But no. That would have been too simple a ruse.' The priest looked genuinely baffled. 'She is the sister of our absent young *enseigne*. She is none other than the Vicomtesse Léonie de Chambois. Her father is a man of some influence at court and her mother — not to be outdone — is part of Marie-Antoinette's household! Our little noblewoman decided to use this expedition to escape a distasteful betrothal and have some adventure at the same time; no doubt she thought it would make her the darling of Versailles when she returned.'

Father Cassel was visibly startled. 'Surely there must have been more to such a decision than a girlish prank?'

François sighed. 'Yes, Yves. Her brother, it appears, was wounded fighting a duel over cards. She thought to take his place and avoid disfavour with her family and the

Minister of Marine.'

'Foolish child.'

François almost laughed. 'I have thought of many epithets since I discovered her duplicity, Father, and I have to say none of them was as charitable as 'foolish'. Stupid, rash, irresponsible, feather-brained, reckless, thoughtless, lunatic . . . '

The priest raised a hand. 'Your point is well made, François. There is no need to hammer it into my poor head.'

'Sorry.'

'So,' the priest resumed, after they had stared in silence at the ocean for a few moments, 'what will you do with her?'

François grunted. 'I know what I would like to do with her. I would like to put her over my knee and spank her little behind.' He could feel the priest observing him thoughtfully and raised his palms in defeat. 'I know it would do no good, but at least I would feel better.'

He turned back to stare out at the night, as frustrated by the expedition's impotence as by his own helplessness.

'Have you ever read the great English poet, William Shakespeare?' Yves Cassel asked. The captain shook his head. 'In one of his plays — *Hamlet*, I believe — he has a line; 'The lady doth protest too much'. Except in

297

your case, it's the good captain who protests with vehemence, don't you think?'

'I don't understand.'

'I wonder, my boy, if you do not have some feelings for the young lady, after all.'

'Feelings! I have feelings, Father, but they are not the ones you suppose.'

'You cared for her when you thought she was Jean-Michel. And if I am not losing my powers of observation — which I may well be at my age — I fancy you were not immune to the attractions of the lovely Hélène de Lisle while we laid at anchor in Port-Louis.'

François was glad of the dark that hid his blushes. 'I did not *care* for Chambois except as one of my young officers. It was merely my responsibility to guide him in his duties.'

'And to purchase certain, ah . . . shall we say 'side benefits'?'

François bowed his head. 'I am ashamed of that, Father. It was wrong of me — even if Chambois hadn't been a . . . a woman.' He sighed. 'How did you know? Isn't there anything in my life that escapes you?'

'I only know what you tell me and what I observe for myself. And I have done much observing, both of young Chambois and of you these past months.'

'Very well, *mon père*. Since you have had

298

so much time to think about all this, tell me what to do.'

'I wouldn't presume, my son.'

'Hah! Since when?'

'Since you are trying to deny what is in your heart.'

'You don't know what you are saying,' he snapped.

The priest's face was impassive. 'You know I do.'

François clenched his fists but the pain was not as strong these days. 'There is nothing in my heart,' he replied after a moment. 'There has been nothing in my heart since Louisa died and took my son with her.'

Father Cassel touched his hand briefly. 'Time is a wonderful gift from God, François. He gives it to us so that we may heal, so that we may overcome our grief and live again.'

'I know what you are saying, Yves. But I will not make the same mistake again.'

'You think your marriage was a mistake?'

'Yes.'

'But you loved her. You told me so yourself the day before I married the two of you.'

'Of course I loved her. But I couldn't be there for her. She needed me, and where was I? At sea, helping the American colonists finish off the English. I was helping men fulfil their political ideals when I should have been at home in Bordeaux holding my wife's hand while she gave birth to my son.'

'You couldn't have saved her, François.'

'I should have been there. She was my wife!'

He felt his voice crack and turned away, crossing to the starboard side before he gave way to the ache behind his eyes. He had come home from America to find two new tombstones in the family graveyard. One bore the simple inscription:

Jean-Paul-Xavier de la Tour
Died 12 July 1782, aged 1 day
Safe in the Arms of Jesus

He hadn't even known his wife was with child. He had never had a chance to hold his baby son in his arms or look upon his face. Alone, his ailing father had buried his daughter-in-law and grandson while François was celebrating the defeat of the English at Yorktown.

He shook his head as the priest joined him at the starboard rail. 'I am a sea captain, Yves.' He waved a hand at the black ocean. 'This is what I know. This is what I do. I cannot be responsible for a wife, and I cannot give up the sea. I have had my chance at marriage, and I will not be coerced into covering up this ridiculous masquerade. If our little viscountess ruins her family, perhaps she will come to her senses and learn something. Perhaps she will even make something of her life if she is barred from court.'

'That is rather harsh, don't you think? She is only a girl.'

'And a reckless one.' He had a sudden thought. What if she was really reckless? What if . . . ? He looked quickly at the priest. 'Father, you don't think she would do something terrible, do you? She wouldn't try to end her own . . . '

But he didn't wait to hear the answer. He ran across the deck and down the companionway toward Roussillon's old quarters, fighting to quell a horrible suspicion that had flared in his mind.

The door was closed and in his agitation, François didn't bother to knock. He threw open the door. The room was empty.

'Damn!' With a quick prayer that he was not too late, he ran down the hallway. As he passed Christian Lavelle's cabin he heard quiet voices. Fear for Léonie's safety dissolved into bitterness. Without pausing to listen to the sounds of the two of them together, he strode on toward his own quarters.

16

Léonie awoke from her nightmares and lay in the hot dark, listening to the silent ship. Though she was exhausted, she was afraid to close her eyes again, for sleep meant to risk more terrible dreams.

She felt for her tinderbox and struck a spark to the wick of the lantern above her bed. The soft light soothed her and she lay back, staring at the low ceiling and trying to think what to do.

Her own fate seemed sealed, for the captain was adamant she would be put off at Batavia in the East Indies. But the damage his reports to the Ministry of Marine would do to poor Christian brought pain to her heart.

It was not fair; none of this was his doing. Had he not been the word of caution in her ear? He was the one who had tried at every opportunity to dissuade her of her mission, right up until they were ready to board the ship in France.

I must do something, she thought. I *must* convince the captain.

She eased herself out of the narrow bed.

302

Her left side was stiff, but troubled her much less than she expected.

Taking a lantern, she let herself out into the hot silent companionway and tiptoed toward the captain's chambers. She knocked softly, but there was no answer. Perhaps he was asleep. Quietly, Léonie turned the handle and stepped into the room.

She held the lantern high so a golden pool of light fell on the captain's pillow. The bed was empty, the covers thrown back. She reached out and touched the place where his head had rested, telling herself it was only to ascertain how long ago he had been here. It was cool, though his scent lingered on the linens. She snatched her hand away, feeling as though she had touched François himself.

She peeped through the open door to his private quarter gallery but the bathroom was empty.

That left only the door that connected the captain's bedchamber to his private study. It was closed. She crossed to the door and tapped quietly with her knuckles. Again, no response. With heart pounding, she turned the handle and peered inside, half expecting to find him asleep at his desk.

But it, too, was unoccupied.

Where *is* he? Léonie thought in despair.

I must talk to him. I must make him understand. She knew he was capable of compassion — she'd seen it when he looked at those poor orphans in Port-Louis. Somehow she had to find the key that would unlock that part of him again.

She wandered into the study, setting her lantern on the desk. She remembered the first day she had arrived on board with Christian and had stood, frightened out of her wits, in this very room, receiving her orders for the first time. She smiled. It seemed such a long time ago, and that Léonie felt like a stranger now.

She fingered the items on the carved walnut desk: quills and ink, an ornate gold knife for sharpening pens, an ivory seal and a stick of scarlet sealing wax. She picked up the seal, admiring the intricate weave of letters, though they were hard to decipher. She could make out the flourishing F and T, but was puzzled by what appeared to be the letter B woven into the design. She set it down again, letting her fingers trail over a small gilt box with a key in the lock.

Then her hand stilled.

In the centre of the desk lay a large leatherbound volume with a silk ribbon marking the open page. Léonie stared at the crisp white sheets covered with the captain's unmistakable writing. His daily log. Part of her didn't want to look, and yet she was so very tempted. She glanced at the door, but no sound came from the becalmed vessel and all the other officers were abed.

If only she were to turn back a few pages, past the lists of the dead and wounded he had clearly just completed, she might find something. Something that told her what he intended to report to the ministry . . .

She reached for the pages and then stopped. What if she didn't like what she found? What then?

★ ★ ★

When François returned from his search for the *vicomtesse* he was in a foul mood, angry beyond all reason that she should sneak away to her lover just hours after he had ordered her to end their liaison. It gave him a reason to despise her, one he needed badly, for his very jealousy showed he cared more for her than he should. God, how he wished the winds would pick up! Once they reached the East Indies he would throw the woman off his ship, then he could breathe easier and regain his sanity.

He saw the glimmer of light beneath his study door, and frowned. He had not been in the room since early that evening when he'd had the miserable task of recording the victims of battle in his log. Had he left his lantern burning then it would probably have run dry of whale oil by now, and he was not one to take such a risk, for fire was the most dreaded enemy on any vessel.

He flung open the door. Standing at his desk was Léonie de Chambois.

François felt momentary confusion, overtaken by a twinge of triumph when he realized it couldn't have been Léonie he'd just heard in Lavelle's room. Then his glance fell to her hand as she pulled it quickly from his log.

He kicked the door shut with his foot.

'Did you like what you read, *Vicomtesse?* I trust you find no fault with my spelling?'

She looked so genuinely afrighted by his sudden appearance, he felt almost sorry for the girl, but his anger was too intense to allow it. She tucked her fingers behind her back and tried to meet his eyes.

'I . . . I did not read your log, Captain. I was merely in search of you. I thought perhaps you were in here.'

'Really? And no doubt when you knocked and I didn't answer you thought you'd just come on in and help yourself to whatever it is you seek?'

Two bright spots appeared on her pale

cheeks, turning her big grey eyes into deep shadows. She looks damnably tired, he thought. He had the strongest urge to wrap her in his arms and kiss her, but no sooner had the thought occurred to him than Father Cassel's words came to mind. He suppressed the urge to comfort her. It was purely physical. The priest was misinterpreting lust for . . . affection. Either way, he wanted no part of it. Or her.

'The dawn *quart* will be on duty soon, *mamselle*. It is not a common time of day for officers to hold conference. Could it not perhaps wait until after breakfast?'

'Of course. That is, I suppose . . . ' She picked up her lantern and stared into the light, her unbound hair tumbling around the shoulders of her simple white nightshirt like a fiery halo. François clenched his fists against the desire that suddenly coursed through him. Was she a witch? How could he have found himself becalmed with this infuriating, captivating woman on his ship?

She looked up. Her eyes bore traces of moisture, but her jaw was tilted in challenge. 'I couldn't sleep, Captain. Nor will I be able to until I have persuaded you of Lieutenant Lavelle's innocence in all this. It was none of his doing and it is wrong of you to punish

307

him for something he himself tried so hard to prevent.'

'A very pretty speech, *mamselle*, but rather perfunctory, don't you think?'

'I . . . I don't understand.'

'Where's the feminine embroidery, *Vicomtesse?* You haven't once swooned, or fluttered your lovely eyelashes at me. Surely a woman of your exceptional parentage can employ some heartfelt devices to render me helpless to refuse?'

His sarcasm was uncalled for, but it gave him a cruel satisfaction to return some of the pain she'd caused him. In return, he expected an outburst of rage, or at least indignation, but instead she did something he was totally unprepared for: she burst into tears.

He stared. He had quite forgotten she was capable of tears. Except for when he had brutally accused her of murdering her own brother, she had never so much as blinked hard in all their months at sea — not even in the height of battle or when he was dressing her wounds. The sight of this indomitable young woman dissolving into tears was his undoing. He took the lantern from her trembling fingers and hung it on a ceiling hook, then unable to stop himself, he gathered her into his arms.

'Hush, Léonie. I meant no harm,' he

murmured as she buried her face in his shirt. She was so light, so vulnerable, he was afraid he would crush her. He relaxed his grip, moving one hand instead to her chin and tilting her face up to his. Her skin was translucent in the lantern light, as smooth as silk. He stroked the ball of his thumb across her cheek, wiping away the tears that fell so freely.

Her sobs slowly faded, save for an occasional gulp, and she stared up at him, wide-eyed. Her lips were soft and red, only inches from his own, and suddenly all the naval regulations in the world couldn't preserve his resolve. He lowered his head and tasted her sweetness, at first gently, and then as he felt her respond, plundering her mouth with his lips and tongue.

Léonie knew he would kiss her. She felt the shiver of anticipation run up her spine and though she knew she should pull away before it was too late, she was mesmerized by the expectation. She wanted him to kiss her. So badly it was almost like a physical pain.

His lips were soft and yet firm, demanding and yet questing. It was quite unlike the few kisses they had stolen on the Île de France. Those had been the embraces of two strangers attracted to each other. This was different. At the first touch of their lips they released a fire that had been smouldering ever since they sailed from France all those months ago. Suddenly it was like opening a volcano.

Desire burned through her, stirring deep in her belly and instinctively making her press herself against him. Dressed in nothing but her thin cotton nightshirt, she could feel his own arousal pressed between their bodies. It made her tremble, whether from passion or fear, she had no experience to say. She twined her arms around his neck, then slid them down slowly, feeling the muscles of his shoulders bunch beneath her palms. His very strength aroused her, drew her like a moth to a flame.

'Oh, Léonie, you have bewitched me since the day we met.' He lowered his mouth and ran a line of hungry kisses along her neck. 'Deep in my heart I always knew you were a woman, but what my eyes didn't see my brain refused to acknowledge.' He ran the tip of his tongue over the sensitive spot behind her ear and Léonie clutched at his shoulders as she heard herself moan with pleasure. If he could have this effect on her just by kissing her, what would it be like . . .

The taste of her hot, sweet skin inflamed François, filling him with a torrent of passion. He groaned with the physical pain of need, and all logic and reason suddenly deserted him. He picked her up bodily, holding her in his arms as though she weighed nothing. Suddenly all that mattered was to assuage the unbearable tension between them, between their bodies. He thought he might explode with need for her. He kicked open the door to his chamber and crossed to the bed.

'I need you, Léonie de Chambois, and by God I'm going to make love to you. If you want me to stop, you'd best tell me now.'

She knew he was offering her a choice, but she wanted him every bit as much. She answered by pressing her mouth to the V of his collarbone, and heard a faint growl from his throat in reply. They tumbled together on to the sheets, then his mouth found hers and plundered its sweetness like a starving honeybee drunk on summer nectar.

He trailed his tongue down her neck, pulling aside the strings of her nightshirt until he could bury himself in the valley between her small well-rounded breasts.

Léonie moaned, arching her back as heat flowed from his touch. Then his tongue found one hard nipple and slowly traced a path around the aureole. Warmth spiralled through her and she cried out, raising herself and lifting her breast to his mouth in an unconscious effort to satisfy the hunger his

311

touch was creating. Then he slowly drew the nipple between his lips and she felt such an exquisite pleasure she cried out in ecstasy.

But he was not finished. He released her breast, cupping it in one hand and gently feathering the nipple with his thumb while his mouth sought her other nipple, repeating the delicious torment until Léonie was clutching at him, tearing away his shirt in her need to feel his flesh, ripping off several buttons in her haste. She ran her fingers over his heated skin, luxuriating in the hot strength of his muscles and the light mat of black wiry hair on his chest.

'Woman, stop!' he moaned. 'You don't know what you're doing to me.'

'But I want to please you,' she whispered, eyes tightly shut against the fire his fingers were trailing across her belly, down, down, sliding toward the central well of her need.

He grabbed her hands, pushing them down on the bed. 'I won't be able to control myself if you do that. You don't understand . . . All these months . . . And then when I thought you were dead . . . '

He stared down at her, his eyes black as ink in the darkened room. Léonie felt a shiver of fear mingle with her need, yet she knew she couldn't refuse him. She watched with a mixture of fascination and dread as he slowly began to pull her white nightshirt up over her legs, over her belly and her bandaged ribs and then higher to expose her breasts. Suddenly, the ship lurched and François lost his balance, crushing her side wound with an elbow as he fell.

Léonie screamed. The captain leapt off her and in a second was on the floor, steadying himself with one hand on the bed rail. Her wound burned as though he'd stabbed her with a hot poker, but worse than that, Léonie felt suddenly horribly naked, exposed to him as though what they had been doing was somehow tawdry. She clutched her nightshirt and tugged it downwards, pushing his hands away and sobbing against the raw emotion she was so totally unprepared to feel.

'Dear God, Léonie. Are you all right?' He grabbed her hands and forced her to let go of the shirt. 'Let me look, damn it!' She kept her eyes shut, refusing to let him see her pain and confusion. 'I am so stupid. What the hell did you think you were doing here in my room at the dead of night, anyway? How could I have let myself . . . ' He yanked her shirt down roughly and turned away. 'It's not bleeding again. I'll get you something for the pain. Wait here.'

'I don't want anything!'

He returned from his study with a bottle

and spoon, poured a generous measure and held it out to her.

'I said I don't want anything!'

'Swallow it!'

'No!' She was crying now, humiliated by his anger, by his violent change of mood. 'If it's so wonderful, you take it.'

She tried to stand up only to be tumbled back on to the bed by a renewed surge from the ship. 'What was that?'

They both stared at the open window, as though suddenly realizing that the *Aurélie* was no longer sitting serenely on a flat ocean. She was being tossed about like a cork. Rain was pouring through the window and the ship was creaking like a demon from hell.

'A storm! We've run into a storm and nobody has called me! Dear God, we're under full sail. If we don't drop the topsails the ship will turn over!' He threw the medicine on to the nightstand, slammed the window and took off out the door, leaving Léonie clinging to the bed, staring after him. He yelled for the first officer as he ran up the stairs to the helm.

The vessel lurched so violently to starboard that Léonie had to press her hands against the wall just to keep from falling face-first on to the window. And then, equally violently, she was thrown to port and fell in an

314

ungainly heap on the floor. She grabbed for the bed, missing it but reaching the leg of a chair. As the ship veered back in its next spasm, the chair flew, crashing with her into the wall. She gasped, but the pain in her ribcage was nothing compared to the terrible peril she knew the expedition was in.

Above the howling wind she heard the sails coming down, the thud of feet as all hands scurried on deck, and the bellowing of voices. After that, the violent bucking of the ship eased a little, settling into a rhythm of sorts and making the storm feel less monstrous. And then she heard it: at first just a rumble, the noise grew until it was like rolling thunder. Léonie's blood ran cold. She'd heard that sound only once before — when they were preparing the *Aurélie* for battle. It was the sound of a cannon rolling across the floor, and it was coming from the wardroom, a few feet from where she lay. The rumbling grew louder and then with a sudden whomp the huge gun ripped away from its lashings and rammed a path through the hull of the ship. There was a half-second of silence and then a great splash as it hit the waves.

The sudden release of eight thousand pounds of iron flipped the ship to starboard, sending everything that was not bolted down in the cabin crashing to the floor. Léonie ducked, covering her head with her hands and waiting while the ship settled back into a pattern controlled more by wild waves than by loose cannon.

She couldn't stay where she was. She crawled to the door, pulling herself up and running drunkenly toward her own quarters. Her door had burst open in the violence of the storm and she tumbled in, trying to use the motion of the sea to aid her passage so she wasn't trying to walk up sudden hills in the floorboards. She shut the window and then struggled into breeches and shirt, pulling on her boots awkwardly with one arm wrapped around her bed end for support.

It was horribly dark when she reached the deck. No one had had time to replenish the lamps, and the boards were slick with rain and seawater. A sharp crack of lightning lit up the sky momentarily, flashing an image Léonie knew she would never forget — scores of sailors crawling in the rigging like a plague of rats, pulling ropes and furling sails as though the Devil himself were at their back. In a second flash, she saw a man lose his grip, scrabbling desperately to grab the ratlines. Above the wind she heard his scream, then he fell headlong into the mountainous sea and was swallowed up by the waves.

'Oh, dear God!' She knew no one could help him. There wasn't even any point in shouting 'Man overboard!' for no one would hear and no one could save him.

Then she remembered the cannon. At least that was something she could do to help. Water would quickly flood the wardroom and officers' quarters unless the hole was repaired, even though it was high above the waterline in calm seas. She grabbed the rail and edged her way toward the helm, stopping often as huge waves washed over the side and drenched her, grabbing at her boots as they towed their way back into the wild ocean.

It took an eternity, but she made it. The captain was standing at the helm himself, barking orders above the storm to his officers and men. He stood feet astride at the wheel, his white shirt flapping in the wind, baring his chest to the full mercy of the storm. Léonie remembered her own hands ripping the buttons from his shirt. It seemed like a lifetime ago. Perhaps the storm was a punishment.

'Captain!'

He turned, his eyes widening when he

saw her. 'Get below, Chambois! That's an order!'

She ignored him, mindful only of the damage done by the loose cannon, and took advantage of the lull between the peak of one wave and the valley of the next to grapple her way to the wheel, where she clung to a post.

'Go below, damn you!' roared the captain.

'Not until I tell you — '

Her words were lost as a renewed squall of rain sheeted down on them. She bowed her head. When she looked up again, his jaw was set and his eyes glittered with anger. Rain ran in runnels down his face, but mostly he ignored it, occasionally wiping his eyes with his sodden sleeve. He looked dangerous and wild, like the storm itself, one minute fighting the wheel to maintain a course, the next barking a volley of orders at those around him. Everyone scurried to do his bidding without question. Everyone except Léonie. She hung back, watching, remembering how those hard angry lips had made her skin flame with desire such a short time before. It caused a flash of heat deep inside her.

'Captain,' she yelled again. 'One of the cannons . . . in the wardroom . . . it went through the hull!'

He glanced at her for barely a moment and then turned his head toward the duty bench, 'Get the chief carpenter to the wardroom on the double! And where the hell is my navigator? I want some readings and I want them now!'

Léonie made it to the duty bench just as Christian emerged from the gloom.

'Sir!' he shouted, with only the barest flicker of recognition that he had seen Léonie. 'We are being blown due west. We must turn about before we are forced too far out into the Indian Ocean.'

'Don't tell me how to sail my ship, Lavelle. If you think you can tack in this blow without sinking us, *you* do it! And where the hell is Grévin?'

'In his cabin, sir. The chief navigator is gravely ill with fever. I fear he's delirious. But I have tried to take some positions — '

'Positions?' the captain roared. 'I'll give you positions! We're in the middle of a — ' Then he saw Léonie.

He signalled to the helmsman to take over and grabbed her by the elbow. 'I thought I told you to get below!'

'I'm an officer on this ship!'

'You're a — '

'Yes, Captain? I'm a what?'

His fingers bit into her elbow through the

thin cotton shirt, but she wouldn't give him the satisfaction of knowing it hurt.

He pulled her down on to the duty bench.

'Your plans were spoiled by the storm, *mamselle*. If you thought that little performance would secure Lavelle's forgiveness, you were greatly mistaken. I don't tamper with my log for anyone.'

'Wha — ?'

'Don't play games with me. I have more important things on my mind. Now return to your cabin and strap yourself into your bunk. As soon as this storm allows, we'll be on our way into port and then, thank God, I can be rid of you!'

Léonie gasped. 'How dare you! One moment you're happy to pass the time playing with me, but now you've got something to do, you throw me off like some old rag.'

He turned back to her, eyes glittering in the rainy night. 'I am not stupid, *Vicomtesse*. I've had women throw themselves at me for all sorts of reasons, but whether you wanted to save your skin or just to have a few thrills with a man who soils his hands for a living, I couldn't care less. You will remain in your quarters until we make port, then you will be offloaded.'

320

'Why don't you just list me as dead, Captain? Then at least you could throw me overboard and be done with me.'

'Don't tempt me, *mamselle*. If the men aboard this ship knew you were a woman, they would blame you not just for this storm but also for the attack by those bloodthirsty brigands. Their superstitions regarding women are deeply ingrained. Your life wouldn't be worth . . . ' He flicked his fingers to emphasize his point and Léonie shivered.

'You wouldn't dare tell them.'

'Will you go below?'

'I will not stay cooped up in that tiny room for who knows how long. There are things I can do — '

But he wouldn't listen. He jumped up from the duty bench and shouted into the dark.

'Sergeant-at-Arms! Take this officer to his cabin and lock him in!'

Léonie felt tears of frustration as she saw the burly soldier approach. 'No!' she shouted, but the captain had turned his back. She suffered the rough hands of the man on her arm, letting him lead her away, and wondered if she would ever see François again.

When she glanced back, he was gone.

17

Marie Beaulieu pushed back the hood of her cloak and let her soft brown hair enjoy the slight breeze, for she was hot from her climb up to the abbey above the village. She paused and looked back down the narrow cobbled street, uneasy with the feeling that someone was watching her. She'd had this strange foreboding all day. It was probably nothing — a mixture of her growing feelings for Jean-Michel and the dread with which she faced her interview with the abbess.

Nothing moved in the village, except a stout Swiss woman hanging washing on a line from a balcony. She could hear a baby crying somewhere in one of the little whitewashed houses, and the sound of cow bells tinkling on the morning breeze from the fields on the mountainside nearby. But all else was still.

Marie chided herself for having too great an imagination and turned resolutely toward the abbey. She crossed a small deserted square where a dog slept in the afternoon sunshine. The smell of boiled cabbage made her wrinkle her nose and she hurried on. She reached the final steps that led to the abbey gate and began to climb, hearing her footsteps echo. The way was narrow, enclosed by small houses that gave directly on to the street. She paused to adjust her cloak. The echo continued. Quickly she turned her head, catching a flash of green as someone stepped into a doorway. With her heart pounding, Marie resumed her climb, though her ears strained for the slightest sound. There it was. A soft footfall, not at all like the noise of her own sabots on the cobbles. Panic began to swirl in her chest, but she forced herself to continue on her way. It was just her imagination. If someone else was climbing the same steps, that was hardly a crime.

As she reached the street that ran around the bottom of the abbey wall, she made a sudden decision and turned away from her destination. If she was being followed, at least she could prevent her tormentor from discovering her mission.

Opposite the gate was a tiny garden with a fountain and a seat that overlooked the village and the mountains beyond. Marie sat on the far side of the fountain where she could be hidden from the abbey gate. Through the veil of water she could watch the end of the narrow street she had just exited. After a moment she heard footsteps and then a tall man stepped out into the sunshine dressed in green velvet with expensive lace at his throat and cuffs. A French nobleman, of that she was certain, for his dress was unlike anything she had seen in Switzerland. She could not make out his features until he turned to stare at the abbey gate. Marie gasped. She would know that profile anywhere. The strong jaw and aquiline nose brought a chill to her bones. The Marquis de Vercours. Though she had never seen him at the Hôtel de Chambois, every young girl in Paris had heard the stories of his cruel ways with women and all knew the devil by sight. They hoped that was the nearest they would ever have to come.

Marie sat as still as a bird, barely breathing, while the Marquis glanced up and down the street. Finally he turned and hurried back the way he'd come, leaving Marie trembling with fright.

★ ★ ★

Alain de Vercours was perplexed by the girl's disappearance. He could tell by her clothes that she was French, and her nervous disposition made him suspicious.

324

The decision to follow her had interrupted his dinner, but when it became clear that her destination was the abbey, he'd felt satisfied that the sacrifice was worth it. But then she had spotted him and disappeared. Now he warred with the idea that perhaps she hadn't been on her way to the abbey at all, and that he had wasted a perfectly good meal.

He lingered on his way back to the inn, hoping to chance an encounter with the girl, but the village was quiet and his stomach was rumbling. He turned back, entering the town square where the modest inn that was the village's only accommodation stood, when he saw her. Vercours stepped back into the shadows.

The girl crossed the square and hurried into the inn. Vercours frowned, for he had thought there were no other guests at the establishment. Indeed he had heard the proprietor discussing the dearth of business.

He decided to wait. His dinner would be spoiled by now anyway. The sun was beginning to set, sending spirals of colour across the mountaintops, and he watched them changing hue as he waited, musing on the puzzle that had brought him to this quiet corner of Switzerland. His faithful Géricault had worked diligently on his behalf and when he finally reported that there were rumours the *vicomtesse* was a penitent in this little-known abbey, he had wasted no time. His interview with the astonished abbess had been illuminating, to him, if not to the nun herself. In short, the Abbaye de Ste-Géneviève had never heard of Léonie de Chambois.

The *vicomtesse*'s disappearance seemed to deepen the more he tried to solve it, yet he held some of the pieces of the puzzle. He knew that somehow, this furtive French maiden had to be connected with her disappearance. Why had the chit been hurrying to the abbey only to turn back without going inside? Had she spotted him? Could she perhaps know who he was or the nature of his business in the canton?

Vercours searched his mind, but could not recall having encountered her before. He was sure he would remember those liquid brown eyes. Amusing himself with such innocent beauties was a favourite hobby and he savoured each memory long after the girls themselves had ceased to inspire. No, if he'd played with this little French mouse, he would not have forgotten.

At last she appeared, but not alone. She was seated on a brown nag with a liveried groom behind her. As the horse and riders cantered out of the lane beside the inn,

Vercours' eyes widened with astonishment.

The man who held the reins had hair as red as the sunset. From this distance there could be no mistake. Servant's livery or not, that groom was none other than the Vicomte de Chambois.

'So, my young buck,' he murmured, 'you are not dead after all. Not yet.'

It took the Marquis de Vercours no time at all to learn who the riders were. Chambois's livery was a gift. According to the innkeeper, who was not averse to having his palm greased with gold, the young man claimed to be one Jean Patou, a groom from the Château Aristide in Franche-Comté. They had asked questions of the landlord regarding the abbey, but otherwise had spoken few words and offered little. The innkeeper shrugged, making an expressive gesture that Vercours had interpreted as meaning who could understand these Frenchmen, anyway?

As he was waiting for his horse to be brought round, the innkeeper's wife offered another tidbit.

'You know, *milord*, the thing that puzzled me?'

He admitted he did not.

'Well, for a stable boy, that lad had the most beautiful hands. Didn't look like he'd

327

done an honest day's work in his life. Probably some nobleman's bastard sent to be out of the way, if you ask me.'

Château Aristide

'I have the horses outside. Are you ready?'

Marie jumped. Jean-Michel's low whisper increased the unease she'd been feeling ever since their return from Switzerland in such a hurry. Her head was in a whirl as they'd prepared to leave. Luckily her uncle hadn't questioned the reason for their hasty departure and had helped Jean-Michel find a reputable dealer from which to purchase two swift but sturdy mounts to carry them back to Paris.

'I have our belongings.' She passed him the leather bags securely tied at the neck with heavy cords. As he took them from her, their hands touched. The fleeting contact burned her skin and brought unbidden tears to her eyes. 'Oh, Jean-Mich, could we not take a post-chaise, instead? I really am not sure — '

'Sweet Marie.' He dropped the bags on the cold flagstones of the kitchen and took her in his arms. 'I wish I could spare you this ordeal, but if we are to reach Paris before Vercours, we must outrun his coach, and we can only do that on horseback. He must have been to the abbey — it's the only possible reason for him to have been in that Swiss village. So he knows Léonie is not there.'

'But what does he care? Why should the marquis be so interested in your family that he would ride across France to search for my mistress?'

Jean-Michel frowned and she could see the question weighed heavily upon him, too. 'That's what we have to figure out. I know he hates our family. He always has. But — '

Marie shivered. She touched a finger to his lips. 'Never mind. My beloved Léonie is in far worse peril than I. If she can sail the oceans with only a shipload of sailors for company, I can surely ride a horse.' She looked down at her man's garb, suddenly amused. 'Do you not think it funny, Jean-Michel, that I should dress as a man to help my mistress while she, too, masquerades in male clothes?'

She blushed when she saw how closely he was observing her, but his eyes were not on her coat of coarse brown cloth, nor upon the simple breeches that she wore so they could travel swiftly and unnoticed through France. She felt her skin heat with a longing that was as powerful as it was new. His eyes roved across her face. *He's looking at my lips*, she thought wildly, frighteningly aroused. And

329

then his mouth was on hers, his lips hot and wild as he caressed her, forcing her lips to answer, forcing her to press her body against him, to acknowledge the warmth that came from deep within.

'Oh, Marie. Good, sweet Marie, I have been so blind.'

He groaned as he slid his hands through the richness of her hair. The bow fell out, letting her curls fall in a silken mass around her shoulders. Marie knew this wasn't the way things should be between them, though she had yearned for it for as long as she could remember. It felt so good. So right. How could she stop him? She had neither the will nor the strength.

His hands slid down her back, crushing her against him. She felt the power of his arousal and it sent her heart hammering in her ribs, filling her with powerful desire.

She tipped back her head, enough to break the kiss. Enough to look at him. Soak in his image so she would never forget.

'*Monsieur*. You must not — '

'I must!' he interrupted vehemently. 'I must kiss you, Marie. I should have done it years ago.' He clutched her to his chest, pressing his cheek against the top of her head. 'I have been so blind. All this time I have thought of you as a childhood friend, as my sister's abigail, as a *copine*. Not once have I ever listened to my heart.'

'Your heart . . . ?'

'My heart.' He gave a short laugh. 'The one I always listen to when it's most likely to get me into trouble. The one I most certainly should not have heard when it urged me to fight Vercours in a duel.' He held her away from him. His gaze burned her, filled her with wild hopeless wanting. 'Marie Beaulieu, will you consent to be my wife?'

Marie stared at Jean-Michel as though he'd taken leave of his senses.

'What — what are you saying? Jean-Michel, this is not something to joke about.'

'I make no jest, Marie.' His eyes darkened as he gazed at her. Suddenly he dropped to one knee on the flagstone floor. 'Forgive me. I have not been a proper gentleman about this.' Marie gasped as he took her hands, pressing them to his lips, and continued without a glimmer of a smile, 'Please, Marie, will you do me the honour of becoming my lawfully wedded wife? I promise I shall love and honour you above all others for the whole of my wretched life. I shall keep you and protect you, give you children and share the sweet darkness of night with you for as long as you will have me.' He kissed her fingers again, one by one, then her palms, then her wrists, while Marie stood dumbstruck gazing down upon a man who was so far above her station that she scarcely dared breathe the same air.

'Jean-Michel!' She pulled her hands away, rubbing them on the rough cloth of her pants to stem their tingling. 'I — I can't — ' She stepped back, almost tripping over their bags. Her mind whirled with a sickening cocktail of emotions. 'You don't know what you are saying. You must not do this to me. It is cruel. How can you hurt me so, after all I have done to help you since we were children?'

'Marie!'

'No!' She held up a hand to stop him coming any closer. 'I am your servant, *monsieur*. You may toy with me, enjoy me as you will. It is the way of your class. But I am not to be spoken of so. My name can never be heard in the same breath as yours.'

He was staring at her as though she were a stranger. It was even more unsettling than his absurd proposal.

'You don't understand, Marie,' he answered softly. He stepped over the bags and reached for her hands, but she tucked them behind her back. He clasped her by the elbows instead. 'I love you. I think I have always loved you. And before you lecture me on my duty as a nobleman, let me tell you what I think. I don't give a fig for my birth. Women make love and produce children the same way, no matter whether their blood be as blue as Marie-Antoinette's or as greasy as a guttersnipe's.'

'Jean-Michel!'

'Your father was a lieutenant in the army. If he had not died on the battlefield, your mother would never have had to go into service. For God's sake, Marie, we were children together. Were you any less of a child than I, or than Léonie? Were you not our dearest friend and confidante?'

He was shaking her, and not just physically. She grasped his hands and pulled them away from her body, pressing them to his chest. 'What you are saying is madness, Jean-Michel. I cannot marry you. It could never be. Léonie would hate me forever for destroying you.'

Jean-Michel swore under his breath and for once failed to apologize when Marie looked horrified.

'Enough of this! There are other choices. We don't even have to stay in France — we can go to America!'

'America!'

'It's perfect. People there can marry whom they please, live as they please.' He stopped

333

suddenly, turning on his heel, and Marie could see the excitement glowing in his eyes. 'I could even work!'

'Work! Jean-Michel, you're a nobleman.'

'That's just it, Marie. In America, there are no classes. A man is a man. His sweat is the measure of his effort.' He jumped, striding across the flagstone floor as he explained, 'In America, a man is what he is, Marie. And a woman is a woman, free to be her best. It would be hard, but we're used to that.' He crossed the floor to where she sat, mesmerized by such strange and heretical ideas. 'Say you'll come, Marie. Promise me you'll be my wife?'

She opened her mouth, but no sound came out. He really means it, was all she could think. He really wants me — *me* — to be his wife. All her life she had longed for something more than the role allotted to her by her birth, but she had disciplined herself not to think such thoughts, not to give in to impossible dreams.

And now it was here, lying before her like a gauntlet, waiting — nay, begging — her to take it up. She gazed at the Vicomte de Chambois but for the first time in her life she saw only Jean-Michel, the man she loved.

'I will come,' she whispered. 'Oh, Jean-Michel, I love you more than my own life. I will go wherever you wish and I will do everything in my power to make you happy.'

She saw his eyes darken with love and felt a happiness unlike any she had ever experienced flow through her. Then she was in his arms, crushed against his chest, and they were laughing and crying together. From outside came the sudden call of a nightingale, drawing their eyes to the open doorway, to their plight.

Jean-Michel turned Marie's face to his with one hand.

'We have a dangerous task before us. Are you ready, my love?'

She nodded. He picked up her hair riband which had fallen out when they kissed and turned her about, tying her hair for her as though it were the most natural thing in the world. Then he grabbed her hand and led her out of the château to where the horses waited in the moonlight.

Marie found riding astride in men's breeches to be comfortable, far more secure than sidesaddle. Though her heart was filled with unspeakable fears, there was no denying a spark of excitement, of daring, of breaking out.

'Ready, my love?' Jean-Michel called from his mount.

'Ready,' she whispered back. In the eerie silence of the witching hour, they urged the horses forward in single file, clipping along the grassy edge of the driveway that led out of the estate to the road.

Marie half turned in the saddle and gazed up at the darkened house, lit by a bright evanescent moon. It seemed to sleep, to let them slip away as though they had never been there, had never found safety within its anonymous walls.

As they passed through the heavy wrought-iron gates and headed west they failed to see the silent observer who kept to the shadows of the trees.

They passed by, side by side, without speaking. After the soft clopping of the horses' hooves had faded, Vercours moved out of the shadows, his soft, mirthless laugh the only sound in the night.

18

Indian Ocean, September 1784

Léonie stayed in her solitary cabin for three more days until the storm blew itself out.

Occasionally one of the servants brought food, but the sight of it made her ill and she often left it untouched. The soup was an unappetizing grey, and the bread, when it came at all, was riddled with cooked weevils. She was puzzled by the rapid decline in food, but as no one came to her room and she was still locked in, there was no one to ask.

She wasn't hungry, anyway. Her wound, which had been healing well, seemed worse, the flesh flaccid and pale rather than the healthy pink it had been. And her legs ached.

Finally the storm abated. She opened her small window and latched it back, drawing in hungry gulps of sparkling air.

'I have to get out of here,' she told a passing albatross, watching its huge white wings hang motionless as it cruised on the soft breezes. She smiled, buoyed by the sight of another living creature.

Léonie poured some water into a mug and picked up her bone-handled toothbrush, wetting it before dipping the bristles into her precious store of tooth powder. Still watching the slow-moving albatross through the window, she began to brush her teeth.

'*Tiens!*' She pulled the brush out of her mouth. 'That hurt.' She could taste blood, but she could see nothing unusual about the brush itself. She spat into the wash basin and picked up Jean-Michel's shaving mirror. Her eyes widened with fright as she peered into her mouth. Her gums were red and swollen, bleeding where she had started her customary vigorous brushing.

Am I ill? she wondered. She resumed her toilette gingerly, for she could not bear to have dirty teeth. It took a lot longer than usual and there was more bleeding, but at last it was done.

She carried the basin into Roussillon's private quarter gallery and tipped it down the toilet, watching the red-stained water tumble into the sea. A shiver ran up her spine, and she closed the door quickly.

Once dressed, she gazed about the cabin, wondering whether she should beat on the door and demand to be let out, or wait until someone came.

Surely Christian would come and visit her? No doubt both he and the captain had been busy during the gale, but surely one of them would remember she was imprisoned here, wouldn't they?

She untied the chair, which she had secured with her belt during the storm, and sat down, gazing about her. Her eyes fell on her foot locker, which had sat unopened since she took over Roussillon's cabin, the letters J-M de Chambois engraved in gilt on the lid. Where was Jean-Michel now, she wondered sadly?

She knelt beside the locker and lifted the lid. Inside was a spare uniform, some shoes, undergarments — all impersonal, male things. She fingered the cloth of the blue frock coat, wishing it were a dress of finest taffeta instead. She rummaged further and found the little package that contained the requirements for her monthly 'curse', though she'd only needed it twice since she left France. She knew she couldn't be pregnant, so she put that particular symptom down to the change of air.

There was nothing. Nothing to remind her of home. Then she touched something leather. Thinking it was just a shoe, she pushed it aside, but it was large and too soft.

'Nounou's bag!' She pulled the leather pouch out from beneath the clothes and stared at it. Tears filled her eyes as she carried the bundle to the bed and with feverish fingers opened the drawstring and tipped the contents on to the blanket.

Inside were two more bags, one made of stout hessian, the other of calfskin. She opened the hessian one first. It was packed with dried herbs. Léonie dipped her nose into the sack and drew in a breath full of the sweet summer scent of flowers. It was like a walk in her parents' orchard and she fought to control the homesickness that swept over her. How she yearned to be there, to see her mother, to talk with her twin brother, to pour out her woes — .

She stopped herself and put the bag down, opening the leather pouch instead. She stared at the shrivelled berries inside and laughed. 'Oh, Nounou! You were trying to spoil Jean-Mich, but I love you for it.'

The dried fruits were *his* favourites, not hers, for she preferred juicy strawberries to cranberries and blackcurrants, but she popped one into her mouth, finding it hard and tart, but surprisingly delicious. With the bag in her hand, she sank back on the bed and lay staring up at the panelled ceiling, sucking blackcurrants until they were soft enough to chew, letting the sharp tang tingle on her tongue.

It was the most wonderful taste she could imagine at that moment, and it made her realize how very hungry she was.

She ate a handful, then carefully retied the bag. She didn't want to waste such a treasure trove. She looked at the herbs, wondering if perhaps the cook might use them to improve the foul flavour of his boiled mutton.

340

When the food came that morning, it was hard biscuit and a slab of mottled grey meat. She gazed at the maggots that were the only garnish and carried the whole mess to her quarter galley. As she tipped it into the great ocean, she wondered if the creatures of the deep were ever desperate enough to eat such stuff.

Then she poured herself a tiny nip of Roussillon's dwindling supply of Cognac, drank it at one toss, and slept.

She was so hungry when she awoke that she ate a few more of Nounou's precious berries, but her stomach ached so she put them away. A soldier brought her the main meal at four in the afternoon and this time she knew she would have to eat it. She asked him for a pot of boiling water and while she waited for him to fetch it, she sprinkled a few herbs into the watery broth that passed as soup, hoping it would impart a palatable flavour. The meat was chicken and seemed free of unwanted visitors, and she wolfed it down, wondering what her mother would think of such unseemly haste.

The soldier returned with the water. She took the pot carefully and set it on the floor, turning to speak to him only to hear the familiar grate of the key in the lock.

I have to get out of here or I'll go mad, she

thought. How long does the captain think he can keep me here? Tears blurred her eyes as she threw some herbs in the pot, hoping to make an infusion that would ease the cramps in her stomach. I didn't ask to fall in love with him, she thought. I tried not to, tried to remember that I was supposed to be a man. How could he use me like that? If that storm hadn't come up, who knows what would've happened?

She knew. He would have made love to her.

He would have taken her virginity.

And then what?

She sat on the floor, stirring the infusion, but not seeing it. In her mind she could only picture François lying beside her, kissing her, trailing his tongue across her breasts until her nipples stood up in stiff little peaks and a fire began to burn in the pit of her stomach. She felt warmth flow through her at the memories, and then grow cold again at the vision of his remorseless expression as he'd ordered her to be taken away by the master-at-arms.

How could he do that? How could he treat her as though she were a precious jewel one moment and then turn on her the next? She bent her head over her lap and squeezed her eyes shut, holding in the tears lest someone else should hear and wonder at an officer who cried like a woman.

A knock at the door made hope flare in her heart. She wiped her eyes quickly on her shirt sleeve.

'*Entrez*!'

The door opened. It was Christian, carrying a jug of wine and two glasses.

He kicked the door shut with his foot, and sat on the bed. 'You look ghastly, my sweet.'

Léonie's heart slowed down again and she sat back on the floor, cross-legged. 'It's wonderful to see you, too, Christian.'

He set the wine and glasses on the bedside table. 'What's that heavenly smell?'

'You like it? I found some old herbs in my locker. Nounou had prepared them for Jean-Michel and I'd forgotten they were there. I thought perhaps they would make a pleasant drink, since the water tastes so foul.'

'It could only help. The men are complaining because they've doubled the vinegar in the drinking water and it makes them gag.'

'Vinegar? No wonder it smells so awful.'

'It's supposed to keep it pure.'

Léonie made a face. 'Let's try this. I think it has camomile, and I can see thin strips of lemon rind, but what do you think this is?'

'Rose hips.'

'Of course! I could smell it, but I wasn't sure.' She poured the decoction into two cups and passed one to him. '*A ta santé!*'

'*Ta santé*' he replied taking a cautious sip. 'Not bad.'

Léonie liked the taste too, and drank half the cup before she asked him about the food. 'What's happened? It never used to be this dreadful.'

He sighed. 'Things are bad, Léonie. The storm has soaked most of the stores, ruining everything. There's some fresh meat from the last of the livestock, but no vegetables and the flour is wet with seawater.'

'But we'll be in port soon, won't we?' she asked, shutting out the knowledge that arriving in Batavia meant the end of the voyage for her. She dreaded it so much that she couldn't bear to think of it. Not until she had talked to the captain once more.

Christian shook his head. 'There's worse. Grévin is gravely ill. I didn't think he'd survive the storm, but he's hanging on somehow. The captain spends most of his time with him.'

'He's a good surgeon. Surely — '

'Grévin's dying, Léonie. Nothing can save him. And the other navigator was killed in the battle.'

'You mean . . . ?'

He nodded. 'That only leaves me.'

'But Christian, that's wonderful!'

'Hah! Tell the captain that. He won't listen to me. I tried to get him to turn about during the gale, but he had other things on his mind.' He looked hard at her.

Léonie blushed. 'What are you saying?'

'We've been pushed far back into the Indian Ocean, away from the coast. The winds at this time of year are coming straight at us, so we'll have to tack all the way.'

'So?'

'So zigzagging takes twice as long. And the men are already weakened by dysentery and lack of food.'

'What are you saying? Are you telling me we're all going to die out here, after all we've endured?'

He crossed to Léonie and wrapped his arms about her, cradling her head on his shoulder. 'Don't worry, my sweet. We'll make it somehow. It's not as far as I had feared. We should be there in two weeks, three at the most.'

'Three weeks!' Léonie trembled. Dear God, how could a ship full of weakened men survive three weeks at sea without proper food? Then she remembered the sturdy little supply ship. 'What about the *Mousquetaire*? She must have provisions that have not been ruined by the accursed storm.'

He shook his head, releasing her and getting up. 'She's gone.'

'Gone!'

'No one knows whether she's simply been blown on a different course, or — '

'Or what?'

'Or whether she's gone down.'

Léonie's eyes widened with horror as she took in this latest piece of news. Without their supply ship . . .

'I have to see the captain. I can't stand it, Christian. I can't bear being locked up like a prisoner. I haven't done anything.'

'You refused to obey an order.'

'It was a stupid order! I only wanted to help — '

'An order is an order, Léonie. Especially in an emergency.'

She knew he was right, but it rankled. 'So let him courtmartial me, if he dares!'

Christian laughed. 'If you want a court-martial, you can have mine!'

'Oh, I'm sorry.' She shrugged, feeling childish in the face of his stoicism. 'That was the reason I went to talk to him that night.'

'No wonder he was so mad. I can fight my own battles, you know.'

The door opened suddenly, making them

both jump. François stood there, his face black as thunder, looking from one to the other. Christian coughed, patted Léonie's knee and got up, excusing himself as he squeezed past the captain.

'Lieutenant Lavelle!'

'Sir?'

'Grévin is dead.'

She saw a fleeting look of sadness and understanding pass between them, but for a moment neither spoke. Then François reached out and touched the younger man on the elbow. 'He was a great navigator. I hope you learned from him.'

'Yes, sir,' Christian replied quietly. 'He was the best.'

'Well, now you're the best, my boy.'

'Sir?'

'You have the sextant, Lieutenant. Use it well and get us into port before I lose too many more men.'

Christian beamed. 'Yes, sir!' He grinned at Léonie and turned to go, then hesitated. 'Does this mean — '

'It means nothing more, Lavelle. I have not changed my mind, though I'm not saying I won't. I'm not an unforgiving man — you'd do well to remember that.'

Christian gave him a speculative look, but left without further comment. When the door closed and Léonie was alone with François she felt fury flame in her breast. 'How can you continue with this ludicrous trial? You have just trusted him with the survival of your ship and yet you persist in persecuting him for something you know he did not do!'

He crossed to her, ignoring her attack and the mess in the room, for there were clothes and cups and wine glasses strewn about. She realized how very unshipshape her quarters appeared, but she tilted her head in defiance.

'Open your mouth,' he said, lifting her chin with one hand.

'My mouth!'

'Just do it, *mamselle*. And turn toward the light. Thank you.'

His skin felt hot and dry. He grasped her jaw with both hands and pulled back her lips, peering in and tilting her head this way and that until he was satisfied.

'Now I know what a horse feels like,' she muttered, rubbing her chin. 'Perhaps you'd care to expla — '

'Show me your wound.'

'No! It — it's fine. Healing well.' It was a lie, but she couldn't bear the thought of him touching her with angry, efficient doctor's fingers. Not after the way he had touched her in his cabin.

He ran one hand wearily across his brow. His face was flushed and there was an unnatural brightness to his eyes, which Léonie put down to his bereavement over the chief navigator. She felt an unexpected rush of compassion and longed to comfort him, if only she knew how.

'Please understand,' he said, not looking at her, 'that I have no desire to . . . to repeat the scene in my cabin. What happened between us was indefensible, irrational — the result of poor timing and unfortunate circumstance. I was not sufficiently on my guard, but I assure you I will not make the same mistake twice.'

'Mistake!' Léonie felt the blood drain from her face. That's all she was to him, a foolish blunder?

'What would you call it? You came to my cabin in the dead of night dressed in nothing but a . . . but a — '

'You flatter yourself, Captain, if you think I came to seduce you.' Two could play at this game, and the wound he had carved in her heart burned far more deeply than any gunshot could inflict. Her stared at her, his eyes black and unyielding as flint.

'I am not in the habit of pleasuring myself at the expense of other men, *mamselle*. Even if that was your intention.'

'My intention!' She curled her hands and grasped them behind her back before she gave in to the urge to slap him. 'My intention was to persuade you of the unfairness of court-martialling Lieutenant Lavelle. It had nothing to do with — '

'I am not stupid, Léonie. You came aboard my ship to escape your obligations to the Marquis de Grise. You came to my room to make certain that he wouldn't have you, even if I do manage to get you back into his loving arms in time.'

'Your sarcasm is misplaced, sir. I joined this doomed expedition for my brother's sake, nothing more.'

'Not for some excitement to spice up a lady's life?' he enquired gently, an irritating smile on his lips. When she refused to dignify that with an answer, his smile faded. 'I have removed the guard from your door. Next time you are given an order, you will obey it instantly, do you understand?'

She nodded mutely, then watched him survey the room once more and leave, closing the door firmly behind him.

'Damn you, François de la Tour!' she sobbed, picking up her pillow and throwing it at the door. She dearly wanted to throw a cup and hear it smash into a million pieces, but she was too afraid of provoking him further. And she was coming to realize that she would rather be near him even if he wanted no part of her, than be unable to see him day after day.

She retrieved the pillow and set the small cabin to rights, before brushing out her hair with hard, savage strokes and retying it with a black riband. Then she made for the deck.

She took the officers' *grande échelle* that led directly up to the poop deck behind the helm. Luckily, only the helmsman was there and he merely nodded as she passed. She was glad not to encounter François. It would be too hard to keep her feelings hidden in front of anyone just now, and she needed a chance to collect her thoughts.

She leaned her back on the mizzenmast and drew in deep breaths of refreshing air. Dusk was falling, the sky deepening to indigo at its zenith, flaming scarlet at the horizon.

'It will be a fair day for sailing again tomorrow, praise God,' came a voice from behind her. She turned to find Father Cassel leaning on the port railing, and crossed the sloping deck to him. They stared down at the curling wake that crested away from the ship.

Their attention was caught by the sound of a hornpipe at the far end of the quarter deck below. The reedy music rose into the darkening air over the heads of the dozen or so men who shuffled about in an aimless circle around the foremast.

'What are they doing?' she asked.

'The master-at-arms is making them dance. It helps to keep their spirits up and prevents sickness.'

'They don't look like they're enjoying it much.'

He shrugged. 'With the storm coming hard on the heels of the battle, it is too late for most. These men are well enough to take part. The rest are either at their duties or unable to benefit.' He sighed. 'I have been below decks for the best part of the day, doing what little I can to help, for the surgeon himself is poorly.'

'Are there many who are sick?'

'Too many.'

'I could help. If you would let me, Father.'

He patted her hand where it lay on the railing. 'Thank you, my dear, but the crew's quarters are no place for you.'

She looked at his hand on hers, eyes wide as she realized he'd addressed her as a woman. 'He told you, didn't he?'

'It wasn't necessary.'

'When did you find out?'

'I think I always knew. Even the day we sailed out of Brest. There was something about you that reminded me of my niece — the way you tilted your head when you spoke, the way your eyes lit up like a little girl when you saw something that delighted you.'

Léonie was awestruck. 'But why didn't you tell the captain?'

He gazed up at the heavens before he answered, as if seeking advice from above. 'Perhaps I thought you would do him good.'

'Good?' She knew she sounded bitter and turned away to stare out at the dark water, watching the sunset paint the waves crimson as they rose and fell. 'I'm sure I've caused him more harm than good. He seems so weary, almost as though he has aged years since we left Île de France.'

'It's hard to look your best when you have scurvy, my dear.'

'Scurvy!' The very word made her blood curdle. 'What are you talking about?'

He looked quizzically at her. 'Officers are no more immune to the scourge of bad sea air than the men below decks. It afflicts all ships when they spend too long away from the healing breezes of the land. Perhaps God did not intend that we should float about like corks for more than a few weeks at a time. We are not fish, after all.'

Léonie wasn't sure she could follow his conversation.

'But Father, what about the captain? Does he have a tonic? Has the surgeon seen him?'

'The surgeon cannot even heal himself, child. There is no cure except to feel solid earth beneath one's feet once more.'

'No cure?' Her breath caught in her throat as she tried to grasp what he was saying. 'Are you telling me the captain will die?'

'We all die, my child. It is God's way.'

Léonie was in no mood for a theological discussion. 'Father, how bad is he?'

The old priest turned to look at her, as though assessing whether to explain. 'He has terrible pains in his legs and he complains of a rash. Certainly there is fever . . . Perhaps that is enough, or do you wish me to continue?'

'No!' she cried, all her anger against the captain dissolving as she thought of him in such a terrible state. Her eyes widened suddenly. 'His gums! Does he have bleeding gums?'

'It's usually the first symptom. Not a pleasant one. I thought perhaps you would prefer me not to mention — '

'That's it!' She grabbed his arm. 'Father, he came to my cabin and demanded that

354

I open my mouth for his inspection. I did have swollen gums that bled when I used my tooth powder, but they're better now.'

He frowned. 'Are you sure?'

'Of course. It's not hard to know when your gums are sore.'

'No, I mean about them being better?'

'Yes. They're fine.'

Father Cassel looked thoughtful. 'I've never heard of such a thing. There are some, like myself, to whom God has granted an exemption from the scourge.' He smiled at her. 'I have never suffered from it, which is why it so often falls to me to tend the sick and bury the dead. A melancholy reward for an iron constitution, is it not?'

'Perhaps I'm like you, Father, for I feel perfectly well.' Then she thought for a moment. 'So does Christian. I wonder . . .' She turned to him. 'Father, did you bring food with you — enough for the whole voyage?'

'A little cognac, some wine, a few sweetmeats — but those I consumed within a week, for I am easily tempted, despite my best prayers.'

'That's not it. Everyone has wine. Is there nothing else?'

He laughed. 'I do have one little eccentricity that I indulge each day after I've said mass.

François always said it showed the peasant in me!'

'What, Father?'

'My passion. Is that the right word, do you think? Priests are not supposed to have passions of the flesh, are they?'

'But what *is* your passion, Father!'

'Oh . . . well. I have a great fondness for parsley. I grow it in stone pots in my cabin. It thrives, surprisingly, for most herbs we grow on board dislike the sea air even more than we, and simply will not perform. Are you fond of parsley, my dear?'

But Léonie wasn't listening, she was staring at the old priest as an idea blossomed in her head. What if it was the herbs? What if Nounou had somehow known? Léonie racked her brains to recall the words the old nurse had spoken when she'd given her the gift as she was leaving Paris. *Something to ward off the foul air at sea* . . .

'Father, we must talk to the cooks. How much parsley do you have? We need everything you can possibly spare. I will bring my herbs and berries. I'll come to your cabin first — I think it might be unwise for me to go down to the galleys on my own, don't you?' She squeezed his arm. 'But first, I must attend the captain.'

356

19

Léonie tapped softly on the captain's door, a candle in one hand and a ceramic jug in the other. Unlike the last time she had stood here in the dark listening, this time the door opened quickly. The captain's new valet stood there, puffed up with pride in his uniform. For a moment, Léonie thought it was Vincent, but this boy was taller and the uniform a poor fit. She realized he was likely wearing Vincent's clothes, and the notion made her sad.

'*Pardon, monsieur!*' the lad said, barring the way. '*Le capitaine* is sick and will not see anyone except the surgeon.'

'The surgeon is sick, too,' Léonie retorted as she pushed past. 'What is your name?'

'Etienne, *monsieur*.' He was flustered, his short-lived authority as the captain's protector already in ruin. She felt sorry for the lad. 'Do you know which cabin is the chaplain's, Etienne? Good. Then go there and wait for me.'

The boy looked around him, but the captain was asleep and there was no one

357

to countermand the order. He disappeared into the companionway and Léonie closed the door.

She set her lantern on the table beside the bed so the light fell on the pillow. François lay sprawled on the bed, one arm flung above his head.

'Go to the Devil!' he growled.

'So, you're awake.' She examined his face, trying to concentrate on his high colour but instead finding herself riveted by his dark eyes.

'What the hell do you want?' he complained. 'I told the boy I would see no one.'

'You are unwell.'

'Your perspicacity amazes me.'

She ignored the barb. 'I have brought you something that might help.'

'Nothing helps. Go away and leave me in peace.'

Léonie took a cup from his cupboard and busied herself pouring a good measure of tea into it. Being so close to him, and in this room, made her flesh tingle in all the places his hands had explored so intimately. She doubted she would ever forget his touch, his caresses.

'Drink this.' She leaned over and helped him sit up a little, putting the cup to his lips, but he pushed it away.

'What are you trying to do, woman, poison me? You needn't bother — I'll die anyway, most likely. Don't you know there's no cure for scurvy?'

'So I've heard. Except setting your feet on solid ground and breathing the fresh air of the countryside. Well, true as that may be, Captain, this infusion is straight from the countryside and will have to do, for there's little hope of landfall in these next few days. Now drink!'

It felt good to hold the whip hand for once. He gave her a black look, but took a few desultory sips.

'It's foul!' he muttered, sinking back onto the pillow and closing his eyes.

'Not as foul as brackish water laced with vinegar. Do you have any Cognac?'

He waved a hand in the direction of a small cupboard beyond the window and she soon found a bottle, barely touched. Clearly, he was not a drinker, which she found curiously pleasing. She poured a stiff measure of brandy into the decoction and with more force than persuasion, managed to get most of it past his lips.

'Now, sleep,' she ordered. 'I will return later.'

His eyes opened briefly. 'Where are you going?'

She smiled. For once he was in no hurry to throw her out. 'I'm going to use your name in vain,' she answered. Then on impulse, she bent over and kissed his lips before she hurried away.

In Father Cassel's room, she administered some of her infusion to Etienne and then sent him to bed, explaining that the captain would sleep for several hours and that by then she would be able to tend to him herself. The boy was clearly overwhelmed by his suddenly exalted company, since until yesterday he had lived and worked in the stinking confines of the lower decks. He looked barely twelve years old and was clearly exhausted.

Léonie and Father Cassel carried their precious medicaments down to the gun deck where the galleys for both officers and crew were tucked into the space between the foremast and the forward stairs. Despite the late hour, they were able to rouse the cooks, who were confused by the sudden appearance of officers in their domain.

Léonie eyed the burly men with some trepidation, but with a reassuring glance from the chaplain, handed each of them a bag.

'This is for the morning meal. You are to put the berries into a stew for the men and make sure everyone has some.' She gave him the second bag. 'And this is to make tea.'

'Tea! Frenchmen do not drink tea!'

'Perhaps not when there is coffee aplenty and no sickness on board,' she retorted with asperity. 'But until we reach port they will drink it twice a day — if the herbs last that long. It will heal their gums and ease the pains in their legs.'

At first the chefs looked doubtful, but when Father Cassel added a generous bunch of parsley to the offerings, they seemed mollified. It was a very long time since anyone on the ship had tasted fresh greens.

'And don't forget,' Léonie added as they were about to leave. 'Everyone must partake every day — both the well and the sick. Captain's orders!'

She caught the priest's eye as they ducked their heads and passed up the companionway again.

'I'm sure God will forgive you,' he murmured.

Perhaps He would, she thought grimly, but would François?

★ ★ ★

Léonie heard the captain moan when she opened the door. She set her candle on

361

the table, and spoke softly, not wishing to awaken the other officers asleep in nearby cabins.

'Captain! Are you awake?'

He lay on the bed, just a light sheet covering him from the waist down, the skin on his bare chest glistening with sweat. His head turned at the sound of her voice, but his eyes remained closed.

She gazed down at him, embarrassed to be in his room with him in such a state, especially without his consent. Just because she was officially a man didn't make it feel right. Should she wake him?

The candlelight cast deep shadows, outlining the planes and angles of his face and the wild tangle of his hair where he had ripped off his riband and thrown it to the floor. His arms were flung above his head, making him appear strangely vulnerable, like a small boy in sleep. But there was no mistaking the very adult stubble that covered his jaw, or the hard muscle in his shoulders that came from years of life at sea.

Léonie turned away, surprised to feel herself blushing. She poured a bowl of cool water from the pitcher beside the bed and dipped a cloth into it, watching the water trickle through her fingers and wondering what it was that drew her to him. Why

362

was she here? What would he say when he awoke?

She studied his flushed features. He looked anything but peaceful but at least he was asleep. If she were to bathe his face, would he awake? For a moment she hesitated.

He groaned, throwing one arm across his face, then letting it fall on to the pillow once more.

She tried again. 'Capitaine de la Tour!'

No response. With tentative fingers, she lay the damp cloth across his forehead, half expecting him to jolt into wakefulness, but instead, it seemed to calm him, for his murmuring ceased briefly.

'You're not asleep at all, are you, my love?' Léonie whispered as she pressed the cool fabric gently to his brow. He seemed so helpless. It was not a thought she would have associated with him before now. His lashes cast deep shadows on his cheeks, hiding those magnificent indigo eyes that had become so familiar, hiding that spark of vitality and desire that she had come to expect in him.

When his eyes remained closed, she became bolder and began sponging his broad battle-scarred chest with water. He mumbled something about America, but she could make no sense of it. With a trembling finger, she traced the line of the scar that ran from beneath his armpit halfway to his navel. It was an old wound, long-healed, the scar faded in parts.

On impulse, she bent her head and kissed the mark, letting her lips follow its path across his chest. He tasted wonderful, salty and musky and . . .

She froze as his hand gripped her shoulder. 'You're awake,' she whispered, raising her head.

But his eyes were still closed. Only a mangled cry came from his lips. He tossed his head this way and that and then fell silent again, releasing her.

'François de la Tour,' she murmured, sitting on the bed and taking his strong fingers in hers. 'You should be ashamed of yourself, getting into this state? Don't you know the men on this ship put their lives in your hands? What good are you to any of us like this? We need you, Captain.'

His forehead was beaded with sweat again. She rinsed the cloth and pressed it to his skin, feeling its fierce heat soak through the fabric in seconds. It worried her. She was not a doctor, nor even a nurse, yet she knew enough to understand that she must cool him down — and quickly.

She began to work frantically to chill his

skin, washing his arms and his chest, dipping and squeezing the cloth over and over. She looked at his long legs, shrouded by the sheet under which he lay, and wondered if she dare . . .

Gingerly, she lifted the sheet from the foot of the bed, rolling it up toward his midriff, keeping her eyes well averted from the center of his torso. With the cloth as wet as she could make it without dripping on the mattress, she began to sponge his legs, quickly and without looking too closely, though it was the hardest thing she'd ever done. Despite her best intentions, she was all too aware of the strong muscles that filled out his calves, of the well-turned ankles, the powerful muscles of his thighs.

'Aah!' She jumped as she felt a hand close around her wrist. His eyes remained closed, but a faint smile played over his lips.

'Come to me!' he murmured.

Léonie put the cloth on the table and allowed him to pull her gently up the bed. 'François?'

'I've missed you, my love. It's been so long.'

She frowned, feeling his forehead. It was still flame-hot, but his eyes opened briefly and he reached for her. She subsided on to the bed beside him, feeling love war with concern, then all other considerations faded into a tenderness that brought tears to her eyes.

'Oh, François, I thought you wanted no more of me, yet I was so certain you held some feelings for me.' She stroked his face softly, smoothing the creases as his face contorted with sudden, inexplicable anguish. 'It's all right, my love. I know my masquerade offended your sense of what is right, but I was not using you to escape my responsibilities, no matter how it may look.'

He didn't respond except to wrap his bare arms around her, pinning her against him so that the fire from his flesh heated through her shirt and into her breasts. She wanted to study his face, but he held her so tightly she couldn't move, and she found herself relaxing in his embrace, giving herself up to the glorious safety of those encircling arms.

He murmured then, something she couldn't quite catch, but the tone was full of pain, there was no mistaking it. She struggled up, searching his face. His lips moved in soundless speech.

'François?'

His eyes opened, his glance flashing about the cabin for an instant, before his lids closed once more.

She realized with a pang that he was

delirious. He didn't even know she was there, not really. Crushing her disappointment, Léonie disentangled herself and resumed sponging him. If she could just reduce his fever she felt sure he would come back —

'Louisa!' He almost shouted the name, startling Léonie into dropping the wash cloth. 'Louisa, wait . . . I'll be back . . . my son, Louisa . . . ' His voice choked into a sob at the end, but she heard the name fall from his lips as clearly as when he'd spoken it the first time.

Léonie stood as still as a rock staring down at him. A million thoughts whirled in her head until her mind became a swirling fog of pain.

'You're married!' she whispered brokenly. '*Nom de Dieu*, all this time I let myself fall in love with you, despite everything, despite how impossible our situations are — and you were married?'

She realized she was crying and brushed the tears away angrily, throwing the cloth into the wash bowl. Damn this stupid ship, she fumed as she tugged open the door and banged it behind her. For once she cared not a fig if she woke the other officers. Why hadn't someone told her? Why not Father Cassel, at least?

She stormed into her room, kicking off her

367

shoes. How could the old priest tell her that he kept her secret only because he thought she would be good for the captain? Could a priest of God condone an adulterous ocean romance as a pleasant distraction for his friend? What kind of morality was that? Didn't she count at all?

She pulled the riband from her hair and threw it down on the desk, slumping on to the bed. The Léonie of old wanted so much to give in to womanly tears, but the Léonie she had become over the past months refused to indulge her. She lay, eyes dry and achy, her face buried in the pillow, trying to think, trying to make sense of it all.

It wasn't easy. The sword in her heart made breathing painful, robbing her of sensibility. She felt rage and betrayal, but mostly it was directed at herself. How could she have been so foolish as to have embarked on this endless voyage? She had never thought beyond the first day or so, that was obvious, but now, she was ruined. She would go home, eventually, lacking not only her social position, but her self-respect, for she had given that to a man who had played with it, and her, as though she were a common harlot.

'I gave you everything I had left, François de la Tour,' she whispered brokenly into the dark, 'and you betrayed me.'

There is only one consolation in all of this, she thought as she lay there rocking with the steady roll of the ship. You left me my body, though no one else will ever want it. For who would ever believe her to be an innocent young woman after all she had seen and heard in the confines of a navy vessel travelling halfway around the world?

★ ★ ★

Léonie stayed in her cabin for the rest of the week, leaving only to join a few officers well enough to partake of their twice-daily meals in the wardroom. Their numbers were growing, however, and she listened to many jokes about the drinking of herbal tea under captain's orders. And though part of her longed to ask after his health, pride prevented the question from leaving her lips.

She had much to do and applied herself diligently to her illustrations which were much behind as a result of all that had happened since the expedition left French India. And Monsieur Duplessis, the botanist, had not been pleased that she had kept until last the final drawings of the phosphorescent lanternfish, a creature whose decaying remains had smelled out her work area for days while she did her best to capture

369

the fast-fading brilliance of its scales. All that remained were sketches covered with hastily scribbled notes detailing exact hue and tone. But the clear memory of that fish's colours, amongst so many species, was gone.

Twice she had drawn the lanternfish, and twice Duplessis had rejected her work.

When the knock sounded at her door, she was almost glad of the interruption, for she had scarcely spoken to anyone, even Christian, since her last encounter with the captain.

'*Entrez!*'

It was Etienne, the captain's valet. He seemed to have gained confidence in his new role and observed her with a cocky tilt of the head.

'Capitaine de la Tour wishes to see you in his study. Monsieur de Chambois.'

She turned back to her work. She had expected a summons at some time, but the news still created a hammering in her chest.

'*Monsieur?*' he asked, puzzled by her lack of response. 'He is waiting.'

Léonie's pen slipped and a blotch of ink splattered on to her latest sketch. '*Nom de Dieu!*'

'*Pardon?*'

She screwed up the sheet and threw it

toward the waste basket in the corner of the room. Like several before it, it missed. Etienne scurried across to collect the missiles and dispose of them properly.

'Monsieur de Chambois?' he asked again, uncertainly.

'You may inform the captain that I am busy.'

'Sir?'

'You heard me.'

'But — but, sir. How can I tell him you have refused an order?'

'Easily,' she began, then through her mind flashed a warning. *Next time I give you an order, you will obey me instantly*. She had learned that disobedience had a price, and much as she disliked the notion of being alone with him again, the sooner he realized they had nothing to discuss, the better.

She pulled on her black boots and followed the valet from the room.

It was not a pleasant interview. The captain let her stand at attention while he lounged in his chair and looked up at her. The pain of his betrayal was so raw that Léonie could not meet his gaze, for to do so would bring forth the tears she had tried so hard to lock away. I will not feel, she told herself. I was a fool, but I will not give him the satisfaction of seeing how much it hurts.

So she stared over his head through the open window at the silvery wake trailing the ship.

'Pray, *mademoiselle*, enlighten me as to your sudden elevation aboard my ship,' he asked quietly, his tone sending a tremor through her.

'I don't comprehend your meaning, Captain.'

'I think you do. If I am not greatly mistaken, did you not promise to take my name in vain a few nights hence?'

'You were delirious, sir.'

'Don't play games with me, young lady. I always win.'

She glanced at him, shocked by the passion and anger she encountered in his dark eyes. They speared her like a butterfly, holding her helplessly while he searched for the truth. Léonie couldn't breathe. This was worse than she had imagined. Much worse.

'Something has happened,' he said at last. 'Since you forced some of your witch's brew into me and pranced away to subvert my ship under my very nose, you have been avoiding me.'

She turned away, though he hadn't given her leave to move, and pretended to examine the brass barometer that hung from a peg on his wall. 'I haven't the least idea what you are talking about.'

He moved so quickly that she gasped as his hand grabbed her shoulders and spun her around to face him.

'Don't trifle with me, Léonie. I was not so out of my mind with fever that I did not feel your kiss. How is it that one day you will nurse me like a babe and the next you cannot even meet my eyes?'

'I did not kiss you!' she responded hotly, feeling traitorous tears threaten. She blinked them back, squirming to release her hands from his vice-like grip. He pressed her to the wall, the warmth of his body firing her imagination with memories she had tried valiantly to suppress. She cursed herself for the weakness of character that made her blood flow with passion for his touch while her mind revolted at the very thought of being embraced by another woman's husband.

'Not only did you kiss me, but you want to kiss me now,' he said, lowering his mouth to within an inch of hers.

'You flatter yourself, Captain,' she replied breathlessly. 'I have no such desire.'

His breath fanned her cheek as he whispered in her ear, 'You little fool. I wasn't really asleep, you know.'

Léonie stiffened. 'Clearly my medicinal infusion has relieved your fever but addled your brain, sir. Kindly release me.'

He stepped back as if stung, his eyes black with anger. '*Pardon, mamselle,* I had forgotten you were so practised at deceit. How foolish of me to expect any constancy in your feelings.'

'Constancy!' How could he use such a word, when he himself was nothing but a — a common philanderer? Léonie rubbed her wrists and cast him a venomous look. 'My feelings are my concern, Capitaine de la Tour. As you have enjoyed pointing out to me many times recently, I am on your vessel under sufferance. Pray inform me when I may relieve you of this burden and find a ship returning to France.'

He turned sharply away, staring out the window with his back to her. When he spoke, his voice was edged with flint. 'We shall make landfall in Batavia within two days. You'll leave the expedition there. I will of course make arrangements for your passage home.'

'That will not be necessary.'

'Nevertheless, it will be done.' He turned to her, his expression unrelenting. 'I made a promise to the king when I received my orders that I would see you home in one piece. It galls me enough that I cannot do that, but I will do my utmost to ensure your return is a safe and swift one.'

Léonie tilted her head. 'Clearly, it was not I you were asked to concern yourself with, Captain. No doubt you were asked to look out for my brother, and since he is not here, you owe me nothing whatsoever. I do not require your patronage.'

He gave a sardonic laugh. 'It is scarcely that, *mamselle*. And you may rail at me and argue your independence until you've used your last breath, but I shall still see you safely aboard a ship — of my choosing.'

'And if I refuse?' His arrogance was unspeakable!

He reached out one hand and tipped up her chin with his fingers. 'Then I will carry you on board myself.'

'You wouldn't dare!'

He made no reply beyond the softest of laughs, and Léonie felt a frisson of fear run through her. She rubbed her hands against the sides of her breeches. 'May I go now?'

'Did you give orders in my name to the galley staff, Enseigne Chambois?'

His abrupt return to the reason for this interview, caught Léonie unprepared. 'Only in everyone's best interests.'

'Luckily for you.' He sat back in his

chair. 'Unfortunately, you have made me a source of amusement among the *matelots*, no less among the officers. It appears I am now considered something of a wizard. Would that I could lay the blame upon a red-headed witch of my acquaintance, don't you think?'

'Sir?' What was he talking about?

'Your infusion. It appears to have worked wonders among the men. There are but few cases of scurvy left, and all of them improving by the day. And as you see, I am myself quite restored.'

Léonie sent him a self-satisfied smile, but said nothing.

'Perhaps you'd care to divulge the recipe? It is still many months before our return to France.'

'I can't.'

'Ah,' he replied enigmatically. 'Don't tell me — it's a secret. You're so good at those.'

Léonie glated at him. 'I was not party to its concoction, sir. It was a gift from Nounou.'

'Let me see, Nounou. Wasn't she your wet nurse?'

If he was trying to make her feel small, Léonie thought, he was doing a wonderful job. But she wouldn't let him see it hurt.

'She made it for my brother, of course, but when she gave it to me in his stead, she told me it was . . . ' she hesitated, 'an English remedy.' He looked dubious. 'But I think I know most of the ingredients. I suppose I could make a list.'

'Pray do. My magic will be quite spoiled without it.' He leaned back in his chair, linking his hands behind his head. Léonie didn't altogether trust the glint in his eye. 'I have one final request,' he said at length. 'Do you think that, in the remaining hours until our arrival in the East Indies, you could refrain from impersonating your commanding officer?'

She looked down, abashed. 'Yes, sir.'

'I am relieved to hear it. Now kindly return to your cabin. You are to see no one except myself, my valet or Lieutenant Lavelle until we make landfall, is that clear?'

'No!' She couldn't bear the thought of being imprisoned in her room again, but his expression showed he would brook no argument. 'Why are you doing this to me?'

'Because I am trying to save your brother's neck, *mamselle*. If you are known to be hale and hearty on reaching Batavia, how am I to write convincingly in my log that I have offloaded you among the sick?'

'Oh. I had not thought of that.'

'But then clarity of thought has not been of paramount importance to you, during our acquaintance, has it, *mamselle*?' Léonie bit back a stinging retort, for despite his sarcasm she was deeply grateful for the efforts he was making to save her reputation.

He went on blithely, 'Your meals will be brought to you by Etienne, and you are to behave as though you're on your last legs whenever he comes, for I cannot vouch for the lad's silence as yet.'

'He is not Vincent,' she said sadly, thinking of the boy they had both been so fond of.

His eyes darkened as their eyes met, and she knew he also was remembering. 'No,' he replied softly, 'he is not Vincent.'

She returned to her cabin, her earlier anger replaced by a painful sadness. For though she knew the captain belonged to another woman, she felt there was something between them, an understanding, that defied it. What had happened to her, she wondered, that despite the unbridgeable gulf separating their backgrounds, she had given her heart to him for safekeeping? Her feelings for him had crept over her with such stealth that she had been powerless to resist.

When Léonie left France last spring, her future had been full of promise and she'd been nearly giddy with the possibilities. Now, only bleak duty remained to accompany the emptiness in her heart. She closed the door of her room and prepared herself reluctantly for the charade of her sick bed, pulling off her boots and breeches and exchanging her chemise for a simple white nightshirt.

20

The *Aurélie* sailed past the soaring volcano of Krakatoa and into the Dutch trading post of Batavia on September 25th. Léonie watched from the open window of her cabin as the anchors were released and the frigate fired a respectable twenty-one-gun salute. From the fort that dominated the walled town, came the return volley and within minutes the longboats were ferrying the first boatloads of men ashore.

She watched with mixed emotions, glad that the eventful voyage from India was over despite the dismal knowledge that this was the end of her adventure.

Christian came in, dressed in his naval uniform.

'I expected you would be first ashore,' she said, smiling at his obvious excitement.

'I'm going soon.' He threw his hat on the bed and picked her up bodily, swinging her around in a great bear hug.

'Christian! Put me down! Is that any way to behave to one of His Majesty's officers?'

'Absolutely.'

'What are you looking so smug about?' she asked, as he set her back on her feet. She straightened her cravat, wishing she could rip it off altogether, for the day was insufferably hot and humid.

'I've just seen Captain de la Tour.'

Her heartbeat quickened at the sound of his name. 'And?'

'And, my sweet, he says I am forgiven.' He ran a hand through his blond hair, dislodging a lock from the riband. 'Apparently, I brought the ship into Batavia days earlier than he'd expected and he's decided to keep me. In fact,' he added, with a gleam in his eyes, 'he's promoted me to chief navigator.'

'Christian! That's wonderful!' She hugged him, relieved that his naval record would be undamaged by her escapade after all. Then as she tucked the stray lock of hair back into his riband for him, she fell to wondering how she and her twin brother would fare, and turned away.

'Léonie?' His brows came together in sudden concern. 'Are you wondering what the captain plans for you?'

'Did he tell you?'

He shook his head. 'He asked me if I would be willing to cover for you.'

Her eyes narrowed. 'In what manner?'

'He thought perhaps I might make an honest woman of you and pretend the whole thing was nothing but an elaborate elopement.' He laughed.

'*Imbécile!*'

Christian's eyebrows rose. 'I hope you mean the captain. I assured him that you wouldn't have me if I were your last hope on earth.'

'Now *you* are being an imbecile, Christian. Didn't you tell him we grew up together?'

'That we were like this.' He held up two crossed fingers. 'I said that even if I had no objection to marrying a woman who fights with swords and pistols, you were as close to me as a sister. It would never do.'

'*Hein.*' She wasn't sure if she liked such an explanation, but at least it had served its purpose. 'So what will he do with me? Will I be arrested when I return to France?'

'What purpose would that serve, pray?'

She pressed her hands together, turning to stare out the window at the brightly coloured fishing boats sailing past. 'Revenge,' she whispered.

'Hardly the captain's way. And whatever you think, he's quite fond of you, you know.'

Fond? Léonie knew who he really cared about. Her name was Louisa and she had a son. Perhaps he looked just like his father, with the same indigo eyes and black locks. What was his name? she wondered.

'He'll be fair, Léonie. He's overcome most of his outrage by now and he's not a man to hold a grudge — after all, your medicine made him a hero. The crew have talked of nothing else and every one of them is willing to continue with the expedition. I doubt a single man will desert.'

She didn't want to think about François any more, so she changed the subject. 'Christian, I am going to be transferred to the Dutch hospital here, until the captain arranges my passage home. As I will have no use for my things, I wondered whether you might offer my boots to Etienne? I think his feet are about my size.'

'Oh, Léonie, don't cry.' He wrapped an arm around her, but she moved away.

'I never cry. Here,' she said with a sniff, 'you'd better have these.' She handed him Jean-Michel's shaving brush and blade. 'They haven't been used.'

'I didn't suppose they had.' He looked

down at the items and smiled. 'You did so well, Léonie. I never thought you'd manage it, you know. I was amazed when you rejoined the ship in Tenerife, let alone in Africa. And then I thought you liked Angélique's company so much that you might stay awhile in the Île de France. I underestimated you. Just like always.'

She touched his face with her fingers, then reached up to kiss his cheek. 'As always, *mon ami*,' she replied sadly. 'I'll tell Jean-Michel of your success. He'll be very proud. And soon we will all be together again.'

He hugged her tightly and she knew it could very well be the last time she would see him alive. Who knew if the expedition would ever return to France, or if it did, whether he himself would survive the journey? So many perils, so much sickness . . .

'*Adieu*, Christian,' she murmured, holding back the tears with all her might.

'Chin up, my sweet. I'll keep an eye on your captain, don't worry. He'll need someone to watch his back now you're gone.' Then he grabbed his hat, sent her a mock salute, and left.

She wiped her eyes on her sleeve and leaned out the window again, watching for Christian. The longboats were back, once more reloading, and she saw his tall figure descend the ladder and jump lightly into one of the rocking vessels. It made her heart glad to see the spring in his step, for he had lost so much weight from worry and bad food these past days that his frock-coat fairly hung from his shoulders.

She looked down at her own frame, lighter by many pounds since Pondicherry. Perhaps it was as well she was to leave the expedition here, since her shape had become willowy rather than wiry. She waved out the window at Christian, who waved back briefly and then was lost among the crowd of men.

She turned away from the window and began tidying the small cabin that had become her home, though little remained to be attended to. She propped the final painting of the lanternfish against her ink bottle and examined it carefully. It was good, perhaps the best zoological illustration she had done. She only hoped it would satisfy Monsieur Duplessis.

By early afternoon, there was nothing left to do and she spent her time staring out the window, watching the high pronged fishing boats and their dark-skinned crews coming and going in the harbour. The heat had lessened with the advent of a sprightly breeze, but finally, tired of waiting in the near-deserted ship, she lay down on her bunk and dozed.

At four, there was a sharp knock on her door.

'*Entrez!*' She jumped up, smoothing her breeches with her sticky palms. Her heart thumped sharply as François let himself in.

'*Bonjour, Capitaine.*'

He dropped a package wrapped in brown paper on the bedside table and stood for a moment letting his eyes travel up and down her figure. 'You have grown thin, *mamselle.*'

'I believe we all have, sir.' She was more comfortable addressing him formally. After all, he was still her captain, for a few more hours at least.

'Well, you will be out of here soon and can enjoy a good fresh meal. My apologies for making you wait so long, but I thought it best if most of the crew were ashore before you.'

'May I — May I know your intentions for me, Captain?'

'You leave Batavia in two days.'

'Two days!' She was aghast. 'But Captain, we have been at sea for two *months*. Surely I may catch my breath before — '

'I have obtained a passage for you aboard a Dutch schooner, the *Nederburgh*. It leaves on Friday. Captain Van Kalken is an old friend. He owes me a favour.'

'I don't speak Dutch.'

'All the better,' he replied caustically, giving her a hard look. 'At least if you can't talk, you will keep your own counsel. It would be unfortunate if anyone aboard that ship were to be in any way suspicious of your story.'

Léonie sat back on the edge of the bed. Her legs felt wobbly. 'What have you told them?'

'All about you,' he said with a wry smile. He perched on her desk and picked up the lanternfish sketch. 'That your name is Michelle Thouars, that you became separated from your family *en route* from China to Europe — due to your severe illness — and that — '

'What illness have you ascribed to this person, Captain?'

He set the drawing down again. 'This is good. Duplessis will be pleased. He will miss you. Illness? Aah, I believe I said that you had the ague. There's a lot of that here, due to the malarial swamps. Van Kalken was most solicitous.'

'I trust I am sufficiently recovered to sail?'

'So I advised him.' He crossed to the head

of the bed and retrieved the parcel. 'You'll need this.' He looked at her quizzically. 'I'm not sure I shall ever forget how you look in those breeches, *mamselle*, but I think it should be the last time you wear them. Such games may have passed the time when you were a child, but I think they get you in a good deal too much trouble now, don't you?'

She blushed, bending her head over the package and occupying her shaky fingers in trying to undo the string.

'Allow me.' He snapped the string with a tug of his hands and the paper opened.

'What on earth . . . ?' Léonie stared at the extraordinary dress as she lifted it from the wrapper. 'Captain, you have bought me a gown!' She didn't know what to say, for she was both touched that he should think of it, and horrified by what she saw. It was livid pink, decorated with ludicrously deep ruffles of orange silk. The échelle bodice was laced at the back with black satin.

She stood up, holding the gown against her. It was extremely revealing and —

'Captain! This is a . . . a . . . ' She felt herself turn white with anger. 'This is a *dancer's* dress.'

'Not quite,' he quipped. 'Actually, I bought it from a *madame* in the market.'

'In her boudoir, more likely!' She threw the thing down on the bed. 'You don't waste much time once you go ashore, do you, Captain?'

'I was in a hurry.'

'So I perceive, but if you have any notions of my wearing such an offensive garment, kindly abandon them. I assure you, even a *petite bourgeoise* like Michelle Toussaint — '

'Thouars.'

'I prefer Toussaint.'

'Perhaps. It hardly describes you, though.'

She glared at him. 'As I was saying, even one such as she would not be seen in such a garment.'

He shrugged. 'It's all I could obtain at such short notice. Shall I help you?'

'No!'

He propped himself on the desk once more, observing her with faint amusement. '*Mamselle*, I believe I have seen every part of you at least once — '

'Kindly do not remind me,' she answered stiffly. How dare he rub that in her face, as if his overbearance wasn't enough of a trial already?

He sighed. 'Léonie, I am sorry you dislike the dress so much, but I had to find something that I could use to get you to the *Nederburgh*. I have taken the liberty

388

of having a lady's . . . requirements sent on board directly in your name. I thought it would simplify your lack of luggage. Your maid — I have engaged a young Irish girl — will be aboard tonight. Her name is Mary-Kate O'Halloran and she speaks very little French, though she can manage some Dutch, I believe.'

Wonderful! Léonie thought, staring at him in defeat. 'So I am to travel for months aboard a ship full of Dutchmen with an English-speaking maid. Are you doing this deliberately to punish me, sir?'

He seemed amused and Léonie felt the greatest urge to kick him. 'Not at all. I thought the rest and meditation would do you good.'

'And what of the Dutch hospital? You gave me to understand that I — that Jean-Michel would be sent there.'

'You are on their books as having been transferred to a sanatorium in the hills, a few miles from the city. The air is ideal for those recuperating from long spells at sea, so I'm told. Jean-Michel will no doubt find his way back to France in due course and be reunited with his family.'

Léonie felt a giant weight lift from her heart. Disregarding her determination not to get too close to him, she crossed the cabin and hugged the captain.

'Thank you, sir. Does this mean there will be nothing in your report to the Ministère de la Marine?'

'Nothing beyond what I have just described,' he answered, smiling down at her excitement. 'However, it is unfortunate that the experience will leave Monsieur Chambois unfit for further service in His Majesty's Navy.'

Her face fell. 'I have ruined his career, then, after all.'

'You mustn't blame yourself,' he said softly. 'You did what you thought was best for his sake, even if it was foolhardy. Now you must carry out your part in his return to France. It will be harder than you think, my dear.'

She stared up at him, his handsome face softened by the golden light from the window, and wished he wouldn't be so kind. It was easier when he was yelling at her.

'Thank you.'

'Don't thank me. Put on the dress and let's get out of here. I have an appointment with a Dutch couturier that you need to keep — unless you wish me to obtain some further gowns on your behalf in the marketplace?'

'No!' She picked up the dress and stared at it balefully. 'Perhaps if I removed this' — she ripped a large orange flounce from the bodice — 'and this' — she tore the black lace from the décollete neckline — 'it would be passable. Horrible, but passable. Did you think to obtain a fichu, Captain?'

'There are some things in the package still,' he replied, seemingly amused by her attack on the garment.

She looked in the discarded brown paper and found petticoats, a fob cap and a length of white muslin. 'This will have to do.' She looked up at him expectantly.

'Ah, I forgot. Now you are learning to be a lady again, you wish to practise modesty.' He stood up and turned his back.

'This robe will make me anything but a lady, sir, and I would prefer you to leave the room.'

'I promise not to peek,' he answered. She could hear the amusement in his voice.

Since he was determined not to go, she stripped off quickly and struggled into the petticoat and gown. It was tight in the waist and very loose in the bust. Clearly, months at sea wearing nothing more restrictive than a man's chemise had altered her curves. Not that she would ever have filled the bodice. She reached around to tighten the stays.

'Problem, *mamselle*?' came the softly mocking question.

'You know there is!' she snapped.

He turned around, his eyes alight with laughter.

'You chose this abomination on purpose, didn't you?' she accused him.

'Actually, I didn't. But perhaps I might help?'

She knew she was blushing to her very roots, but she held her head high and turned her back, ignoring his glance where it fell on the low neckline, even more exposed than intended since her removal of the offensive lace.

She felt his hands pulling the cord through the stays and took a deep breath as he tugged the gown in at the waist.

'That's not too tight?' he asked.

'No — no,' she said, trying to hold her breath lest she explode. He tightened the laces to the top and tied them. Léonie had never been dressed by anyone but an experienced lady's maid and to have a man's hands on her body in such a way was strangely arousing. She stepped away quickly when he had finished, and picked up the fichu, draping it around her shoulders and tucking it into the bodice so that it hid most of her exposed breast and filled out the dress a little as well.

'Quite an improvement,' he murmured, then frowned as he observed her bare feet.

392

'I seem to have overlooked a small detail.'

'I can't go without shoes.'

She slipped on her navy shoes and fluffed the skirt out to cover them.

'It will do for now,' he said, 'but you must wear the cap. If someone sees your hair when you are leaving the ship, you will be recognized for certain.'

Léonie pulled off her riband and wound the hair up in a loose roll on her head, easing the cap over it and letting the lacy brim fall around her face.

She had just tucked the last tendril into place when there was a quick knock on the door, which opened almost immediately. André de Montauban, the ship's surgeon, stood there. His startled glance shot from Léonie to the captain and he turned beet red.

Léonie looked away, her heart pounding.

'Oh, *pardon*, Monsieur le Capitaine!' the ageing doctor flubbered. 'I was in search of young Chambois. I hear he is to be sent to the Dutch hospital and I wished to examine him.'

Léonie, who had been watching him surreptitiously, suddenly realized that Jean-Michel's uniform lay on the bed. She gently sat on it, smoothing out her skirts to cover the articles.

'Chambois is gone already, *mon vieux*,' François replied. 'He won't be joining the ship again, sadly. I believe the Dutch doctors are sending him to the hills for rest and clean air.'

'Very wise, very wise.' He looked at Léonie, then back at the captain, a knowing grin on his face. 'You never cease with your surprises, Captain, I do declare. Don't waste much time, do you, eh?'

But François was herding him out the door. He leaned his back on it when it was closed, his shoulders shaking with laughter.

'Captain!' Léonie reproved him, for she did not find it in the least funny.

'I'm sorry.' He laughed again, then spread his hands in defeat. 'The old boy was quite fooled. You'll do, Léonie. That ensemble may not be quite what your heart desires, but if it'll convince Montauban, it'll suffice well enough. Let's go ashore and get that dressmaker's fingers busy.'

Léonie received some exceedingly curious stares from the *matelots* who rowed the longboat to the walled city, but they appeared not to recognize her and she kept her eyes downcast, allowing the cap to shadow her face.

The residence of the dressmaker stood in a narrow cobbled street east of the great

394

Kasteel. The woman, who introduced herself as Madame van der Nuyt, quickly covered her shock at Léonie's attire and got busy with her assistant. Fortunately the woman spoke a few words of French and while her fashion sense was far more utilitarian than stylish, anything was preferable to that ridiculous pink gown.

'*Mademoiselle* cannot wear this pink . . . ensemble,' she said emphatically when the measuring and selection of fabrics was complete. 'It is not at all proper.'

Léonie cast the captain an 'I told you so' glance. He shrugged.

'But I have nothing else,' she said to the woman.

'Nothing?'

'I was — I was robbed, *madame*.' She cast her eyes down, trying her best to blush. 'And — much worse . . . ' She wiped an imaginary tear from her eye, causing the dressmaker to tut-tut effusively.

'But how terrible! Come, child,' she said emphatically. 'You shall have something of my daughter. I fetch you to it. You wait here please, *Capitaine*.' And she bustled away. Léonie looked back at the captain as she followed the woman from the room, casting him a triumphant little grin.

The woman produced two dresses, both

very modest creations in light cotton. 'You choose, please,' Madame van der Nuyt said, holding them up.

Léonie was touched. 'I would be very happy to borrow a gown until mine are ready,' she said. 'The blue, perhaps?' Madame van der Nuyt beamed and helped her change. Léonie gave her the pink and orange monstrosity to dispose of.

When they returned Léonie felt François' appraisal, and turned around so he could survey the result.

'What do you think, Captain?'

'Most suitable.' In a low voice that only she could hear, he whispered, 'I think it becomes you far more than breeches, my dear.'

Then he bowed to the woman and took up his hat. 'Have the gowns ready by tomorrow evening, *s'il vous plaît, madame*.'

The woman nodded in a no-nonsense way, though Léonie privately wondered how she would manage it in so short a time.

As François helped her into the carriage he had hired, she said, 'No doubt you have paid her well that she will make such haste.'

His face was impassive as he signalled the driver. 'It is taken care of.'

'François, it is one thing for you to arrange everything for me, but I can pay my own expenses.' Then she realized how very little money she actually had left. 'That is — I will ensure that you are reimbursed, if you will give me an account of your expenditures.'

'That's not necessary.'

'But I insist! Surely it is enough that I must allow you to dictate my every move. Pray allow me the dignity of compensating you for your trouble.'

His eyes grew distant and his jaw tilted. He turned, flicking aside the curtain to stare out at the narrow streets. 'We are almost there. We won't discuss it further.'

Léonie felt something snap inside. '*I* will discuss it, sir, and I believe you will do me the honour of listening.'

'I'll do no such thing, *mamselle*. I made a promise to look after you and I intend to do just that. Please don't make it any more difficult than you already have. I shall dine with you this evening and tomorrow I shall see you on board the *Nederburgh*.' He leaned back in the seat and shut his eyes. 'Then perhaps I can be rid of you. I am a sailor, not a nursemaid.'

Léonie's outburst of rage came just a split second before her hand flew at him, slapping him across the cheek. She felt his iron grip snatch her wrist and gasped at both her own audacity and the speed with which he moved.

'I advise you to control your temper, *mamselle*, before I lose mine.'

He pushed her roughly back against the seat, his eyes glittering. Then he reached in his pocket and withdrew a small leather purse. 'Here! This is yours.'

She untied the string with shaking fingers and poured the gold Louis on to her hand. Though the money was all that she could possibly require to get her back to France, she felt soiled by the gift. She tipped them back into the bag and threw it on the seat beside him. 'I don't want your money,' she said, just barely holding the tears at bay. How could he insult her so? Had she not suffered enough, losing her heart to this man when he was already given to another? Why did he have to treat her with such contempt?

'You little fool,' he growled, picking up the purse and forcing it into her hands. 'This is your navy pay! I think you've earned it, even though I would gladly have strangled you on half a dozen occasions.'

Tears filled her eyes as she stared down at the money. 'I'm sorry,' she mumbled, sniffing. She took the kerchief he proffered and blew her nose.

'Better?'

'Much, thank you.' She looked up. All

the anger on his face was gone, replaced by a softness that took her breath away. She was helpless as he reached out, taking her shoulders in his hands and pulling her gently into his lap. He smelled of sandalwood and sea air, and filled her with sweet longing. She turned her face up to him and closed her eyes as his lips met hers, brushing them softly with feathery kisses. She heard herself give a little moan and felt his touch become more urgent, more demanding. Deep inside, Léonie felt herself begin to melt with liquid heat and she clung to him, entwining her hands around his shoulders and neck, pulling him to her as though she were drowning. He whispered her name against her mouth, then his lips plundered hers once more, exploring and delving with a passion that set fire to every inch of her body.

'François, François,' she cried, forcing a little space between them, but his lips only moved to the sensitive spot beneath her ear, and she closed her eyes in ecstasy. This was like nothing she had ever felt before, nothing she had ever been able to imagine. At that moment Léonie knew she wanted François de la Tour. More than that, she knew she wanted to give herself to him, body and soul.

'Stop!' Tears stung her eyes as she realized

what she had just admitted to herself. He belonged to Louisa. He belonged to his son. She pushed herself away from him, back to the opposite bench.

'Dammit, woman,' he muttered. 'What troubles you now?'

'You can't . . . you mustn't.' She wiped her eyes on his kerchief, which lay on the seat beside her. 'I — I am leaving tomorrow, remember? Who knows if I will ever see you again? Who can say whether I — or you — will ever live to see France again?'

'Léonie, don't!' He pulled her into his arms again, crushing her to his chest. 'You mustn't upset yourself. The future holds what it holds, close to itself. We do no good trying to outguess our own fate. If we could see into the future it would only drive us to madness.'

'Then I must be mad. For I can see too much already.'

He turned her face up and looked into her eyes. 'What do you see?'

'If I were to tell you that, Captain, I would endanger your expedition — if your theory is correct.'

'I'll risk it.'

She shook her head, for the black images that she saw in her own future were not ones she wished to speak aloud. She stared out the window as the carriage approached the Kasteel, then gasped as she spied a tall ship sailing into the harbour. 'Captain, look!'

Way out in the bay, dropping anchor not fifty yards from where the *Aurélie* rested on the blue waters, was their little supply ship, the *Mousquetaire*.

'Dear God,' François whispered as he took in the sight. 'So she didn't go to the bottom after all.'

He called the coachman to stop and Léonie followed him into the late sunshine, shading her eyes to watch the ship fire its guns in salute. She couldn't help feeling a small upwelling of hope. It seemed so like an omen.

21

François and Léonie dined in private that evening and, though he had hoped for more, he found her mood strangely distant and measured. She was spending the night in a Dutch inn on the outskirts of the walled city, a modest establishment as befitted a bourgeoise of limited means, and away from danger of encountering anyone who knew her from the *Aurélie*.

They ate capons and fresh pork, with an abundance of fresh greens that seemed even more inviting than the farm-fresh meats. And there were many different fishes from both the sea and the rivers, flavoured with exotic spices that in Europe only the rich could afford. It was a companionable enough meal, yet there was an undercurrent of tension. After the sweetmeats and coffee had been served, François passed her a letter, sealed with his mark.

'This will simplify your return to France,' he explained. 'It is addressed to the Mother Superior at the convent of Sainte-Agnès in Bruges.'

'I am going to Flanders?'

'For a few days only, *en route* from Holland to Paris. The nuns will look after you.'

'May I know its contents?'

'No.'

Their eyes met across the candle that flickered on the table. Léonie tried to judge his determination from his gaze, for she itched to know what he had written. Finally she looked down. 'Ah well,' she sighed. 'No doubt I would only hear ill of myself.'

He chuckled. 'Do I detect that you are mellowing at last, *mamselle*?'

'Not at all,' she retorted stiffly. 'But you may credit me with the intelligence to know when I have met my match.'

His eyes softened. 'Have I been such an ogre?'

You have been too many things, she thought, and I have loved them all. Then she thought of his deceit and her eyes clouded with pain. She jumped as he reached across the table. His large hand enveloped hers and she pulled back as if burned.

François watched her rummage in a small reticule she had with her, wondering how such a beautiful woman could ever have passed herself off as a man in front of his very nose. It seemed incredible now when he looked at her in the candlelight, her vibrant hair like a flame as it curled softly around her face. Her skin was smooth and golden from the sun, yet so obviously feminine, and the curves of her slender body made his palms itch. He tried to remember her as Jean-Michel, the argumentative young *enseigne*, but it was as though they were two separate creatures, one he admired, the other he desired. Or was it more than desire?

'I want you to have this, Captain. I didn't know if I should give it to you, but since it means nothing to anyone else — '

'It's beautiful!' He gazed at the small

watercolour with genuine delight.

'I don't know if you recall — '

'Of course I do. It's that little valley where we went horse riding on the Île de France.' He looked up, seeing her uncertainty and wondering that she could display such diffidence. 'It's a fine sketch. May I keep it?'

'I meant for you to have it.' She was toying with her wineglass, avoiding him. 'I hope you won't consider it an impertinence.'

'Impertinence be damned! Léonie, what has put you in this strange mood? You know I am delighted to have such an elegant reminder of — ' He stopped. Reminder of the time before she was really herself, the time she gave up her disguise as a man to take on the disguise of another woman. 'I'm so stupid.' he murmured, rubbing her chilled fingers in his. 'I am still greatly fond of *la belle Hélène*, you know. Even if she wasn't quite real on the surface, underneath — '

'Stop! Please, Captain, you are beginning to make me regret my decision to give you the drawing. I had it in my belongings, and simply thought you might enjoy it. Please don't take it to mean more than that.'

His eyes narrowed and he sat back in his chair, lifting his coffee cup to his lips and sipping thoughtfully as he regarded her. 'I'll do my best.' Damn, why was the woman so twitchy?

He watched her pick a ripe mango from the huge dish of fruit the innkeeper's wife had set before them. She seemed unsure what to do with it, finally cutting it in half with her knife.

'Cut out the stone,' he said, amused by her innocence. It was hard to believe this was the same person who had worn the uniform of a French officer only hours before, let alone one who had wielded a sword like a fiend. She looked up and their eyes met for an instant, hers dove-grey in the soft candlelight. Then she bent her head over her plate and began to scoop out some of the aromatic yellow flesh with a silver spoon.

'Do you like it?'

She nodded. 'What is it?'

'Mango. It's a pity they don't keep, or we could make quite a stir in Paris with them, don't you think?'

He watched as she popped another morsel into her small pink mouth, giving him an overwhelming urge to reach across the table and plunder the sweet fruit from right between her lips. He coughed and picked up his brandy glass instead, concentrating on the swirling cognac in the glass, making it twist and turn and catch the light. He downed it in a single gulp.

'Captain!' Her tone was reproving. 'You are drinking like a *matelot* let loose on the town.'

He smiled wryly. 'Whatever will I do without you as my conscience, *Vicomtesse*? By the time I reach France again I shall have lost all vestige of civilization.'

'Fiddle!' she answered. 'You'll be much better off without a woman bringing bad luck to your expedition.'

'*Touché*,' he replied wryly. 'Though I think you brought the *Aurélie* more good than bad.'

That caught her attention. She set down her spoon and wiped her fingers on her serviette. 'Do you think I did? I should like to think I was able to make some contribution, no matter how small, as recompense for the trouble I caused.'

'Your contribution was considerable, *mamselle*. You have furnished some of the finest sketches of plants and animals that I have ever seen on a voyage, and you avenged young Vincent as though you were the Devil incarnate. Not forgetting your magic brew that got us all here alive in the face of scurvy. I would call that a worthwhile contribution, wouldn't you?'

'Do you think the *Nederburgh* will call in at Port-Louis?'

Her abrupt change of tack confused him for a moment. 'I don't know. They may wish to trade there, or replenish supplies. Why do you ask?'

'I promised the children I would bring them back to France. They have no one. I could give them work, an education, some chance in life.'

'If you like, I will pass your request on to Captain Van Kalken.'

She looked down again. Clearly she was not satisfied. 'If . . . if the Dutch captain refuses my request, I don't know — '

'Are you needling me into bringing them on the *Aurélie*?' he asked. 'You should know by now my attitude to women aboard ship.'

Her lip trembled and he cursed himself silently. He couldn't cope with her in tears, and she probably knew it, but damn, he couldn't help himself.

'All right, *mamselle*! If Van Kalken won't call there, I'll find a corner for them.' He shook his head, wondering how he managed to get himself into these messes.

'Thank you, sir.'

'Don't look at me like that. It's nothing. Think no more about it.' I shall certainly try not to, he thought, looking down at his empty glass and wondering whether to fill it again. There was a knock at the door. The innkeeper came in, a rotund man well on in years, with an apron tied around his waist.

'Well, man?'

'Sir, I beg your pardon, but there's a message — '

François took the letter and waved the man away. He broke the seal.

'What is it?' Léonie asked.

'A piece of good fortune. I believe. It seems there is an English vessel in the harbour, recently arrived from the Pacific under the command of a Captain Hargest. He has news of Barron's expedition.'

'What news?'

He scanned the page quickly. 'It says little here. Just that there have been natives in the Admiralty Islands seen wearing French naval uniforms, and some talk of a ship broken up in a storm.' He stopped, bowing his head at the thought of so trite an end to such a brave explorer. 'Poor — ' He looked up, red-faced. 'I beg your pardon, *mamselle*. What I meant was, it's a sad way to end so illustrious a career, losing your ship to a storm and then having the natives pick the clothes off your corpse — or worse.'

He saw Léonie shudder, and wished he'd been more circumspect. Then he tucked the letter into his breast pocket. 'I'm afraid I must take my leave. I must speak with Captain Hargest as soon as possible, and then consult with the captain of the *Mousquetaire*. But I will return tomorrow to see you aboard the *Nederburgh*. Meanwhile, I suggest you get some sleep on dry land. It will be a while before you enjoy such a novelty again.'

'Indeed, sir,' she replied rather stiffly. 'At least I will have no need to regain my sea legs, for the earth seems to rock and sway constantly for all its solidity.'

He laughed. 'It takes many days to recover one's equilibrium.' He bent low over her hand, kissing her fingers but not trusting himself to do more. He had already played with her emotions too much, feasting on the glorious feel of her arms about his neck and the taste of her sun-ripe mouth. He knew if he had another taste of that forbidden fruit, he would have to have more. And she was not the sort of woman he would consider taking to his bed and then walking away from. No, if he did not keep his head he would be back where he started — responsible for a woman but without the power to protect her. He had nothing to offer one such as the *vicomtesse*, and she needed to know that. As for himself, he thought as he jumped into the waiting carriage, he wouldn't be safe until the *Nederburgh* had departed Batavia and had taken Léonie de Chambois with it.

★ ★ ★

Léonie slept badly, then as dawn crept into the sky, fell deeply asleep. When she finally awoke it was nearly ten and Madame van der Nuyt's messenger had already delivered three gowns to her rooms. She bathed quickly then chose a soft apple-green gown *à l'anglaise* with elbow-length sleeves deeply edged with folds of white lace. It was an elegant creation, and Léonie felt decidedly feminine wearing it — a novel sensation after so many months in breeches. She began to feel more like herself, was aware of a quickening in her step, as though her legs only took to striding when encased in gentleman's attire. She tucked her short hair under the fob cap and surveyed her reflection in the cheval mirror.

She was brown, too brown. Several months at sea had served to tan her skin to a deep golden hue, not at all *à la mode*. She would have to be careful to stay entirely out of the sun for the journey back to France. Perhaps by then her complexion might have regained its former creamy colour, for it would indeed be awkward to explain how she had come by such a bronzing while enclosed in an abbey's sombre walls. Meanwhile, there was nothing to be done, for she had no powders or ceruse to whiten her features.

In a short while, she was ready, and sat at the small table by the window partaking of a dish of sweet tropical fruits while she waited for François. Her stomach fluttered and her hands trembled slightly, but she made herself eat if only for something to do. She knew she was as jittery as a debutante at the thought of seeing him, and that such emotions were quite unsuitable, but she couldn't help herself. The very sight of him set her aquiver. She dug into a sweet yellow mango, having quickly developed a passion for the aromatic fruit, mindful of François' instructions to first remove the stone. She had to think of him like that, watching and guiding her, sparring with her, or she would never be able to face the finality of this departure. The absoluteness of their separation had kept her awake hour after hour last night, and she didn't wish to spoil her last moments with the captain thinking about her barren future.

From the window she saw his carriage draw up in front of the establishment and jumped up, wiping her fingers on her serviette. She adjusted her cap and the white muslin fichu

411

that modestly hid her neckline, then surveyed the room to ensure all her belongings were packed away ready for the *Nederburgh*. Then she ran downstairs to meet him.

'Father Cassel!' She was surprised and yet genuinely pleased to see the old priest again. 'Have you come as well to wish me God speed?'

He looked rather ill at ease and Léonie, having ordered her bags brought down to the carriage, turned to study him more closely. 'Where is the captain, Father? Did he come with you?'

'No, my dear. I regret he has been detained this morning.'

'Detained? But he will meet me at the *Nederburgh*?'

'He will try, but I fear it may not be possible. You see, the Englishman who has information concerning the whereabouts of Auguste de Barron is leaving Batavia on the same tide. If François is to investigate his claims fully, it must be done before they weigh anchor.'

Léonie felt panic rise in her breast. 'But I can't go without saying goodbye!'

'Let us go to the harbour, my dear, and await him there. I'm sure he'll make every effort.'

Léonie felt a black weight settle on her

412

heart. He wouldn't come. Perhaps she'd always known it. This was his way of creating a chasm between them. What did she expect? It showed he at least had more sense than she, who insisted on keeping alive some small spark of hope that their differences in status and marital circumstances might somehow be resolved. There was no solution. There never had been.

She followed the chaplain into the carriage and watched the walled city roll past the windows without any interest, for she felt numb. Father Cassel had to shake her quite hard to gain her attention.

'I'm sorry, *mon père*, what did you say?' He was holding out a small package. 'What is this?'

'A gift for you, my dear. I think perhaps you had better open it.'

She frowned, pulling at the string to loosen the wrapping. Inside was a small ceramic box, the lid enamelled with a scene reminiscent of a Watteau painting showing lovers in an elegant garden, the sides decorated with flowers of every description. 'Why, it's beautiful!' she exclaimed. 'But Father — '

'Look inside,' he urged.

She opened the box carefully, wondering how the priest could possibly have the means to — She gasped. Inside lay a pair of ivory

413

combs, decorated with gold and set with pearls and diamonds.

Léonie started at the priest. 'Father, I can't possibly accept these. Even if I understood what service I might have rendered you, I could never accept something so . . . ' — she almost said expensive, but caught herself before she could cause offence — 'so very fine.'

He was laughing. 'My dear Léonie, you are as perspicacious as ever. The compensation awarded to chaplains would I fear not reach this, were it to be squirrelled away for years.'

'Then — '

'It's from François, my dear.'

Léonie felt her eyes blur, but while the beautiful gift filled her heart with love, its meaning was only too painfully clear. She shut the lid and shoved it back at Father Cassel.

'I cannot possibly accept it. Kindly return the gift to Capitaine de la Tour with my regrets.'

The carriage had stopped at the wharf. Léonie jumped out quickly, sniffing back the tears that she would never let fall. How dare he! Giving her gifts as though she were his mistress! Was it for services rendered? If so, she deserved no payment, for she had never delivered. Or was it a bribe that he might enter her bed-chamber on those rare occasions when he might be in port and yet not enjoying his nuptial bed? She felt cheapened.

'You don't understand, my dear . . . er . . . Mademoiselle Thouars,' he added, smiling at the people gathered about waiting for the longboat to carry them to the *Nederburgh*.

'I understand perfectly, Father. The captain did not wish to face me himself, so he sent you with this — this enticement!' She felt herself blush as he caught her meaning. 'You may take a message back with you to Captain de la Tour.' She lowered her voice so she would not be overheard. 'You may tell him that Mademoiselle le Vicomtesse de Chambois is not so desperate that she would throw herself away for the occasional pleasures of a sea captain and his pretty baubles.'

The priest stepped back as if stung. 'He will be deeply saddened, *mamselle*. Can you not find it in your heart to accept his gift — '

'Never! Whatever madness led him to purchase such an item may I hope be ameliorated by its return.'

'It was not obtained here, my dear,'

answered the priest sadly. 'It has been in his possession a long — '

'Pray spare me the details, Father.' Léonie knew what he was going to say: that the gift had been meant for the captain's wife. That would hurt even more abominably were she to hear it spoken aloud.

Several Dutch ladies were being assisted into the longboat, and Léonie knew it was time to leave. For all the bitterness she felt toward François, she loved the old priest and did not want him to think her disfavour extended to him.

'Father, I must go.' She took his hands and smiled. 'I trust your journey to the Pacific will be safe and speedy, and your return to France less eventful than the outward passage.'

He smiled, though his eyes betrayed the sadness her refusal of the gift had caused him.

'Please, *mon père*, you are in no way to blame for François' thoughtlessness. I will always think of you as a dear friend and confidante. Why, without you aboard the *Aurélie* I should never have retained my sensibilities, and I wonder how I shall fare cooped up in a boat full of people who do not speak my language. I shall have to pray a lot!' she teased, grateful to see him relax a little.

'A fine idea, *mamselle*. I believe God speaks French passably well.'

She laughed and hugged him, receiving a rather awkward hug in return.

'When you get home, Father, will you promise me something?'

'If God allows.'

'Will you come and visit me?'

He smiled, taking her arm and leading her to the now-filled longboat. 'It will be my pleasure. I think this will be my last voyage around God's earth and I shall be looking for a quiet village in which to serve out my declining years.'

'Then you shall come to the Loire, where my family home is. We should be glad of a man as wise as you to guide us. Perhaps you can curb some of the more exuberant spirits among us.'

'If they are like you, my dear, I very much doubt it, but I am grateful for your offer.'

She settled herself into the longboat and smiled up at the old man as the vessel was pushed away from the wharf and the oarsmen leaned to their task. As the boat moved out into the harbour toward the waiting schooner, he grew smaller and smaller until she could see his face only as a blur. Then he turned and climbed into the carriage, failing to see her hand raised in a final wave.

22

Paris, Late September 1784

It was hot the day Marie and Jean-Michel
rode into Paris. Marie was thirsty from
their dusty ride so they stopped at a water
pump in the street. She watched Jean-Michel
as she sipped the cool, slightly brackish
water, noticing how tense he seemed now
they were back in the throng of humanity.
It was impossible to feel truly safe, truly
anonymous in such a crowded place. She
would be so glad when Léonie returned and
this nightmare was ended.

She stood up and stretched her stiff back.
Just then, a black carriage caught her eye
as it turned down the street, the emblem
of a silver falcon on its door flashing in the
sun. For an instant she froze, not wanting
to believe what she had seen.

Was she mistaken? Could that possibly
have been the livery of the Marquis de
Vercours? Marie gazed at the street, filled
with bustling peddlers and farm wagons.
Nothing seemed out of place. Nothing

seemed unusual. Perhaps she had imagined it.

She mounted her horse and rejoined Jean-Michel who was waiting on the opposite corner.

'Are you all right, my love?' he enquired closely. 'You look like you've seen a ghost.'

Marie laughed as best she could. 'The water was not too pleasant, that's all. I've become accustomed to the sparkling waters from country streams, I suppose.'

They carried on their way, though Jean-Michel looked thoughtfully at her from time to time.

No one gave more than a passing glance to the two young farmhands riding their muddy nags through the crowded streets, and they found their way to the Rue d'Atoine without difficulty.

Marie's uncle and aunt were overjoyed to see her again, once they'd overcome their horror at her mode of dress. They were more prepared for the viscount's appearance, since it was they who'd helped him escape to the countryside months before, and they were grateful for the fresh chickens and vegetables they had brought as gifts.

That night, Marie lay pretending to sleep in the corner of the attic bedroom she shared with her two young cousins, until she was certain they were asleep. Then she crept out of bed, dressed in her best gown, and let herself out into the street. She knew she should tell Jean-Michel where she was going, but she could not do so without alerting the entire household, for he was sleeping at the opposite end of the house.

Once in the street, Marie called for a chair. Though her precious store of money was fast dwindling. If she could just talk to the Marquis de Vercours and persuade him to give up his vendetta against Jean-Michel and his family, it would be money well spent.

The Hôtel de Vercours was an imposing edifice, overlooking a quiet tree-lined boulevard. Marie stepped nervously from the chair and mounted the six white steps to the door.

She blessed herself quickly and rang the bell, hearing the chimes toll deep within.

For a minute there was no response and then the door opened.

A manservant stared at her with distaste. '*Mamselle?*'

'I — I wish to speak to Monsieur le Marquis de Vercours,' she said hesitantly. 'It is a matter of some importance.'

The butler raised his eyebrows. 'The marquis does not receive visitors at this hour.'

'Oh, please!' Marie protested, horrified that her mission could be so abruptly foiled. 'Tell him it concerns' — she hesitated, for to speak the words was to admit so much — 'Mademoiselle la Vicomtesse de Chambois.'

The man's eyes narrowed, but before he could respond, a voice came from within.

'Géricault, where are your manners? Pray, invite the lady in!'

The sound of that voice chilled Marie to the bone as she stood on the step. But it was too late now. The lackey took her cloak and ushered her into a dark hallway, lit by a single brace of candles, and thence into a salon where a fire glowed in the grate, casting soft light on the walls.

She looked about, but only on second glance did she perceive a long pair of legs protruding from a wing chair near the fire, crossed at the ankles and dressed in gold breeches and silk stockings. Gold buckles glinted in the firelight atop dusty black shoes. Over the arm of the chair, one hand was visible, long pale fingers, adorned with emeralds, tapping a slow rhythm on the pink brocade.

'So,' said a voice from the chair. 'You decided to brave the lion's den.' He rose from his hiding place and Marie's eyes widened at the state of his dress. The Marquis de Vercours' exquisite green faille coat was travel-stained, his cravat awry and his silk shirt and waistcoat unbuttoned to the navel. She looked away quickly.

'Hah! Don't tell me you've never seen a man's chest before, little maid. Not after the company you've been keeping these past weeks.'

Marie stared at the marquis in dismay. She could not tell if he was guessing in order to trick her, or whether he really knew something. Surely it was not possible that he knew.

'You're surprised,' he continued, crossing to her and reaching out to tilt up her face. She had no choice but to look him in the eyes. 'You should realize by now that I know everything. Sooner or later.'

Marie forced herself not to cringe as he stroked his thumb back and forth across her bottom lip. She longed to pull away from the evil man and run outside, back into the cool, clean night air, but she had come here with a purpose and she would not be swayed.

'I wish to speak to you, sir,' she said carefully, easing back from his grasp, 'on a matter of honour.'

He dropped his hand and reached into his pocket for a tiny silver snuff box. 'Your honour or mine?' he asked, a faint smile on his lips. He dipped two fingers into the snuff and touched them to one nostril.

'Yours, sir.'

He raised one eyebrow. '*My honour.*' He sneezed into a white silk handkerchief, then folded it meticulously and replaced it in his pocket. 'You interest me immensely, little maid. I had not thought there remained much honour attached to my name.' He waved her toward a chair and summoned the lurking servant from the shadows. 'Refreshments, Géricault. The lady is out past her bedtime and requires sustenance.'

'I require nothing but your attention, sir.'

'Indeed?' He flicked out the tails of his dusty coat and sat down once more, languishing in a manner that made Marie feel distinctly uneasy. 'Then you shall have it — just as soon as we have wine. I do not listen well without a glass in my hand.'

Marie fidgeted while they waited, feeling like a butterfly about to be speared for his collection, rather than a lady's maid who had no business being seated in such a fine room. Her heart warmed at the thought that such notions meant less than nothing to Jean-Michel. The thought of his plight brought a flush of love and she returned the marquis's stare with all the determination she could muster.

At last Géricault returned. Vercours took the tray and placed it on the sideboard, pouring the drinks himself and dismissing the servant. He passed her a glass of wine.

'No, thank you,' she said, wanting only to state her business and be off.

'But I insist. It's my finest Madeira. I import it for just such occasions as this.'

Marie didn't understand what he meant, but she took the glass for the sake of politeness and sipped it. The rich, sweet wine was the best she'd ever tasted — even during prankish visits to the Chambois cellars with Léonie and Jean-Michel when they were children — and it calmed her nerves. She found she was drinking rather too much and set the glass upon the table at her elbow.

'I have no wish to impose upon your hospitality, *monsieur*,' she said, folding her hands in her lap. 'I came here to appeal to your honour as a gentleman — '

'You came alone?'

'Why, yes, indeed. My plea is made for those I love, and it is made out of love. No one has sent me, of that you may be sure.'

He smiled into his wine. For some reason, the look on his face made Marie shiver. She straightened her shoulders and went

424

on, 'Monsieur le Marquis, I know you have been searching for . . . for my mistress.' She almost gave Jean-Michel's name and chided herself for such a lack of concentration. 'I also know you have not found her.'

She had his whole attention now and it was unnerving.

'What makes you think that?' he asked quietly.

'I — I saw you. At the abbey in Switzerland. You couldn't have found her, because she's not there.'

'Indeed?' A crooked smile touched his lips. He rose and came to her, picking up the decanter of wine and refilling her glass. To Marie's consternation, he then knelt in front of her, pressing the glass into her hands and holding it there with his own. 'Perhaps you came to tell me where I might find the little viscountess. My friend the Marquis de Grise would be most appreciative were I to find his wayward fiancée. His heart quite pines for her.'

'No! That is — I cannot. I made a vow.' She saw the flicker of anger in the hard angles of his face, but her love for Léonie was stronger than her fear. 'I came to ask you to abandon your quest. It is . . . a family matter, and of no concern to others.'

'Perhaps that is a matter of opinion.' He

got up, turning his back for a moment, but not moving away. Marie noticed the travel grime on the back of his coat. Clearly he had arrived too recently to change his attire. They had beaten his coach and horses to Paris, but not by much. The man must drive like the very Devil, she thought.

He turned, staring down at her with unbridled malice. 'And that young whelp, Jean-Michel de Chambois? Was it his family who sent him to live in the country as a common servant?'

Marie gasped, spilling some wine on her lap. He had seen them together! All that time they had travelled believing the marquis unaware of Jean-Michel's presence in France — but he'd known all along! And if Vercours knew, perhaps everyone did.

My mistress will be ruined, she thought miserably. It has all been in vain. She stared at the dark stain on her blue gown without really seeing it, feeling suddenly weary and struggling to focus her eyes.

'You almost killed Monsieur le Vicomte in a duel. Surely you have done enough. Why can't you let him alone? What has the Chambois family done to you that you must persecute them so?'

'Persecute? Not at all. I am merely . . . interested. I went to discover if the little redhead could actually be wearing out her knees in a convent. It was such an improbable notion, don't you think? It did not surprise me to find that the abbess had never heard of the fair Léonie.' He reached out one finger and traced the shape of Marie's chin. 'And then I saw you. If you'd hoped to beat me to it and cover your mistress's tracks, you underestimated me. All I had to do was watch you — you led me straight to your lover. It was most illuminating.'

'My lover!'

'I may be a gambler and a womanizer, *mamselle* but I am not without intelligence.'

'Jean-Michel was — '

'Ah! So he is Jean-Michel to you, is he?'

'We grew up together!'

'Of course you did.'

'My mother was his nurse. He was hurt. He could not sail and — ' Marie wiped her eyes with the back of her hand, for she was feeling abominably tired and wasn't sure she was making sense.

'And — '

The marquis was leaning over her, taking the glass from her hand. Marie's tongue felt thick. She was disoriented, and oh so tired.

'I — I m-must go. Please, would you help me find my c-cloak . . . ?'

She felt Vercours' hands encircle her waist,

cringed as his mouth brushed against her ear, though she was strangely powerless to push him away.

'You are going nowhere, *mamselle*,' he murmured. 'I rather fancy keeping you here and seeing if Monsieur le Vicomte comes to find his little songbird. Who knows, we may be able to pleasure each other while we wait.'

★ ★ ★

Marie lay on her back not sure whether her eyes were open or shut. Her head felt thick and her tongue was stuck to the roof of her mouth. She groaned, rolled over onto her side and sought the floor with her feet.

In the faint gloom that confirmed her eyes were open, she could make out wooden boards beneath her toes. She pushed herself up until she was sitting and put her feet flat on the floor, letting the cool surface calm her.

After a minute she looked up. Across the room, heavy brocade drapes allowed the faint light of dawn to penetrate the dark.

'How long have I been here?' she wondered groggily, putting a hand to her forehead. 'That wine! It was so strong!' And then she knew. It took more than a few sips of

Madeira to leave her senseless.

With alarm, Marie gazed around her. The small chamber in which she had been placed was wholly unfamiliar. A simple washstand, the plain bed with threadbare blankets, she recognized such items well enough.

'This is a servant's room.'

She got to her feet gingerly, waited while the dizzy feeling in her head cleared and then walked slowly to the door, not bothering to put on her stockings and shoes which had been taken from her and lay at the bottom of the bed. With trembling hands she turned the knob. It was locked.

Panic was rising from deep within as the fogginess lost its grip on her mind.

'Stay calm, Marie,' she told herself, crossing stealthily to the window. She eased back the curtains and looked down. Below was what looked like a cook's garden, a small area laid in a pattern of stone slabs and herbs. But she was a full three storeys above. She was imprisoned in an attic.

She fought a temptation to scream, recalling whose house she was in.

'I'll not give him the pleasure,' she muttered under her breath, easing open the window. Leaning down to look cheered her spirits a little, for she had never been afraid of heights.

She turned back to the room, yanking the blanket off the bed and pulling at the sheets. They were old and soft with washing, but they were all she had.

As she began feverishly tying the worn sheets into a makeshift rope, Marie heard creaking from somewhere in the house. Her heart pounded so loudly in her breast that she thought she would faint, but she struggled on, forcing herself to tie the bulky linen. But the knots went wrong and unfurled when she tugged on them. She hadn't done anything like this since she was a child. Why couldn't her fingers remember how to make knots that would hold?

There were more sounds. Footsteps this time. With one last despairing tug at the useless rope, she dropped it on the floor and fled to the window.

She looked down. Below the balcony, heavy vines grew up the brickwork. One floor below, they were sturdy, as thick as any rope, but up here they tapered to leafy twigs and would never take her weight.

She heard a key scraping in the lock and knew she must risk a jump into the vines. Who knew what would become of her — or of Jean-Michel — were she to remain in her prison? Perhaps he had already been

430

alerted and was at this moment being led into the trap.

She gathered her skirts about her, wishing that she still had the convenience of men's breeches, and swung her leg over the balcony.

Vercours opened the door and looked toward the bed, smiling as he thought of the unexpected prize he had stored there. In an instant his eyes took in the discarded sheets and their clumsy knots, then the open window.

'You little wretch!' he bellowed, lunging at the open window. She looked back just as she was about to leap for a handhold on the creeper. It was her undoing.

With an exultant grin, Vercours snatched at her skirt, grabbing a secure handful, and then relentlessly reeled her back.

But she fought. My, how she fought. He had to duck — twice — to avoid her little fists.

'Let me go, you devil! You have no right to imprison me here!'

He let her struggle while he carried her bodily across the room, then threw her on the bed, standing over her and breathing hard. 'On the contrary, my dear little viper. I have every right in the world. You are nothing but a little serving wench who thought herself too clever. You came to my house in the dead of night when all decent people are properly asleep in their beds, and all but offered yourself to me.'

'Offered — ' she sputtered. 'I did no such thing. I came to ask you to behave like a gentleman, like a man of honour.' She stared contemptuously at him. 'But I found out you have no understanding of such a word.'

He laughed. 'On the contrary. I understand men of honour well. They are bores, cheapskates and drones. They prattle on in polite circles wasting money and feeling superior. They purport to live clean, God-fearing lives while they cheat on their wives. They even cheat on their lovers — the ultimate irony, don't you think?'

Marie was so angry — mostly at herself for having wasted the only opportunity she would probably get to escape — that she could only glare at him.

'I am not like them, my dear, as you have so rightly said, and I thank you for that observation.' He straightened up, though his legs still held her to the bed, and threw off the heavy silk robe he wore. Marie's eyes widened, for he wore only a pair of buckskin breeches beneath. '*I*, on the other hand, never pretend.'

His voice brought a chill of real fear to Marie, and she clawed at the mattress,

432

pulling herself as far from the man who stood over her as she could.

'I will shout out. I will wake the household if you lay a finger on me!' she warned, wishing her voice wouldn't tremble so.

'Shout, eh? Be my guest. You wouldn't be the first. But my staff are painfully aware who pays their wages.'

He leaned over and with a force that belied the casual tone of his voice, yanked her back to the edge of the bed. Marie brought up her feet to kick him, while her fists pummelled him, but he was expecting the moves and with his free arm, picked her up and flipped her face down on the bed. His voice was low and angry then, making her whimper with fright.

'Do you really imagine you can best me in my own house, you little whore? Make this easy on yourself.'

She crawled away again, turning to face him, but he ripped the neckerchief from the bodice of her dress in one motion, exposing her breasts. His eyes were hot and evil, showing a lust that Marie had never witnessed on any man's face.

'Please, *monsieur*,' she pleaded, 'I will give you what you want. You do not need to take it.'

His hands stilled in the very process of

lifting her skirt. 'Oh? To what do I attribute this change of heart?'

'You — you may do as you wish. If I may have what I ask.'

Vercours stared at her. 'You astonish me, *mamselle*. Are you seriously proposing that I may have my way with you if I give up my search for the truth about the Duc de Chambois's twin brats?'

Marie's temper flared to hear her beloved family described in such a way — and by such a man — but she forced herself to remain calm.

'It's a fair exchange.'

'Fair!' He laughed, throwing back his head. 'That potion I gave you last night must have addled your brain, my pretty. No, your offer does not excite me in the least. You cannot possibly afford to buy my silence. I have far bigger fish to fry than the likes of those auburn-haired troublemakers.' He reached out a hand and in one swift movement pulled off her drawers.

Marie shrieked, leaping away from him across the bed and cowering against the wall, feet tucked beneath her and her hands wrapped tightly around her skirt-covered knees. 'Don't you dare touch me! You will never get away with this.'

'My goodness, you are behaving like a

434

little virgin,' he responded, throwing the drawers on the floor and advancing toward her.

She refused to answer. It is all over, she thought, feeling her strength ebbing away. He will take the one thing I had been saving for my only love. Oh, Jean-Michel, forgive me for my foolishness!

As the marquis grabbed at her, pulling her beneath him and burying his face in her breasts, tears of remorse filled her eyes. She felt limp, now, powerless in the face of inevitability. What stupidity had led her to this monster's house? What arrogance to think that she stood any chance of protecting those she cared about?

She felt Vercours' hands pulling up her skirt, sliding up the inside of her thighs, and squeezed her mind shut against the horror that was about to happen. But when his lips encircled her nipple, they brought back a flood of sweet memories of a starlit night in the apple orchard with Jean-Michel — a night when they had controlled their passions for the sheer delicious anticipation of waiting until their nuptial eve.

As much to avoid being forced to watch what he was doing, Marie turned her head away. Beside the bed on a small table stood a brass candlestick. She wrapped her fingers around it and smashed it into Vercours' temple.

He grunted and slumped on top of her. Marie sobbed with relief as she rolled him off her body. Without waiting to retrieve her undergarment, she ran to the window and climbed over the balcony.

★ ★ ★

The Marquis de Vercours felt the terrible pain in his head a second before his eyes opened, and for an instant he was tempted not to bother subjecting them to the glare of daylight. Then he remembered the girl, and pushed himself up off the mattress in a rage, just in time to see her climbing over the railings.

He rolled off the bed and dived at the window. As he reached it, his eyes met hers. She was caught, snared in the wrought iron by the skirt of her gown. Her wide brown eyes reminded him of a rabbit frozen with fear in a hunter's snare.

He leaned out and reached for her, feeling victory rise in his throat. But just as he sought to grab her waist and pull her back into the room, the cloth gave way, tearing loose from the metal and sending her tumbling downwards.

Marie shrieked, grabbing at the rail, but she was too far down. Arms flailing, she fell into the ivy, but it barely broke her headlong tumble. Vercours watched her snatch wildly at the vines as she fell toward the ground, saw her almost gain purchase and then lose her grip.

The last few yards were bare of growth and with a final scream, she fell into a large patch of lavender bushes and lay still.

Vercours stared down at her for a moment, then straightened up and shut the window.

'Stupid tart,' he said.

23

Jean-Michel was frantic when he discovered Marie had not slept in her bed and could not be found. In the busy market street in front of the row house, a night-soil collector remembered a young woman asking for a chair to take her to the Marquis de Vercours' house, despite the late hour.

'Pierre!' he bellowed to the eldest of Marie's cousins, who was hovering nearby, anxious to have everyone in the street know he was somehow connected to this commanding stranger. 'Fetch my horse!'

The teenager took off at a run, leaving Jean-Michel pacing up and down in a state of fury. He knew he was angry with Marie. Angry and yet fearful for her safety. What could she be thinking? Doesn't she know Vercours cannot be trusted?

He turned at the sound of hooves behind him, but it was not Pierre with his mount. His eyes widened with shock as he recognized the Vercours livery on the groom's uniform. But when he saw who lay slumped across the saddle of the horse the man was leading he gave a bellow of anguish.

'What has he done to you?' he groaned, lifting Marie's head gingerly from where it lay motionless over the stirrup. Her clothes were torn, her neckerchief missing, and she was covered in bruises. Her beautiful brown hair hung upside down from her head, hiding her bloodied face. He pressed his lips to her neck, for his hands were trembling too much for him to feel for a pulse. The skin was cool, but not cold, and he could feel the faint throb of life.

'God in heaven, Marie. How could the monster do this to you?'

In a sudden rage, he turned on the marquis's groom, grabbing him by his black lapels and tossing him bodily into a nearby watering trough for horses. When the man came up for air, he grabbed him again and swung a huge punch at his jaw, knocking him senseless on to the street.

'Pass that on to your precious master,' he spat, turning on his heel and going to help Marie's family lift her from the horse.

* * *

It was barely eleven when the Duchess de Chambois's maid announced her unexpected visitor.

'The Marquis de Vercours? Here?' She felt a frisson of uneasiness and shuddered physically to dispel the unpleasant sensation. Memories. That's all.

She turned to her mirror, smoothing her hands down the sides of her buttercup-yellow gown.

'Why should he ask to see me?'

'I — I have no idea, Your Grace. But he was most insistent.'

The duchess looked past her own image in the mirror to stare at the girl, who was clearly quite agitated. 'Is my husband at home?'

'No, Your Grace. He left an hour ago. I believe he has some business with the Agent Général.'

Eléanore snorted. 'Talleyrand is forever

lobbying to have the church excused from paying taxes. I wonder he can say his prayers at night.' She touched a hand to her ebony hair, checking almost unconsciously for the presence of telltale grey. There was none and she was glad she had decided to leave her coiffure unpowdered. 'Very well. If I must see the odious man, I might as well do it now.'

He was in the small salon. The duchess paused at the sight of him, tall and forbiddingly attired in a frock suit of such dark green as to be almost black. The buckles of his high-heeled shoes were encrusted with diamonds, his hands adorned with heavy emeralds, and he wore a smallsword at his waist.

'*Monsieur le Marquis*,' she said formally, refusing to offer him the courtesy of a seat.

'*Madame la Duchesse*, you are so precisely as my memory has preserved you.' He bowed low over her hand, making a great deal of showing some leg. When she made no response, he took her hand and pressed it to his lips. Eléanore felt a shudder but controlled it.

'Perhaps you would care to state your business, *monsieur*. I have little time for civilities this morning.'

'So I perceive,' he replied equably, smiling

in a way that unnerved her. 'I, on the other hand, have the greatest inclination to outstay my welcome and pass a pleasant hour or two in your company — shall we say, for old times' sake?'

Eléanore blanched, insulted that he should dare raise the issue. 'The past is gone, *monsieur*. I have no wish to revisit old mistakes.'

'Ah! So you admit turning your back on me was an error? I thought as much. Never fear, dear lady, I have the solution to that problem, and I think when I have explained my errand, you will welcome it with open arms.'

The duchess doubted that, but she would not play cat and mouse with him. She seated herself on a giltwood *fauteuil* without inviting him to do likewise — and waited. It pleased her to see him catch the snub, though he covered his annoyance masterfully.

'You have something you feel I should know?' she asked.

Giving her a hard look, the marquis turned to the French windows. 'It concerns your beloved offspring, *madame*.'

'Which of my children, sir? I have four.'

'The twins.'

She had suspected it were so, but to hear it from his lips gave Eléanore a deep foreboding. Jean-Michel she did not fret for, since he was at sea in the care of Captain de la Tour, and they regularly received his letters, full of wondrous doings. But her only daughter, Léonie, the child she had always held most dear, had vanished from the face of the earth. Just to think of her brought pain and anguish, for she had no idea whether her child was alive or dead.

She felt Vercours searching her face for a hint of what she knew and felt. Then he turned away and began to expound some strange tale about encountering Jean-Michel with a serving girl as his lover, somewhere in Switzerland. Nothing made sense, but she listened, becoming more and more convinced that the man had lost his mind. Finally, he was finished, gazing triumphantly like a dog waiting for a bone.

'Your tale is entertaining sir, but I think you have taken leave of your senses. If you are finished I will have you shown out.'

'Finished!' he bellowed, making Eléanore jump. 'You think I have invented this preposterous story? To what possible end, *madame*? Your precious son is not aboard the *Aurélie*. He is here in Paris. His little paramour, some silly chit called Marie Beaulieu, threw herself off my balcony last night and broke her neck!'

'Marie!' The Duchess felt suddenly faint. How could he know Marie's name? And what was she doing at his house?

'Marie is dead?' she whispered. The girl had been like a second daughter to her all these years, despite her station. Must she endure her loss as well? Her eyes filled and through the veil of unshed tears she saw Vercours turn away.

'How is it that this family bears such high regard for children of the gutter?'

'Marie . . .' The duchess blinked rapidly, searching for a kerchief in the pocket of her yellow gown. 'She was — '

At that instant there was a great commotion in the hall, then the doors of the salon burst open. To Eléanore's absolute astonishment, her son Jean-Michel stood there, clearly drunk and dressed as a servant.

'Goddamn you, Vercours, you murdering blackguard! Draw your sword!'

Jean-Michel raised his arm showing his father's razor-sharp rapier clenched in his hand.

'Jean-Michel!' cried the duchess, throwing herself at him, suddenly horribly aware that everything Vercours had recounted could well be the truth.

'Stand back, *ma mère*. The marquis and I have unfinished business.'

443

'My pleasure, you young braggart,' Vercours responded, drawing his own sword with the ominous grating of steel on steel as it withdrew from its scabbard.

The two men advanced across the room — a mere three paces each — only to find the duchess, purple with rage, standing between their tips. 'Jean-Michel, you will go to your chamber at once. How dare you draw a sword in my house — and drunk at that! Pray relieve us of your presence until you are properly attired and sober enough for church!'

Her son looked at her, his eyes wild with pain and passion, but her words had the desired effect, and he dropped his arm. Eléanore took the rapier with distaste and handed it to the butler who was hovering, eyes agog, near the door. 'Please escort *Monsieur le Vicomte* to his room and attend to his toilette. And return this to its — its proper place.'

When the door had closed upon them, she turned to Vercours.

'I believe you were ready to leave, *monsieur*,' she said coldly.

'On the contrary, Duchess. Now that I know you believe my tale, I think we have many things to discuss.' He thrust his sword back into the scabbard at his hips.

'You are playing with fire, sir.'

'I am not afraid to ignite a few sparks, Your Grace, if you would let me.'

Eléanore turned away, eyes blazing. 'May I remind you that you are a mere marquis in all this. I have rather . . . special connections at Versailles that you would do well to keep in mind.'

'You mean that foreign trollop, Marie-Antoinette?' He laughed at her stiff-necked censure. 'Yes. I know. You are so fine now, aren't you, my dear? A lady-in-waiting to the most powerful woman in Europe. Would you have gained such elevation if you had married me instead of that — that frumped-up excuse for a nobleman!'

Her eyes widened. 'I love my husband, *monsieur*. And I have never — never, you understand — been sorry that I refused your hand. No,' she said resolutely, 'I made the perfect choice. Jean-Alexandre is a good man and a considerate husband.'

'I am pleased to hear you say so,' he answered evenly, closing the gap between them so that he stood mere inches from her. 'Your affection for his good name is just as I hoped it would be.'

'I do not take your meaning.'

'It is just this, Eléanore . . . ' He bent his head, letting his hot breath flutter the

445

tendrils of hair at her nape as he pressed his lips to her neck. She jumped away, rubbing the tingling skin with her fingers.

'How dare you!'

He laughed softly. 'I dare much more, my dear. You see, we are each caught in a bind. I must tread carefully lest you disown me to the queen; you on the other hand' — he stretched out and languidly wrapped a finger around a black curl of hair over her shoulder — 'must beware that I do not bring you and your husband into disfavour with that same lady and her husband the king.'

Eléanore felt faint. She stepped back, reaching behind her for the chair and eased herself into it. But he followed, kneeling before her as though he were about to propose.

'I don't want much,' he murmured, lifting her hand to his lips as his eyes held hers. She felt a shudder of loathing that a man of such wealth could stoop to blackmail.

'How much do you want?'

'I have no need of money, *Madame la Duchesse*. You have something far more valuable.'

She frowned. 'Such as?'

'Yourself,' he whispered. 'I want you to take me as your lover. Openly. Officially. So that all the world will know you only married the Duc de Chambois for his money and his title. So they will know that it was really me you loved.'

'But that's a lie!' Eléanore was so appalled by his suggestion that her brain had trouble understanding him. 'I love my husband. I have always loved him. Never — never have I taken a lover. It would hurt him too much. And what would my children think?'

'They would think you were following fashion, Your Grace. And your precious secret would remain between the two of us, where it couldn't hurt your daughter or your son. Not even your husband need know of it.'

She stared at him, wanting so badly to strike him that the pain of restraint was almost physical. 'You are a despicable example of humankind, Alain de Vercours, and I thank God I married the man I did and not you.' She jumped up, pacing across the room and twisting her fingers together in agitation. But then an idea came to her, and she stopped, turning to look straight at him. For a second, she vacillated, for it was a great risk, but she loved her family dearly and there seemed no other way. She took a deep breath. 'Very well, for the sake of my children and my husband, I agree to your terms.

447

But I require time to prepare myself. You may call on me from the first of next month, but meanwhile, should you breathe a word of this to anyone, I vow you will rue this day for the rest of your life.'

Vercours smiled, unable to conceal his exultation.

'I have waited more than twenty years, wondering how I should ever share your bed. A few more days will only sweeten my anticipation.' He bent over her hand, pressing it to his lips with a warmth that startled her. 'You never believed that I loved you, all those years ago, Eléanore, but I truly did. And I have never been able to care for another woman since. Not one ever measured up.'

When he was gone, she sat down, stunned by all that had transpired. Then she scrubbed her hand on the edge of the seat to wipe away the lingering sensation of his mouth and ran from the room.

Jean-Michel was home. Whatever he had been up to, at least he was alive and well, and if anyone knew the whereabouts of her daughter, it was he.

She fairly flew up the stairs to his room.

★ ★ ★

'Jean-Michel!' stormed the duchess as she burst into his chamber. 'Where is my daughter? What has happened to my beloved Léonie?'

'*Maman!*' The viscount was about to step out of his bath, but at the sight of his enraged parent storming across the room, he ducked back under the water. 'Couldn't this wait until I am at least dressed?'

'I don't care about that,' she said impatiently, waving his valet away and taking the towel herself. 'Here, if it will speed your tongue, I will turn my back.'

Jean-Michel took the towel and wrapped it around his middle.

'*Bien,*' said Eléanore, turning around again. 'Now explain yourself. What is this filth of lies that I have been subjected to this morning and why do you appear like a ghost from nowhere dressed like a like a — '

'Groom, *Maman*. I was dressed in the livery of the Château Aristide.'

She stared up at him as though he were a stranger. 'I think I should sit down. Although I am not fond of fainting, I may as well be prepared.' She seated herself on an embroidered stool. 'Very well, *mon fils*. I am listening.'

Jean-Michel gazed balefully at his mother. Most of the time she was fully occupied with the business of court, with shoes and hats and coiffures. But when she was riled, she became like a ferret, snapping her sharp little teeth at everything and spearing her prey with those sharp grey eyes. One of his least favourite things in all the world was to bring his mother's wrath down upon his head.

A drop of water rolled down his leg and he rubbed it absently with his other foot. 'I — I don't really know where to begin, *ma mére*.'

'Then begin by telling me what has become of my daughter.'

'As far as I know, she is alive and well.'

'Oh, thank God!' The Duchess squeezed her eyes shut and blessed herself. After a moment, she opened them and though they were filled with tears, Jean-Michel could see the joy that shone through. 'Then where is she? Why have I heard not a word or a line from her all these months? Does she not care that she has broken my heart?'

'You are right, of course. That was stupid of us. We should have thought to get letters to you.'

'We? Jean-Mich, what is going on?'

'She is with Christian, *Maman*. At least, she is under his protection.' He squatted in front of his mother and took her hands, holding them tenderly and thinking how like his sister's they were. When she heard where Léonie was, she would likely wish the girl had died instead. 'She is aboard the *Aurélie*. She took my place. Léonie is pretending to be me, Mother.'

Absolute silence greeted his words. His mother's eyes grew round as she stared open-mouthed at him, trying to take in his meaning, to make sense of what he was saying.

'You are not going to faint, are you, *Maman*?'

She shook her head, but no words came. Jean-Michel released her hands and raked his loose red hair back from his face. He stood up, pulling the towel tighter around his midriff.

'I think perhaps I had better explain how all this started.'

'I — I think that would be a good idea,' she replied faintly He poured her a large glass of cognac and helped her to drink it while he recounted the sorry tale. By the time he had finished, the glass was half-empty and his mother's eyes were glazed with shock.

'And now, Mother, I must know what that vile monster Vercours was doing in your salon this morning, for I swear I am going to kill him this time.'

451

'No!' Eléanore seemed suddenly to snap into focus again. 'He came here to make accusations, some of which, it would seem, were well-founded, though I doubt he knows all you have told me. However, now he knows you are not at sea, he will waste no time checking the navy records. He will soon know that you were listed as being aboard the *Aurélie*, and Vercours can put two and two together as well as I can.'

'I don't care about that, *Maman*. What I am concerned with is Marie and what he did to her. She has agreed to marry me and sail to America, where we can live without censure. Now — '

The duchess jumped up from the stool. 'Oh, my dear boy, I am so sorry.' She took his hands. 'That abominable man told me she had fallen to her death from his balcony last — '

'Death? She is not dead, Mother, though she wishes she were. She is lying gravely ill at her uncle's house on the Rue d'Antoine. I want to bring her here, but I am afraid the move will kill her.'

'Then we must send the surgeon to her at once.' She ran to the door and opened it, calling for her maid, who had clearly been hovering nearby in case she was needed. 'Hurry, child. Fetch the surgeon to — '

She turned back for her son to tell her the address, and then instructed the girl. 'And send Héloïse to my salon. Quickly now.'

Jean-Michel leaned past her and pulled the door closed for a moment. He had vowed to avenge himself on Vercours, and his mother had to understand why, though for Marie's sake he didn't want the whole household to know. 'He tried to rape her, *Maman*. Half her clothes were torn off and she had been drugged. The man is not fit to breathe God's air.'

The duchess's eyes sparked with anger. 'That is for God to decide, not you! You will leave the man alone. I will take care of Alain de Vercours, never fear. You would do better to concern yourself with how we are to save your sister from absolute ruin if this gets out.'

He thumped the door with the flat of his hand. '*Maman*! Much as I love my sister, she is strong. She can take care of herself. But I love Marie and I made her a promise! What kind of man would I be if I allowed such a vile act to go unpunished?'

'Jean-Michel, I absolutely forbid you to lay a finger on the Marquis de Vercours. Do you hear?'

★ ★ ★

Jean-Michel could not contain his anger or his frustration. He threw on the clothes and hat his valet brought him and mounted his horse in a fury, whipping it to a gallop through the cobbled streets and on to the road toward Versailles. The exercise eased his violent mood and by the time he reached the palace he knew what he must do.

He spied his father in the royal gardens engaged in conversation with Talleyrand and some ministers of the government. Jean-Michel hung well back, tricorne low over his face, knowing that his presence would create a stir if he were recognized. Then his father looked up and their eyes met. The duke stared incredulously for an instant and then turned to his friends, excusing himself before strolling toward the trees by the Grand Canal to where Jean-Michel waited in the shadows.

'*Bonjour, mon père.*'

'Jean-Michel. Why don't we take this path? There's a very agreeable view of the lake through the trees further along.'

They walked in silence for a moment until they were beyond earshot of a group of young ladies dressed to the nines in ruffled Polonaise gowns. Jean-Michel ignored their flirting glances and stared straight ahead.

'Well, young man. Perhaps you would like to explain why you are not somewhere in the

Pacific doing those scientific illustrations that are making you famous.'

'Illustrations, Your Grace?'

Jean-Michel stared uneasily at his father, wondering why he'd never been able to lie to him. He seemed to see right inside people sometimes, as though he could peel away the layers.

'What game are you playing, *mon fils*? Don't you know your mother has spent these past months trying to accept that her daughter is dead? She disappeared the same day you sailed for the Pacific, taking her maid but none of her belongings, and leaving some cock-and-bull letter about becoming a nun. He stabbed a finger into Jean-Michel's shoulder. 'I have had France searched stone by stone, and yet I can't find one hair from her head. I don't give a fig for why you are suddenly here when your ship is somewhere in the Pacific. But as God is my witness if you know where your sister is, you will tell me now or I will not be responsible for my actions.'

Jean-Michel could not remember ever seeing his father so angry. He could scarcely blame him.

'I was not aboard that ship, *mon père*,' he replied, resigning himself to the worst. 'It was Léonie.'

In the silence that followed, Jean-Michel saw the full implication of that statement flowering in his father's eyes. Then for the second time that day, he recounted the story of his sister's disappearance and his own flight with Marie. The Duc de Chambois' face grew more and more grim but he made no comment until Jean-Michel was finished.

'And your mother received Vercours, you say?'

'This morning. She says she will take care of the monster, but I wish she would let me do it. I'm afraid she has made a deal with the devil, but if she thinks she can rely on his word of honour, she will rue her decision, I am sure.'

'Your mother is not your concern, Jean-Michel. Nor is Vercours. They shall be taken care of.'

'He must have found a way to blackmail her, though why he would be in the least in need of money, I cannot imagine!'

The duke stared at the shimmering waters of the Grand Canal through the trees. 'Oh, he will be in great need of money when this is over, that I promise you, young man.' He turned to his son and the wrath in his father's expression made Jean-Michel's palms sweaty. 'As for you, you have brought

456

disgrace upon this family. Your behaviour has been reprehensible, and that of your sister utterly foolhardy.'

He turned away, pacing up the path and back like a caged tiger. 'She is finished. No one will offer for her now. If she knows what is good for her, she will stay on the other side of the world, for she can never have a life in France again.'

'But surely there is something we can do, Your Grace? No one knows, yet.'

'Except Vercours, who knows enough to ruin her, even if he hasn't guessed it all. No, it is too late for that. After twenty years of struggling to instil some sense into the pair of you, I count myself a failure. No matter. The facts of the situation cannot be altered. You must leave France.' He held up a bejewelled hand to stem Jean-Michel's instant objections. 'You will remove yourself this very day to the coast and take the first boat you can find to England. I do not wish to see or hear of you again until I summon you do you understand?'

Jean-Michel clenched his fists behind his back. 'I will not leave without Marie, and she is too ill to travel.'

'Your fondness for the girl shows you have some redeeming qualities, *mon fils*, but you will still go. She will be taken care of. No doubt your mother has already seen to that. Did anyone see you coming here?'

The viscount shook his head. 'I don't think so. I came through the outer gardens and it was quiet.'

'Then leave the same way. You are not to return to Paris. I shall send my man, Boucheron, to set you safely on a boat.'

'To be my gaoler, you mean,' Jean-Michel murmured, but cast his eyes down, quelled by his father's glare.

The interview seemed to be over. Jean-Michel made a formal bow to the duke and turned back up one of the paths that led diagonally through the woods. His father's voice stopped him.

'Jean-Michel!'

He paused and looked back.

'Thank you for coming to me.'

Jean-Michel nodded, then turned and walked away.

★ ★ ★

He waited fifteen minutes at the gate for Boucheron to arrive, then it occurred to him that his father had taken the hint about needing a gaoler.

'You old dog!' he muttered and turned his horse away. It both pleased and disquieted him that his father had decided to trust him after all. He was fond of his rather overbearing parent, but was determined to avoid going to England at all costs. He would write to Marie and explain, and as for Vercours, he rather pitied the fellow. Facing the combined wrath of the duke and duchess was not something to be envied.

He rode into the back streets of Versailles and had little trouble exchanging his clothes for the simple, inconspicuous attire of a tradesman. Then he turned his horse west toward the naval shipyards at Brest.

He would find a vessel heading for the Pacific and bring Léonie home himself.

Paris, 1 October, 1784

The soirée had been a great success, but the Duchess de Chambois felt utterly drained. Going through the pretence that she would openly acknowledge Vercours as her lover during the evening had sickened her and strained her self-control to the limit. Were it not for the support of her husband she doubted she could have maintained the sham. She stretched her stiff back and wandered through the empty salon toward the French doors. She was bone weary, yet even after the last guests had taken their leave she had been unable to think of sleep. At least it had been worth it, in the end. She wandered out on to the terrace at the back of the Hôtel de Chambois and watched the sun rise over the chestnut trees.

'Where are you, Léonie?' she murmured to the sky. 'Are you really alive, somewhere on the other side of the earth?'

She blinked against the threat of tears, silently reprimanding herself for such foolishness. Her daughter was strong, and even if she was sometimes impetuous, she was a good girl and would do everything she could to protect her own virtue.

'But even if you succeed, my dearest, will anyone believe you?'

She turned back into the house, thinking of another young girl whose innocence had been taken from her. She had some good news for Marie, and despite the hour she could wait no longer to share it.

She climbed the stairs to Léonie's room, where she had insisted the injured girl be moved, let herself in and crossed quietly to the window to open the drapes.

'Your Grace?'

'Hush, child. Don't sit up.' Eléanore sat on the edge of the bed and took Marie's hand in hers. 'How are you this morning?'

'Better, thank you. I can return to my room today — '

'I will not hear of it. It comforts me to have you here. Having this room empty all these months has merely aggravated my distress.' She fingered the lace-edged sheet, smoothing the wrinkles. 'When I heard how close to death you were, I realized that I had come to think of you as one of my family, Marie. You can't fill the place in my heart left by my daughter, but having you close eases my sadness.'

'Your Grace is so kind.'

'Nonsense.' The duchess stroked Marie's brow, tracing her fingers across the ugly bruise that marked her forehead. 'I have some news for you, *petite*. About Vercours.'

Marie turned her head away and Eléanore felt her cringe beneath the covers. 'You can rest easy, my dear. The monster has been thoroughly thwarted.' She looked down at the girl, so fragile and broken, after five days still unable to eat for the pain in her jaw, one arm broken, several ribs cracked, covered in cuts and bruises, and worse than all the physical damage, feeling unbearably soiled, used, unclean. She wondered what indomitable spirit was keeping the girl alive.

'It was a splendid soirée, Marie. Everyone was there to enjoy the spectacle, and our

461

friend-of-a-friend proved more than his worth at the card table. The marquis was quite taken in.'

'He wagered with him, then, as you had planned?'

'Once he started, he seemed unable to stop.' The duchess smiled with satisfaction. 'You see, he thought this was to be his night. He believed he was the guest of honour, and was keenly anticipating announcing his conquest over my affections, and then we allowed him to meet this supposed upstart from the provinces who bragged about his talent at cards and obviously possessed more money than skill.'

She laughed. 'Monsieur Vercours couldn't resist. At first he won. Then he got greedy. Then, just when he thought he had acquired half of Normandy, he began to lose. Oh, Marie, I was hugging myself with delight, yet I was mortally afraid Vercours would somehow turn the tables. But our man was gifted beyond my wildest dreams. As Vercours began to lose, so he would let him win — but just a little, to raise his hopes again. Then he went in for the kill. Vercours could not escape. He was doomed.'

'Did he lose very badly?'

'Badly? No, he did not lose badly. He lost abominably. For what he did to you — and to many young girls in Paris — and for what he tried to do to me and my daughter, he lost everything, Marie. Everything.'

'But he still has — '

'He has nothing but the clothes he stood in. His opponent let him keep his horses and carriage — so he could flee France. Pride almost made him refuse, but pragmatism won the evening.'

'He is gone?'

'To who knows where. And may he never return,' the duchess announced with satisfaction. 'I was almost disappointed the blackguard didn't have the decency to blow out his brains, but I think your mother would've fussed about such a mess on the rug, don't you?' She patted Marie's hand. 'Now, you must rest. I shall have some breakfast sent up to you, but I think it is time I went to bed!'

At the door, she turned. 'Marie, my son told me of his offer of marriage. I want you to know that I have thought about it, and that I will make no objection.'

'Your Grace! But — but it's impossible!'

Eléanore frowned, coming back to the bedside. 'Why do you say that, child?'

Marie's eyes filled with tears, and though she said not a word, the duchess understood.

'Marie, this was not your fault. Vercours

is a monster. He is vermin, and I hope this night has rid us of him forever. But his actions defile himself, not his victims. You are not belittled by the horrible consequences of your efforts to help my children.'

Marie turned away, her tears falling freely on to the feather pillow. 'Please do not think me ungrateful, Your Grace, but it can never be.'

Eléanore stood looking at the girl for a moment, then sat once more upon the bed and reached out to turn Marie's face to her.

'Marie, do you love my son?'

'Yes,' she whispered. 'I have always loved him.'

'Well, then, there's no more to be said. If there's one thing for which I am grateful to the Marquis de Vercours, it's that he reminded me how lucky I was to have married a man I also loved. And since I am quite certain my son loves you, I shall look forward to having some American grandchildren!' She bent over the bed and kissed Marie.

'Now, sleep until your broth comes, and try to eat if you can.'

As she left the room, Eléanore felt more at peace than she had since her daughter disappeared.

24

February 1785

The voyage home passed slowly, its boredom ameliorated by the enlivening company of Léonie's Irish maid, Mary-Kate O'Halloran — or Marie-Kate, as Léonie called her in her best approximation of the girl's name. Through her, Léonie learned not only how to be a lady again and wipe away every last vestige of her months as a man, but how to converse in halting Dutch with her fellow travellers. Mary-Kate's facility for different tongues amazed the *vicomtesse*, for contrary to what the captain had told her, she spoke French and Dutch with surprising ease.

Together, they occupied themselves during the long months at sea by sewing garments suitable for a European winter. François, at Mary-Kate's urging, had purchased numerous bolts of cloth from which gowns and capes could be concocted, and as time passed, her bitterness toward him faded, leaving only painful memories.

The *Nederburgh* made port in the chill

waters of the Maas at Rotterdam on February 4th. Snow was falling and Léonie pulled her pelisse tightly around her as she stood on the busy wharf awaiting her belongings.

'Are you sure you won't come with me, Marie-Kate?'

The Irish girl shook her head with a broad smile and hugged Léonie fiercely. Then she pulled up the hood of her cloak and hurried away along the pier. Léonie watched her go, knowing she would miss the girl.

She turned to the waiting diligence. The footman helped her inside where she squashed herself between one of the larger Dutch matrons from the *Nederburgh* and a thin wiry gentleman she'd not seen before. On the opposite seat sat two small children with their harried mother. The children talked nonstop all the way to Bruges, in what Léonie assumed was Flemish, for it was quite like the Dutch her ears had grown accustomed to on the voyage home.

She was grateful to be deposited outside the gates of the Convent of Sainte-Agnès in the ancient city. Her request to be admitted seemed to surprise the gateman, but he obliged her by carrying her boxes and she was escorted to the mother superior.

'What may I do for you, my child?'

Léonie handed her François' letter with its

unbroken red seal, and waited patiently while the woman perused its contents.

'Well,' said the *réligieuse* when she had finished, her eyes examining Léonie rather too closely. Léonie dearly wanted to know what the letter contained that would cause such a reaction, but she was too proud to enquire. 'You may stay with us for three nights. That should suffice for you to find your 'land legs', as the captain suggests, though why he should employ such a nautical term, I am at some loss to comprehend.'

Léonie sighed with relief. Clearly François had said nothing of her adventures, and as she was not about to enlighten the mother superior, she merely smiled.

She was taken to a Spartan room, informed that food would be brought to her, advised of the time for prayers and mass and the saying of the Angelus, all of which reminded Léonie of how little she had attended to the health of her soul while at sea, despite Father Cassel's daily celebrations. She decided she would fill her obligatory three days at the convent by absorbing as much of the life as she could — at least it would facilitate her answering the many questions she would no doubt encounter in Paris.

By the end of three days, one thing Léonie knew for certain was that she could not have borne such an existence for one month, let alone the ten she had passed away from home.

She was relieved when her private carriage arrived. As she farewelled the mother superior she made a generous donation from the money François had given her, for she would have no need of it in Paris.

If the driver thought it strange that a lady should travel unaccompanied, he gave no indication, and Léonie found such formality cold after the warmth and friendliness she had experienced as a member of the bourgeoisie. No matter. She was not a bourgeoise any longer. She was a duke's daughter returning to her family after a time for meditation and solitude in a Flemish convent. She shut her mind to all else and tried to convince herself that all she had seen and done these past months was but a dream.

As mile after mile of dreary winter farmland passed, that task became increasingly easy.

★ ★ ★

Dusk fell early the day Léonie's carriage rolled through the gates of the Hôtel de Chambois and came to a stop in front of the wide marble steps. Light rain had begun falling as she entered Paris, darkening

468

the winter gloom and blurring the skyline, creating a contrast as great as any Léonie could imagine with her memories of Batavia.

But at last she was home. She gazed at the creeper-covered house with smoke spiralling into the damp air from several chimneys. It was almost as though she'd been away for no more than an hour or two, so unchanged did everything appear. And yet as the door opened and an astonished Gaston ushered her inside, she felt like a stranger.

She threw off her travelling cloak, letting it fall to the floor. 'Nounou!' she called, too excited to wait while Gaston fetched her. 'Nounou, where are you?'

She turned at the sound of someone at the top of the stairs. 'Marie!' she gasped. 'Why are you here?' Clearly, something was not as it should be.

'*Sainte Vierge!*' Héloise Beaulieu cried, blessing herself as she scurried toward Léonie. 'God has brought you home safely to us at last, child!'

'Dear Nounou, how I missed you,' she replied, returning the old nurse's fierce hug with equal warmth. Then Marie was there and they were all hugging and crying.

'Come, come,' Héloise urged them, 'you are tired and hungry. I shall fetch a tray for you from the kitchen. Marie, take your mistress into the salon and let her warm herself by the fire.'

'Nounou, I am not a porcelain doll!' Léonie protested, but she was chivvied along regardless.

A cheerful fire crackled in the huge grate and Léonie stood gratefully before it, warming her fingers and toes, which were numb after days in the draughty carriage. Marie hovered about, more anxious than Léonie had ever seen her, until her mother finally left in search of sustenance for the prodigal mistress.

'*Mamselle*, please tell me now,' she said, the instant the door closed, 'for I cannot bear to wait a moment longer.'

'What on earth are you talking about, Marie? And what has happened to you? You have a terrible scar on the back of your hand.'

'' 'Tis nothing. I will tell you later.'

Léonie lowered her voice, lest there be servants nearby. 'Marie, answer me this — why are you here and not hiding with Jean-Michel until my return? I thought we'd agreed that you would pretend to be with me in my incarceration in the convent — Oh, Marie, I could no more have stood life there than have sprouted wings and flown to the moon! It was so closeted. After sailing the vast oceans, I thought I should suffocate if I stayed another minute!'

Marie sat dejectedly on the sofa. 'He didn't tell you, then?'

'Tell me?' Léonie felt a sudden prickle of uneasiness. 'Who didn't tell me what, my dear friend? You are talking in riddles.'

'Oh, dear heaven!' Marie dissolved into tears. Now utterly perplexed, Léonie passed her a kerchief.

'Marie, I think you had better explain everything.'

The girl wiped her eyes. 'Jean-Michel went to find you, *mamselle*. No one knows but I. Please, promise me you will tell no one? Not even my mother knows.'

'But I don't understand. Surely they think he is aboard the *Aurélie*?'

Marie shook her head, sniffing. 'No, your parents know it was you.'

Léonie felt the floor tilting and braced herself for a wave before she remembered where she was. She sat on the sofa next to Marie and took a breath to calm herself. 'How could this have happened?'

'It is a very long tale, *mamselle*. I shall explain later. But His Grace — your father — was very angry with Jean-Mich and sent him away. To England. But *Monsieur le Vicomte* would not go. He went to Brest to find a ship bound for the Pacific. He said he would find you and bring you back himself.'

'*Mon Dieu!* This is a disaster, Marie! He will never find me, nor word of me, for I was in disguise throughout my journey home.' At that moment, Nounou returned bearing a steaming tray, and they fell into silence.

'Come, child. Get some of this chicken broth inside you.' She set the repast on a small table at Léonie's elbow. 'Now, there's rolls fresh from cook's oven, and butter, and a nice slice of pigeon pie. Marie, get your mistress some wine! Sup your broth, *mamselle*. My, you've grown so thin I thought you'd forgotten yourself and sent your shadow home to us instead.'

'Nounou!' Léonie laughed, despite her anxiety for her brother. It felt so like old times to have the woman fussing about. She sipped the steaming soup. 'Delicious!' For a while, she gave in to her hunger, for she hadn't eaten since breakfast. She devoured two rolls with her soup, followed by half the pigeon pie, before she sat back with her glass of wine and gazed affectionately at the two women.

'I can't express how glad I am to be back,' she said. 'But there is so much I want to know. Firstly, where are my parents, and are my brothers well, and what did Alphonse, the Marquis de Grise, say when he heard I'd run away to a convent when I should have married him last November?'

'One question at a time, child,' Nounou answered, picking up the tray. 'Your parents are at court, but I have despatched a messenger to tell them the happy news. Your poor mother, she thought you were dead for so many months, until — ' She glanced at Marie, then pressed her lips together before continuing. '*Tant pis*. No doubt Their Graces will be here by first light. I shall have to air their rooms, and cook will want to prepare a special breakfast.' She bustled out with the tray.

Marie seemed to have recovered her equanimity, and smiled indulgently at her mother's back.

'She hasn't changed,' Léonie observed with an answering smile.

'Just a little older. She worried terribly for you, but I know she'll rest easier now you're safe.'

'I wouldn't be here if it weren't for her sack of magic herbs and berries,' Léonie said. Héloise returned at that moment.

'What's that, child? I've never indulged in magic, as well you know. I'm a God-fearing woman and don't hold with such nonsense.'

Léonie laughed. 'Dear Nounou, do you not remember the bag of herbs you prepared for Jean-Michel to take on his voyage? You gave them to me.' She recounted the ordeal of many weeks at sea, of the storm-ruined food, and the loss of the supply ship, carefully omitting reference to the battle and to her ministrations to the captain, though he filled her mind, despite her best efforts to forbid him entry.

'So you see, His Majesty's Navy owes you a great deal, Nounou, if only it knew.'

Héloise pooh-poohed the notion, but Léonie could see she was flattered.

'As for your question concerning Monsieur Alphonse,' Marie said, 'he was most put out when you disappeared. He even made a wager with the Marquis de Vercours — ' She stopped, turning away abruptly and fingering the scar on her hand.

'There, there, child. You must forget all that. The monster is gone,' said her mother, putting an arm around Marie's slim shoulders. Then she looked up at Léonie, who was feeling more and more confused. 'Marie does not wish to hear that vile monster's name again, *mamselle*, if you don't mind.'

'Nor do I, *je t'assure*,' replied Léonie, knowing that if she were to obtain the full story it would have to wait until she could be alone with Marie. She yawned, feeling incredibly tired after all the excitement. The food and wine and the crackling fire had soothed her and she was struggling to stay awake. 'You must forgive me, but I am greatly fatigued after my journey. If my parents are to be here in the morning, I shall need some rest.' She grimaced at the thought of what was to come, for she had not prepared herself for their full knowledge of the ruse. But just now, she was too tired to think.

'Oh, *Maman*,' Marie cried. '*Mamselle*'s room?'

The two women started at each other in dismay.

'It matters not,' Léonie said. 'If the room is not made up, I doubt it will worry me. After all the time I've spent at sea, a blanket on the floor would be restful enough.'

Marie looked quickly at her mother. 'I will remove my things,' she said, and hurried away.

'Her things? Nounou, what is she talking about? I fear my brain is still going up and down with the tide.'

'Don't fret, child. After Marie was so grievously hurt, your mother insisted. She'll be out of there in a moment.'

Marie hurt? Léonie could stand this double talk no longer. Brushing past the old woman, she ran from the salon and followed Marie up the stairs to her old bedroom.

★ ★ ★

Sleep had to wait for Léonie that first night. The discovery that Marie was occupying her own mistress's bedroom at the insistence of the duke and duchess flabbergasted Léonie. The two young women sat on the heavy silk bedspread like the girls they'd once been together and Léonie listened with astonishment to the whole sorry tale. The idea that her parents were content to consider Marie as a future daughter-in-law made Léonie realize how little she really knew them. If only things had been different . . . if only François de la Tour had not been married . . .

But such notions, for the time being, she kept to herself. At her own insistence she had her belongings installed in Jean-Michel's room, and fell exhausted into his bed, just as she had occupied his bunk aboard the *Aurélie* for so many months, without the slightest equivocation.

And as she slept, her dreams were gently rocked by the rhythmic motion of an elegant

French frigate sailing across an endless ocean.

It was noon when she finally awoke. She opened her eyes to find her mother sitting on her bed. Léonie lay quite still, staring into her face, into the soft grey eyes that were so like her own, and feeling terrible remorse at all the pain she must have suffered.

'*Maman*,' she whispered.

The duchess smiled gently, reaching out to touch her cheek, and then with a sob, throwing herself into her daughter's outstretched arms.

★ ★ ★

Dinner at the Hôtel de Chambois that evening began as a rather strange meal. The duke seldom ate with his family, and Léonie could only presume that her return had prompted the event. After the tearful but joyous reunion with her mother, she had not known what to expect from her father.

They ate grouse and goose, as well as rich, succulent beef brought in from their country estates, accompanied by so many side dishes that it seemed excessive to her sailor's eye.

All through the meal, Léonie had felt the duke quietly watching her, not speaking, but regarding her with something so akin to amusement that Léonie, who had expected outrage, found it disconcerting. Her mother, on the other hand, appeared subdued and overly solicitous, occasionally patting Léonie's hand across the table.

While they awaited the bringing of fruits to cleanse the palate, her father finally broke his silence.

'I received some items of curious news today, Léonie.'

Her pulse quickened. 'On what subject, Your Grace?'

'If I am not much mistaken, the subject was you.'

'Oh?' She wanted him to come out with it, but he was playing cat and mouse, a game she knew he enjoyed whenever he had the upper hand. 'May one enquire from whom you received this news, Your Grace?'

He inclined his head, though his eyes held a spark of intrigue that belied the indifference he was trying to convey. 'From the Ministre de la Marine.'

Léonie put down her serviette, feeling herself grow pale. He seemed not to notice.

'He informed me that my *son* has received two commendations for his service as part of the de la Tour expedition.'

Léonie's heart pattered sharply at the

mention of François' name, but she managed a smile.

'But how, my dear?' enquired the duchess. 'Are you saying that our dear daughter acquitted her brother so well that — '

'So it would appear,' he answered, selecting a golden pear from the silver dish placed before them. 'The king has himself congratulated me on the fine artistic skills of Jean-Michel, whose excellent depiction of a mountain named Krakatoa has been chosen to embellish the publication of the expedition journals.' Léonie saw her mother's eyes fill with pride. 'Furthermore,' continued His Grace, with a quizzical look at his wife, 'it seems your son earned a commendation for his skill in battle.'

The duchess gave a little squeak of horror. Léonie peeked at her father and couldn't suppress an impish grin. He returned her look gravely.

'But my dear child,' Eléanore said in alarm, 'are you saying that you fought with — with swords?'

'Yes. *Maman*. Everyone did. It was most exciting.'

The duchess frowned. 'I am sure it was no such thing!'

'Oh, but it was. We were caught in a thick fog when suddenly out of the mist came this

479

huge black ship, swarming with brigands. We had to fight for our lives. And I was only wounded a little.' From the corner of her eye, she saw she had finally piqued the duke's interest. She hid a little smile and calmly selected a few cherries from the dish.

'I do not believe,' said His Grace, 'that such information was conveyed to me. What was the nature of this injury?'

'A bullet wound, Your Grace. But it was not so bad,' she assured her mother, who was looking quite unwell, 'the bullet went right through.'

The duke, who was in the process of lifting a slice of pear to his lips, set it back upon his plate and wiped his fingers on his serviette. 'I think we have endured sufficient detail, thank you, child.'

Léonie suppressed a smile. It was rare that she could best her father. 'You had other news, Your Grace?' she asked, picking up the cherries and trying to decide which to eat first.

He sipped his wine, watching her over the rim of the glass in a way that reminded her painfully of the captain when he was displeased. 'I do. But first I require something of you.'

Léonie had a feeling she wasn't going to enjoy the rest of her meal. She put the cherries back on her plate untouched. Her appetite seemed to have vanished.

'I require your promise that you have satisfied the wild *enfant* in your breast and that we may enjoy the company of a wise and dutiful daughter in her stead.'

'I — I will try my best, Your Grace.'

'Your best does not always suffice, child. I believe I would prefer obedience.'

Léonie felt herself losing control, as ever when she came up against her father in such a mood. She nodded meekly, stealing a glance at her mother, but Eléanore's eyes were lowered.

'You must understand that given your extraordinary disappearance and its unlikely explanation, all of Paris — and indeed Versailles — was agog for news of you. The abandonment of your obligation to the Marquis de Grise did not win you many admirers.'

'I — I am sorry about Alphonse, Your Grace, but he caused me such revulsion . . . ' She shuddered.

Her father appeared unmoved. 'An unfortunate attitude, but one you could have sought to overcome in time.'

'No!' she replied, meeting his eyes brazenly. 'It would have made me ill to share his bed.'

She saw the ice-cold look in her father's eyes and sat back in her chair, stung that he should have so little compassion for his own daughter's happiness.

'Since the matter is resolved, we will speak no more of it. De Grise has married a rich widow from Chantilly and is, I hear, admirably suited to the lady's charms.'

Léonie giggled. 'You mean she is as unsightly as he?'

Her father continued as if he hadn't heard. 'You, on the other hand, were quite likely to remain unspoken for, having gained something of a reputation for lack of self-discipline.'

Léonie said nothing, thinking how François had so often echoed that sentiment. Her father continued, 'However, to my considerable relief, that is not to be. Today I received a letter requesting your hand in marriage.'

Léonie's head shot up. 'Someone wishes to marry me?'

His Grace coughed gently. 'Your dowry is considerable, child, and I believe there are those who would still not object to a connection with the house of Chambois.'

Léonie's head was spinning. 'May I ask who this person is?'

Her mother reached across the table and squeezed her hand. 'He is a duke, my dear!

Just imagine! And we had thought it would be impossible to find anyone who would take you after the fiasco with Alphonse and your disappearance. People thought you had eloped, of course, but they could not perceive with whom, which was just as well.'

'Mother! You're not making any sense.' She turned to her father. 'Who is this duke and, pray, why is he so desperate that he must seek out such soiled property as everyone perceives me to be?'

'His name is Béligny. I met him some years ago and thought him rather handsome, but he's seldom at court — I seem to recall him telling me he preferred his estates in the Gironde.'

Léonie took a deep breath, for her heart was thumping painfully. 'How — how old is he, Your Grace?'

'He gives no indication in his correspondence, which is entirely proper, and I am not impertinent enough to enquire. Fifty-five, perhaps a little more. He's been widowed some years, I believe.'

'Fifty-five!' She sank back in her chair, feeling her eyes burn with tears. It's my own fault, she thought bitterly. And anyway, what possible difference could it make? The only man she had ever loved was somewhere on the other side of the globe, probably wondering at this very minute what his beloved wife and son were doing. No, if it was a choice between life in a convent and life as the dutiful wife of an ageing duke, the latter at least offered her some hope. As long as she could bring herself to satisfy his wants from time to time, he would probably leave her alone and she could carry on a pleasant enough existence. Perhaps she could even conceive a child? The idea filled her with a sad kind of hope, and she looked up at her father with more composure.

'Very well, Your Grace. I shall marry him if you ask me to.'

His Grace seemed surprised, and cast a quick glance at his wife. 'I am delighted to hear it. He has suggested April 22nd.'

'But that's so soon, Léonie,' cried the duchess, jumping up from the table. 'There is so much to do. We must order your gown tomorrow . . .'

Léonie got up from the table and went to her father, kissing his cheek to show that she would do her best not to disappoint him this time, though she felt numb inside.

'I'm surprised you haven't asked when you may meet him,' her father commented.

Léonie had not the slightest interest in doing so, since she was agreeing to this purely to satisfy her duty.

'Perhaps it's just as well,' he continued, 'since it won't be possible. His correspondence alludes to some business he is engaged in. He says he'll try to get here before the day of your nuptials, 'tis all.'

'Thank you, Your Grace,' Léonie answered automatically, and followed her mother out of the room.

25

Spring came early to Paris, with warm winds blowing from the south and dusting the chestnut trees with green. Though it was only April, Léonie was often out of doors, enjoying the gentle sunshine and escaping the endless hubbub that her forthcoming nuptials seemed to cause.

For six weeks now, she had been doing her best to face the future as the Duchesse de Béligny. She had let her mind dwell on the possibility of children, for even if the duke were as old as her own father, she herself was young and healthy and she longed for a baby of her own, maybe several.

Also, she knew her social standing would be impeccable. Since her return, she had been invited to several soirées at all the fashionable houses, but whenever she attended, she had felt like a freak at a county fair. Everyone wished to express their delicious horror that she had escaped her betrothal to Alphonse de Grise by running away to a convent. After a while, she stopped going, for she seldom found anyone worth conversing with, and she missed the real conversations she had enjoyed as a 'man'.

Mostly, she worried about Jean-Michel. Just that morning her father had expressed some concern that his son had not returned from England, and that in six months, he had not called on the duke's London bankers. Finally, Léonie had explained that her brother was not, as instructed, in England, but at sea trying to intercept the *Aurélie* in search of her. She understood the duke's displeasure, for not only was her twin's action against his father's express wishes, but he had gone to sea on his behalf without the protection of the French Navy.

But there was nothing anyone could do except wait and hope. The duchess appeared fully occupied with Léonie's forthcoming nuptials and had excused herself from the palace and her duties as one of Queen Marie-Antoinette's entourage in order to put all her efforts into the event. Léonie expressed the wish that it could be a small affair, but to no avail.

She sat on a cold stone bench and watched the fountain spraying water from the mouth of Neptune into a small pond. As the days wore on, she was finding it harder and harder to accept, and the more she felt her father watching her, the harder it was to face her wedding with equanimity. She had believed that by the time she reached France, her feelings for François would have faded, would have assumed their correct perspective. She had been so hoping that what she felt for him was a passing emotion sharpened by the exotic places and events they had experienced together, and that a return to normal life would render it no more than a bittersweet memory.

But that was not to be. Even here, she was constantly reminded of his presence. She found herself wanting to talk to him about things people said, about the way they viewed the world, about how she felt concerning obedience and honour and her place in society, for she needed help to make sense of what was happening.

She heard someone approach along the crunchy gravel and was surprised to see her mother away from her endless organizing.

'My dear child,' the duchess said reprovingly,

'it will not be so bad, you know.'

Léonie smiled at her. 'I can never love him, *Maman*.'

'Perhaps not. But if you try, you may find that age is not the barrier you make it now. A good man is much more than youthful looks and a fine leg. He is companionship and sharing, and a sense of the rightness of the world.'

'Rightness? *Maman*, if you and Papa are so concerned with what is right and proper, I wonder that you seem content for my twin to marry my abigail!' She knew the words were petulant, and she leapt from the bench and bent to pick a few stones from the path and toss them into the fountain.

'Marie is a gentlewoman by birth, Léonie,' her mother replied. 'It is only her father's untimely death that brought her to her present station.'

'And because Jean-Mich loves her, she is acceptable?'

'She risked her own life — and nearly lost it — for the honour of our family, Léonie. We owe her much. But aside from that, Jean-Michel is a man, and if he plans to make a new life for them both in America, her status in France will not disbar them from happiness.'

Léonie felt lost in her mother's logic.

'So if I were a man I would be able to choose a spouse from' — she stared at the round stones in her hand, for she had yet to speak these words aloud — 'from the bourgeoisie?'

'Certainly, child.' Léonie was stunned, but her mother continued as if she hadn't noticed. 'As long as you were content to be ruined socially. The world would cut you off, naturally, but you could still be comfortable enough. Léonie, why are you asking me these questions?'

'Me?' Léonie turned away, tossing the last of the pebbles into the water. 'No reason, *Maman*. It just seemed strange, that's all.'

'Life is seldom fair, my dear, though sometimes it offers serendipity when we least expect it. Like your betrothal to the Duc de Béligny.'

Léonie bit her tongue, for she could think of no reason to consider the match a stroke of good fortune.

'By the by,' her mother said, getting up and taking Léonie's arm to lead her back to the house. 'Madame Desjardins was here this morning. Her husband, you know, is something high up in the Ministère de la Marine.' Léonie found herself suddenly listening very closely. 'She mentioned the captain of your expedition, what was his name? De Tours?'

'De la Tour,' Léonie supplied, pressing one hand against her bodice to stem the wild fluttering his name had caused.

'De la Tour, yes, that was it. His ship returned to Brittany a few days ago, I believe.'

He was safe! Léonie closed her eyes in a moment of heartfelt thanks, then opened them again, rebuking herself for her concern with the welfare of someone else's husband. She tried to focus on what her mother was saying.

' . . . and suffered a great sadness while he was serving in the Americas.'

'He was there with Lafayette,' she added automatically.

'Indeed. A fine man.'

Léonie stopped suddenly. 'What sadness, Mother?'

The duchess bent to pluck a fragrant jonquil from a bed of spring bulbs. She teased her nose with it, inhaling the sweet scent before she answered. 'Something to do with his wife. I believe she died in childbirth while he was away. Is this not the most heavenly scent?' She cast Léonie a despondent look. 'The poor man didn't even realize his wife was with child and

490

he lost them both before he knew it. She said he's been mad about work ever since, quite driven they say. Hardly stays ashore a minute between expeditions if he can avoid it. He seems well thought of, though.'

Léonie's head was reeling. She stared straight in front of her, hearing only the pounding of blood in her ears. She thought of François, delirious with fever from scurvy, clinging to her hand and calling out for his family. If only she'd seen it.

'My dear child, are you quite well?' her mother asked.

Léonie stared at her mother, trying to control the outpouring of emotions that her news had brought. Without another word, she turned and fled into the garden, seeking refuge in the high-walled maze which she and Jean-Michel, alone in all the family, could navigate blindfold.

She ran through the narrow hedgerows until she found her favourite hiding place, a small wooden bench set in a dead-end. Then she sank on to it and gave way to her sobs.

After a while, she felt better and sat up, wiping her eyes on her sodden kerchief. She brushed the dirt off the hem of her gown and sat staring at the narrow green space around her. She could hear a lark singing high above, its trilling notes fluttering down to her on the clear morning air. Shading her eyes with one hand, she tried to spot it, but as usual it flew too close to the sun and too far above the earth to betray its little heaven.

'Lucky bird,' she said. 'Why can't I just fly away and be as free as you?' She looked down again, suddenly aware of how confined she was in the thick green maze. It was claustrophobic, and yet to run out into the gardens was to encounter another form of prison, for the whole property was enclosed in a ten-foot-high wall, cutting it off from the city and keeping its occupants safely inside.

And when she was married? What then? Another set of walls? Another duty to perform?

When does *my* life begin? she thought, feeling suddenly indignant that she should have been brought to this as a penance for refusing to imprison herself with Alphonse de Grise.

And then there was François, driving himself like the Furies because he couldn't face his own demons. Was that why he kept pushing me away? she wondered, for she was sure he had cared for her. Somehow, he could never quite let go.

Was it because she was a duke's daughter and he was a sea captain? He'd made no secret of his attitude toward those who spent their lives at court. She wandered through the maze trying to stop the pain that tore at her heart, trying to understand why he would toy with her emotions and then toss her aside in so cavalier a fashion, even sending a priest to say goodbye in his stead. It was as though her position were pure poison to his nature.

She plucked a twig absently off the hedge, thinking of Port-Louis and how good it had been. There they had met as equals, with no such barriers to divide them. It seemed so unfair that Marie and Jean-Michel were able to —

She couldn't stop the idea once it began to take shape in her mind: if Jean-Michel and Marie could have a future in America, why couldn't she and François? Perhaps her father would even grant her part of the dowry he was planning to offer the Duc de Béligny? That should be enough to get them started.

Léonie knew precious little about life in America, but she could learn. And who better to teach her . . . ?

By the time she had found her way out of the maze and returned to the house, Léonie had made up her mind. She would find out where Capitaine de la Tour lived and she would go to him, throwing off all the trappings of her birthright until she was no more than the bourgeoise she had been in Port-Louis. In her heart she already mourned the loss of her family, for they would surely cut her off forever, but she was determined that she would never consent to be another man's wife unless she was certain that François de la Tour didn't want her.

★ ★ ★

Léonie confided her plan to Marie, who was both delighted at the prospect of having her beloved mistress close by in America and yet horrified that she should contemplate defying her father yet again.

But by April 21st — the day before her wedding — Léonie had learned no more about François' whereabouts than that he came from a village called Blaye near Bordeaux. She was awake at dawn, having packed a few belongings the night before and sent Marie to hide them in a light carriage she had secretly purchased. She was determined that she would travel to Blaye and find him herself, and to that end had taken up riding every fine morning between ten and noon, with only a young, inexperienced groom for an escort; that was when she would make her escape.

It was barely eight when there was a

commotion in the courtyard in front of the house. She ran to the window and looked down.

'Marie! Marie! Come quickly!'

Marie followed her mistress to the grand staircase, but Léonie flew down the stairs and reached the front door before even Gaston. She flung it wide and threw herself into the arms of a man standing on the doorstep about to press the bell.

'Jean-Mich! Jean-Mich! I thought you were dead!'

'Steady on, *ma soeur*, must you weep all over my cloak?' He swept her up in his arms and swung her into the hall, hugging her fiercely. 'Dear God, Léonie, I began to think I should never see you again. Let me look at you! You've lost weight. And I hear you're going to be married — tomorrow, isn't it?'

She nodded glumly as he set her back on her feet. 'I must talk to you, Jean Mich.'

But she saw that he had raised his head and discovered Marie waiting quietly on the stairs. 'Later, *ma soeur*.' He took the steps two at a time and crushed Marie into his arms, kissing her long and deeply. Léonie watched them as Jean-Michel led his love down the stairs and out into the garden. They were so much in love, she thought, despite all the problems they faced. She felt her resolve to find François harden, despite the pain of having to leave so soon after her brother's return. At least she knew he was safe, and he had Marie now.

She returned to her chamber to dress for riding.

★ ★ ★

It was a glorious morning. A sparkling frost still crackled in places beneath the horses' hooves, apple and almond blossoms drifted to the grass like confetti, and narcissi nodded in the sunshine. Léonie rode sedately a few yards in front of the groom. When she reached the middle of the park, she dismounted and fiddled with her saddle. André jumped off his horse and came to help, but she immediately took his hand and slipped two gold louis into it.

'*Mamselle!*' he gasped.

'Ssh. There is something very important I wish you to do for me.'

'I will do whatever you ask, of course. It is my duty.'

'You may not think so when I explain your task,' she murmured. She looked around, but there were few people about, and no one near. 'I wish you to ride to the west gate of the park and wait for me there till noon, do you understand?'

The groom's face paled. 'But *mamselle*, it is barely past ten. Her Grace made me vow I would stay with you whenever you were out. I would lose my position if they discovered I had not done so.'

Léonie looked at him speculatively, wondering if he was as timid as she had hoped when she first chose him to be her daily escort.

'Perhaps I have not made myself clear, André. It is necessary that you do exactly as I ask, and that you tell no one. Perhaps you have not heard below stairs, that I have been known to kill men bolder and braver than you — '

Her lips twitched with wry amusement as André took a rapid step backward, his eyes suddenly wary.

'Very well, *mamselle*. I shall expect you at twelve.'

'At the west gate.'

'At the west gate,' he confirmed.

Léonie watched him mount his horse and hurry away. Then she turned and headed toward the east gate where her inconspicuous carriage awaited, drawn by a mismatched pair that were sturdy but had seen better times. No one would ever suspect her origins if they saw her arrive in Blaye in such a vehicle. The driver she had engaged sat dozing on the box, but he straightened at her approach.

Léonie tethered her mare to a tree, knowing she would eventually be found, and with another glance around her to make certain she was unobserved, pulled open the carriage door and stepped up.

She gasped as someone grabbed her, pulling her into the carriage. A hand was clamped over her mouth, choking off a scream.

'It seems that you're running away from your obligations once again, *mamselle*,' said a voice close to her ear. 'This is becoming an unfortunate habit.'

The hands fell away and Léonie turned to look at her attacker.

'François!' She tumbled on to the seat and stared at him in total disbelief. He wore his navy uniform but his boots were thick with dust and his cravat awry. She couldn't believe he was really here, that *he* had found *her!* Her heart was beating a wild tattoo in her breast.

Before she could gather her wits, he tossed something wrapped in velvet on to her lap. 'I gave this to you once before. Kindly do me the honour of accepting it this time.'

Wordlessly, she unwrapped the box Father

Cassel had presented to her in Batavia. The lovely ceramic painting made her catch her breath once more. Inside lay the matched ivory combs studded with pearls and diamonds.

'This time, I want to see you wear them,' he said.

Her eyes were misted with unshed tears. 'I thought you had meant these as a gift for your wife. Why didn't you tell me you were widowed?'

He touched her cheek with one finger, wiping away a tear that had escaped. 'You didn't ask. And the pain was still raw. It wasn't until after you'd sailed on the *Nederburgh* that I knew I should have told you.'

'And if you had? Would you still have sent me away?'

He set the box on the seat and took her trembling hands in his strong warm ones. 'I didn't want to, but I had no choice, for your sake. When you were gone, I told myself I could concentrate on my first love, the sea. But the oceans were just vast empty saltwater without you. I knew then that the sea was no longer my home.'

'What — what are you saying, François?' She dreaded asking him, but a spark of hope had caught alight in her heart and was growing into a fire. If he were to quench her hopes, she wanted him to do it now, before she lost herself.

His eyes were midnight blue as he gazed at her. 'My ship was empty without you, and so was my life, Léonie. These last seven months have been hell. I've sent everyone mad, even Father Cassel, driving them to get back to France as fast as the ships could sail. But I knew I couldn't spend the rest of my days without you by my side.' He looked down, and Léonie was almost certain he was blushing. 'The old padre gave me rather a tongue-lashing, brought me to my senses.'

'Father Cassel? Where is he now?'

'At your father's house, I believe, waiting to marry us. That is, if you'll have me.' He reached out and drew her on to his lap, cupping her face with one hand. 'I love you, Léonie de Chambois. But I must warn you, I also love Hélène de Lisle and Michelle Thouars. Do you think you could stand to share me?'

Léonie laughed. 'I love you too, François, more than life itself. I can't help myself. I tried everything, but you seem to have — ' Her words were cut off as his mouth descended on hers, crushing them into a kiss rich with passion and hunger. She opened her lips to him, letting his tongue plunder the sensitive recesses of her mouth. Her hands curled in his hair, holding him to her as though she were drowning.

She heard herself moan, heard his breath quicken in response, when suddenly their situation returned full-force to her mind like a dose of cold water.

'François, wait!' She pushed him away and sat back on the bench seat.

'What is it, my love? Are you becoming a prude now you're back on shore?'

She looked up at him. 'François, you're a sea captain. And if I were to marry you, Father would never let me have my dowry. How will we live?'

'We'll manage,' he answered enigmatically.

'But how?' Then a thought occurred to her and she giggled. 'Unless of course, you sign me on as chief artist on your voyages, and then we would have two salaries!'

'Hah!' he snorted. 'Never again! I learned my lesson the first time. Anyway, I'm not going back to sea.'

'Not going back! But — but what will you do?'

He kissed the top of her head. 'You worry too much.' He ran a finger down the neckline of her riding habit, feathering little circles on her skin. Léonie felt the heat in his gaze and held her breath, feeling a quivering deep inside.

'Perhaps,' François suggested, 'we could make the duke a grandfather. Do you think that would persuade him to part with your dowry?'

Léonie's heart filled with such joy that she could no longer argue. She allowed him to tug her forward, turned her face up to welcome his kiss and met his lips with a fervour that spoke of all the achingly lonely months they had been separated.

'How many children would it take?' François murmured as he pressed his lips to the tender skin on her neck.

'Several.' She wound her fingers into the hair at his temples.

He kissed her nape, then trailed a row of tiny teasing bites around her neck to her chin. 'How soon can we start?'

Léonie laughed. 'Aren't you being rather hasty for a man without any means of support?'

He lifted his head and looked seriously at her. 'Does this mean you'll marry me?'

His question wiped away the fairytale they had been weaving around them. Her eyes filled with tears.

'I want to, my love, oh so very much. That's why I was coming to find you, to see if you . . . cared. But — '

He kissed her lightly on the lips. 'Does that answer your question?'

She blinked, laughing and crying at the same time. 'But you don't understand. I've promised to marry someone else tomorrow.'

'Who?' François answered calmly. 'Tell me his name and I'll kill him.'

Léonie stood up, shocked. 'You can't! François, he's a duke. They'd send you to the scaffold! You must not joke like that.' She sat in the corner, suddenly realizing how hopeless everything had become. 'I promised my father I would keep my word this time, but I can't. That's why I'm here. When I discovered you were back, I knew I couldn't marry another man if there was a chance you'd have me. I only agreed to the marriage because I believed you already had a wife. But then *Maman* told me you were a widower . . . Oh, François, what am I to do? He's so old — older than my father!'

'How do you know?'

'Papa met him once. He's been married, but his wife died a long time ago. I didn't dare ask if he had any children — they'd probably be older than me.'

'Probably.'

'François, you're not taking this seriously!'

He gave her a quick smile, then banged

his fist on the roof. The carriage began to move. 'Why don't we go back to the Hôtel de Chambois and talk to your parents.'

'No! They'll throw you out and lock me up till the wedding tomorrow.'

But François just sat back in the carriage, took a large white kerchief out of his pocket and used it to flick the dust off his boots.

'Anyway,' Léonie said as they rumbled on to the cobbled streets outside the park, 'how did you know I was here?'

'Marie told me.'

'Marie?'

'She thought that since you were running away to find me, and I was already here, it would save the horses' legs. She's quite a sensible girl.'

Léonie's face fell. 'Then all my family knows I was trying to escape.'

'I don't believe so. Jean-Michel seems to think I'm a decent prospect as a brother-in-law, so he persuaded her to tell me all — in privacy.'

'You know my brother?'

'I found him on the wharf at Cape Town and brought him home. His red hair gave him away, along with the pugnacious manner with which he was attempting to obtain passage on a vessel bound for India. He reminded me rather strongly of someone else

I know.' He leaned over and kissed the tip of her nose. 'I had to make him wear a wig on the *Aurélie*, of course, or there would have been no end of trouble.'

'So nobody recognized him?'

'Luckily. And since you had bullied me into collecting your orphans, I thought I should bring all your strays home with me at once, lest I get my ear bitten off.'

'You brought Danielle and her brother? Oh, Captain, thank you!' She threw her arms around him and kissed him soundly, hearing a deep chuckle in his throat.

'Where are they now?' she asked at last.

'I believe the inestimable Nounou is feeding them vast quantities of sweetmeats in your mother's kitchen. How did you ever survive childhood without becoming as rotund as she?'

'She's getting softer with age,' Léonie answered, 'unlike my father.' Her happy smile faded into worry as she thought of the forthcoming confrontation with the duke. She stared out the window, biting her lip. The day didn't seem so pretty any more.

'Don't be afraid, my love,' he said softly, drawing her to him and straightening her riding gown. He passed her the plumed hat she had thrown on the floor and watched while she positioned it on her simple coiffure.

'Your hair has grown, and I see you've lost your *matelot*'s tan.' He grinned. 'Just as well, I expect, since it seems Paris has been unable to prove you were anywhere other than inside the Convent of Sainte-Agnès all those months.'

'Thanks to you,' she said, smiling shyly at him. 'I don't know what you said in your note to the mother superior, but she was the soul of discretion.'

'Father Cassel said she would be entirely trustworthy — especially if I made it worth her while.'

The carriage drew up in front of the imposing house before Léonie could query that statement.

'Take nice deep breaths, my love, and don't forget your little trinkets. I want to see them in your hair when you marry me.'

She slid the little box into the pocket of her gown as he took her elbow and steered her into the house.

'Good afternoon, Your Grace, *mamselle*,' said Gaston with his customary bow. Léonie glanced about her nervously.

'Is my father here, Gaston?'

'In the grand salon, I believe, *mamselle*, with Her Grace and your brother.'

Léonie looked oddly at him, but François was guiding her swiftly toward the salon. A

506

footman opened the doors and without a moment to compose herself, she was ushered inside on the captain's arm.

'Christian!' she exclaimed delightedly. Lieutenant Lavelle stood by the fireplace in his naval uniform. He sent Léonie a quick smile, then bowed stiffly to the captain.

The captain responded with a bashful grin, and Léonie looked from one to the other, wondering what was going on. Then her mother crossed to her, resplendent in a morning gown of crimson damask.

'Léonie!' she exclaimed. 'Is this not the most serendipitous event! Imagine, His Grace has brought Jean-Michel back to us as well. Why did you pretend you did not know him, child? It is most vexatious of you. We were quite expecting François' father, but it appears the old duke was poorly for some time before he succumbed. So unfortunate.'

She took the captain's arm and propelled him to a *fauteuil*, offering him a glass of sparkling champagne. Léonie stood glued to the spot, staring at François as if a thunderbolt had hit her.

He turned, a mischievous glint in his blue eyes. 'Won't you have some wine, my love, to celebrate our betrothal?'

Still she couldn't move. François, a duke. No, not a duke. *The* duke. The Duc de Béligny. The *fifty-five-year-old* Duc de Béligny! About the only true thing she had heard about him was that he was widowed.

How could he have misled her like that? Anger flashed through her and she stormed across the salon, snatched the glass of wine from his hand and threw it at him.

François was spluttering with gratifying rage, the duke and duchess were yelling, Marie was running for a cloth and Jean-Michel was howling with laughter, but Léonie merely stood there, letting the hubbub storm around her while she stared over François' head to the corner of the room where Father Cassel was calmly watching, a faint smile dancing across his lips.

'I see you have lost none of your fighting spirit, *mamselle*,' the old priest said. Everyone stopped and looked at him. He sent François a wry shrug. 'I've been telling the captain for years that it's all very well not to use titles aboard his ships, but he did carry it rather too far this time.'

François sent him a baleful glance and then looked up at Léonie who was still standing in front of him. She looked into his eyes. Slowly a smile spread across his face and she smiled back.

'What did I tell you?' he said.

Léonie threw herself into his arms, not

caring that her riding coat was getting wet with wine. He hugged her tightly, and she wrapped her arms around his neck and buried her face in his chest. 'I love you, even if you are the Duc de Béligny — and an utter rogue!'

'Does this mean you'll marry me after all and won't run away with some impoverished sea captain?'

She lifted her head and gazed into his eyes, laughing. 'Mmm, it's tempting. But I am rather fond of my sea captain.'

'Vixen!' he replied, kissing her soundly on the mouth.

His lips were sweet with wine and Léonie gave herself up to the heady joy that filled her. She had suffered such agony believing she could never be his, then trying to accept that she must share the bed of some old duke. Now that the barriers to their love had fallen away her joy was almost more than she could bear.

When they drew apart, finally, the salon was empty. They looked around them and laughed.

'I think our passion chased them away.'

'Good,' she said. 'I had to share you with a whole shipload of sailors all those months. From now on, I want you all to myself.'

'And so you shall, my love.' He traced the

curve of her lips with a finger. Her heart felt so full that she knew she'd never been happier in her life.

'I loved my first wife,' he said, 'in a quiet way. Her name was Louisa.'

'I know,' she replied. 'You called out her name when you had the fever. Her death must have caused you much pain.'

'I did that? Oh, my love, no wonder you were so strange after that.' He kissed her quickly but with such passion that the last of Léonie's doubts dissolved into happiness.

'Louisa made me feel protective,' he continued, as though he needed to explain, to set things to rights between them. 'I liked that, but not enough to give up my life at sea. Then you came along and changed everything. I never thought I could care for another woman, and I'd convinced myself that I would never be responsible for one again. I couldn't look after a wife if I was away all the time, and I wouldn't give up my career.'

'Then you mustn't my love. You know I'm strong. I can look after myself while you're away.'

He raised one eyebrow. 'Are you suggesting I leave you alone to get up to who knows what? Not a chance, my dear Duchess-to-be.' He kissed her lips lightly, laughing. 'I'd worry that you'd be out sword-fighting the minute my ship had sailed.'

'So you're giving up your ships to stay at home and be my gaoler?'

'Maybe,' he answered with a provocative kiss. 'But since my father died there is much to do in Blaye. I was rather hoping you would help.'

'Doing what?' she giggled. 'Pressing grapes with my feet?'

He laughed, his eyes alight with love. 'I thought we might leave the winemaking to the experts and see how good we are at making babies.'

'Sons,' she said, kissing him full on the mouth. 'Twin sons. After all, they do run in families.'

'With red hair,' he added, kissing her back.

'And dark-blue, captain's eyes.'

Then she lost herself in those eyes, in the sensations of his tongue as he nuzzled a kiss beneath her ear, seeking out the magic spot that sent the breath rushing from her lungs and made thinking impossible. She squirmed in his lap, turning so she could wrap her arms around his neck and feel the muscles of his shoulders beneath her fingers. His hand traced the curve of her breast through her gown, and she arched her back as he slid his fingers beneath her fichu and sought out her nipple, slowly rubbing a path around the aureole until she was breathless with need of him. A powerful hunger stirred deep in her belly and she moaned his name against his neck. Then his hand left her breast and moved to her knee. Slowly, he inched the hem of her gown up her leg, his warm fingers burning a fiery trail through her silk stockings. Then he stroked the tender flesh of her thigh and she drew a sharp breath as liquid heat flowed through her, filling her with physical longing.

She heard him laugh softly, apologetically, and felt his hand retreat, easing her gown back down over her legs.

'Much as I would like to continue, I would hate to be interrupted by someone coming to clean champagne off the carpet,' he said.

Léonie tried to laugh, but found herself staring into his eyes, hot with passion.

'They say anticipation flavours the pot, Your Grace,' she whispered, kissing him softly on the lips. She climbed off his knee and crossed the salon to put some distance between them, for she knew if he pressed her, she would go to his bed at his slightest bidding. She tried to think about something else to calm the beating of her heart.

'When I'm a duchess, I'll be able to do as I please, won't I?'

'Why does that question fill me with foreboding?'

'I have no idea,' she replied with a teasing laugh, hearing him approach behind her. 'May I wear breeches?'

His hands captured her waist and he turned her to face him, bending to feather kisses on her temple. 'Only when you're . . . ' — he rained kisses over her cheek — 'teaching our sons . . . ' — he nuzzled her ear — 'to fence with swords.'

She pulled back and looked up at him in surprise. 'But surely you will do that?'

'Certainly not. I'm skilled, but you have a knack. In fact, when the mood takes you, my love, you're downright devious.'

'Indeed, Your Grace? Then let me show you quite how devious I can be.' She took his hand and led him out through the open French doors into the sun-filled garden, laughing with delight.

'Let me take you on a guided tour of the maze,' she said.

We do hope that you have enjoyed reading this large print book.

Did you know that all of our titles are available for purchase?

We publish a wide range of high quality large print books including:
Romances, Mysteries, Classics
General Fiction
Non Fiction and Westerns

Special interest titles available in large print are:
The Little Oxford Dictionary
Music Book
Song Book
Hymn Book
Service Book

Also available from us courtesy of Oxford University Press:
Young Readers' Dictionary
(large print edition)
Young Readers' Thesaurus
(large print edition)

For further information or a free brochure, please contact us at:
Ulverscroft Large Print Books Ltd.,
The Green, Bradgate Road, Anstey,
Leicester, LE7 7FU, England.
Tel: (00 44) 0116 236 4325
Fax: (00 44) 0116 234 0205

HIJACK
OUR STORY OF SURVIVAL

Lizzie Anders and Katie Hayes

Katie and Lizzie, two successful young professionals, abandoned the London rat race and set off to travel the world. They wanted to absorb different cultures, learn different values and reassess their lives. In the end they got more lessons in life than they had bargained for. Plunged into a nightmarish terrorist hold-up on an Ethiopian Airways flight, they were among the few to survive one of history's most tragic hijacks and plane crashes. This is their story — a story of friendship and danger, struggle and death.

THE VILLA VIOLETTA

June Barraclough

In the 1950s, Xavier Leopardi returned to Italy to reclaim his dead grandfather's beautiful villa on Lake Como. Xavier's English girlfriend, Flora, goes to stay there with him and his family, but finds the atmosphere oppressive. Xavier is obsessed with the memory of his childhood, which he associates with the scent of violets. There is a mystery concerning his parents and Flora is determined to solve it, in her bid to 'save' Xavier from himself. Only after much sorrow will Edwige, the old housekeeper, finally reveal what happened there.

BREATH OF BRIMSTONE

Anthea Fraser

Innocent enough — an inscription in a child's autograph book; a token from her new music teacher, Lucas Todd, that had charmed the six-year-old Lucy. But in Celia, Lucy's mother, it had struck a chill of unease. They had been thirteen at table that day — a foolish superstition that had preyed strangely on Celia's mind. And that night she had been disturbed by vivid and sinister dreams of Lucas Todd . . . After that, Celia lived in a nightmare of nameless dread — watching something change her happy, gentle child into a monster of evil . . .

THE WORLD AT NIGHT

Alan Furst

Jean Casson, a well-dressed, well-bred Parisian film producer, spends his days in the finest cafes and bistros, his evenings at elegant dinner parties and nights in the apartments of numerous women friends — until his agreeable lifestyle is changed for ever by the German invasion. As he struggles to put his world back together and to come to terms with the uncomfortable realities of life under German occupation, he becomes caught up — reluctantly — in the early activities of what was to become the French Resistance, and is faced with the first of many impossible choices.

BLOOD PROOF

Bill Knox

Colin Thane of the elite Scottish Crime Squad is sent north from Glasgow to the Scottish Highlands after a vicious arson attack at Broch Distillery has left three men dead and eight million pounds worth of prime stock destroyed. Finn Rankin, who runs the distillery with the aid of his three daughters, is at first unhelpful, then events take a dramatic turn for the worse. To uncover the truth, Thane must head back to Glasgow and its underworld, with one more race back to the mountains needed before the terror can finally be ended.

ISLAND OF FLOWERS

Jean M. Long

'Swallowfield' had belonged to Bethany Tyler's family for generations, but now Aunt Sophie, who lived on Jersey, was claiming her share of the property. It seemed that the only way of raising the capital was to sell the house, but then, unexpectedly, Justin Rochel arrived in Sussex and things took on a new dimension. Bethany accompanied her father and sister to Jersey, where there were shocks in store for her. She was attracted to Justin, but could she trust him?